DREAM RIVER

Dorothy Garlock

POPULAR LIBRARY

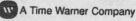

An Imprint of Warner Books, Inc.

A Time Warner Company

POPULAR LIBRARY EDITION

Copyright © 1988 by Dorothy Garlock
All rights reserved.

Popular Library® and the fanciful P design are registered trademarks of Warner Books, Inc.

Cover illustration by Sharon Spiak

Popular Library books are published by
Warner Books, Inc.
1271 Avenue of the Americas
New York. N.Y. 10020

Visit our Web site at
http://warnerbooks.com

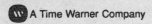 A Time Warner Company

Printed in the United States of America

First Printing: April, 1988

10 9

"I've not kissed any man but you," Amy confessed.

"Kiss me again." Rain's voice drawled those unreal words, and Amy lifted her hands to his hair, wound her fingers into it, and pulled his head down toward her uplifted face and ready-parted lips.

Rain set his mouth against hers. At first the kiss was gentle, sweet, hesitant, as if waiting for an invitation to deepen it. Amy's mind fed on the new sensations created by the feel of his body against hers, the firm but gentle lips, open and exploring and caressing. Her lips met his with a hunger equal to the hunger that heated her blood, and with a craving from some unknown thing that was her soul.

He made her world spin. A wild crescendo rose within her, and she knew that if he truly made love to her, if she became one with his rock-hard body, the world would stand still.

☆

DREAM RIVER
Book II of the Wabash Trilogy

☆

"A sprawling, gutsy saga...the Wabash trilogy promises to continue a career of shining triumphs."
—"Ann's World," *Hearst Cablevision*

"Vivid and real...there is joy, laughter, sadness, and tears in these pages...a gripping, endearing, and exciting read that is full of surprises and written in Garlock's own magical style."
—*Affaire de Coeur* on *Lonesome River*

Books by Dorothy Garlock

Published by
WARNER BOOKS

This book is dedicated to my readers:

The Anns, Betties, Margarets, Lindas, Beckys, Virginias, Marys, Berthas, Janets, Marians, Marcias, and Stephanies. Ladies, I cannot possibly name you all.

This book is also for: Gene Hoffman, Bob, Raymond, Lester, Ray, P.K., Paul, Merv, Carl J., and so on.

And for my bookseller friends: Jean, Marilyn, Linda, Dee, Glenn, Gloria, Paula, Connie, Beverly, Mary G., Jennifer, Francis, Mary Lynn and Len, Ellen, Genny, Odell, Barbara, Bea, Gayle, Nancy, Ann, Judy, and so many more.

With this dedication go my love and thanks.

D.G.

PROLOGUE

2:30 A.M. December 16, 1811

Beneath a cloudless sky, all was quiet in the Indian village that lay along the banks of the Mississippi River in the Missouri Territory. No moon lit the night, but the stars shone brightly against the blackness. Under his warm robe, Rain Tallman, a youth of eighteen summers, slept peacefully in the *weigius* of his stepfather, John Spotted Elk.

Suddenly the earth shuddered. Swiftly, with a deep, terrifying rumble, the violent temblor shook the slumbering village. A hundred heads lifted at the fierce grinding sound, and panic struck the hearts of the bravest men. Clay vessels smashed as they hit the hard-packed earth; lodge poles came crashing down; screaming women clutched their children. Land birds roused from their roosting places and cawed in fright, flapping their wings frantically. Horses squealed with terror as they were thrown to the ground where they rolled about, unable to regain their balance. Herds of bison staggered to their feet and stampeded in panic.

The waters of the Mississippi River danced, great waves breaking erratically on the shores. The riverbank caved in and huge trees toppled in a continuous crash of snapping branches. Boulders broke loose on hillsides, cutting swaths through trees and brush as they hurtled into the valleys. Towering trees, uprooted by the heaving earth, overturned, meshing their branches in a giant tangle.

From the area where the Ohio River meets the Mississippi, where Tennessee, Kentucky, Arkansas, Missouri, and Illinois come together, the ripples fanned out, splitting the earth, and huge tracts of land sank out of sight. Above the Indian village a tremendous bluff broke loose, crashed down, and swept the inhabitants into the muddy waters of the Mississippi River. The river swirled and eddied, hissed and gurgled, and flowed backward for a time.

At length, when the earth ceased its trembling, the face of the land was revealed—changed forever. Water covered thousands of acres of forests. Entire sections of land were inundated as others that once had been riverbed were left high in the air. Fish flopped away their lives on the muddy beds that remained after the water had been sucked from the river.

Rain Tallman woke with the first tremor. "Father! What is happening?" he mumbled, disoriented.

At that moment the lodge pole came crashing down. "Father!" he screamed and thrust out a hand to save himself.

He wrapped his arms around the pole as the earth beneath him began to slide. Terrified, he hung on to the pole as it carried him toward a solid black curtain. Downward he plunged into the expanding coils of pitch-black darkness.

From behind the black curtain he slowly emerged into another eerie darkness. He heard squawking and recognized the sound. Birds were circling in the darkness overhead looking for a place to roost. Gradually his mind cleared. He lay very still and waited for the earth to ripple beneath him again.

The faraway sound of a horse's whinny reached him. It was such a familiar, everyday sound that Rain almost cried out with relief. For in those first few seconds of consciousness, he was sure that only he and the birds had lived through the unfathomable horror. He lay on his stomach, his arms locked around the lodge pole, the lower part of his body buried in thick river mud.

Through the mist of his rising consciousness, awareness of danger penetrated. *He was about to be sucked under that quivering mass!*

In a near panic, Rain gradually pulled himself up out of the mud and onto the riverbank. He lay panting and holding on to his side for a moment. Then he pushed himself to his feet and stood swaying. The mud had sucked the knee-high moccasins from his feet and legs. He was barefoot and trembling . . . but alive!

Had John Spotted Elk, his stepfather, survived too? Scarcely daring to hope, Rain turned dazed eyes to the left and to the right and then to the sky, trying to determine his location by sighting the great North Star. It shone brightly, but he still didn't know where he was. He was sure the mudslide had carried him downriver, but how far? He sank down on the trunk of a fallen timber, tears of helplessness flooding his eyes.

Rain and his stepfather, John Spotted Elk, had been in the camp less than a week. The two of them had left the North Country a month before and had traveled south at a leisurely pace, enjoying each other's company and reminiscing about the past. John had shared his memories of the time he had bought Rain, a lad of three summers, and his mother, Caroline, from the Sioux who had raided a frontier village in the north, killed the men, and stolen the women and children to sell as slaves.

John had fallen in love with Rain's young fair-haired mother and she had returned that love passionately. Never again had she spoken of her former life. The boy's Christian name was changed to Rain Tallman because the day he and his mother were bought from the Sioux there had been a cloudburst, and because he was exceptionally tall for his age. John had raised the boy as his son. When Rain's mother lay dying, she had asked John to send Rain to their friend, Farrway Quill, who had a homestead on the Wabash River. She wanted him to live as a white man for a while so he could decide which world he preferred, the white or the Indian.

Rain recalled how reluctantly he had gone at age twelve to live at Quill's Station; but Farrway Quill and Juicy Deverell, an old mountain man, became his second family. He met Colby Carroll, the son of the man who had raised Quill, and Colby helped him to adapt to the white man's ways. In time he became so fond of his foster family that he found himself living between the two worlds.

When a war between the settlers and the Indian tribes seemed inevitable, Rain, unwilling to fight against either his white friends or his Indian brothers, had left Quill's Station. After this visit with John Spotted Elk, he had intended to go west into new territory.

Now Rain sat on the log, wet and shivering with cold. Minutes seemed like hours as he waited for dawn to break. A cathedral-like silence hung around him on all sides, broken only by the rustle of leaves as birds tried to make themselves comfortable in the few trees left standing and the hissing of confused snakes that had been routed from winter hibernation and were searching for warm dens. Rain broke a branch off the log he was sitting on and thrashed the ground around him to frighten away the snakes.

When light finally came, Rain looked upon a new world. Devastation was everywhere. Trees lay in a tangled mass for as far as he could see. Huge cracks in the earth had created streams where before there had been none. The river had changed its course. The water was thick with mud and debris of every description floated on its surface. Smoke rose in the sky from fires in the white village of New Madrid across the river. Two surviving horses stood enmeshed in the tangles of branches nearby. Making his way carefully on bare feet, Rain pulled away the branches and freed them. He mounted one, led the other, and began his search for his Indian father.

During the next two days he searched for John Spotted Elk. Of the one hundred people in the Indian village, no more than two dozen had escaped with their lives. When he was sure there was no hope of finding his stepfather alive, Rain turned north, his heart like a stone in his breast.

The earth had made the decision for him. From now on he would live his life as a white man. Those he loved were gone. His Indian way of life had vanished. He was on his own, he told himself. He would have to think his own thoughts and follow his own counsel. No sign of the constriction in his throat showed on his face as he looked back one last time on the desolate face of what had once been his home.

Rain followed the Wabash River north toward Quill's Station. Along the River of White Foam, as the Indians called it, the signs of devastation left by the earthquake were less severe. Occasionally he would pass a house or a barn that had collapsed. More often the well-built structures had withstood the tremors. Rain began to hope that all would be well with Farrway Quill and his family. He had to know if they had survived the quake before he turned his horse toward the western frontier. He was convinced the earthquake was the omen Tecumseh, the Shawnee chief, had predicted would unite the tribes against the whites. In a village where he traded one of the horses for moccasins and a blanket, the young men were preparing for war.

Two days' distance from Quill's Station, Rain's horse went lame and he turned it loose. He forged steadily northward on foot, sustained only by a fat partridge he had killed with his knife as it rose wobbling into the air on an injured wing. He thought about Liberty Quill, Farr's beautiful blond wife whom Tecumseh called the White Dove of the Wabash. And he thought about Amy, Liberty's young sister, and the kiss she had given him just before she was wed to Juicy Deverell. Her marriage to the eighty-two-year-old mountain man had been arranged to keep the father of the twelve-year-old girl from marrying her to a cruel and vengeful man. Juicy had married her to watch over the child and give her time to grow up. When he was gone, he had told them, Amy could choose her own man. Remembering now, Rain thought of the meaningful look Juicy had directed his way.

All these memories filtered through Rain's mind as he approached the station. The stockade was still standing, but parts of it tilted precariously. He went through the gate and up the path to the house, happy that it appeared to have withstood the earthquake without damage.

The door was flung open and Amy ran from the house. Like a long-legged colt, holding her dress up to her knees so she could run, her hair flowing out behind her, she ran to him and threw her arms around him.

"Rain! Oh, Rain! You've come back! Oh, I prayed you would! We were so worried about you."

It was Christmas Eve.

CHAPTER
One

Christmas Eve, 1818

It was bitter cold and growing colder by the minute. The storm swept down across the Illinois plains with brutal intensity. Cruel winds raked exposed flesh with icy fingers and threatened to suck the air from the lungs of the big, wide-shouldered man riding the rangy, dun horse. He hunched his shoulders against the savage bite of the wind and pulled his beaver cap down over his ears. The sharp north wind beat at his face, and wind-driven snowflakes settled on the fur collar of his coat.

Glancing back over his shoulder, he looked at a white wall of snow. He turned the dun horse northeast and headed into the wind. It gave him little comfort to know that whoever was following him was also being battered by the storm.

"Come on, horse," he muttered. "We'd better find a place to dig in or we'll freeze to death."

Rain Tallman lowered his head to shield his face from the wind and patted the neck of the straining dun with his fur-gloved hand. When they came to a gully, the horse plunged belly-deep in snow. Rain lifted his head. The wind whipped at him, stinging his eyes. He forced the dun through the ice-covered brush. It slid and stumbled. When it regained its footing, he turned it east along a frozen creek bed whose high banks shielded him from wind.

He came to a drywash, followed it and soon found what he was looking for. A boulder, one that might have been heaved up by the last earthquake seven years before, had caught logs and brush as they washed downstream. When he pulled the brush away, he uncovered a cave of sorts, big enough for him and the horse. Rain led the dun inside and then, working swiftly, closed the entryway and set about starting a fire.

He built his fire next to the boulder. As the blaze mounted higher, he added more fuel, then dragged in a large log and placed the end of it in the fire. Quickly he built a second fire a good yard from the first one. Later he would scoop the burning embers onto the first fire and unroll his bed on the warm ground. It was an old wilderness trick. He could survive here even if the blizzard worsened.

Rain unsaddled the horse and carefully rubbed him down with a piece of old blanket. The supply of shelled corn he had bought in Cahokia was almost gone. He emptied what was left into the feed bag and hung it over the horse's nose, patting the big dun affectionately.

"This is about the last of it, Horse. I'd hoped to be at Quill's by now, but the storm slowed us down a bit, and now the dog on our trail will delay us even more."

The fire soon warmed the boulder and the heat was reflected back into the cave. Rain took a large tin cup from his pack, filled it with snow, and set it on a flat stone beside the fire. The wind howled and worried the leafless cottonwoods until their branches creaked and groaned. Rain's thoughts turned to the lone man who had been on his trail for the last two days.

On the day after he had crossed the Kaskaskia River, he

had looked down from a bluff above the river and seen a man on a buckskin horse studying his tracks. This morning he had caught sight of him again. The man must be carrying a grudge against him, Rain mused. Or else he was getting paid a hell of a lot of money to get him. What else would cause a man to follow him in such weather?

"We'll just wait right here and let him come on, if he's got a mind to, won't we, Horse?" Rain lifted the empty bag from the horse's head and gently rubbed the space between the perked ears.

Slow anger built in him as he shaved jerked beef into the cup of hot water. He didn't like being hunted this way. It was hard for him to be patient. He knew what lay ahead, knew it was kill or be killed. A man didn't trail someone in this weather for the fun of it. A couple of advantages were on Rain's side. The man on his trail might not know that he'd been observed or that Rain had found shelter for himself and his horse.

Rain had learned seven years earlier, during the first few months he was on his own, that a man had to use his wits and make quick decisions if he expected to live very long.

Restless, he stirred the beef in his cup with the tip of his knife, then peered out through the opening in his hastily constructed shelter. There was nothing he could do now but wait and think . . . and remember.

One cold but bright day, seven long years before, shortly after he had left Quill's Station on his journey west, he had been plunged into a situation that required a quick decision. He had stopped to water his horse at a small spring that seeped from a rocky cliff when two trappers and an Indian came silently out of the woods and were within yards of him before he knew they were there. One trapper carried a long rifle in one hand; wrapped around his other was the end of a leash. He was leading the Indian who was bent almost double by the huge pack on his back. The other man carried a small pack, and the only weapon on him that Rain could see was a knife in his belt. They were disreputable-looking men with hard faces and dirty, unkempt clothing.

"Howdy."

"Howdy." Rain swung into the saddle and moved the horse away from the spring.

Suddenly, one of the men lunged forward and grabbed the bridle, jerking the bit cruelly. The horse squealed with pain and tried to rear, but the man clung until the tortured horse realized that resisting caused the pain.

"Well, looky here, Hopper. This'n ain't nothin' but a wet-eared kid!" The ruffian grinned at Rain. His tobacco-stained lips spread, showing stubs of rotting teeth. The putrid odor of something long dead wafted from his unwashed body.

"A kid ain't got no business with a horse when we ain't got nothin' but this here heathen to tote fer us. Ain't that right?" The other man jerked on the leash around the Indian's neck.

A coldness grew at the back of Rain's neck, and then a thin wave of heat washed over him. He knew with certainty that they meant to kill him and take his horse and gun. John Spotted Elk had always said to trust his own instincts. Rain's dark eyes studied the men. He did not want to kill them, yet he did not want to die.

"I'm takin' this here horse. We done 'bout wore that Injun down to a nubbin. I'm goin' ta have me that gun, too."

The man lifted his brawny arm to sweep Rain from the saddle. In the same instant Rain's hand lifted as swiftly as a striking snake. The long, thin blade he held glinted briefly in the sunlight before he plunged it into the man's throat.

"I don't think so," he hissed as he withdrew the knife and focused his full attention on the other man, who was trying to get his gun in position to fire while still holding on to the leash.

The Indian jerked just before the gun was fired at its target and the shot went wild. Rain felt a sharp sting on his earlobe as the bullet struck him. He lifted his rifle, coldly took aim and fired back. The force of the load knocked the trapper backward. In his death throes he pulled on the leash and dragged the Indian with him. As the exhausted Indian fell, the thong looped over the huge pack drew the noose tighter about his neck.

While the shots still echoed through the hills, Rain leaped from the horse, raced to the choking Indian, cut the thong and set the man free to breathe. Then he quickly reloaded his rifle, as both Juicy and Farr had told him to do immediately after firing. The two trappers lay sprawled, their arms flung wide in that last minute when death came sharply. Rain held a cloth to his ear to keep the blood from running down his neck and looked at them. A strange calmness took possession of him.

"It was them or me," he muttered aloud.

The Indian, a Shawnee from a village in the north, helped him bury the men. Then, taking the dead man's gun, the Indian silently slipped away, leaving Rain with the pack of valuable furs.

Rain traveled west and sold the mink, otter, marten, sable and fox furs in Saint Louis to Manuel Lisa's Fur Company for a considerable amount of money. He banked the money with the company and went to work as a crewman on one of the keelboats that traveled up the Missouri River.

He grew to be a man in a hard land where only the strong survived.

Rain's thoughts came back to the present. His long fingers touched the lobe of his ear, feeling the nick left there by a bullet fired during that first year. Since that day by the spring he had lived by the gun and the knife, killed swiftly and mercilessly, but only in order to save his own life. He had little hope of dying peacefully in bed. Perhaps someday he would die quickly, if he were lucky, he thought now as he munched on the tough meat and drank the hot broth. He had chosen his way of life, and he had lived among men who understood no other.

Rain kept his two fires going, counting on the heavy snowfall to absorb the smell of the woodsmoke so that it would not lead the hunter to him. He sat between the fires during the long afternoon hours. When finally darkness set in and he became drowsy, he spread his blanket on the warm ground and went to sleep.

He awakened suddenly. The wind had died with the coming of dawn. The silence was eerie. He lay without moving except for the hand that slid to the scabbard against his thigh. Slowly he drew his knife and palmed it. He heard again the sound that had awakened him, the scrape of something against the frozen brush outside his shelter. He thought for a moment that some wild creature was seeking the warmth of his fire, then he noticed the twitching ears of the horse. Born and bred in the mountains, the dun had a strong survival instinct.

Rain rolled out of his blankets. He had lived by his own instincts for a long time. In the hard years behind him, he had learned that things were not always as they seemed to be. He had known careless men and had helped bury some of them.

Head up, listening, Rain waited. The firelight cast a rosy glow inside the cave. He edged out of its light. The brush that covered the entry began to move. Rain inched over until he was behind the horse's rump.

Suddenly the brush was swept away and a man lunged into the cave, rifle in hand. At that instant Rain sent his knife spinning through the air with the precision of a well-aimed bullet. The blade pierced the man's shoulder, the force of the blow turning him halfway around. He cried out and fell back. The rifle dropped from his hands. Desperately he grabbed for his gun, but it was out of his reach.

Rain walked out from behind the horse, his rifle ready. He didn't know why he had, at the last instant, aimed high. Such consideration for his attacker would get him killed. Yet in the instant when he glimpsed the boy's face, he had known he couldn't kill him. Even though it was a mere boy who was trying to kill him, he told himself cynically, he would have ended up just as dead. Someone like this boy would kill him someday.

Rain's face assumed the mask of stillness worn by the Shawnee he had lived among when he was young. His black brows remained straight and unmoving, his dark lashes shaded his eyes against the snow's white glare. His face was as immobile as if it were etched in stone.

That the wounded boy was a long way from being a man was apparent from the smoothness of his cheeks. He had fallen back against the deadfall. Blood stained his worn wool coat and seeped on to the snow. Rain looked down at him, hating him for delaying his journey, hating him because now he'd have to take care of him. The frightened face that stared up at him was that of a half-starved kid.

"Go ahead. Kill me!" the boy snarled.

"I should have," Rain said coldly. "Why were you trailing me?"

"You ought to know, you . . ." The boy sank his teeth into his lower lip and refused to continue. The silence lasted for a full minute. Finally he said, "Well . . . what're ya waitin' for? If yo're agoin' to kill me, do it!"

"I can wait. I can get my knife after you bleed to death," Rain answered without emotion. He saw the look of terror con tort the young face. "You can tell me who sent you or I'll leave you to die right here in the snow."

"The army man," the boy blurted. "Said he'd give me fifty silver dollars if'n I brung in that ear of yores with the nick in it."

"You'd murder a man for fifty dollars?"

"I'd kill ya for free, ya bastard!" the boy yelled, his voice echoing in the ravine. "Yo're one of 'em that killed my folks . . . my sisters . . . my brothers—"

"Who said I did?"

"The militia, that's who! They're huntin ya—" Tears flooded the boy's eyes and he began to shake. His bare hand clenched into a fist, coloring the snow with his blood.

Rain knelt down beside him, and before the boy could guess his intentions, jerked the knife from his shoulder. The youth let out a cry, squeezed his eyes shut and cringed.

"I'm not going to kill you. Open your eyes, damn you! Tell me who sent you after me. If I ride off and leave you here, you'll be dead and stiff as a board in a few hours."

The boy's eyes flew open. They were filled with lethal hatred. "I won't tell ya a goddamn thing . . . ya murderin' scum!"

Rain sat back on his heels and studied the young face. The boy was hurt and scared. He was also full of hatred.

"You were sent to kill a murderer." It was a statement, not a question.

"A white man who'd ride with Indians to kill 'n rape women 'n girls is worse than . . . than . . ." The words clogged the boy's throat and he ended with a sob. Although his eyes were filled with tears he glared at Rain defiantly.

"Where did this happen?" Rain asked quietly.

"Ya know where, damn ya! Up on the Missouri."

"How far up?"

"Up near Franklin."

"I was there in August."

"Ya were there in September, too!"

"I spent September with Nathan Boone."

"Yo're a liar! The Boones wouldn't have nothin' to do with the likes a you."

"Do you want to lay there and argue about it? Or do you want me to help you with that shoulder?"

"I don't need . . . ya . . . to . . ." The boy's jaws shook so hard he couldn't talk.

"Stubborn and proud. Being proud and bullheaded won't keep you alive, boy. Can you walk?"

Without waiting for him to answer, Rain got behind him and lifted him to his feet. Then, with a hand firmly gripping his arm, he helped him enter the cave. The boy sank down close to the fire, and Rain threw his blanket around him to retain what warmth his body could develop.

"Where's your horse?"

"Off to the right a ways."

Rain snorted. "You didn't find shelter for your horse? I'll have to give you a few lessons in survival if you're going into the ambush business." He threw more fuel on the fire and waited until it blazed. "I'll get your horse, then I'll pack that shoulder." He led his own horse outside the shelter and tied him where he could paw the snow away to reach the dried grass.

He found the buckskin behind a clay bank, standing with his tail to the wind. Beside a deadfall he found the boy's belongings: a worn saddle, a bag half filled with grain for the horse, and a couple of ragged blankets.

Back at the cave the boy was too weak to protest when Rain dressed the wound. The wound itself wouldn't kill the kid, Rain decided, but the loss of blood and the cold might. Afterward he heated water in his cup, poured a generous amount of whiskey in it and made the boy drink it.

"You've followed me from Cahokia. Why did you wait so long to make your move?"

"I ain't tellin' you nothin'."

"You didn't much like the idea of shooting a man in the back, even for fifty dollars. You'd better find another line of work."

"I could kill ya with my bare hands—"

"You're not real sure I did it, are you?"

"Captain Perry said ya did."

"I figured Hammond Perry sent you. Didn't you wonder why Perry didn't call in the soldiers and have me arrested? If I was a criminal it would have been a feather in his cap," Rain pointed out. "He's not with the militia anymore. He was cashiered out of the regulars a few years ago. I'm not sure why, but old 'Rough and Ready' must have had good reason."

"He's a captain," the boy said stoutly. "He works for Major Taylor doin' secret, important things like findin' murderers like you."

"He's nothing and works for himself!" Rain said and snorted. Then he added, as if to himself, "I knew I shouldn't have entered that rifle shoot. I saw Perry there. That's where he pointed me out, wasn't it?" Rain took off his fur hat and ran his fingers through his dark hair. "But I hadn't kissed the sweet lips of Black Betty for a long while and I had a powerful thirst. You're drinking some of my prize."

"Ya should've stayed for the next round. The prize was a night with the town whore," the boy sneered.

Rain grinned. "I saw her. That's why I left. I was afraid I'd win." Rain kicked snow on to the fire to put it out. "Get on the horse. We'll start out for Quill's Station. I can't leave you or you'll starve or freeze, and I'm not staying here with you."

"I'm not goin'! I ain't hookin' up with no . . . murderer!"

"Listen to me, boy. I've put up with your mouth about as long as I'm going to. Call me that again and I'll backhand you. Understand?"

The boy tried to get to his feet, but his legs wilted under him. He gave Rain a sullen look but accepted his help. Rain boosted him into the saddle, then wrapped his own and the boy's blankets around him.

"You've lost a lot of blood. I don't want you to die on me, it's too damn cold to dig a grave."

Rain followed the frozen creek bed, leading the boy's horse. His breath and that of the horses rose in clouds. The boy rode with his face buried in the blankets. Even though there was no evidence of activity, Rain exercised caution, approaching every blind spot with care. In the open places he had plenty to think about.

Why would Hammond Perry, Farr's old enemy, want him dead? Rain had thought it no more than a coincidence when he had seen him again in Cahokia after having spotted him just a few days earlier in Saint Louis. Perry owned several large keelboats that took freight downriver to New Orleans and smaller ones that went up the Missouri and the Arkansas. It was said he also owned stores in a half dozen forts up and down the rivers. Nathan Boone had told Rain that Perry had been in Arkansas for the past year. Was he planning to move in and set up a trading post on the Arkansas River below the fort at Belle Point? Rain wondered.

Hammond Perry and Will Bradford, Rain remembered, had both served in the Ninth Military Department with headquarters at Belle Fontaine, fifteen miles north of Saint Louis. Will Bradford had been ordered to ascend the Arkansas River to the Poteau and build a fort at Belle Point— the important job Perry had hoped to get—but instead he had been dismissed shortly after Bradford and his company left on their assignment. If Perry had learned that Rain had gone to fetch Will's bride, that was probably the reason he had set the kid on him. Anything, Rain decided, was possible when Hammond Perry was involved.

He glanced back at the boy. How like Perry to get a down-at-the-heels kid to do his dirty work! He had actually convinced the boy Rain was one of the raiders who had killed his family. To a backwoods kid, a rich man like Perry must have seemed as reliable an authority as the governor of the territory, Rain mused. He didn't blame the boy for trying to kill him, but he wasn't going to let him keep him from spending Christmas at Quill's Station.

Quill's Station. Would Amy still be there? Rain remembered the way she had cried when he left the station seven long years ago. He had held her, kissed her, and promised to come back for her someday after Juicy had passed away. She had promised to think about Rain every day and to wait for him no matter how long he was gone. They were kids' promises, he thought now with a silent chuckle, although he had really meant them at the time. She was the first white girl he had known, the first girl he had talked to alone, the first one he had kissed. He remembered his surprise that her body had been so soft and her breasts so firm when he held her against him. She had smelled so fresh and clean that the memory of it lingered for days.

At times during the first few years he had thought about her, especially at night when he was on the keelboat feeling lonely, cut loose from everything that was familiar to him. As the years passed it became harder and harder to visualize her face, and gradually he stopped thinking about her.

Little Amy with the long skinny legs and freckles on her nose would be grown up now. When Farr's letter telling about Juicy's death reached him a year earlier, Amy had already been a widow for more than a year. Two years. That was a long time for a pretty woman to remain unwed among the woman-hungry men in the wilderness along the Wabash.

Pretty? Now why did he think that Amy had grown into a pretty woman? Because her sister looked like an angel didn't mean she would too. More than likely she had married again, turned to fat, and had a child or two.

Somehow the thought didn't sit well in his mind.

CHAPTER
Two

"This turkey is as old as I am!" Liberty Quill pushed the pan containing the huge bird back into the wall oven and gave her husband a disgusted look. "And he's as tough as shoe leather."

"You said you wanted a big one, love."

"Fiddle faddle! I didn't think I'd get one as old as the hills."

Farr sat in the rocker holding his four-month-old daughter against his shoulder and watched his wife with loving eyes. Sanctuary and peace existed for him in that sweet woman. Her white-blond hair was drawn in graceful wings to a knot at the back of her neck, framing her pale oval face. Her blue eyes flashed him a bright, happy smile. As she moved he caught the scent of her, the clean sweetness of her hair and skin. He never ceased to marvel that she was his and that she loved him. The baby burped and Farr felt something wet on his shoulder.

"Ah, shoot, Libby! She puked on me again."

Liberty laughed. "Serves you right for pounding her little

back so hard. Mercy, fetch your papa a cloth. He's complaining about a little puke."

Nine-year-old Mercy, whom Farr had found in a burned-out homestead seven years before, tugged on a strand of his hair at the nape of his neck as she passed behind him on the way to the wash stand.

"Someday I'm going to tan your backside, young lady," Farr growled menacingly.

"You always say that, but I know you won't." Mercy wrinkled her nose and gave him a saucy grin.

"But he ought to. It'd take some of the sass out of you." A tall youth called out as he came in the door, quickly closed it behind him to shut out the cold and stood on the rag rug stamping his feet to rid them of snow.

"Just hush up, Daniel Phelps. You're not giving orders around here!"

"No bickering on Christmas Eve, Mercy. That goes for you, too, Daniel." Liberty gazed fondly at the boy, and her husband gazed fondly at her.

"Tell *him*. He's always saying, 'do this, do that'." Mercy tossed her blond head and behind Liberty's back stuck her tongue out at Daniel.

"Shhh . . . I did tell him. Be quiet or you'll wake up the baby."

"Papa, Daniel's back! Ya done the chores, Daniel? Can we go out and fire the shots, Papa?" A towheaded boy scampered down the stairs from the loft. His shouts woke the baby, and she let out a screech.

"Oh, Zack! We can see that Daniel's back. Must you always shout?" Liberty spoke loudly to her five-year-old son so she could be heard over her daughter's frightened cries. Zachary, named for Major Zachary Taylor, was a big, robust child with his father's green eyes and his mother's light hair.

"Take Mary Elizabeth, Libby, and I'll get these younguns

out from under your feet." Farr stood and passed the crying infant over to her mother.

"If you're going to make a racket, go far enough from the house so you won't scare the baby. There, there, darling . . ." Liberty crooned.

"We'll just fire off a few shots to celebrate." Farr shrugged into his coat. His green eyes twinkled with laughter. The lines about his eyes and mouth attested to the fact that he smiled often. "We're suppose to make a little racket on Christmas Eve. I bet your Liberty Bell is ringing in Philadelphia right now."

"Silly man! It isn't *my* bell; I'm just named after it. Folks in town will think you're crazy as a loon to waste all that good powder."

"Since when do you care what folks think, Mrs. Quill?" His eyes mocked her.

"I guess I don't, now that you mention it."

"I'm going! I'm going to shoot the gun too!" Mercy pulled her coat from the peg on the wall and tried to wiggle around Daniel to get out the door.

"Hold on there, you stupid girl!" He yanked on her arm to stop her, then shoved a cap down on her head. "Put your coat on before you go out."

"Dan, Dan, the bossy man!" Mercy chanted and stamped her foot. "Oh, you make me so mad! Papa!" she shrieked when Daniel wrapped a scarf around and around her neck and drew it tight. "Make him leave me be."

Liberty watched with a tolerant smile. Daniel had been looking after Mercy since the day they had found him, a four-year-old boy, sitting beside his dead mother. She had tossed him into hiding in the berry bushes to save him when their caravan had been attacked by river pirates.

"Daniel's right this time, Mercy. If you're going with us, put on your cap and mittens and wrap that scarf around your neck. If you get sick it will spoil your Christmas." Farr helped his young son into his coat and shoved a fur cap down over his ears. "Put on your mittens and let's get out of here before Mama loses her temper and calls off Christmas."

"Calls off Christmas? Can Mama do that?" Zack asked with a fearful look over his shoulder at his mother.

"Your mama usually does whatever she sets her mind to." Farr opened the door and a puff of cold air came rushing in. "Get the sled, Daniel, and let's go." While ushering the children out, his eyes, soft with twinkling lights, rested lovingly on his wife's face.

After the door closed, Liberty pulled the rocker up close to the fire, sat down and opened her dress. The baby's seeking mouth found the nipple on her breast and sucked greedily. She hugged her small daughter to her and rocked contentedly. She had caught the look her husband had given her before he closed the door. He had sought her eyes, and she his, as they did a hundred times or more each day. He did not have to touch her or even move toward her to let her know she was wrapped in his love.

Liberty could hear her sister moving around upstairs. Amy had been quiet and restless lately, no doubt dreading their father and stepmother's visit the next day. Amy had not forgiven her father for trying to force her when she was only twelve to marry Stith Lenning, a man so cruel and devious that Farr had later been forced to kill him. Amy had married old Juicy Deverell instead. Now her father wanted her to marry Tally Perkins, his stepson. Tally had proposed marriage almost immediately after Juicy had died two years ago.

Amy came lightly down the steep stairway. Unusually tall for a girl, she was amazingly slender and graceful, with a long neck, arms and legs. She wore her hair loose today. It hung down her back in shimmering reddish brown waves. The most arresting feature in her fragile, finely sculpted face was her eyes. They were pure amber, large and thickly fringed with long, brown, gold-tipped lashes. Juicy had once described her as quick as a cat, smart as a whip, and wild as a deer. The old man had married her, given her his name for protection, and treated her like the beloved granddaughter he'd never had.

The last years of Juicy's life had been devoted to Amy. He taught her to load and shoot the gun in half a minute; and more important than speed, he taught her to hit what she shot at. He taught her to use a knife, a whip, and to follow a track through the forest. The old man took great pride in the fact that she could handle a canoe, hunt, and trap almost as well as Farr, who was the best he had ever known. In general, Juicy taught her the things he would have taught a grandson. Amy, in turn, gave to him the love and devotion she had never felt for her own father, and she missed him terribly after he died.

"I can smell the turkey."

"It'll have to cook all night. The partridges won't take so long. I'll put them in early in the morning. All we have left to make are the pies. Ah . . . Mary Elizabeth, I'm soaking wet. Why couldn't you have done that when your papa was holding you?" Liberty lifted her daughter and put a folded cloth beneath her. The baby spit and cooed and smiled. Liberty held the chubby infant to her shoulder and watched her sister roam around the room.

"It's stopped snowing." Amy let the curtain fall back in place, turned and put her hands on her hips. "Why do I always look for him on Christmas Eve?"

Liberty knew who "he" was—Rain Tallman, the boy Amy had loved since she was twelve years old.

"Because the year of the earthquake he came on Christmas Eve. In his letter to Farr he said that he was coming back sometime this year."

"Well, the year is about over, damn it," Amy said crossly and turned back to the window.

"Don't swear, love."

"Why not? Sometimes I feel like swearing. He knows Uncle Juicy is gone. I've waited two years for him to come back!"

"Rain won't be the same boy who went away seven years ago, Amy. By now he's a man who has seen more country than a dozen men put together. He may have . . . married, put down roots, had children—"

Amy spun around and glared at her sister. "If he has, I'll kill him," she said slowly and venomously. Then her voice softened and the anger went from her face. "I'll be an old maid before he comes back!"

"You'll never be an old maid. You're a widow, remember? There are a dozen men in the territory who would come running if you blinked an eye in their direction."

"They're all clods like Tally Perkins! If Papa even mentions his name to me tomorrow I'll throw up. I wish he and Maude weren't coming for Christmas. We'll have to listen to Papa tell about his bad back and how *he* runs the farm. They'll bring Tally and Walter, who's every bit as boring as Tally, and it'll just spoil the day."

Liberty laughed. "Maude has done a good job handling Papa these past seven years. I'm glad she's the one who has had to put up with him and not us. She sees to it that he does his share of the work, and I think he's been happy with her in spite of it."

"She's welcome to him. He did nothing but complain all the way out here when we were traveling from Middlecrossing. He was a grump! You had to do everything. I don't know how you stood him, Libby. Or how I did either, for that matter. You're strong. You know what you want and set about getting it."

"So do you, love. I've not seen you back down from anything yet."

"I just feel like I'm suspended here . . . waiting—"

"Oh, honey! I don't know what to tell you. Seven years is

a long time. And if Rain does come back he'll not be the same. Heaven only knows where all he's been. My, my, when I think of him going all the way up the Missouri on a Keelboat, and him only a lone boy. It's just a marvel that he lived through those first years."

"Rain was never a *boy*, Libby. I think he was born a man! Remember how stubborn he was? He'd get his mind set and no one could change it. He said he was going away to find out what kind of man he was. How long is it going to take him, for goodness sake?"

"It took courage for him, a boy who hadn't even shaved yet, to leave here all by himself and go west where there are hardly any settlers at all."

"He didn't want to fight against his people. Not that the Shawnee were his people, even if he was raised by John Spotted Elk. There wasn't much trouble around here anyway. Some people say we had some peace because of Farr's strong connection with Tecumseh. I think it was because the Shawnee respected you. They called you the White Dove of the Wabash for good reason."

"I think it was because Farr had organized the settlers so well and built the stockade." Liberty stood and gently placed the sleeping child in the cradle.

"I get scared when I think about how easily Rain could have died during the earthquake." Amy was looking out the window again. "All of his village was wiped out except for a dozen or so. We're his family, now. Damn him! He was always bullheaded—"

"I remember. Stubborn and proud. The first year he sent back money to pay for the gun and the horse he rode away on. Help me move the cradle into the other room, Amy. Farr and the children will be back soon. They're so excited about Christmas they can't possibly be quiet. Mary Elizabeth will never be able to sleep in here with all the racket."

"What can I do to help with the fixings, Libby?" Amy

asked after they had settled the baby in the spare room, built up the fire to keep the room warm and returned to the kitchen. "Making pies isn't my favorite thing to do, but I need to be doing something."

"You'd rather be in those buckskin britches with your gun in your hand. My but Juicy ruined you for homemaking chores." Liberty smiled fondly at her sister. "You look awfully pretty in your blue dress with your hair hanging down. Are you going to wear it tomorrow? If you do, poor Tally won't be able to eat a bite for looking at you." When she got no response to her teasing, Liberty pulled the pan out of the oven and poked at the big bird with a two-tined fork. "Maybe it's going to tender up after all. I may even have to apologize to Farr." She looked over her shoulder to see her sister peering out the window again. "Are the presents wrapped for the children?"

"Every last one of them," Amy said absently and let the window curtain fall back in place.

A blizzard blew in toward evening and intensified during the night. Amy lay in her bed and listened to the wind tormenting the frozen branches of the oak tree beside the house. Another Christmas Eve had come and gone and Rain had not returned.

She flopped over on her back and stared into the darkness. Through the open gateway through which her imagination rushed, she could see his lean, dark face, straight black brows and deep-set eyes so blue they seemed at first to be black. His hair was black and thick and slightly curled on the ends. He walked with his head up, his back straight, assuming an air of utter indifference. Yet his eyes bored into everything with an intensity wholly at variance with his relaxed stance.

Amy's eyes became slightly damp as her mind swung back, remembering the last time they were together, remembering his softly spoken words.

"Don't cry, little Amy. You're married to Juicy. He'll keep you safe until I come back."

"But I don't want you to go. I'll . . . miss you . . ."

"I've got to go. I've got to find out what kind of man I am."

"You're a good man. Rain. The best man I know. Farr and Juicy think you're a good man and I . . . I love you."

"Ah . . . Amy. You're just a kid. You're not ready for grown-up love."

"How do you know I'm not, Mr. Smarty?"

"Because I'm not ready, and I'm older than you are."

"Please don't go—"

"I've got to."

"But why?"

"You know why. I'll be back—"

"I'll think about you every day, Rain."

Amy turned restlessly in the bed. "I'm not waiting much longer, Rain Tallman," she whispered aloud. "I don't want to live the rest of my life in my sister's house. I want a home of my own." She flopped over on her side. "You . . . mule's ass. If you've gotten married and have a parcel of kids I'll shoot you! Damned if I won't!"

The storm blew itself out in the night, and when morning came the sun shone on bright new snow.

Amy awakened to find Mercy's bed empty. She should have known, she thought with a bemused smile when she heard voices downstairs. Mercy had awakened Daniel and Zack so they could eat an early breakfast, something Liberty insisted they do before they open their presents. Amy threw back the covers and shivered as a blast of cold air hit her warm body. Her feet found the fur slippers on the floor beside her bed and snuggled into them. She slipped her dress on over her nightgown, threw a shawl about her shoulders and hurried down the stairs.

"Hurry up, Amy. We're waiting for you." Mercy stood beside the table gazing at the wrapped packages. "Mama said this is mine." Her fingertips caressed the paper-wrapped bundle tied with a yarn string. "Mama opened hers already. Looky, Amy. Embroidered silk. Papa sent all the way to Philadelphia for it." The blue silk Mercy held up for her to see shimmered in the lamplight.

"All the way to Philadelphia?" Amy's fingertips brushed the material. "I've never seen anything so pretty."

"Mama gave Papa the pipe she had Uncle Colby send—"

"Why don't you hush up, Mercy, and let Zack tell something?" Daniel stood back from the table of gifts as if he were too old to get excited over presents, but his dark eyes strayed often to the package with his name on it.

"I don't have to hush up till Papa tells me to. So there!" Mercy wrinkled her nose in an attempt to make an ugly face at Daniel.

"We'd better look at the calendar again, Liberty." Farr had a serious look on his face. "Is Christmas today, or is it tomorrow? We might open the presents on the wrong day."

Zack looked from his father to his mother, waiting anxiously for her reply.

"Of course it's Christmas," Liberty said quickly. "Shame on you for teasing."

"If you're sure it's Christmas, we'd better get started." Farr sat down in the chair beside the fireplace, reached up and pulled Liberty down on his lap. They watched as the children opened their gifts.

Mercy was first. She squealed with delight when she saw a hand mirror, brush and comb set. Also tucked into the package were store-bought stockings and a length of ribbon. Daniel had a new skinning knife and a scabbard. In Zack's package was a sack of marbles, a ball made of leather and a storybook.

Amy waited until the children's excitement waned, then opened her package and lifted out a pair of soft, leather gloves. She slipped her hand inside and made a fist.

"They're lovely! And, oh, so soft—"

"They came from Philadelphia too," Liberty said.

From where she was seated on Farr's lap, Liberty watched her sister and noted her forced gaiety. Lately she had often seen a look of despair on Amy's face. If only she could see Rain Tallman once again, Liberty thought. He would be either the person Amy remembered and loved or a stranger made hard by the life he had led. If that were the case, the ties would be broken and Amy would be free to find happiness with someone else.

Liberty's hand caressed the back of her husband's neck absently as she wished fervently that her sister might someday have the love and contentment she had found.

A sleigh pulled by two prancing, steaming horses came up the lane from the road about mid-morning and stopped at the front of the house. Maude and Elija Carroll got out, baskets on their arms, their cheerful greetings on the cold air. Maude's two sons remained in the sleigh to take it and the horses to the barn.

Liberty was holding open the door when they reached it, and Maude's chatter preceded her into the room.

"My, what a fine ride it was. When the storm blew in last night I was afraid we'd not get to come. Smells pretty in here, Libby. I'll just bet it tastes pretty too." She pecked Liberty on the cheek. "Come on in, Elija. She can't hold the door open all day. How's the baby? My but I can't wait to see how much she's grown."

"She's fine. Hello, Papa. Hang your things there on the pegs. Give me the basket, Maude, so you can shed your coat."

Liberty genuinely liked her father's wife. Maude was pleasant, if snoopy at times. Best of all, she ruled Elija with a strong but gentle hand. Although Amy refused to have anything to do with Maude, she seemed not to mind. She and Mercy, however, had a special relationship. She liked to sew and Mercy liked pretty things.

Tally and Walter came in followed by Farr, who winked at Liberty when he saw Tally's mouth drop open at the sight of Amy in spite of the fact that she had refused to put on a dress and had braided her hair into a long plait that hung down her back to her waist. She wore her usual clothes—a shirt that came down to her knees and was belted about her narrow waist, fringed leather pants, and warm, fur-lined moccasins that were elaborately fringed and beaded.

Amy helped Maude and Liberty prepare the Christmas dinner. They chatted about the amount of food Maude had brought and speculated as to which moment the turkey would be done just right. Maude passed on what news she had.

"Florence Thompson didn't last long after Harriet ran off with that peddler man. He was a Jew fellow and real smart, so George says."

"He couldn't be *too* smart if he took up with Harriet," Amy murmured.

"Harriet wasn't really so fat and lazy after George clamped down on her," Maude said. "Florence didn't change. She was a bigot until the day she died. I've heard that George is courting a widow in Vincennes."

"I hope he can be happy. I believe he was embarrassed when Florence acted as if she was so much better than the rest of us. Do I have enough places set at the table?" Liberty asked. "I'd better count again."

"There'll be ten of us," Maude said. "Have you heard from Willa and Colby Carroll lately?"

"They're still at Carrolltown. Farr thinks Colby wants to come back to Quill's Station and build a gristmill."

"A gristmill? Wouldn't that be grand? My my, when I think how fast time has gone by. Only a few years ago there was nothing here but a small house and a storage shed. Now you've got five rooms with real glass windows and a town growing up around you."

Liberty laughed. "Farr couldn't wait to tear down that stockade. He hated being fenced in. The town just seemed to sprout after he built the merchandise store. Now we have the sawmill and the inn. Farr could run the sawmill twenty-four hours a day if there was daylight. Everyone wants sawed boards."

"Have you ever counted the people who have moved in here since the war?"

"Over one hundred and fifty. I have eleven children in school not counting our own. But at times I think it's getting to be too crowded here for Farr. I've seen him standing on the porch looking off toward the west."

"Heavens! He wouldn't pull out and leave you here. He thinks you're the sun and the moon."

"Of course he wouldn't. If he should decide to go, I'd go with him."

"You couldn't do that, Libby," Maude scoffed. "You've got the school to think of."

"I've got my husband to think of, Maude. He comes first, last and always with me."

Maude passed out gaily wrapped packages before they sat down to Christmas dinner. Elija had carved an elaborate whistle with two finger holes for different sounds for Zack and a turkey-calling whistle for Daniel. Maude had made a bonnet for Mercy, the brim edged with lace and ribbons. Mercy put it on and danced over to Amy so she could tie ribbons beneath her chin. There was a bean bag for Mary Elizabeth, handkerchiefs for Liberty and Amy and knitted socks for Farr.

Whenever Amy glanced over at Tally Perkins, he was staring at her as if he could not believe, draw breath, move or speak. His mouth was agape as if he were catching flies. Amy could scarcely suppress the desire to stick out her tongue, put her thumbs in her ears and wiggle her fingers at him. Compared to Rain Tallman, Tally Perkins was a milk-sop. She wouldn't have him if he were served up on a silver platter with a silver ring in his nose, she thought angrily. He was the most boring person she had ever known.

Amy regarded her sister and Farr. Farr had paused behind Liberty and was nuzzling her ear with his nose. He wasn't ashamed to show love for his wife. He never passed her without touching her. It was as if he couldn't help himself. Liberty turned to look at him and between them passed a unity of thought, a rapport cemented in love and friendship. Amy looked away quickly, afraid she would cry. When a man looked at a woman the way Farr looked at Liberty, she had everything, Amy thought.

Suddenly Amy was swamped with despair, and dark thoughts vied for possession of her mind. Oh, God! What if it was her lot to spend the rest of her life with someone like Tally Perkins? She wouldn't do it! She wanted a love like Liberty and Farr shared. She could have it with Rain. She knew he would be changed when he came back for her, but she knew what he'd be like. He'd be hard, tough and lonely —and he'd want her, as much as she wanted him.

The day passed slowly for Amy. Somehow she managed not to be cornered by Tally, but late in the afternoon she was cornered by her father.

"It's time ya took a man, Amy. Come on home with me 'n Maude, get to know Tally, start ya up a family. Tally's a good, strong man. He'd be good to ya——"

"Start a family of what? Dumb-heads? I'd sooner bed down with a warthog."

"Hush up that talk! It ain't fittin'. Ya ain't got no cause ta be a burden on Libby when ya got a pa and a ma and a man willin' to wed ya."

"Ha! Burden on Libby? You rode her back all the way from Middlecrossing! Maude isn't my ma and Tally's not a man to my way of thinking. I suppose he's got the parts, but that's all he's got. He's got no backbone or he'd be doing his own talking."

"Ya've got to where ya talk plumb bawdy!"

"It's no concern of yours how I talk."

"I can order ya ta do as I say! Yo're a unwed daughter——"

"You just try ordering me to do anything! I'm not a child of twelve——"

"Yo're still carryin' that grudge, ain't ya? We didn't have us no home, no nothin'. I'd knowed Stith back home 'n I was tryin' to make a place fer us."

"For yourself you mean. I'll never forgive you for trying to sell me off to a mean, low-down bastard like Stith Lenning. And I'll not forget that Farr and Juicy stepped in and saved me. I'll tell you, Papa, although it's no business of yours, I'm not a burden here. Juicy left me with enough money to pay my way. Is that what you're after? Do you want my money for yourself, or for Tally?"

"It'd give ya and Tally a fine start. Tally's a good hand, a settled man——"

"Tally's a stupid dolt who does whatever you and Maude tell him to do. Now stop pushing him at me!"

"Yo're hard, Amy. Yo're makin' talk of yorself ramin'

'round in britches ahuntin' like a man. Folks'll think ya ain't had no bringin' up a'tall."

Only by closing her eyes for a moment was Amy able to keep her temper under control. What angered her the most was her father's total lack of regard for her feelings. He hadn't cared a flitter for her when she was young, and he didn't care for her now. It was Maude he was trying to please. She was pressuring him to get her to marry Tally. These were her thoughts as she stood before him, fists on her hips.

"I'd not have had any bringing up at all if not for Libby. You were too busy complaining about your back and trying to get out of work," she said cruelly.

"Yo're hard," he said again. "Ya ain't ort a talk like that to yore pa."

"Does the truth hurt, Papa?"

Elija snorted through his nose. "I know what yo're up to. Yo're thinkin' that kid what was raised by the Injuns'll come back. Yo're just lollygaggin' 'round waitin' fer a man what's got the wanderin's. He jist up 'n pulled foot—"

"Hush up! Don't say another word or I'll never speak to you again even if you are my papa!"

Amy's head was up, her shoulders rigid. She met his gaze squarely, looking at him as if he were something beneath her contempt. The change in her manner was even a shock to Elija. Her body was as stiff as a board, her eyes hard as stones and glowing fiercely. She snarled her words as if she hated him.

"Elija, it'll be dark soon. We'd better be going." Maude had heard enough of the conversation to know Elija was pushing too hard. She took his arm and gently pulled him toward the coats hanging beside the door. "Come see us, Amy. I'm making a dress for Mercy. Maybe you can bring her for a fitting and spend a day or two."

"No," Amy said bluntly. "Daniel can bring her." She turned her back, and from the set of her shoulders Maude knew there would be no reasoning with her that day.

"All right, dear. Come along, Elija, and help me with the baskets."

As soon as they went out the door, Amy slid her feet into heavy, fur-lined moccasins and put on Juicy's old fur coat. She pushed her hair up into a wool cap and slipped out the back way. She had been cooped up too long in the house with too many people. She needed solitude, the scent of the woods, freedom.

The setting sun transmitted rays of red and orange colors across the white snow that crunched beneath her feet. She cut through the woods, walking with her head up, as Juicy had taught her to do. The sights and sounds and smells of the woods made her realize how precious her freedom was; how much better this was than the prison walls of a cabin, and how much better than being tied to a dull man like Tally Perkins for the rest of her life.

Her eyes grew misty, filled and spilled over.

Amy came out of the woods and started down the road leading to Mr. Washington's ferry. It wasn't Mr. Washington's now, but she still thought of it as his. The giant black man who built it had been killed during an Indian attack, and the ferry was now run by the Harmonists, members of a strict religious group under George Rapp who had moved in from Pennsylvania a year or two ago and established a colony just across the river on the Indiana side.

She rounded a bend in the road and saw two riders coming toward her; the sound of their horses' hooves were muffled by the soft snow. A man in a heavy wool coat and fur hat was riding a dun and leading a buckskin carrying a blanket-wrapped figure leaning on the horse's neck. Probably a drunk, Amy thought with distaste. Down-and-outers moved through there all the time on their way to Vincennes. In the summer they came by boat; in the winter by horseback or on foot. If they didn't have money to stay at the inn they would bed down in the barn. She moved off the road toward the timber and slipped her hand inside her coat where her knife was tucked in her belt.

Amy had intended to turn into the woods again, but the men had seen her. She had no fear of them; but if they meant her harm, she could lose them in the deep thicket. She continued on along the edge of the woods a good two dozen feet back from the road.

The man on the dun horse pulled up. He was big and had a black stubble of beard on his face. The horse moved restlessly as if wanting to go on. The man held him with a light hand on the rein.

"Boy," he called. "Is this Quill's Station?"

Amy nodded. There was something about his voice and the way he sat the saddle that kindled a spark in her memory. A deep frown wrinkled her brow.

"It's changed," he said as if to himself. "Ruined. Hell! It's a regular town." He dipped his head at Amy, kicked the dun, and the horse moved on down the road.

Amy stood for a full minute looking after him. A tingling started in her legs and moved upward as the knowledge of who he was slowly seeped into her senses. She froze, then her muscles tensed and she began to shake. Her heart stopped and then began again, thundering in her ears.

"My God . . . it's him!" She lost her breath. "Rain! Rain has come back!" She pressed a clenched fist tightly against her mouth to keep from calling out, and her eyes blurred so that she could scarcely see him as he rode on down the trail.

Boy! He had called her boy! He hadn't recognized her.

Jubilation, fear and anxiety vied for possession of her mind. She had to get back to the house and out of her britches before she saw him again. She darted into the woods and ran as if she were being chased by a pack of wolves.

Her heart sang, He's back! He's back! It's Christmastime and Rain has come home!

CHAPTER
Three

Rain tugged on the lead rope, glanced at the boy who rode behind him, and moved the dun on down the road toward the settlement.

Everything but the slow smoke that rose from a dozen chimneys was still in the cold evening. Quill's Station was a convenient stop, he had heard, for those traveling between the Ohio River and Vincennes. A town had sprung up where seven years earlier there had been only the log cabin, the shed and sawyer camp. Nothing was familiar to Rain except the bend in the road. He rounded it and recognized Farr's place by the big oak tree in front and the barn and stone well house behind. The light of a lamp shone through a glass windowpane. During the years he had lived here, the window had been covered with deerhide scraped paper-thin to admit the light. Civilization, he mused, had come to Quill's Station.

Rain was a man who never rode without caution, never approached even a friendly place without care. Now his eyes roamed and caught movement as he stopped the horse a few yards from the front door. He saw the boy in the fur coat running from behind the barn, heading for the back of the house. At that moment the front door swung open and Farrway Quill, a broad smile of welcome on his face, came to meet him.

"Rain!" An older and slightly heavier Farr wrung Rain's hand in a hearty handshake when he stepped from the saddle. "It sure is good to see you." There was genuine gladness in his voice.

"It's good to see you." A smile creased Rain's tired face, and his dark eyes shone with pleasure.

Farr took a step back to look him up and down. "My God! I can't believe it. What happened to that skinny kid who left here?"

"Either I've grown some or you've shrunk. How in the world are you?" The two men stood grinning at each other, hands clasped to each other's shoulders.

"Fine, Rain. Just fine."

"And Libby?"

"She's fine too." Farr shook his head in amazement. "You're taller than I am." He looked past Rain to the second horse and the figure lying against the horse's neck. "What've you got here?"

"A boy who needs a bed and some attention to a knife wound. I saw a sign that says there's bed and board up ahead. I can take him there."

"You'll do no such thing. You move one foot from here and Libby will have my head on a platter. She'll take care of him."

Rain untied the wounded boy from the saddle and helped him to the ground. "Can you walk?"

The boy groaned and held on to the saddle horn. "Hell yes, I can... walk!" he gritted. "If... ya give me a minute."

Rain scooped him up in his arms. "You ornery, stubborn little cuss. You don't know quit."

"Take him on in the house, Rain. Daniel and I will take care of the horses."

Liberty was at the door when they reached it. She was even more beautiful than Rain remembered. She smiled at him. Huge tears glistened in her eyes.

"I'm . . . going to hug you and kiss you . . . later, Rain Tallman. Then I'm going to hit you for staying away so long."

"I'm going to hold you to that first part, Libby." Rain's dark eyes smiled into hers.

"What's the matter with your friend?"

"He's got a knife wound in his shoulder and he's half starved."

"My goodness! Bring him in here. Get a lamp, Mercy." Liberty led the way through the main room and into another room that held three bunks, one attached to each of three walls, and a fireplace on the other. She turned back the covers on one of the bunks and Rain eased the boy down.

Mercy came with the lamp and set it on the table in the middle of the room, then stood back and gazed wide-eyed at the giant of a man in the heavy wool coat.

"Let's get his coat and boots off and get him in bed." Liberty gently eased the boy's arms out of his coat, opened his shirt and removed the blood-soaked bandage Rain had wrapped around his shoulder. "The bleeding has stopped. But he's shaking like a leaf." She pressed a clean cloth to the wound and tucked covers around him.

Rain removed his own coat and fur cap and looked down to see a towhaired boy with big green eyes gazing up at him. He was about the size Daniel had been when Rain saw him last.

"Howdy," Rain said and held out his hand. A small hand went into it.

"Howdy. Are you Rain Tallman?"

"That's my name. What's yours?"

"Zachary Taylor Quill. I'm five years old. Papa told me about you. He says you can whip every bear that growls in the bushes."

"Well, I don't know about that."

"Papa says you can show me how to Indian wrestle."

"Zack, there will be plenty of time for you to talk to Rain. Go rock the cradle so Mary Elizabeth will go back to sleep. But gently," Liberty cautioned.

"Ah, shoot! That old . . . poot spoils ever'thing."

"Zack Quill! I'll see to you later. Go tend to your sister. Rain, we've got to get this boy warm." Libby went to the door and called, "Amy." When there was no answer Libby prodded Mercy in the back. "Honey, run and tell Amy I've got to have help. Oh, there's Farr. Fill the warming pan with coals, Farr. We'll wrap it and put it at his feet. Put some whiskey in a mug, Daniel, and pour in some hot water from the teakettle."

Rain stood back and watched as the family all worked to help the stranger he had brought into their home. When Daniel brought the mug, Liberty held the boy's head and forced him to drink the whiskey. He coughed and sputtered and tried to avoid the mug being put to his mouth.

"Drink it all," she commanded sternly. "You'll be warm in a minute."

Rain held out his hand to Daniel. "You've shot up like a weed, Daniel."

"I guess I have. But I've got a ways to go to catch you."

Liberty spoke over her shoulder. "What's this boy's name, Rain?"

"I don't know. I just met up with him this morning."

Rain was looking over her head as he spoke. His eyes were on the girl who stood in the doorway and her eyes were on him. She was tall and slender, with high, firm breasts and a small waist. She wore a blue dress and her hair hung down her back in shimmering reddish brown waves. When Amy was young she had reminded Rain of an unsure, long-legged colt. Now she was more like a poised, high-spirited filly. The thought crossed his mind that he had seen prettier women, but this one would draw attention in any crowd, not only because of her height but because of the light way she moved: chin up, shoulders back, and a proud lift of her head on that slender neck. Her eyelashes were long and her lids drooped a bit, hiding her eyes. She came into the room, walked briskly past him as if he weren't there, and set a basin of water on the floor beside the bunk.

"What's the matter with him?"

Her voice is different too, Rain thought. It was no longer shrill, but soft and musical.

"He's got a knife wound in his shoulder." Liberty dipped the cloth into the warm water and pressed it to the wound.

"Who knifed him?" Amy whispered to Liberty, but her voice carried across the room to Rain.

"I did," he said and moved forward to lift the end covers so Farr could put the warming pan to the boy's feet. "He was laying for me."

"Thunderation!" Liberty exclaimed. "He's a boy not much older than Daniel." She brushed the hair back from his flushed face and clucked her tongue sorrowfully.

"He's old enough to pull a trigger," Rain said dryly.

"He's right, honey." Farr placed his hand on his wife's shoulder. "Can you and Amy take it from here? I'll fix Rain something to eat."

Amy, kneeling beside the bunk, looked up and met Rain's dark eyes. The light from the lamp on the table touched his face, turning his cheeks into dark hollows and his eyes into shadows beneath black, level brows. His mouth as much as his eyes set the tone of him. It was firm and unsmiling. He looked big, hard and tough. He was a man who needed no one, she thought with a sudden pang. The mark of the loner was on him.

"Hello, Amy."

"Hello, Rain," she murmured softly and turned away.

Rain followed Farr into the other room. Zack stopped rocking the cradle. Mary Elizabeth let out a shrill cry of protest.

"Old bawl-baby!" Zack said with disgust. "All she's good for is to bawl and mess her *pants*."

Farr picked up his daughter and the screeches stopped instantly. "You're spoiled, young lady," he said with a chuckle. "This is Mary Elizabeth, Rain. We lost one between her and Zack."

Rain looked at the small face and a slow grin shifted the tired lines of his face. "She's not much bigger than a skinned jackrabbit."

Farr chuckled again. "No, but she can make a hell of a lot more racket. Do you want to get Rain something to eat, Mercy, or hold Mary Elizabeth while I do it?"

"I'll get Rain something to eat." Mercy flashed Rain a smile. Papa didn't know it, she thought gleefully, but Mary Elizabeth *had* messed her diaper.

Because of Rain's homecoming, Zack and Mercy were allowed to stay up far later than their usual bedtime. They both protested vigorously when Liberty finally insisted that they say good night and climb the stairs to the loft.

"Why doesn't Daniel have to go to bed? He's just a *boy!*" Mercy said scathingly.

"What Daniel does or does not do has nothing to do with you, young lady," Liberty said sternly. "Run along."

"Papa, can't I stay?" Zack looked beseechingly up at his father.

"Mind your mother, son. You can talk to Rain tomorrow."

"Oh, all right."

Liberty took the baby into the other room to nurse her, and Farr took his pipe and tobacco from the mantel shelf.

"Smoke, Rain?"

Rain went to the saddlebags that Daniel had placed just inside the door and took out his pipe. "You've got quite a family, Farr."

"Yes, but I still miss Juicy. He was a part of my life for a long time."

"I was sorry to hear he was gone. He taught me a lot."

"Me too. I've wondered where I would be and what I would be doing if not for Juicy. I was mighty lucky to have had him when my grandfather died."

"He lived longer than most men." Rain drew on the pipe, leaned back and stretched his feet to the fire. "I hardly recognized the place, Farr. You've got a regular town here."

"Every week or two someone moves in. It's good . . . in a way. But—" He hesitated and looked into the fire for a moment before he spoke again. "I'd gladly change it back to the way it was before people started moving in if I could."

"Town life isn't for me, either."

"You said that boy in there laid for you," Farr said after a companionable silence. "Seems like he was taking a big chunk to chew for a kid."

"He thought he had a right. His family was killed by a raiding party, and someone convinced him I was one of them. It was your old friend, Hammond Perry, by the way."

"Perry? I haven't heard anything about him since he went west with Zachary Taylor."

"Taylor got rid of him. He's in the keelboat and trade business now. I saw him in Cahokia a few days back. That's where he set the kid on me."

"I was sure someone would've killed that bastard Perry by now," Farr snorted, remembering how Perry had tried to get him hanged for treason seven years earlier.

"He'll get it. He doesn't have the protection of the militia behind him now."

With knowledge born of long experience, Rain's trained ears picked up the sound of soft leather whispering against the plank floor behind him, and his eyes caught a shadow on the ceiling. Even without the faint aroma of rose water he would have known that Amy had come into the room and moved to the far corner behind him. Seconds later he heard the creak of ropes as she seated herself in a chair. Suddenly he had a prickly feeling on the back of his neck, a feeling born from years of caution. Amy's eyes were on him.

"Perry set the boy on you, huh?" Farr broke into his thoughts.

"This ear with the nick in it was worth fifty dollars in silver to the boy." Rain touched his earlobe and flashed his friend a shy grin.

"How come you aimed high? You could always put a blade where you wanted it."

"It was an instant decision. The kid didn't look like a killer. He looked hungry and scared and kind of reminded me of myself at that age."

Farr chuckled. "If you were ever scared you didn't show it."

"I was scared plenty of times during those first years. Not quite so often now, but it comes on once in a while."

"Do you have any plans for settling down?"

"A few. I've been as far west on the Missouri as I want to go, and as far north on the Mississippi. I've got a liking for a warmer country, where the streams run all year, the summers are long and the winters short."

"I've thought of it myself when I break the ice on the pond so the animals can drink, and when I watch the honkers going south for the winter."

"I found a place that suits me. It's wild and free, Farr, with clear streams, mountains, game, grass that reaches the belly on a horse, and trees that grow straight as an arrow. It's a place untouched by man." Rain's expression softened and his eyes came alive as he spoke.

"This place was that way when Juicy and I first came here. Only the Indians had been here before us."

"I didn't find even Indian signs in my mountain valley, although there are plenty of Osage and Cherokee in the area."

A murmur of voices came from the other room. The boy had called out in his sleep and Liberty was soothing him. It had been a while since Rain had been in the midst of a family. The peace of sitting in a warm cabin in front of a fire on a cold night with the sounds and the smell of women and children about brought forth a restlessness in Rain.

"Farr, do you still have the yen to cross rivers and climb mountains?" Rain asked quietly. His words were like a searching hand reaching out.

Farr was looking into the fire as if his mind was somewhere far away. "At times," he said slowly.

Rain leaned forward and knocked the bowl of his pipe against the stone of the fireplace.

"I had a letter from Colby waiting for me when I got to Saint Louis. He wants to move on and make a place for himself. I thought to tell him he was welcome to come with me to Arkansas if he had a mind to."

"He spoke of coming here and building a gristmill."

"He mentioned that too."

"I've heard of Arkansas. Is it filling up as fast as it is here?"

"People are moving into the southeastern section and planting cotton. My mountain valley is to the west and south of the Arkansas River. I spent two years in the area with Will Bradford. Last year he established a fort at Belle Point to keep the peace among local Osage, Cherokee and non-Indian settlers who have tried to take up land in the Indian Territory."

Farr's head rested against the back of his chair. "How far west is your valley?" he queried softly.

"Three, maybe four hundred miles west of the Mississippi and about that many miles south."

"Rivers and mountains," Farr said, low-voiced.

"Clear sparkling streams and tall pines." Rain stared into the fire. "It's peaceful and quiet. Deer came down to drink not a dozen feet from where I sat on the bank of a stream watching fish as long as my arm. It's a land of resinous pine, cedar, juniper, long green meadows and unexpected canyons. I spent a month there. The only smoke I saw was from my own fire. I didn't want to leave."

Rain glanced at Farr. He seemed to be totally absorbed in his thoughts and he wondered if by speaking of his valley he had stirred up a buried restlessness in his friend. He remembered the plans the two of them and Colby Carroll had made years ago during the long winter evenings. He remembered how distance had called to them. They had talked of strange valleys, of canyons where no man had gone, of far heights and lonely places. They had dreamed of climbing mountains, crossing rivers and trekking to the shore of the great water that was said to be beyond the mountains.

"I suppose you'll be heading back in the spring," Farr said, breaking the long silence.

"I'm hoping to get an early start, but first I'm going to Louisville. Will Bradford has asked me to escort his intended bride and her aunt to Belle Point, which means it will take me almost twice as long to get back there."

Farr chuckled. "Escorting a bride? I don't envy you the job."

"Hell! I'd not do it for anyone but Will Bradford. I owe him a favor. He can't get away for at least another year. The girl is a second cousin and alone except for the aunt. Will thinks a wife would help bring some refinement to the fort."

"If all he wants is a woman, I'd think he could find one closer than Louisville."

"It's more than that. Will doesn't even know Miss Woodbury, but he feels responsible for her. He'll wed her and kill two birds with one stone. He sent money to outfit a wagon. I'm hoping to find a couple of good men to go with me."

"And if you don't?"

"I'll go it alone."

Liberty came into the room and placed Mary Elizabeth in the cradle. She covered the sleeping child and pulled the cradle back away from the light.

"The boy's name is Mike Hartman," she said when she turned. "The homestead where he lived with his family was attacked by a band of renegades who have been raiding up and down the Missouri River. Everyone was killed, the homestead burned. He blames himself because he was in Franklin at a turkey shoot and not at home to help protect his family. The way his mother and sisters died is tearing him apart."

Farr caught her hand as she passed him to go back into the room where the boy lay.

"Sit with us for a while. Daniel will call you if the boy needs you." He pulled her down on his lap and she rested in his arms. Her head dropped forward against his chest. His lips touched her forehead, his cheek lay for a moment against her hair.

"I feel so sorry for him," Liberty murmured. "He's really alone. All his kin are dead."

"He's lucky it was Rain he was after, sweetheart. Any other man would have killed him." Farr placed gentle kisses on his wife's brow and played with her hand.

"I know. But I think it has just now come home to him that he's alone, and he's scared."

Rain turned his eyes away from the couple in the chair. Their demonstration of affection was something new to him. He'd seen trollops fondled in taverns, but this was different. Every gesture, every look that passed between Farr and

Libby spoke of their love for each other. They shared their thoughts, their sorrows, their dreams.

Rain's thoughts turned to the more intimate side of married life. How would it be to have a woman come into his arms so willingly, share his life, his love, his bed? He had seen a lot of country, and he had learned a lot, but what was the use of that unless it could be shared with somebody? When the first sap of youth was in him he had wanted to challenge the world, but there was a time when any man worth his salt wanted a wife and a home and a son. The thought surprised him. He had to admit that he liked the warm feeling of the house, the sound of the fire, the comfortable sounds of a woman moving about. A man had to put down roots, build something to call his own. He would do that in his mountain valley. What was a life worth if it was wasted in idle drifting?

Amy hadn't moved since she came to sit in the back of the room. Rain remembered how talkative she used to be. What had happened to change her? Had she remembered the last private words that had passed between them and was now embarrassed? Rain hadn't expected to see her in Farr's house. She must not have remarried after Juicy's death. He wondered why. In a place as settled as this, there were five men to every woman. More than likely several woman-hungry men had camped on the doorstep before Juicy was laid in the ground, so it couldn't be for the lack of opportunity that she had remained unwed.

Behind him the rope chair squeaked. Rain heard the swish of slippers on the board floor, and then smelled the faint aroma of rose water as Amy passed.

"Good night," she murmured.

"Stay and visit with us, Amy." Liberty would have gotten up, but Farr held her on his lap.

"No. I think I'll go to bed. Call if you need me to help with the boy."

Rain watched Amy go up the stairs. She was no longer the coltish girl, but a woman who moved with a casual, natural grace that was pleasant to watch. Like a blade of tall prairie grass swaying in the wind, he thought. He felt a stirring in his body and had to remind himself that she was just a pretty woman he'd known a long time ago when she was a child.

Amy felt Rain's eyes on her back. She held her head up and forced her trembling legs to carry her up the steep stairs to the loft. She felt her way along the wall to her bed and sat down, holding her palms to her cheeks. Her chest hurt, her throat felt as if a hand were squeezing it, and her eyes burned. For years she had dreamed of Rain's homecoming and it hadn't been at all as she had imagined it would be.

Rain, the stubborn dark-haired boy she had known and loved, had changed. He was taller and heavier than Farr, but more than that, she had seen in his eyes during the brief time she had looked into them that he was different on the inside as well. He wanted no one, needed no one, depended on no one but himself. He was strong, very strong, not only with the muscular strength that came from living in the wilderness, but with an inner toughness like tempered steel that would bend but not break.

He had changed, but she could still see glimpses of the boy she had loved. His hair was still as black as a crow's wing, his eyes still saw everything without seeming to. He still moved with the grace of a wildcat; head up, proud and aloof. And, like a wildcat, Rain Tallman would never be tamed. Inwardly he would always have that toughness of purpose, that leashed fury that could break loose, as it must have done when he knifed the boy. Amy remembered another time when Rain, the boy, had sprung as quick as a cat on to the back of a man who had taken an unfair advantage of Farr. He would have plunged his knife into the man's throat had Colby Carroll not intervened.

Amy stood, and despite the cold, undressed slowly. She

pulled her nightdress from beneath her pillow, slipped it over her head, crawled between the blankets, and consoled herself with the knowledge that Rain hadn't married. If he had, he would have surely mentioned it to Farr.

Rain was home. Her waiting was over and she was more miserable than she had ever been in her life. Tears of disappointment flooded her eyes. One of the foolish dreams that had sustained her since Juicy's death had been of herself running down the lane to meet Rain when he returned. He would see her coming and open his arms. She would run into them and he would swing her high into the air and laugh joyously before he smothered her with passionate kisses. He would tell her he had come to her as soon as he heard she was a widow, and now nothing on earth would keep them apart.

Rain's homecoming had been the very opposite of her dream. He had not even recognized her when they met on the road. Amy rolled over on her stomach, buried her face in her pillow and gritted her teeth. He had scarcely looked at her when she came into the room. All he had said was hello, Amy. I'm surprised he even remembered my name, she thought angrily.

He hadn't come *home* at all! He had just stopped by on his way to Louisville, then he was going back to his damned valley! Amy felt a spurt of anger for the wasted years. She was nineteen years old and she had waited for him for seven years. She wouldn't wait any longer. She hated him, she told herself. He was so self-centered he didn't know the first thing about loving or needing anyone. A stubborn, independent, know-it-all jackass. That much about him *hadn't* changed.

"Damn you, Rain Tallman," she cried silently. "I made a real fool of myself putting on a dress, splashing myself with rose water, letting my hair hang down. I did it so you'd notice me and all you said was, 'hello, Amy.' Oh . . . I wish I didn't love you!"

She fell into a fitful sleep and dreamed of a tall, thin boy with serious dark eyes who whispered close to her ear. "Don't cry, Amy. I'll be back."

CHAPTER
Four

An hour before dawn Amy slipped out of the house and went to the barn to milk. While doing so she came to a decision: She would not make a fool of herself by wearing the blue dress again or letting her hair hang down as she had done the night before. If she did, Mercy would be sure to ask her, no doubt in front of Rain, why she was getting all gussied up. He would know then that she was doing it for his benefit. Even if she was, she couldn't bear for him to know it, she thought, her heartbeat quickening.

Amy looked down at her worn buckskins and moccasins and wished Uncle Juicy were here to tell her what to do. Rain wasn't like any other she had known. He was not even like the boy she used to know. He had always looked at her with those fathomless eyes and read her every thought. He would be sure to know how her heart ached for him. . . .

"Yo're jist as purty as a button, Sis. Ya ain't agoin' to have no trouble a'tall gettin' any man ya want after I'm gone. Jist don't be in no hurry choosin', 'n jist don't be lettin' the one ya want see how good ya can shoot, if'n ya like him a'tall," Juicy had said one afternoon after she had brought down a duck on the wing. "Fellers ain't alikin' to be bested by a button of a gal."

"Oh, poo! That wouldn't bother Rain," she had replied.

"I'm atellin' ya fer yore own good, missy. If'n ya set yore sights on a man, don't be ashowin' him up. Not that I reckon ya could best Rain at anythin' a'tall. Stay soft, missy. Ya can get more flies with honey than ya can with vinegar."

"I put the dress on last night and it didn't do a damn bit of good," she hissed aloud to the old man's image that floated in her mind. "So much for being soft. I can't be what I'm not, not even for Rain. I'm me. Amy. He'll know it if I start playacting."

Amy placed the bucket of milk on the doorstone, ran her sweating palms down the smooth, soft leather of her long shirt and tightened the belt at her waist. Her insides were shaking, but her features were composed when she lifted the doorlatch, picked up the bucket and went into the kitchen.

Liberty was bending over the iron spider where breakfast meat was sizzling. Farr and Rain sat at the table. One quick glance told her Rain had shaved and was wearing a soft linen shirt instead of the buckskin he'd worn the night before.

"Morning," Amy said to everyone in general and put the bucket on the counter. "What can I do, Libby?"

Liberty looked up, saw her sister's still face and noted that she wore the britches and long shirt. Her heart lurched with pity. There was no coyness or pretense in Amy. She was no longer the outspoken child who blurted her feelings. She would hold them inside, waiting for Rain to make a move. Liberty hoped and prayed he had a special feeling for her sister and would tell her so. He and Farr were so busy talking he had scarcely looked up when Amy came in the door.

"You can get a crock of milk out of the cellar."

Almost before Liberty had finished speaking, Amy was lifting the trap door in the floor. She took a candle from the mantel and went down the steps into the cold cellar. Knowing it would be foolish to linger and let the cold air up into the kitchen, she picked up the crock and went quickly back up the steps. Her eyes met Rain's as she came up into the kitchen. She stopped breathing for an instant. Then his dark eyes left her face and moved back to Farr's as if she were no more than a stranger.

Amy would have been surprised to know the thoughts that raced through Rain's mind: Well, what do you know? Little Amy in britches. Rain had seen only one other woman wearing men's pants, and she hadn't looked half as fetching as Amy. She was the woman of a French voyager who was as big and as rough as her man. He had to admit that there was no comparison between Amy and the Frenchman's woman. He wondered what folks here in the settlement thought about a female in pants. It must be a good topic of conversation for the ladies as well as the men, he mused. Then it occurred to him that Amy was the "boy" he had met down the road. Had he changed so much she hadn't recognized him? he wondered.

With an effort Rain brought his attention back to what Farr was saying.

"Liberty teaches reading. Amy teaches writing and ciphering. Besides our three, there are a dozen other children. Mercy teaches some of the young ones. Someday there'll be a real schoolhouse, but for now they come here three mornings a week."

"You've made a lot of progress here, Farr."

"Yes, but the challenge is gone. Libby and I talked about it last night, Rain. We're boxed in here and we're considering going on west, across the Mississippi and into the Missouri Territory." Liberty stopped behind her husband and placed her hand on his shoulder. He reached up to cover it with his. "We'd like to know more about your high valley, Rain, if you've got a mind for our company."

The words dropped like a stone in the quiet room. Amy straightened, her head turning to look over her shoulder at the two men at the table. Liberty looked quickly at her sister and saw the frozen look on her face.

"I sure as hell do have a mind for your company! I was hoping you still had the yen to cross rivers and climb mountains, but was afraid—"

Farr chuckled. "Afraid Libby would hold me back? Not on your life! She's the one that suggested we pull up and go with you. She's afraid I missed out on something by marrying her and tying myself down with a family. Even if I'd not met Libby, and God forbid such a thing would have happened, I still couldn't have left Juicy. He had been ailing for years and deserved some comfort in his old age."

"The country's opening up. A man with trade goods can do business anyplace along the river."

Amy turned her back to lift plates from the shelf. A chill touched her spine. Would Libby and Farr pull out and leave her here? If Rain didn't invite her to go, what would she do?

"What do you think, Amy?" Farr's voice broke into her thoughts. "Do you have a yen to cross rivers and climb mountains?"

Amy turned slowly. Her eyes passed over Rain and settled on Farr's smiling face. "I . . . hadn't given it much thought."

"Of course, if you've got plans to marry Tally Perkins . . ." he teased.

"I've no plans to marry that jelly-head and you know it," she said quickly.

"Well then?" Farr's green eyes were alight with excitement.

"I don't exactly favor staying here by myself," Amy said crossly.

Rain watched Amy and listened to the exchange. He wondered why she was snapping at Farr. Did she have her cap set for Tally Perkins after all? Maybe he hadn't asked her to wed him and she was hacked. Rain remembered Tally as a towheaded, big-toothed, clumsy kid. Even back then he seemed to be always trailing after Amy.

Daniel came in from the side room and spoke to Farr in low tones. "The feller's awake and he's got to go."

"I'll take care of it," Rain said and stood.

As soon as Rain and Daniel went into the other room, Liberty put her hand on her sister's arm.

"What's the matter, Amy? I thought this was something you would want to do too. Farr and I feel we've become boxed in here. We're looking forward to going to a new land where there's plenty of room. It isn't as if we were greenhorns like we were when we came out here from Middlecrossing. Farr and Rain will take care of us."

"Oh, I've no doubt Rain can take care of most anything that comes along," she said sarcastically. "I just don't like feeling like a third thumb, tagging along uninvited."

"Uninvited?" Farr got up from the table. "Hell, Amy, you're part of our family."

"I'm a grown woman living in my sister's house, and that's the bald truth of it."

"You're a partner in all we have. Juicy and I started this place together. If we can't sell it, we'll have to use your cash money to buy stout wagons and pay for river crossings. Colby may come here and take over. If that's the case I'll take his note and it'll be a while before we see any coin."

Amy looked from Farr's face to her sister's. Liberty had a worried look on her face. She was feeling sorry for her, Amy thought. Oh, Lordy! She knew how she had looked forward to Rain coming back. Libby knew she expected him to be as glad to see her as she was to see him.

"I'm sure Rain assumed you'd go with us," Liberty said softly.

"Assumed? Why in hell should he assume anything about me? He acts as if he doesn't even know me." She kept the hurt out of her voice by sheer willpower. A thousand words filled her throat, all things she wanted to say about the years she had waited for Rain to return, but nothing came out. Her hands shook as she brushed her hair back from her face and picked up a cloth to pull the pan of bread from the baking oven.

"Is this something you want to do or not, Amy?" Farr asked. "If you'd rather stay here—"

"I'll go, if . . . if you want me to."

"You'd better be sure, Amy. I'll not bring you back if you change your mind. This is my last trip across the big river." Rain had come back in the room and stood with his thumbs hooked in his belt.

"If I decide to come back, Rain Tallman, I'll not ask you to bring me," she snapped.

"Are you pining for someone besides . . . jelly-head?" Rain didn't know why he asked that. He just had the sudden urge to rile her. "I'd like to look over whoever it is you want to bring along. We'll not carry any dead weight on this trip."

Blazing amber eyes met Rain's dark, serious ones. "You haven't gotten one bit smarter, Rain Tallman. You're still just as dumb as ever if you think I'd tie up with a stupid dolt. The man I tie up with will be as much—or more—of a man than you are."

Rain lifted his brows and shrugged. He turned his back and sat down at the table.

Amy's hands were shaking so hard she could scarcely hold the pan of bread and Liberty took it from her.

"Heavens. I'll have to fix something for that boy in there to eat. Daniel," she called, "come to breakfast."

Amy was aware of the years that had passed when she was seated across the table from Rain. She was no longer a twelve-year-old listening with rapt attention to what the tall, quiet boy had to say when Farr or Juicy drew him into the conversation. Rain still spoke quietly, but he was far more confident than he had been seven years before. Cool, remote and confident. In fact, she'd never seen a man, other than Farr, who was so sure of himself.

"I'll get the kid out of here as soon as he can ride. He seems a mite better this morning. Good biscuits, Libby. Guess you can tell I've had a bellyful of my own cooking." Rain speared another biscuit and grinned at Liberty. Smile lines changed his stern features drastically, and Amy wondered if he knew how handsome he was.

"No hurry about the boy leaving," Farr said as he passed the meat platter. "When do you plan to head back?"

"March. But now that I know you're going with me, I can wait a few weeks if that's too soon. I'll go on and fetch Miss Woodbury. I told Will I'd be back by the first part of June. You could run into trouble with Hammond Perry, Farr. I heard he's moving in along the Arkansas River."

Farr frowned. "I've been wondering if I could leave Libby and the children at the fort until I get a place ready."

Before Rain could answer, Liberty spoke with a firmness she used when there was absolutely no chance of her changing her mind.

"You can forget that. You're not leaving me and the children anyplace at all, Farr Quill. Our place is with you, and with you we'll stay. We've handled Hammond Perry before. We can do it again. Have some honey with the biscuits, Rain." Smiling gently at Rain, she pushed a small crock across the table.

Farr gazed lovingly at his wife, then lifted his shoulders. "You see how it is, Rain? When the White Dove of the Wabash sets her mind, there's no changing it."

Rain looked from Farr's smiling face to Liberty's and remembered the day long ago when Farr had calmly announced at the same table that he and Liberty had been wed by the Sufferite preacher down the road. Liberty and Amy had planned to take over the abandoned homestead, but an old enemy had followed them from New York State and had taken over the place. They had had no place to go. Rain wondered if Farr had loved Liberty then or if love had come to them after they were wed. There was no doubt that she was now the center of his world and that he loved her fiercely.

"The only settlement is at the fort. There are eight women there who are married to or living with soldiers. They serve as laundresses. It'll be a hard trip, Libby," Rain said quietly.

"I know. But it'll not be nearly as hard as the trip Amy and I made out here from New York. We'll have Farr with us. And Amy is no slouch at—" She stopped speaking abruptly when she saw the quick frown on her sister's face.

Zack came down the stairs holding up his nightshirt and rubbing his eyes.

"Ma, the pot's full."

Liberty started to get up from the table, but Farr reached over and put his hand on her shoulder.

"Sit still, love. I'll take him." He swooped his son up in one arm and went into the room where the injured boy and Daniel and Rain had slept. "Your feet are like chunks of ice, son. Didn't you have time to put on your shoes?"

Amy bent over her plate, trying to hide her red face from Rain's amused gaze. She'd caught his eyes when Zack first spoke and had seen the amusement there. He had changed, she thought. At one time he would have flushed with embarrassment, but now he smiled good-naturedly at her own confusion.

Farr and Rain left the house immediately after breakfast to walk down to the sawyer camp and then to the river so that

Rain could see the place Farr thought suitable for a gristmill if Colby was still interested in building one at the station.

While Zack and Mercy ate, Liberty told them about the plans to leave Quill's Station and resettle in the mountains of Arkansas. Zack went into a frenzy of excitement at the prospect, but Mercy was quiet for a long moment before she spoke.

"I'll never see Grandma Maude again if we leave here."

"It will be a long time, if ever," Liberty said gently.

"Why don't Grandma and Grandpa come with us?"

"No!" Amy spoke more sharply than she intended and all eyes turned to her in surprise. "They've got their own farm and they're too old to pull up and move into the wilderness." Heaven forbid, she thought. She would not be able to endure her father's complaining all the way to Arkansas as he had done coming from New York State. And having to look at the cowlike expressions on Tally's face every day would make her sick.

"I know why you don't want them to come with us. You're afraid Tally will spoil your chances with Rain," Mercy said saucily with the wisdom of an observant nine-year-old female.

"You've got a smart mouth, Mercy." Amy was stung to speak sharply again. "If you don't want your bottom whacked, keep your opinions to yourself."

"I may not even go. So there! I may stay with Grandma Maude."

Daniel had been watching quietly, as was his way. He, more than anyone, understood Mercy's feelings. He had come to terms with the fact that he was an orphan and not a real son of the family, but of late her not being a blood relative had began to eat on Mercy, especially since the birth of Mary Elizabeth.

"You're talking silly," he said quietly. "You're going with

us. Ma and Pa won't leave you with Grandma. She'll spoil you rotten."

"She will not! She loves me. She loves me more than anyone does," Mercy said defiantly as tears filled her cornflower blue eyes. "She said she always wanted a little girl."

"Ma and Pa love you too, stupid!" Daniel saw the hurt look on Liberty's face. "Why do you think they sat up with you all night when you were sick? Or take care of you, put up with your sass, and *try* to teach you some manners?"

"But they've got . . . Mary Elizabeth . . . and Grandma don't have a little girl—"

"Oh, Mercy!" Liberty pulled the child onto her lap. "Did you think that because we have Mary Elizabeth we don't love you? If I had a dozen little girls you would always be special to me. Long ago I chose to keep you with me even when Amy and I had nowhere to go. I was going to keep you and Daniel with me no matter what. I loved you right from the time Farr came walking into our camp with you asleep on his shoulder. Remember? I told you about that. It would break my heart if you wanted to leave us and go live with Grandma Maude."

"I . . . don't want to."

"There, there, don't cry, honey. We're going to take a long trip, see new sights, meet new people. I couldn't love you more, Mercy, if I had given birth to you like I did Mary Elizabeth." Liberty crooned to the child and hugged her.

"She'll go. She just wanted you to beg her," Daniel said impatiently on his way to get his coat. He jerked it on, and slammed his hat down on his head. "I'll go tell the kids there'll be no school today."

"You just shut up, Daniel Phelps. Hear me? You don't know everything!" Mercy shouted from the safe haven of Liberty's arms. "Oh, sometimes he makes me so mad!"

Liberty smiled into Mercy's blond hair. Daniel and Mercy reminded her of Rain and Amy long ago when she and Amy first came to Quill's Station. Then Rain had been as protective of Amy in his quiet way as Daniel now was of Mercy.

Before the day was over, Mike Hartman was able to sit up on the edge of the cot. The wound in his shoulder throbbed painfully, but he was free of fever.

"I'll be goin' as soon as I can, ma'am, and I'm obliged to ya," he said when Liberty came into the room before suppertime to see how he was doing.

"You don't have to be in a hurry about leaving, unless you want to go. We have plenty of room here, and I think Daniel likes your company."

"I ain't got no money to pay my way."

"Who said anything about pay? This isn't an inn, Mike. Rain is like a part of our family. He brought you here. You're our guest."

"I was goin' to kill him—"

"He told us. The man who pointed the finger at Rain was mistaken. It's perfectly understandable that you'd want to kill him if you thought he'd done those terrible things. If Rain was that kind of man he would have killed you. He could have, you know. He can whack the hairs out of a man's nose with his fighting knife without drawing blood. You're lucky it was Rain you were after."

"I know it now, ma'am. I was jist so lonesome 'n full a hate that when the man said it was him what done it, I believed what he was sayin' was gospel." The boy looked up at Liberty, his eyes swimming with tears.

Liberty's soft heart went out to him. She smoothed the shaggy hair back from his face with gentle fingers.

"I know how you must have felt. I've been lonely myself and could have killed someone who had done me wrong. Things can only get better, Mike. You're welcome to stay here with us until you get your strength back. Who knows? Maybe you'll get to liking us and decide to go with us to Arkansas."

"I heared ya talkin', but why'd ya want to leave this place, ma'am? I jist never seen a place so nice as this'n. There ain't no cold a'tall comin' through cracks in the walls, 'n there's a wood floor 'n two fireplaces."

"Yes, it's nice. But my husband has always dreamed of the mountains across the big river. He's had his face turned to the west for a long time. What we have here is nothing compared to my love for him. I'll leave this place gladly and live in a wagon for the rest of my life if it's what he wants."

"I jist ain't never heared of the like."

Liberty laughed. "Someday you'll fall in love and then you'll understand. Now, lie back there and I'll have Daniel bring you in some supper."

After the children were put to bed, Farr, Liberty and Rain sat at the table and planned the trip.

"I'm figuring on taking four wagons, Rain, two with goods for trading." Farr was listing the things they would take with them. He dipped the quill in the ink horn and wrote painstakingly on a sheet of paper.

"Oxen can pull a heavier load than horses or mules and we'll be going into mountainous country," Rain said.

"I'd thought of that. We'll need tools, extra wheels, seed, salt—"

"Plenty of powder and shot," Rain added.

"I suppose Liberty will insist on taking her rocking chair and her clock," Farr said and smiled teasingly at his wife.

"And some cookware if you're planning on eating on the way," Liberty shot back.

Amy listened but took no part in the conversation. Rain had announced that he would leave in a few days. He would go to Carrolltown to see Colby and then on to Louisville to get Miss Woodbury and her aunt.

Farr had spent the afternoon talking with George Rapp, the leader of the Harmonist colony across the river. They had taken over the ferry and were interested in acquiring the store, the inn and the sawyer camp. Rain would carry the word to Colby that the place was his if he wanted it, but if he didn't, the Harmonists would take it.

Rain had invited Daniel to go with him to Louisville, but Daniel was worried about going off and leaving Farr with all the work of getting ready to move.

"You should go with Rain, Daniel," Liberty had said. "We'll just have to keep Mike here to do your work. By the time you and Rain are ready to leave, he'll be almost as good as new."

The talk went on for hours without Amy uttering a word. Rain looked at her several times and wondered at her silence. It was hard for him to associate this silent, brooding girl with the boisterous, happy Amy of long ago who had laughed at the drop of a hat. Each time he caught her looking at him, she turned her eyes away quickly. Something was eating at her, and he wondered what it was.

After Amy said good night and went up to the room in the loft, Liberty and Farr sat at the table and worked on the list of things they were taking to Arkansas. Rain sat in the chair with his legs stretched out, smoking and thinking. It was almost as if somehow he had upset Amy's plans by being here. She hadn't taken any part in the planning; she didn't seem to have any enthusiasm for the trip. Damn her, Rain thought irritably. She was a grown woman; if she didn't want to go, why didn't she say so?

* * *

The day broke cold and clear but infinitely warmer than it had been for the past week. Amy rolled out of bed at first light and dressed swiftly. There were soft movements downstairs. Liberty was up, and Farr would be with her. Her sister never left the bed with her husband in it. They retired together and got up together. When Amy came down into the kitchen, Liberty was sitting in the rocking chair nursing the baby and Farr was starting the morning meal.

"Morning."

"Morning, Amy. Farr's got the coffee going. Do you want a cup before you milk?"

"I don't believe so." Amy shrugged into her coat and pulled a wool cap down over her ears. She was slipping the bail of the milk bucket over her arm when Rain came in from the other room.

"Morning," he said, looking directly at her.

"Morning." She nodded her head as she spoke, surprised that her voice was able to come up out of her tight throat. Needing desperately to escape his intense dark gaze, she lit the lantern and went out the door.

Dawn was breaking, but a few stars still shone brightly. The early morning air was crisp, even though the weather had turned quite warm after the blizzard, above the freezing point. Ice and snow were melting rapidly all over. Wood smoke came from every chimney in the settlement as fires were rekindled for morning meals. Amy burrowed her face in the collar of her coat and headed for the barn.

The two milch cows were waiting patiently and lowed as she neared them. Hanging the lantern on the end post, she pulled up an overturned bucket to sit on.

"Bossie, Bossie," Amy said tiredly as she rested her head against the side of the cow. She liked the smell of the barn, the cow, and the warm milk. Life was so uncomplicated for a cow, she thought as she nudged the udder and squeezed the cow's teat. Milk shot into the bucket she held between her feet. She milked for several minutes. Her strong, slender fingers squeezed and pulled in rhythm. "All you have to do is stand here, Bossie, and someone will come and give you relief from an aching udder," she murmured.

"Talking to yourself, Amy?"

Rain's voice was close to her ear and so startling that Amy jumped to her feet and almost kicked over the bucket of milk. She whirled and glared up at him.

"That's a good way to get yourself shot," she spat out angrily.

"Did I scare you?"

"I don't like someone sneaking up on me."

"I didn't sneak. I just walked in."

"You always moved about like a . . . a cat."

"Speaking of cats, you're the one with your back up and your claws out."

The sight of him lounging against the barn post brought back memories of another time they had talked in the barn. He hadn't smiled then either. She had been the one to follow him, she recalled. She had thrown herself at him and begged him not to leave. The thought of that brazen action brought a flush to her cheeks. She had to tilt her head to look up at him then, just as she did now. She felt weak in the knees but stood with her eyes fastened on his. She could feel the warmth of the telltale blood that rushed into her face. To hide it, she bent her head and looked at her hands clasped in front of her.

"You're taller," she murmured.

"So are you." Silence, then, "I was sorry to hear about Juicy."

Her head came up sharply. "Why were you sorry? He was

an old man and in constant pain. Dying was a release for him."

"It's been two years since he died. I thought you would be married again by now."

"Well, I'm not! Not that it's any business of yours, Rain Tallman."

Smile lines appeared at the corners of his eyes. "That sounds like the Amy of a long time ago. Some things about you haven't changed."

"Everything about you . . . has."

"It was bound to happen."

"If I remember right, you left to find out what kind of man you are. Did you?"

"I think so. I learned I was man enough to take care of myself."

"Why haven't you married, or don't they bother to do that out west?" She stared up at him through thick, gold-tipped lashes, all her nerve ends tingling under the scrutiny of his dark eyes. She fervently hoped that he would not notice how breathless she was.

"Some do, some don't. I aim to . . . someday."

Rain's firm lips flattened against his even white teeth when he smiled. She watched the firm line of his mouth curve in a smile that softened the hard contours of his face. His smile was wicked, teasing, and jarred her to her senses. She wanted to say something, but his eyes on her face were almost like warm hands caressing her cheeks. She could feel them to the marrow of her bones. Color tinged her cheeks as his gaze traveled over her face, taking in the freckles on her nose, the wisps of curly hair that had escaped from the braid. She stared at him, her gold-flecked eyes holding a definite shimmer of defiance against the effect he was having on her breathing. All her defenses were raised. There was an inner need to protect herself from more hurt from this man. But was it possible? she asked herself.

"What do you want, Rain?"

"In a wife?"

"No! What do you want *here?*"

"Nothing. I came to see about my horse." His dark eyes held hers.

"Oh . . ." With an effort she turned away and sat back down on the bucket. "Well, see about him."

"I aim to, but first I want to know why you're running around in britches like a boy."

Her head swiveled. She met his gaze and for an instant she thought he was teasing her, but his gaze was disconcertingly sharp. She struggled back from the edge of that yawning pit of rage and misery stretching before her. Forgetting the discipline, both mental and physical, for which she had fought so hard since he had followed her into the barn, she answered with a scathing look in her eyes.

"That, too, is none of your damn business, Rain Tallman."

She would have had to be blind not to see the annoyance that flashed in his jet black eyes.

"Wearing britches *and* swearing. Juicy must have let you run wild," he said softly.

"Don't you dare say a word against Uncle Juicy. He married me and saved me from Stith Lenning. It was more than you were willing to do." The words were out before she could trap them in her throat.

"I was a kid. I had no way of taking care of you."

"You . . . didn't even consider it. You had mountains to climb and rivers to cross," she snarled, wishing he would leave before she lost control and the tears that were so close to the back of her eyes spurted forth and shamed her.

"That was a long time ago. Why are you so hostile to me now? You've been like a bear with a sore tail ever since I got here."

Amy nudged the side of the cow with her head and began

to milk again. The only sounds in the barn were the swishes as the milk shot into the bucket and the contented grunts of the cow. She ignored his question and asked one of her own.

"When are you leaving?"

"Have I overstayed my welcome?"

She was quiet for a long moment, then murmured, "It isn't my place to say. It isn't my house."

"Is that what's eating you?" he asked softly. "Are you jealous of your sister?"

His words caught Amy off guard. She drew in a quivering breath, closed her eyes and continued to milk by instinct only. When she finished she stood and turned. His hard, intense gaze was fastened to her face. She was acutely aware of his broad chest and lean, muscular body. He radiated energy, strength, confidence. She gazed back at him blindly, her own amber eyes fixed on his.

He cared nothing for her at all.

The thought echoed in her mind, causing her heart to sink like a rock in her chest and nerves to knot in her stomach. She thought she would be sick. In spite of her roiling emotions, when she spoke, her voice was quiet and as solid as steel.

"You *have* changed, Rain. Back when I knew you you wouldn't have even thought of such a thing." She looked at him with disappointment and pain in her eyes and in every line of her face.

"What do you think I meant?" he asked in a soft, puzzled tone while his steady gaze held hers.

"Maybe you'd better tell me."

"I was wondering if you were jealous of Liberty because she has a home of her own, a husband and children. I'm sure you could have all of that if you wanted it."

"You must not have a very good opinion of me if you think I begrudge my sister her family." Pride kept Amy's voice steady, although she never felt more like crying in her life.

"I don't know what to think of you . . . now."

"You didn't know what to think of me back then."

"We're not kids anymore. We should be civil to each other . . . for Libby's sake."

"I'll try to stay out of your way." With her smooth brows raised, Amy picked up the bucket, moved around him and started for the door. "Blow out the lantern when you leave," she said over her shoulder.

"Amy! What the hell's the matter with you?"

"Nothing, Rain. I'm the same as I've always been."

Rain knew her attitude had something to do with him. He had seen her teasing Daniel and Mercy, laughing with them. But when she realized he was nearby, she closed up. Now he groped for words and could find none. He was a man who had spent much time alone, given to expressing himself in action, and the few words he used were usually associated with action. He wanted to grab her and tell her not to walk away from him.

"If you don't want to come west with us, say so. Don't put a damper on it for Farr and Libby," he called after her, knowing instinctively that he was saying the wrong thing.

Amy didn't answer. She kicked the barn door open, went through it, then kicked it shut with such force it failed to catch and bounced back open. She heard the low murmur of curses that came from inside the barn and felt a brief flash of satisfaction.

CHAPTER
Five

Rain watched Amy leave the barn. He was surprised to find himself so angry he wanted to pound the stall posts with his fists. He wondered why the hell he was so riled up. No answer came readily to his mind as he tossed hay into each of the stalls. He didn't know why Amy's attitude toward him disturbed him. He hadn't expected her to be at Quill's Station, and the sight of her that first night had stirred an unfamiliar emotion in him. He'd been too long without a woman, his logical mind reasoned.

He finished the chores and blew out the lantern. In the semidarkness he could still see the look of hurt on her face. He wondered if he had been too close to the truth when he asked if she were jealous of Libby. She had lived here all these years with Libby and Farr, he thought, and even as a kid she was so fond of Farr that he was the first one she ran to when something went wrong. Had she fallen in love with her sister's husband? Was that the reason she hadn't married again? The thought was so depressing that he wanted to saddle up and ride out. But he didn't. He headed for the house.

* * *

The day passed quickly. Rain and Farr spent much of the afternoon at the store where Rain helped Farr select goods suitable for trading along the Arkansas River. They decided on hard-bottom candles with cotton wicks, salt, cider vinegar, beans, flour, and five hundred pounds of good hard soap along with bolts of cloth and seeds. Rain suggested they take whiskey, tobacco, knives, needles, beads, thread, vermilion, lead, paints, powder, guns, blankets, flints, knife handles, gun screws, wampum belts, and the like.

At the sawyer camp they looked over the heavy freight wagons Farr planned to use to carry his trade goods and his family west.

"The bottom boards are two inches thick and the sides only slightly less. They'll need to hold a heavy load if I take tools to trade and tools to set up another sawyer camp. What do you think, Rain?"

Rain knelt down and peered at the angle iron straps that reinforced the bottom.

"I never saw a better built wagon bed. If you mount it on fifty-two-inch, iron-rimmed wheels you'll be able to ford most streams without getting the bottom wet."

Farr rested his hands on the back wheel of the wagon and gripped hard.

"At times I think I'm out of my mind to be uprooting my family and taking them into unsettled land. My God, Rain! If anything happened to Libby . . ."

Rain shrugged. "I've told you what to expect, Farr. It's your decision."

"It wasn't mine alone. Libby wants to go. She's excited about it."

"Some women take to trail life and setting up a homestead. Some women want to stay put."

"Most women would hate pulling out and leaving a comfortable home. Libby says home is where family is, not the other way around."

"I hadn't thought about it like that."

The word *home* had never meant much to Rain. He had not had a home—a real home—of his own. At first he had lived in John Spotted Elk's *weigius*, and then he had come to be with Farr and Juicy. After that home had been wherever he could throw down his blanket. It would be different in his high valley, he thought. The cabin he built would be his, and the woman he brought to it would be his woman—

"Don't worry about Amy. She'll come around."

Farr's voice broke into Rain's thoughts and he turned to look at him with a puzzled frown.

"I'm not worrying about her." Even as he said the words, he knew they were not true. Always honest with himself, he admitted that he would be disappointed as hell if Amy decided to stay at Quill's Station.

"Her pa's pushing her to marry Tally Perkins."

"I can't see her being pushed into anything. She's not a kid now."

"No, she's not a kid now." Farr turned away and they started walking toward the house. "She was devoted to Juicy and cared for him like a baby at the last."

"I thought she'd be wed again by now. Women aren't all that plentiful, even here."

Farr laughed. "She could've had her pick of the best and the worst of the lot. Every unwed man within miles called on her the first week. Some were on the doorstone before we buried Juicy. She gave the first few a good tongue-lashing for courting her before she'd put her husband in the ground. Juicy would have had a good laugh out of that."

"Juicy should have kept a tighter hold on her," Rain growled.

Farr looked at him quickly. "Do the britches bother you? Folks around here are used to her. Oh, she turns some heads once in a while." Farr chuckled. "Our Amy is quite a girl. She can do most things as good as a man."

"I saw a woman in britches once before. She was as hard as nails and as tough as boot leather. I like a woman to have a little softness about her."

Farr slapped Rain on the back. "Like Libby?"

Rain grinned at his friend. "Like Libby."

At the end of the week Rain left Quill's Station to go to Carrolltown to see Colby Carroll. On the way back he would stop at Louisville to get Miss Woodbury and her aunt. He made no attempt to see Amy alone until the last morning. He went to the barn just as she was finishing the milking.

"Morning, Amy."

"Morning."

"It's going to be a nice day for traveling. With luck, I'll see Colby within a week."

"Tell him and Willa hello."

"I'll do that."

"Good-bye." She picked up the bucket and moved past him.

"Amy . . . wait."

She turned, lifted her brows and tilted her head so she could look up at him. Hope that sprang in her heart died when she looked into his dark, fathomless eyes. Deep crinkly grooves marked the corners, put there when his eyes had squinted against the sun. There were other lines too that experience, tiredness, or harsh winter weather had made.

They were hard, penetrating eyes with no softness in them for her.

He continued to look at her, and she felt herself becoming unnerved by his intense scrutiny. She racked her brain for something to say. Damn him! Why didn't *he* say something? She straightened her back stubbornly and decided to say nothing, but her eyes seemed to be drawn to his, and he held them with a probing stare before moving from her face to her hair, then down the full length of her body.

Amy set the bucket of milk down, still keeping her eyes on his face.

His voice was softer than she expected when he finally spoke. His lips barely moved, but she heard his words distinctly.

"Do you remember the last time we said good-bye? You kissed me."

Her face turned brick red. He was not smiling, so he was not teasing. It suddenly occurred to her that he wanted to embarrass her—that he blamed her for the silence that had been between them during the past week. She was silent for as long as it took her to fight down the angry words that sprang to her lips. The thickheaded fool! Didn't he know her love for him was tearing her apart, that she couldn't even look at him without wanting to cry? In spite of her thundering heartbeat, she tossed her head in a gesture of indifference and concentrated on keeping her poise.

"I was a child. Children do foolish things."

"It didn't seem foolish at the time."

"Oh, well—" She shrugged and bent to pick up the bucket. His hand on her wrist stopped her.

"Amy . . . let's do it again." His words reached into her consciousness through the blood pounding in her ears.

She was too stunned to answer and her lips parted softly in surprise. The glitter in his eyes made her feel as though her heart might leap from her breast, and she stared at him in total panic as his arms slid around her.

Amy watched his mouth moving toward hers and instinctively splayed her fingers against his chest. His lips pressed hers gently, then took slow, deliberate possession. Her lips parted invitingly beneath his as if she had no control over them. She could feel the scrape of his whiskers on her cheek and feel the pounding of his heartbeat against her palm. His fingers caressed the nape of her neck and a wave of gladness made her pulse leap. Her hands moved beneath his arms to his back and she hugged him tightly to her.

Her surrender seemed to trigger a deeper need in him and the quality of his kiss exploded into a passionate demand that caused something warm and powerful to throb in the area below her stomach. His warmth seeped into her; she luxuriated in his strength.

Rain lifted his head a fraction until their noses were tip to tip and looked at her with glittering eyes. Then his mouth tenderly and almost reverently planted another kiss on her lips before his hands on her shoulders gently moved her away from him.

"It was better than I remembered."

The words were spoken so softly that Amy scarcely heard them. She closed her eyes against momentary giddiness. There was a tightness across her chest and a fullness in her throat. His hands on her shoulders tightened. She had an incredible urge to throw her arms around him and beg him to take her with him. Fear that she would do something foolish and irreversible brought her back to reality. When she bent to pick up the bucket, his hands fell to his sides. She turned to leave.

"Amy . . . I'll be back."

She heard the familiar words and glanced at him over her shoulder. Years rolled away and he was a tall, thin youth holding tightly to the reins of a borrowed horse. Unable to speak, she nodded her head and walked quickly to the house.

The following weeks were filled with frenzied preparations. Farr was away from the house much of the time. He was having one of the heavy freight wagons fitted out for the family to live in and three other wagons reinforced to carry supplies, trade goods and the tools he would need to set up a sawyer camp and a blacksmith shop. Both he and Liberty vowed to take enough land for themselves so they would not be boxed in as they were at Quill's Station.

Liberty selected the things she wanted to take with her to her new home and the things she wanted to leave with Maude and her father.

"We'll take the spinning wheel but leave the loom. We'll take all the feather ticks. Laid flat they'll serve as a mattress or a cover. Of course, we'll take the clock, the good pieces of pottery, the rocking chair, and the trunks. What are you taking, Amy?"

Liberty paused amid the clutter and looked inquiringly at her sister. For a time after Rain left, more than a month ago now, she had been more like her cheerful self, but gradually she had become quieter, spending more and more time alone.

Amy, working on a buckskin shirt that would come to her knees, glanced up, then back to her work.

"Clothes, rifle, knife, blankets."

Liberty looked at her sister with a worried frown. Faint lines of strain had appeared lately between her brows and at the corners of her eyes and mouth. Her face often had a pensive look, with shadows of worry beneath her eyes. Her wide mouth, its lower lip fuller and softer than the upper one, was often turned down at the corners, reflecting her less-than-happy mood. Liberty was sure her sister's depression was due to Rain's attitude toward her. She had tried to talk to her about him, but Amy refused to discuss him.

Mercy, coming down from the loft, broke into Liberty's thoughts.

"When will Rain and Daniel be back?"

"Not for another couple of weeks. I swear, Mercy. You've asked me that every day. If I didn't know better I'd think that you miss Daniel."

"I don't! I don't miss him at all! I like Mike better. He doesn't boss me all the time. I'm glad he's going with us to the Arkansas."

"So am I. Farr says he's a willing worker and learns fast. He'd good with a hammer and saw."

"Better than Daniel?"

"No. Farr wasn't comparing the two boys."

Liberty glanced quickly at Amy and saw her brief, knowing grin. They both knew that for all Mercy's complaining about Daniel, she would get riled up if anyone else criticized him. A few months back she had launched herself at Tally and kicked his shins when he shoved Daniel out of his way.

Mercy bent over Mary Elizabeth's cradle and wiped the baby's chin. "She's slobbering all over, Ma."

"She's cutting teeth. It'll be like that for a while. Give her the sugar-tit to chew on."

"I'm going to have lots of babies."

"You'd better grow up first," Amy said, looking up and smiling fondly at the fair-haired girl.

"Silly! I know that!" Mercy gave Mary Elizabeth the sugar-tit, then sat cross-legged on the floor beside the cradle and rocked it gently. "Why don't you get one, Amy? I bet Rain would help you."

"Mercy!" Liberty exclaimed. "For heaven's sake! What kind of talk is that coming from a little girl?"

"I know about things like that. I know how a cow gets a calf. When I was at Grandma Maude's, I saw Tally put a cow in with a mean old bull. I saw what he was doing before that bossy old Daniel made me get out of the barn. Grandma said the cow would get a calf and I could name it."

"Daniel was right to make you leave. That isn't a sight for a little girl to see." Liberty turned away before Mercy could see the smile she was trying to suppress.

"Did Papa do that to make you get Zack and Mary Elizabeth?"

"Mercy!" Liberty whirled. She looked first at Mercy's innocent face and then to Amy's for help.

Amy stretched her long legs out in front of her and crossed her moccasined feet. She reached behind her and pulled the long, thick braid over her shoulder before she rested her head against the back of the chair and folded her arms over her chest.

"Tell us, Libby."

"Oh, you! You're no help at all." Liberty glared at her sister.

"I know it doesn't happen when you sit on Pa's lap." Mercy tilted her head and smiled knowingly up at Liberty. "Because your dress isn't up. So there!"

Liberty threw her hands in the air. "Oh, for goodness sake!"

"I think you and Mercy had better have a talk," Amy said, trying to keep the laughter out of her voice.

"If somebody don't tell me I'll ask . . . Mike." Mercy got up and started for the door.

"Come back here, young lady. Don't you dare say anything about this to Mike."

"Why not? I asked Daniel and he said I was too young. Mike won't think so. He said I was as tall as his sister and she was almost fourteen."

"Being tall has nothing to do with it."

"Well! Pearle Jackson wears rags every month and I'm as tall as she is."

Liberty looked helplessly up at the ceiling. "I guess it is time you and I had a talk. Put on your shawl and we'll walk down to the spring."

The next morning a wagon carrying Elija, Maude and Tally came up the lane. The dog barked and Amy went to the window.

"Oh, for crying out loud! It's Papa and Maude. Why that worthless dog doesn't get up and bite them is beyond me."

Liberty laughed. "Old Pike wouldn't bite anyone if they were carrying off the house."

"If Papa starts in on me again about marrying Tally—"

"He will and you know it. Just tell him firmly that you've made up your mind and then ignore him. Be nice, honey, we'll be leaving soon."

"Be nice!" Amy threw up her hands in disgust. "Being *nice* doesn't get you anywhere with Papa when he's got his mind set."

Liberty went to the door. Amy stood by the window and watched the source of her irritation pull to a stop in front of the house, then she went to her room in order to delay as long as possible the meeting with her parent.

"We've come to help you get things squared away for the trip," Maude said brightly in the way of a greeting, and handed down several baskets of food. "Tally, take the horses to the barn and see what you can do to help Farr. Elija dear, carry the baskets into the house."

Elija obeyed, then began grumbling as soon as he was sure Farr was not in the house to hear him.

"I'll swear, Libby. I thought ya had more sense 'n what ya got. By jigger! The idea of pullin' foot 'n agoin' off to the wilds is pure harebrained."

"Tell it to Farr, Papa," Liberty said evenly.

Elija looked at her with a disapproving scowl. "A man aroamin' here 'n yon is one thin', but a woman traipsin' off with a bunch a younguns pure fogs a body's mind. It's plum dosey, is what it is."

Liberty ignored him and turned to peek into Maude's basket.

"You've brought dried apple pie," she exclaimed. "My it's been many a day since we've had apple pie. Would you like cream on it, Papa?"

"Thin's just ain't like they was back in my day," Elija continued. He had a way of closing his ears when he had something to say. "I tell ya. I got my shortcomin's jist like other folk, but I ain't never done nothin' so downright fool-hardy as what yo're adoin'." He moved about restlessly, coughing and muttering his complaints in a droning voice.

"I swan to goodness, Mary Elizabeth! Come here to Granny." Maude lifted the baby from the cradle. "Elija, look how this baby has grown. I declare! She's goin' to be a beauty is what she is."

Elija grunted and glanced at the baby. "If'n she ain't scalped by the heathens," he said dismally.

Amy came down from the loft where she had retreated before her father came in. She walked past him and went to the door.

"Sister, ain't ya got a howdy fer yore papa?"

"Howdy."

"I got a thin' to say, Sister—"

"I figured you did." Amy snapped her teeth together and grimaced.

"As yore pa, I got a right to say my piece—"

"A cyclone couldn't stop you from saying your piece," she said crossly. Amy turned to face him, pushed her hands into her pockets, hunched her shoulders and waited.

"Ya ain't got no business goin' off into the wilds without a man to look out fer ya. I'd feel a mite easier if 'n Tally went along—"

"If that's all you've got to say, I've heard enough!"

"I knowed ya'd get yore back up. There ain't no reasonin' with a woman like ya are."

"You're right about one thing, Papa. I'm a woman, not a child. I choose my own man."

"Ya think ya know it all, dad-burnit! Ya get yoreself all up in the air if 'n I try to give ya some advice."

"I don't care a hoot for your advice," Amy said cruelly. "Besides, Libby says advice is like croton oil. It's good as long as someone else takes it."

"Ya ain't got no call to be saying that," Elija whined, and his shoulders rose and fell expressively.

"I don't want to argue with you, Papa," Amy said in a kinder tone and turned away.

"I got my wind up 'n I'll have my say!" Elija shouted so loud it frightened the baby and she began to cry.

Amy turned on him with an anger that threatened to make her eyes go out of focus.

"You can have your wind up all you want and you can have your *say*, but it doesn't amount to a tinker's damn!"

"There ya go. Ya always got ta belittle—"

Amy swore under her breath, spun on her heel to walk away, but turned back with an angry scowl on her face. She pointed her finger at her father.

"Listen to me for once in your life, Papa! I'm sick and tired of you pushing that jug-head at me. You try sending him along and I'll fill his butt so full of shot he'll never sit on it again!"

Elija sucked in his thin cheeks and pursed his lips. His gaunt shoulders sagged in defeat. "It's a blessin' yore ma ain't livin' to hear ya."

"You always resort to that! It wasn't my fault she died having me. She was just twice as old as your seven-year-old daughter when you married her. Men!" Amy snorted. "You couldn't wait to get her to bed. No wonder you were willing to give me to Stith Lenning when I was only twelve years old."

The tension that had been building in Amy for days had mounted to produce a splitting headache; all she wanted at that moment was to slip outside the house and disappear into the quiet woods. She pressed her fingertips to her temples and turned to the door. Elija's words stopped her.

"I aim to send Tally—"

Amy whirled. Her clenched fists rested on her hips and her voice was shrill with anger. "Can't you get it through your head that I don't want him? If he comes with us I'll stop off in Saint Louis and take a boat downriver to New Orleans. You'll never hear from me again."

"Yo're hard, Sister." Elija shook his head sadly. "By Jupiter yo're hard."

"Confound it! Keep your nose out of my business or you'll find out how hard I am." Amy picked up her rifle and slammed out of the house.

"Glory be! Women! They never listen to a man, but they can sure shoot off their mouths. I tell ya, ya'll all go to rack 'n ruin. I jist don't know what gets into Sister. She gets herself in a plaguey hobble over nothin'."

"Amy does seem rather irritable today," Maude said, and cast Elija a sympathetic smile.

Maude had put Amy's mood mildly. She was furious, and as soon as she was alone, she allowed herself the luxury of several swear words. She took the path to the river, reached it and turned to walk along the rushing white water until she came to the knoll where Juicy was buried. For a moment she gazed down at the headboard Farr had so painstakingly carved. She concentrated on breathing deeply, hoping to calm her nerves. The old man who lay beneath the headboard had been father, grandfather, teacher, and the best friend she had ever had.

Blinking away the tears, she ran her hand caressingly over the top of the board before she moved to stand at the head of the only other grave in the small glade, that of Fawnella Quill.

Juicy had told her the story many times of how Farr, when he was a young boy, had taken the girl from a pair of crazed trappers. She could not speak and was never able to tell them anything about herself. Farr was devastated when she was killed by a Frenchman while he and Juicy were away from the cabin. For that reason, Juicy had been determined to teach Amy how to defend herself.

After a while Amy walked back down the path. At times she looked forward to the day Rain would return, and at other times she dreaded it. It was now near the end of March, and they had received no word from him or from Colby Carroll. She could tell that Farr was beginning to feel uneasy. He had hoped to be on the way by now. The March winds had dried the trails, and the farther south they traveled the warmer it would be.

Amy went down to the sawyer camp where Farr and Mike were working on the wagons. She was too late to turn back when she realized Tally was with them. He seemed to forget what he was doing when she approached and stood gawking at her with his mouth open.

"Hello, Tally."

"Hel-lo, Miss Amy." He always stammered when he spoke to her.

Amy could have almost liked Tally if not for Maude and her father. He worked hard and did what he was told. He was a big, strong man and not really unpleasant to look at, if she could forget about the placid, cowlike expression he usually wore on his face. He was not overly bright, but not really dumb, either. It was almost as if he didn't have enough mind of his own to make a decision.

The thing about him that irritated her was the fact that he was so much under his mother's thumb that he never spoke without first looking at her to get her approval. She wondered why they were willing to let him leave the farm and trail after her to the Arkansas. Did Maude and her father think she would be so desperate for a man she would marry him, and then he would have control over the money Juicy had left her? She decided to set him straight about that right now.

"I want to talk to you, Tally."

"Yes, ma'am." His eyes widened in surprise and he began to smile as he followed her a short distance from the loud rasp of the two-man saw Farr and Mike were using.

"I'm not going to marry you, Tally. Not ever." Amy said the words bluntly and distinctively to be sure he understood them.

"Oh . . ." The smile faded from his face and a sorrowful look took its place.

"I don't love you, and you don't love me. You've let your mother and my father push me at you until you've not even looked at another girl. You should make your own choice. Not let them choose for you."

"I chose you, Miss Amy."

"But I don't choose you," Amy said kindly. "I don't want to hurt you, Tally, but I want you to get all thoughts of marrying me out of your head."

"There ain't nobody pretty as you."

"Pshaw! What about the Luscomb girl, or one of the Cash girls? And there's Tom Treloar's daughters. Susie is pretty. So are Betsy and Katy. Court one of them."

"Ah . . . I couldn't."

"Why not?"

"Well, Ma said—"

"There you go! 'Ma said,'" she mimicked. "How old are you, Tally? Twenty-two? You're a man, for land's sake. Act like one and tell your mother to go suck eggs, that you'll marry who and when you want to." Amy wheeled and walked away from him.

"Miss Amy," he called. "I sure would like to see the mountains."

Amy gritted her teeth in frustration and didn't answer.

Maude and Elija left in the middle of the afternoon, amid promises to return in a week. Amy had stayed away from the house most of the day to avoid another confrontation with her father. Tired and hungry, she returned in time to wave good-bye.

"You shouldn't let Papa keep you away," Liberty admonished. "Come have something to eat."

"He makes me so mad I can hardly see straight."

"Papa has a way of doing that. When I was younger I thought at times I hated him. Now I can only feel sorry for him."

"Sorry for him! Lord have mercy, Libby. He's never cared for anyone in his life but himself."

"He cares for Maude."

"I don't believe that for a minute. He cares for what Maude has—the farm."

"He works hard. She sees to it."

"Then why is he wanting to send Tally off with us to the Arkansas? He's the one who does the work out there. You can bet Papa does as little as he can get away with."

"I've thought about that. They must plan on Tally getting settled out there and then they can come out. Papa really doesn't want to be separated from us, Amy. We're some sort of security for him."

"Well, name of a name! Is it never to end?"

Liberty laughed. "You've just got to stop letting him bother you."

"That's easier said than done," Amy retorted dryly.

A squeal outside the house caused both women to look up sharply.

"Ma! Amy! Ma! Amy! Daniel's comin'! Daniel and Rain are comin'!" Mercy's shouts reached the house before she did. She flung open the door with such force it bounced against the wall. "They're comin'," she exclaimed breathlessly.

Mercy's words rocked Amy. Blood drained from her face and her heartbeat slowed to a dull thud, then raced like a galloping horse. She got to her feet on numb legs and moved to the window to look out.

Two riders, followed by a wagon, were coming up the lane. A woman in a bright blue dress and bonnet sat on the wagon seat beside the driver. Amy's eyes moved over her and fastened on the big, black-haired man on the dun horse. His words of more than two months ago echoed in her head.

Amy . . . I'll be back.

CHAPTER
Six

"They're coming! Rain and Daniel are coming! Will the lady stay here with us, Ma?" Mercy shouted.

"Don't shout, honey," Liberty cautioned. "Of course she'll stay with us. We'll not be leaving for a week, maybe two."

Amy leaned against the doorjamb and watched the procession approach. Her eyes rested on Rain, and the pleasure she felt when she looked at his tall, erect body blinded to her all but him. She loved the way he held his head, slightly to one side as if he were listening. She had thought about what had happened in the barn before he left. Until now it had seemed to her it had been something she had dreamed, a very pleasant, wonderful dream.

Daniel, wearing a new, round-brimmed hat, rode beside Rain. He was growing up so fast, Amy thought with a pang. Was that a new rifle he was carrying? Behind them the wagon came on at a steady clip. The woman who sat on the seat beside the driver wore a bonnet with a high crown and a folded back brim. Two men on tall, rangy mules rode behind the wagon.

Farr and Zack stood waiting beside the lane that curved in front of the house. Mike stood back under the oak tree, and Amy wondered if he was feeling a little uneasy about meeting Rain again. He had filled out considerably during the last two months. Like a hound dog he had attached himself to Farr.

Farr stepped forward to shake Rain's hand when he slid from the saddle.

"Glad to see you back, Rain. By jinks damn, Daniel! I swear you've grown a foot." Daniel had a wide grin on his face. Farr shook his hand, then threw his arm across his shoulders and gave him a hug. "You were sorely missed, boy."

"He's a good man to trail with," Rain said. "Howdy, Mike. You've perked up considerably. Did Farr work your tail off?"

"Well . . . almost." He shook Rain's hand with a relieved grin on his face.

"It doesn't look like it hurt you any."

"Daniel," Zack shouted. "Mike made a gopher trap!"

Daniel's young face was radiant. He grabbed for Zack, lifted him up, then set him down. Liberty came out from the house, put her arms around Daniel and hugged him.

"I missed you, Daniel. Oh, I missed you. I'm so glad you're home." She smiled up at Rain. "Hello, Rain. Can I hug you too?"

"It wouldn't make me mad at all, Libby," he said and gave her a brief hug.

Mercy stood primly beside Liberty, her hands clasped behind her. After Daniel had greeted everyone else, he drew a small package out of his pocket and thrust it into Mercy's hands.

"Here. I bought you something in Louisville."

"For me?" Mercy squealed.

"I got something for you too, Zack. It's in my bedroll."

Daniel squatted down to fondle the dog. "Did you miss me, Pike? Did you?"

When the wagon rolled up, the driver pulled the team to a halt. Rain went to the wagon and reached for the woman who stood and waited for him to help her down. He put his hands on her waist and swung her easily to the ground. She was a slim woman whose head scarcely came to Rain's shoulder. He took her arm and escorted her to where Liberty stood beside Farr.

"This is Miss Woodbury, Libby."

"Hello," Liberty extended her hand. The woman put hers into it and smiled, but didn't speak.

"Miss Woodbury's had a bad time, Libby," Rain said. "Her aunt died just before we left Louisville."

"Oh, I'm sorry to hear that. Come in and meet my sister while the men get things squared away. As soon as you're rested we'll have supper."

Amy eyed Eleanor Woodbury as she approached the door. She was the prettiest woman she had ever seen. She was small, like a tiny doll. Her hair was black, her skin white, and her eyes a lavender blue. The small lines at the corners of her eyes and mouth told Amy that her age was somewhere between hers and Liberty's. She didn't give that much thought, however, because she was swamped with the feeling of being tall and awkward and decidedly shoddy in her buckskin britches and homespun shirt. Amy shot another look at Rain. He had turned away to talk to Farr without giving her as much as a glance. She moved back into the house ahead of Liberty and her guest, the cold lump that was her heart throbbing in her throat.

"I can't thank you enough for taking me into your home, Mrs. Quill. Although it was a hard trip, Rain was as sweet as pie. He's just the nicest man." Eleanor removed her blue bonnet with the black mourning band around the crown, lifted small white hands and patted her hair in place. "Poor

Aunty took sick just before he got there, and she suffered so. I just couldn't leave her and so we waited . . . until the end." Her voice dropped to a whisper.

"There was nothing else you could do," Liberty said. "This is my sister, Amy."

The black-fringed lavender eyes flicked over Amy and then away. A slight bob of her head was her only greeting.

"Sit down, Miss Woodbury," Liberty invited. "Rain or Daniel will bring in your trunk; you can share the room upstairs with Amy and Mercy for the time being."

"Oh, Rain will take care of my things. But I don't want to be any bother, ma'am." Eleanor backed into the rocking chair, sat down and spread her skirts until only the toes of her soft slippers showed beneath them.

Every time Eleanor used Rain's name with such familiarity it sent a shiver of dread through Amy. She began to stoke up the fire, trying to ignore her pumping heart and wishing for an excuse to leave the room so she could think, but nothing plausible came to mind. There was nothing to do but to stay and help Liberty get a meal on the table.

Farr and Rain stood beside the wagon and watched while Daniel played with the dog.

"I think Daniel's glad to be home." Farr chuckled as Pike ran to fetch a stick Daniel had thrown.

The man driving the wagon came to take Rain's horse.

"Farr, this is Gavin McCourtney. He hired on to go with me to Belle Point."

When Farr held out his hand, it was clasped by a larger one. Sharp blue eyes looked directly into Farr's as each man took the other's measure. Gavin was a big, homely man. Everything about him was too big—mouth, nose, ears, hands, shoulders. His hair was an ugly brown on top, weathered and sunned; it was caught at the nape of his neck with a thong. His nose leaned to one side and his chin and cheeks showed signs of many barroom brawls. In spite of all this, Farr recognized basic integrity. When he looked into Gavin's wide-spaced eyes they were steady and honest.

"Howdy."

"Likewise, to be sure." The man answered in a deep Scottish brogue. "Would ye want that we leave the wagon here or pull it yonder aside the house?"

"This is a good level place. Mike will help you with the team."

"Jonas, Albert," Rain called to the two men standing beside their mules. "Come meet Farr Quill." Aside he said to Farr, "They were long hunters with an outfit I was with going up the Missouri. They can abide a mountain trail as good as any men I've seen."

"Howdy." Farr shook hands with each man. Both were tall and gaunt with shaggy hair and weathered faces. Both looked him in the eye. Farr recognized the look. If they didn't like him, they'd not work for him regardless of the pay. "Welcome. If Rain says you're hickory, it's all I need to know. Water your mules and put your tucker in the barn. Supper call will be soon." The men nodded and walked away. Farr turned to Rain. "You were a long time coming. I was about to give up on you."

"It couldn't be helped. Miss Woodbury's aunt was sick when I got there, and it was plain she was on her death bed. We pulled out the day after the burying."

"I figured you'd get here when you could."

Rain's eyes followed Gavin as he watered the team, then turned to Farr. He grinned. "I got him out of a tavern in Louisville after he'd broken a few heads and before the deputy of the watch got hold of him to throw him in a cell."

"He bears the signs of a brawler, but I've met reformed rogues who turned out to be pretty good men."

"I don't know if he's reformed. So far I couldn't ask for a better man. However, we didn't have any trouble to speak of. I went up the Missouri with the other two men a year or so back. They're reliable and trailwise, and they don't back off from trouble. I didn't promise them anything."

"I'll talk to them tomorrow. I've not run into anyone here who's anxious to go except Tally Perkins. How are things in Carrolltown?"

"Good and bad. The good news is Colby and his pa want to buy you out, and the bad is Willa is in the family way and having a hard time of it. Colby figures he can't leave Carrolltown until the first of May."

Farr frowned. "That is bad news."

"It wouldn't be if I hadn't promised Will Bradford I'd be back by early June. It'll be hard to get there by that time even if we leave tomorrow. Will thought a transfer might come through that would send him south. I want to get Miss Woodbury to him before that happens. I'd hate like hell to have to take her down into Mexican Territory."

"You'll have to go on without us."

"I've been thinking about it, Farr. I'll have to go on, but I can draw out a map and you can follow as soon as you get loose of this place. That's one reason I brought Albert and Jonas. They know the country."

"It's about the only thing I can do. I can't leave the station or it would be looted before Colby got here. There's no one here I'd want to put in charge of it. Besides that, Sloan and Colby will pay cash money, and I'll need it to get set up again." Farr broke a twig off the oak tree and stuck the end in his mouth.

"Jonas said he heard Hammond Perry had bought out a trading post on the lower Arkansas. Before you know it, he'll cover the whole damn river as thick as hair on a grizzly and run nearly everybody else off."

"I'm not interested in the fur trade. Settlers will be moving in and they'll need supplies. Lumber and a mill will be needed."

"With the two men I brought in and Mike and Daniel, you'd be five guns. That's a pretty strong force, but you may want to pick up another man or two who'd stay on after Jonas and Albert leave. They're not settling kind of men."

"You're forgetting Amy. She can load and shoot as fast as any man I've seen."

"Shooting at game is one thing, shooting at someone shooting back at you is another," Rain said dryly and stuck his foot on a wheel spoke. He leaned his elbow on his thigh. "That brings up another matter. Do you suppose Amy would be willing to go along with Miss Woodbury? It wouldn't please Will at all to know his bride traveled cross-country with a couple of men and no woman to keep her company. He was counting on her aunt to be with her."

"That's something you'll have to take up with Amy." Farr eyed his friend keenly. "After you deliver Miss Woodbury, what about Amy?"

Rain's foot came down off the wheel spoke. "She could stay at the fort until you and Libby get there. I'd not let any harm come to Amy. Christ, Farr, she's like my . . . my sister."

Farr raised his dark brows and his face creased with a wide grin. He let out a bellow of laughter and slapped Rain on the back.

"You've got a funny way of kissing your *sister*. You were so busy doing it the day you left here you didn't even hear me open the barn door."

Rain felt as though he had been caught with his hand in the sugar jar. He wondered if he looked as foolish as he felt. He did. He looked uneasy and shifted his feet like a man who had pressing business elsewhere. To make matters worse, Farr was openly enjoying his discomfort. It was one of the few times he had seen his friend so disconcerted.

"Gavin and the other two can bed down in the barn," Rain said gruffly. "If you don't want Albert and Jonas, you can send them on their way tomorrow."

Farr's green eyes twinkled with silent laughter. "If you say I can depend on them, Rain, I'll hire them on. Tell them to wash up and come on in to supper. I'll go on in and make sure Libby has plenty of grub."

Rain walked slowly to the barn feeling he had made a complete fool of himself. Thoughts of Amy had clung to his mind like burrs while he was gone. He wondered if Farr had teased her about the kiss and if that was the reason she had not even acknowledged him when he arrived. With shocking suddenness he realized how disappointed he was. He paused and looked toward the river as thoughts flooded his mind. He had been anxious to get back to see her again and had almost expected her to come running to meet him, as she had done that time so long ago.

"You damn crazy fool," he muttered. "You'd better put a stop to this before it gets out of hand."

Eleanor sat across the room in the rocking chair while Amy and Liberty waited on the table. Mercy dangled the new bright pink ribbon Daniel had brought her over the cradle. When the baby cooed and gurgled and tried to grab it, Mercy laughed happily.

The five men and three boys ate with gusto. The two long hunters had come in with water still on their whiskered faces and their hair slicked down. They were ill-at-ease sitting at a table. Liberty did her best to ignore their bad manners and to make them feel comfortable. Gavin McCourtney had shaved and put on a clean but ragged shirt of soft, white homespun. He said very little but handled his eating tools skillfully and chewed with his mouth closed. Every so often he would glance up from his plate and his sharp blue eyes would slowly and intently circle the room. One time they rested on Amy's flushed face as she forked slabs of deer meat onto a platter. They stayed there a long while. When she looked up and met his eyes, he didn't look away.

Rain caught the look that passed between them and a deep, inner restlessness flickered to life in his stomach. By God! McCourtney had better not take any liberties with Amy. He had been respectful to Miss Woodbury, and Amy would get the same treatment. If McCourtney thought she was any less a lady because she was wearing britches, he would soon set him straight or bust his head. Rain's eyes narrowed slightly. Not a flicker of emotion showed on his face, but for a moment he had heard nothing of what Farr was saying.

"Usually by the middle of May the river is down." Farr's voice pierced Rain's consciousness. "The snow was light up north this year. It didn't raise the river more than two feet."

"You shouldn't have any problems with crossings," Rain said absently. He tried to switch his thought to the problems Farr was facing, but he was too sharply aware of the interest Gavin was showing in Amy.

Farr leaned on his elbow, waiting until the last man had cleared his plate before he pushed back his chair and got to his feet.

"We can smoke outside and give the women a chance to eat in peace."

"Sure was a fine supper, Libby." Rain followed Farr to the door.

"Twas as fine a meal as ever I sat me down to, Mrs. Quill," Gavin said. "Is there nothin' I can be doin' in the way of pay?"

"Heavens, no! But thank you." Liberty picked up the meat platter and failed to see the sharp look Gavin gave

Eleanor, who was sitting in the rocking chair, making no move to help the women clear the table.

"I will be goin' then. G'night to ye."

"He's a nice, mannerly man for all his rough looks," Liberty said after the men had left the house and closed the door behind them.

"I suspect he was putting on airs, trying to impress you and your sister. You see a lot of his kind on the river, Mrs. Quill," Eleanor said. "Rough, tough, hard drinking Irish and Scots who are glib of tongue but quite unscrupulous."

"Oh? Did he act improperly on the way from Louisville?"

"He didn't dare act improperly. Rain watched every move he made and never left me alone with him."

Amy decided then and there that she did not like Eleanor Woodbury. It was evident that Eleanor thought she was too good to rub elbows with the likes of Gavin McCourtney and the two long hunters. More than likely, Amy thought, she was looking down her dainty little nose at the rest of them too. If Eleanor wasn't the intended of Will Bradford, Rain's friend, and if Amy weren't sure Rain would be furious, she would just accidentally dump the gravy bowl she was carrying to the table into Eleanor's lap.

"Come to the table, Eleanor."

Liberty never let anyone's snooty ways bother her. Amy was sure her sister had deliberately called Miss Woodbury by her first name. It was Liberty's way of letting her know she was no better than the rest of them. Amy, however, doubted the woman was quick-witted enough to realize it.

"Thank you, ma'am. I am hungry. It's been a fierce day. I'm so tired I think I'll eat and then go to bed."

"I'll fix Mercy's bed for you. She can sleep in with Amy."

"It's kind of you, ma'am." Eleanor seated herself at the table. "Rain says we'll be going on after tomorrow."

"I doubt that. I don't think Farr can be ready by then." Liberty brought a fresh loaf of bread from the oven.

"Rain confided to me that he isn't going to wait for Mr. Quill. He feels a smaller party would make better time, so he's taking me on to Major Bradford. Aunty's being sick and all has delayed us. Willy will be worried about me."

"This is freshly churned butter, Eleanor. Have some." Liberty set the small crock in front of her guest with downcast eyes. The news that Rain wished to go on without them was shocking. She felt the hurt and disappointment that Farr would feel when he heard the news. Seeing the look on Amy's face tore her heart.

Eleanor dipped into the butter, smeared it on the warm bread and took a dainty bite.

"Oh . . . this reminds me of Mammy. Mammy always made sure I had butter for my bread. She said it made my cheeks rosy and my hair shiny. Mammy took care of me after Mama and Papa died. Mammy and Aunty. Then Mammy sickened and died, then Aunty . . ." Her voice trailed away and huge tears glistened in her eyes. "Everybody who . . . loved me is . . . dead."

"You've got Major Bradford," Liberty said absently, her mind still on the news that Rain planned to leave at once. "He must love you if he sent Rain all the way to Louisville to fetch you."

"Yes. Willy loves me fiercely. He used to come to see Papa a long time ago when I was just a little girl. Aunty wrote to him after Papa and Mama died and, of course, he wanted me."

Of course he did! Amy thought. Most men were stupid when it came to a pretty face. But why a man on the frontier would want a useless bit of fluff like Eleanor Woodbury was beyond her understanding. Her thoughts turned to Rain. Damn him! Farr had worked his tail off these last two months. Now Rain wanted to go on without them. How would Farr take this news? Amy looked at her sister and saw that she was having a hard time carrying on a conversation with her guest. Mercy was hanging on to every word, but then Mercy couldn't see beyond the woman's pretty face and fine clothes.

"Did you live all your life in Louisville?" Amy asked, deciding to take the burden from Liberty, leaving her to think her own thoughts.

"Heavens no! Our plantation was in the Carolinas. At one time my papa had three hundred slaves, miles and miles of cotton and tobacco, and a big house. My mama was the darlin' of society in Charleston." Eleanor's lavender eyes shone through tears as she talked of her former home.

"Why did you leave it then?" Amy asked bluntly.

"'Cause there wasn't anything left, ma'am, after the big storm came from the sea and ruined everything. Waves almost a mile high came crashing in. The wind uprooted the trees and tore the roof right off the house. It carried away most all the slaves and left our house sitting in a lake of water. Papa just barely managed to get me and Mama and Aunty to safety. He went back to find his fields flooded and his crops washed away. It was just awful."

"Oh, my!" Mercy said. "Did a lot of people die?"

"No, just slaves."

"And they're not people?" Amy asked, stabbing a piece of meat from the meat platter with unnecessary force.

"Well, in a way. But not like us."

"Of course not," Amy snapped. "They don't love their children, feel pain or get sick. They're just worked to death, like dumb beasts."

"Why, whatever do you mean?"

Liberty could see the sign of anger on Amy's face. She remembered how fond Amy was of the black man, Mr. Washington, who had run the ferry when they first came to Quill's Station.

"What did you do in Louisville, Eleanor?" Liberty smoothly slid into the conversation.

"Nothing, ma'am. Whatever could I do?"

"I guess I meant what did your father do after he lost his plantation."

"Papa didn't do anything. He wasn't brought up to *work*."

"I see. He must have salvaged enough from the plantation for you to live on."

"Just barely. He did, finally, let Mama teach young ladies to play the spinet, but it vexed him something awful for her to take money for it." Eleanor placed her spoon carefully beside her plate. "I've eaten just every bite I can hold, ma'am. If you'll tell Rain to bring in my trunk, I'll go to bed."

"How about telling him yourself?" Amy looked directly into wide eyes that showed surprise, then hardened and grew cold.

"I can do that," Eleanor said with a jerk of her chin. "I can certainly do that."

"Then do it. We all carry our own weight here." Amy's eyes were shards of ice.

"Rain said I would be welcome here. I hope I don't have to . . . to tell him on you, ma'am."

"Stop calling me ma'am. Unless I miss my guess, you're older than I am."

"Well, I never!" Eleanor exclaimed as the age barb hit home. "Rain said you were widowed. How long were you wed? Ten years? Fifteen? Backwoods women marry so young."

"I married at twelve. I was wed for five years. My husband died two years ago." Amy's chin came out and her look defied Eleanor to comment on her early marriage.

"Well then, you can't very well be called a miss. Your correct title is ma'am."

"I don't like it."

Eleanor flashed her a cold, taut smile. "Very well, but I

don't believe we are sufficiently acquainted to call each other by first names."

"If you *must* call me at all, call me Mrs. Deverell." Amy's cold smile was even colder than Eleanor's.

"I can't imagine why I would need to call you. I've had a limited experience with women who do not know—or want to know—how to dress properly. I've known none who wear . . . britches."

"Don't you wear britches under your skirts? My . . . how convenient!" Amy felt desperate anger take her, and met the other woman's eyes fiercely. She wanted nothing more than to slap the smirk off her pretty face.

Liberty got up from the table. "Mercy, run out and tell Rain or Daniel to bring in Miss Woodbury's trunk." She took a candle from the mantel and lit it. "I'll show you to your bed, Miss Woodbury."

"Thank you, ma'am. I'm most grateful for your hospitality." She shot Amy a defiant look, lifted her skirts and followed Liberty up the steep stairway to the loft.

Amy was clearing the table and putting the dishes in the washpan when the door opened. She glanced over her shoulder and saw Rain come in with a small trunk on his shoulder. He had to come through the door sideways and she turned her back before he saw her looking at him.

"Where do you want this?"

Amy heard the familiar voice and a trembling got into her throat and jaws. She clenched her teeth to steady them before she answered.

"*I* don't want it anywhere," she snarled. "*She* wants it upstairs." She gave her head a suggestion of a toss toward the stairway.

Rain went up the stairs until his shoulder was even with the loft floor. He slid the trunk on to the floor, gave it a shove, and backed down the stairs.

"Thank you, Rain," Eleanor called.

Amy kept her back turned, but she knew when he came to stand behind her, knew every step he had taken, every move he had made since he came into the house. She held her breath and thought about moving away. A small, quick jerk on the braid that hung down her back brought her head around.

"Look at me!" His words were as sharp as a pistol shot. His hands on her shoulders turned her around.

Every line of her body from her pulsing throat to her clenched fists was rigid with anger, left over from her spat with Eleanor Woodbury and from his decision to go on to the Arkansas without them. She had to look up. His dark eyes and hawklike face were too close; she tried to take a step backward, only to come up against the table. The thought came to her that not only was Rain a handsome man, but he was strong, capable and . . . ruthless.

"What do you want?"

"I want to talk to you."

"Why?"

"Goddamn it, Amy, does there have to be a reason?"

"I already know you're leaving the day after tomorrow."

His brows came together in a frown she recognized as one of irritation, and a little pleased flutter punctuated her already rapid heartbeat.

"I wanted to tell you myself."

"Miss Woodbury did it for you."

"No one speaks for me. I do my own talking."

Amy waited until she was sure she could speak normally. "I've got to help Liberty."

"After that, come outside."

"It'll be time for bed."

"Why are you being so damn mule-headed?" He glanced at the clock on the mantel. "Be outside before that clock strikes again or I'll come in here and drag you out." His cold, brittle eyes held hers.

"All right." She tried to meet his gaze coolly. Because the anger she was using to hold back the tears was about to desert her, she dredged up Eleanor Woodbury's words. *Rain confided to me he isn't going to wait for Mr. Quill.* She drew in a shaky breath. "All right," she said again.

"You'll come out?"

"I said I would," she said crossly. "Now get out of here so I can get my work done."

"I meant what I said. You come out before that clock strikes again." He waited a full moment, and when she didn't speak, he stomped to the door. It opened just as he reached it and Mercy came in. He went by her without a word and closed the door.

"What's he so mad about, Amy? I wouldn't want Rain mad at me. He looked madder than a cornered polecat." Mercy leaned on the table and tried to look into Amy's face, but she kept it turned.

"Wrap the bread in a cloth, honey, and hush your chattering or we'll wake Mary Elizabeth. There'll be enough bread for breakfast in the morning if we make a pan of cornbread to go with it."

The words that came from Amy's mouth and her thoughts had no connection. Questions swirled in her mind. What did Rain want to talk to her about? Had Mercy run out and told him she had been rude to Miss Woodbury? That was it, she thought. It had to be that. What else would make him so angry? Well, she wasn't going to apologize. The sooner he took the high-and-mighty bitch and left Quill's Station the better she'd like it.

That's not true, Amy Deverell, an inner voice told her sternly. You're heartsick because she's so pretty and next to her you look like a . . . cow. Rain had spent a couple of months with her and could already be in love with her, even if she was engaged to marry his friend. How could any woman want anyone else when she could have Rain? Damn

Rain Tallman! She would not kowtow to that brainless creature. She had too much pride for that. A second thought
crowded in on the first. Pride would cause her to lose him.
Well, it was too late now. If Rain Tallman didn't like her the
way she was, there were plenty of others who did. That
Scotsman for one. She saw admiration in his eyes, and he
didn't try to hide it.

Amy's thoughts brought her to a plateau of misery which
resulted in a blessed state of numbness. She sank into that
state of mind and worked automatically. Liberty came down
from the loft and joined her. There was no need for words
between the two women. Each knew what the other was
thinking.

CHAPTER
Seven

The night was extremely dark. Mike and Daniel had built a small fire in the clearing beside the woodpile and the men sat around it, smoking and telling yarns.

"That thar grizzly was ten feet high if'n he was a foot," Jonas said. "I was up as far in the aspen as I could get 'n he was areachin' up 'n strainin' to pull down the tree. I had me a whopper of a chaw in my mouth. When the aspen begun to crack, I knowed what I had to do. I spit that wad right square in that grizzly's eye. He let out a roar ya could a heard if'n ya'd been dead, 'n let loose his hold on the tree. The tree flew up so hard I was throwed off my perch. I tell ya, I flew through the air like'n I was a bird 'n landed right slap-dab in the middle of the river. Course I can't swim none 'n was pert nigh as bad off as I when the grizzly treed me, but then this here big old elk come aswimmin' by. I grabbed on to his tail 'n hung on—"

"Ah, shoot!" Daniel said. "I was about to believe the part about the grizzly."

"Don't ya ever believe no tale Jonas tells ya, young

feller," Albert cautioned. "He jist sits round dreamin' up lies to tell when he can get a ear to hear 'em."

"The one I tell 'bout the catfish ain't no lie, Albert. Ya know it ain't. Ya was thar."

"Tell it, Mr. Jonas. I don't care if it's a lie or not." Mike spoke as he placed several small sticks on the fire. It blazed up, showing that Zack had fallen asleep on his father's shoulder.

Gavin McCourtney had sat quietly, smoking a long-stemmed pipe, chuckling occasionally at one of the tall tales the long hunters were telling.

Rain watched the doorway of the house, waiting for Amy to come out. He had heard the clock strike the hour several minutes ago. He would give her a while longer, he decided, before he went in to get her. He wasn't going back on his word and he wasn't going to let her go back on hers. Since he was primed to talk to her, he would do it tonight.

"Mr. McCourtney knows some good stories," Daniel said. "He told me one while we were on the keelboat coming down the river. Tell them about the leper—uh—"

"'Tis leprechauns ye're thinkin' of, laddie."

"Tell them, Mr. McCourtney," Daniel said. "Tell them how they live in the trees, and if you can catch one, he'll lead you to a treasure."

"'Tis a tale the Irish hand down from generation to generation. Some swear to the truth of it. In the woods on a moonlit night tis said ya can see the wee creatures dancin' in the moonlight. On their heads are tall pointed caps and on their feet shoes with tinkling bells . . ."

The door opened and candlelight spilled out into the darkness. Amy stood for an instant in the doorway before she stepped out and closed the door behind her. Rain got to his feet and walked swiftly across the yard. She stood with her back to the wall of the house, almost invisible in her long buckskin shirt and britches. Without hesitation Rain took her arm and propelled her toward the road.

"Come. We'll walk a ways."

"What do you want to talk about?" Amy asked because she thought she had to say something.

"What do you have to say?" The question stunned her and she stopped. His hand on her elbow put her feet into motion again as they walked on.

"About what?"

"About what Miss Woodbury told you."

They reached the old barracks building that had been used during the Indian wars to house patrols. Farr used it now for a storage building. Amy pulled her elbow from Rain's grasp and moved away from him.

"I'm disappointed . . . for Farr and Libby."

"Did Miss Woodbury tell you why we'll go on ahead?"

"Oh, yes. She said *Willy* would be worried about her, and that you said you could travel faster if you went without the rest of us."

"What she said is true, but it isn't all."

"It's enough."

Rain took her arm again and pulled her to a stop. "Why can't we talk without snarling at each other?"

"Who's snarling?"

"You are. Come sit down. I want to tell you about Colby and Willa."

Amy sat on a felled tree trunk and Rain stood in front of her with his foot on the log as if he expected her to jump up and run. There was a long silence while Amy waited for him to speak again. She could feel his eyes on her face and was glad he couldn't see the flush that flagged her cheekbones.

"Well?" she asked when she couldn't bear the silence any longer.

"Colby wants to buy out Farr, but because of Willa's condition he can't leave Carrolltown until the first of May."

Patiently, using more words than he normally used, he told her the reason why Farr would stay and wait for Colby and then come on to the Arkansas with Jonas and Albert. He told her he had chosen the two mountain men because if anyone could see Farr through they could. He also told her why he had to get Miss Woodbury to Belle Point as quickly as possible. "I'd sure as hell hate to get there and find Will has been transferred. I figure to get to Belle Point, then double back and meet Farr somewhere near Davidsonville. That's a settlement in the northeast corner of the Arkansas Territory. It means I'll have to travel fast and light."

"Why tell me?"

"Because I want you to come with me."

Amy was stunned for a moment. When she spoke, her teeth chattered. "Why?"

"Will had counted on Miss Woodbury's aunt traveling with her. It won't look good for her to arrive at the fort in the company of two men."

"No."

"No?"

"No." Amy stood and moved away from him. "I'll not be a nursemaid to that empty-headed little snob! Take her to her Willy yourself. The sooner she's gone the better I'll like it." The hurt that followed that first little surge of hope gave her voice a distant, chilly quality.

"I'm not asking you to nursemaid her. I'm asking you to go with us for appearance's sake. I spoke to Farr and he said it would be your decision.

For appearance's sake. The words were a blow to her pride.

"I told you, I'm not going."

"Think about it before you decide."

"I don't have to think about it. I don't like her."

"What's that got to do with it?"

Amy didn't answer. She turned her back to him and

folded her arms across her chest. She was shaken by Rain's request and desperately hoped that he didn't know it. She felt as if she were standing on the edge of a cliff and if she moved she would topple into oblivion. Her head felt tight, her eyes smarted, and for the first time in her life she wanted to crawl off into a hole and cry.

Rain's hands fastened on to her shoulders. She tried to shrug them away, but they tightened and drew her back against him. His breath was a warm caress on her ear.

"You used to . . . like me a little. Have I changed so much, Amy? We used to be able to talk to each other."

"I talked. You didn't say much."

"I was shy and trying to find myself." His voice was a mere whisper against her ear.

"A lot of time has gone by. We've . . . both changed." Her voice had raw feeling in it and she drew in her lower lip to stop its quivering.

"I still see traces of the old Amy."

"You . . . said that in the barn that day."

"I never say things I don't mean."

He turned her around to face him. She felt his eyes probe fiercely all the way down to her legs that were suddenly cold and shaking.

"I'll not urge you to come with us, if you're dead set against it, but I wish you would."

They stood looking at each other. An owl hooted in a tree down by the river and a squirrel stirred restlessly in the new nest she had built to raise her family. Sounds of muted laughter came from the fire beside the woodpile. It suddenly occurred to Amy that she had never before heard Rain Tallman ask anything of another person—not even Farr.

"Rain . . ." Her hands came up and grasped his elbows. "I wouldn't make a good companion for someone like Miss Woodbury. She and I are as different as daylight and dark."

"I know that. You need only to be civil to her, that's all.

You and McCourtney would take turns driving the wagon. It's light and we'll move fast."

"But . . . Farr will need me."

"I need you more." His voice came quietly out of the darkness.

"Don't wheedle me, Rain."

"I won't ask you again."

Amy stood with her head bowed and her eyes closed. Gradually, Rain's hands on her shoulders pulled her closer until her forehead rested against his shoulder. She rolled her head back and forth.

"I don't know what to do."

"Are you afraid to go? I can't tell you it won't be a dangerous trip. It's a rough country, even rougher and more uncivilized than it was here when you and Libby first came. But if I didn't think I could keep you reasonably safe, I'd not take you."

"Uncle Juicy taught me to take care of myself."

"We had the same teacher. Remember?"

Amy didn't know when his hands slid from her shoulders and down her back to cross and splay over her rib cage. It seemed so natural to be standing there close to him, enfolded in his arms, leaning on his strength. This was Rain, her beloved Rain. Her hands moved, her arms went around him and she hugged his great, hard body to her. She felt the gentle pull of his beard when he bent his head and pressed his cheek to hers, heard the thump of his heartbeat, smelled the familiar smell of his buckskin shirt. This was *home*. It was like she imagined heaven would be. She wished with all her heart that she could stop time and stay there with him forever.

"I'll come with you, Rain."

His arms tightened around her until she was pressed into every curve of his body.

"I'm glad." His voice rasped roughly and his warm breath

tickled her ear. "I want to leave at first light the day after tomorrow."

"I'll be ready."

"Do you think we know each other well enough to share a kiss?" He spoke against her ear.

"Do you?"

He chuckled softly, lifted his head and looked into her eyes.

"Amy, Amy! I knew you when your mouth and eyes were too big for your face and you talked all the time." His hand caressed her back and then moved up to the nape of her neck beneath the long rope of hair.

"You didn't like me."

"I was scared to death of you. You were the first white girl I knew, the first girl I kissed."

"I've not kissed any man but you."

"Am I the only one you cornered in the barn?" he teased.

"You cornered me last time."

"Yeah, I did. Kiss me again."

His voice drawled those unreal words and she lifted her hands to his hair, wound her fingers into it, and gave a slow tug. And then, with a wonderful feeling of freedom, she trailed her hands down his cheekbones, feeling the drag of new beard against her palms, and brought her fingertips lingeringly across his mouth to trace his firm lips. Then she pulled his head down toward her uplifted face and parted lips.

Rain set his mouth against hers. At first the kiss was gentle, sweet, hesitant, as if waiting for an invitation to deepen it. Amy's mind fed on the new sensations created by the feel of his body against hers, his firm but gentle lips, open and exploring and caressing. Her lips met his with a hunger equal to the hunger that heated her blood, and with a craving from some unknown thing that was her soul.

He made the world spin.

When he deepened the kiss with mounting urgency, she welcomed the feel of his teeth, his tongue, the fresh taste of his mouth, the rough drag of the whiskers on his cheeks, and even the hardness of his nose lying beside hers. Her fingers caressed his ears and tugged gently at the hair at the nape of his neck. A wild crescendo rose within her and she knew that if he truly made love to her, if she became one with his rock-hard body, the world would stand still.

His lips softened, caressed and clung with a leisurely sweetness that held still the very moments of time. He lifted his head and looked into her eyes. He was breathing hard. Puffs of warm breath touched her wet lips.

"That was a lot better than that first one in the barn." His lips touched her nose lightly. "Don't say anything," he cautioned softly. "Don't say anything at all."

With his arm behind her and his hand on her waist, they walked back to the house.

Rain stretched out on his bunk and listened to the sounds of the house creaking and the branches of the oak tree scraping the roof. Now that it was settled that Amy would go with them, he was filled with a quiet unrest. Not often did he question his decisions as he did now. He knew how Farr had felt that day by the wagon when he had suddenly gripped the wheel and said that at times he thought he was out of his mind for even considering taking his family into the unsettled land.

If anything happened to Libby... he had said, and Rain had seen the fear that entered his eyes.

Things happen, Rain thought. Things no one can control. Accidents, Indian trouble, renegades, river crossings ... He flopped over on his side. He realized that suddenly Amy had become very dear to him. If anything happened to her on this trip, would he be able to endure the pain? The thought of losing her caused fear to flood over him like an icy wave.

After long moments of staring into the darkness he began to speculate on how it would be to be with Amy day and night, to have her look at him with love as Libby looked at Farr. He had not known love since his mother died. John Spotted Elk had cared for him. Juicy, Farr and Colby Carroll had liked him. But love such as Libby and Farr had for each other was a rare, wonderful and illusive thing. Did he dare hope it could be his?

A warmth flowed through him as he thought of the way Amy's soft body had fit against his, the way her lips clung, her arms hugged him to her. Never had he felt so close to anyone. It was as if, for that short time, they were a part of each other. He hadn't wanted it to end, or for words to shatter the sweetness they had shared.

He forced himself to think of practical things. He would have to set Gavin McCourtney right about Amy. If Gavin thought she was fair game he would soon find out how wrong he was. Rain thought for a moment of leaving him to travel with Farr and asking one of the long hunters to come with him. After careful deliberation he decided against it. Albert and Jonas had been together too long and knew each other's ways too well to break up the team. It would be best to leave them with Farr.

The sound of an owl in the oak tree above the house drew his attention for a moment. Caution was bred deep in Rain. The habit of years was hard to break. He listened with all his senses attuned to the night sounds. His sharp ears heard the flapping of wings, then the squeak of a small animal caught in the powerful claws of the owl. A natural event had occurred—the strong feeding on the weak.

Rain's last thought before he drifted off to sleep was that he would have a talk with McCourtney in the morning.

* * *

Amy told Liberty the news while they were preparing breakfast. Farr had taken over the milking chore that morning because of the men sleeping in the barn.

"Rain asked me to go, and I said I would," Amy said, trying to keep the joy she was feeling out of her voice. "What do you think, Libby?"

"I think it's grand! Oh, honey. I just knew that Rain cared for you!"

"He didn't say that!"

"He will. Just mark my words. He loves you." Liberty finished pinching off the biscuits from the pile of dough in the bowl. She shoved the heavy iron baking pan into the oven and covered her flour bowl with a cloth before setting it under the workbench.

"Shh . . ." Amy giggled and pointed to the room where Rain slept with the boys.

"He isn't in there. He went out early this morning. I knew something exciting had happened when you came down. Your eyes were shining like stars."

"I hardly slept a wink. Oh, Libby, I'll have to get along with Miss Woodbury and . . . I don't like her."

"Don't let her bother you. You're ten times the woman she is. Slice more meat, honey."

"But she's so pretty." Amy put several more slices in the skillet and slid it along the grate until it was directly over the flame.

"So are you. You're real. She's just fluff and lace."

Farr came in and set the milk bucket on the workbench. "The men will be in after they wash up."

"We'll be ready. Did Rain tell you Amy is going with him?"

"He told me. He and McCourtney have been up for a

couple of hours switching the wheels on the wagon and adding heavier iron rims."

"So that's what they've been doing by lantern light. What do you think about Amy going, Farr?"

"I think it's fine if it's what she wants to do. Rain can take care of her if anyone can. We'll miss you, Amy."

"I'll miss you too."

"This is the first time we've been away from each other," Liberty said as it suddenly occurred to her.

"You're forgetting the time you went to Vincennes for a few weeks when Hammond Perry arrested Farr."

"That worm! We showed him who not to mess with." Liberty tossed her head and her eyes sought those of her husband's.

Farr laughed softly and moved toward his wife as if he had no control over his feet. "I love you, Mrs. Quill," he said softly for her ears alone.

"And I love you, Mr. Quill," she murmured. Then she said sternly, "There's a straw floating around in the milk pail. I wonder what else went in unnoticed."

Rain had his chance to talk to Gavin while they were working on the wagon.

"There will be four of us making the trip, McCourtney. Mrs. Deverell is coming along as a companion for Miss Woodbury."

"Aye."

"She's a woman with a mind of her own, and one I have the utmost respect for."

"Aye."

"She'll be under my protection the same as Miss Woodbury."

"What're ye sayin', mon? Spill it out."

"I'm saying she's a lady and will be treated like one."

"Ye're thinkin' I may be thinkin' less of the lass because of the britches?"

"That's what I'm thinking."

"Have no fear, mon. If'n there's one thing I know tis the ones what will and the ones what won't."

"I'm glad to hear it. I know next to nothing at all about women."

"I know when a lass is deep and true, mon. I was bonded to such a one when I was a wee lad of eight, though it didna last to see me up and on me own."

Gavin planted his feet wide apart, stooped and lifted the heavy wheel. Rain guided the hub on to the axle. The big man was scarcely breathing hard when he stepped back.

"The women are to be left alone . . . unless they invite your attention.

"I willna lust for your lass, for tis plain to see her heart is yours."

Rain felt a flush of pleasure on hearing his words, but spoke firmly. "The women are under our protection. Remember that."

"Aye. Now, to my way of thinkin', the other lassie is one to be needin' a strong hand on her bare bottom." A mischievous light came into Gavin's blue eyes, and his lips spread to reveal remarkably fine, white teeth considering the battering they had taken over the years in numerous barroom brawls.

"That may be," Rain said and looked into the other man's eyes. "But it isn't your job or mine to correct her ways. That will be Major Bradford's responsibility."

"Aye. That is true. The mon has his work cut out." Gavin shrugged and went back to fixing the wagon.

* * *

The morning passed with incredible swiftness. No one bothered to tell Eleanor Woodbury that Amy was going to travel with them. She first heard it mentioned at the noon meal. She had not come down to the kitchen for breakfast until after the men and the children had been fed. Then she sat at the table daintily picking at the meat and biscuits Libby had kept warm on the hearth as she chatted with Liberty about parties she had attended in Carolina before hard times fell on the family.

Amy spent the morning at the storehouse with Rain choosing food supplies and other necessities for the trip.

"Is there anyone you want to say good-bye to, Amy?" Farr asked when the men were seated at the table and she and Liberty were serving the meal.

"No."

"If you want to ride over to see your father this afternoon, Mike or Daniel will go with you."

"Thank you, but I don't want to go," Amy's eyes went to Rain's before she turned back to the hearth and swung the teakettle away from the flame.

Eleanor sat in the rocker with a piece of needlework in her hands. She heard Farr's words to Amy and saw the look that passed between Amy and Rain. Her hands stilled, and she sat quietly watching, her eyes going from one face to the other.

"Amy made a tab of the supplies she took from the store, Farr. We'll settle up before we leave." Rain took a paper from his shirt pocket and passed it to Farr.

Gavin's sharp eyes saw the nostrils of Eleanor's shapely nose quiver and knew the exact moment she became aware that the other woman was going with them. She was angry but was making every effort to keep it from showing on her beautiful face. Gavin's eyes filled with admiration for the little woman, and he looked down at his plate before she looked at him. He was sure the prim and proper Miss Woodbury would do everything in her power to keep the lass from going. She was in for a comedown, he thought gleefully. Rain Tallman was not a man to be swayed by a pretty face or a woman's tears.

As soon as the men finished their meal and began to leave the table, Eleanor got to her feet, just as Gavin expected.

"Mr. Tallman," she called softly. "May I speak with you? Please?" She stood with her hands clasped demurely in front of her. The dress she wore was of fine lavender cotton that matched her eyes. An edge of cream lace at the high round neck touched the raven hair at her nape and her white jawline. Her hair was puffed and coiled on the top of her head and held there with a beaded comb. All eyes were on her and she was aware of the picture she made.

She looked like a beautiful china doll, Amy thought with a sinking feeling.

Rain nodded and stood with his hands on the back of his chair while the other men filed out. Eleanor lifted a white shawl from the back of the rocker and put it about her shoulders. Without a word she went to the door. Rain followed her out into the yard. When they were beyond hearing distance of the men who were still working on the wagon, she stopped and turned to look up at him, her eyes wide and innocent.

"Mr. Tallman, it has occurred to me that something is going on that I haven't been told about."

"You mean about Mrs. Deverell going to Belle Point with us?"

"Exactly. I feel I should have been consulted before such a decision was made."

"Why do you think that? I'm in charge. I don't have to consult you about anything."

"Oh, but I think you do. You were employed by my fiancé."

"But not by *you*, Miss Woodbury."

Eleanor chose to ignore Rain's blunt words and used a different tactic. She raised her hand hesitantly and placed it lightly on his arm.

"I feel perfectly safe with you. Willy thinks you are very trustworthy or he wouldn't have sent you to fetch me."

"It isn't a matter of safety. It's a matter of appearances. Had your aunt lived, she would be traveling with you. I don't think Will would be pleased if you arrived at Belle Point without a woman companion."

Eleanor's mouth tightened. "Will paid you to bring *me* to Belle Point, not your Mrs. Deverell."

Rain shrugged her hand from his arm, crossed his arms on his chest and looked down at her upturned face. The thought of Gavin's words about her needing a strong hand on her bottom almost brought a smile to his lips.

"I'm repaying a favor to Will by taking you to him. He gave me money to outfit a wagon and buy supplies. Now understand this: It matters not a whit to me if you want to travel with Amy or not. She is going, and you had better be civil to her or you'll answer to me."

"Well, of all things! Are you threatening me?"

"Call it what you want. I'm telling you to behave yourself or you'll have a mighty unpleasant trip."

"I'll not be told what to do by a . . . a hired hand! I'll tell Willy!"

"Tell him. But you've got to get there first, don't you?"

Eleanor realized she would get nowhere with this man by trying to bully him. There had to be another way. She allowed her eyes to widen and her lips to tremble. She summoned images of times past in order to bring tears to her eyes. She dabbed at them with a handkerchief she drew from her sleeve.

"I don't think you understand, Rain. I've not been raised like other girls. I was always so protected. Aunty and Mammy did everything for me ... while they lived. It will be difficult for me to share quarters with someone like Mrs. Deverell."

"Why is that, Miss Woodbury?"

"Well ... I don't think she likes me, and she'll not give me a chance to be friends with her."

"It's true. Amy doesn't like you. She told me so when I asked her to go with us. It will be up to you to change her mind."

Eleanor's control almost deserted her again. *"You* asked *her?* I don't want her with me. I want that wagon to myself. Hear me?"

"What I said about being civil goes. We're leaving in the morning." Rain turned on his heel and walked away.

Eleanor stood for a long moment with her fists clenched and her face a mask of fury. Damn him, she thought. Nothing had gone right since Aunt Gilda took sick. Then she had to die and leave her to face all this alone. Knowing that she had to get herself under control before she went back into the house, Eleanor walked for a short way down the lane and then back.

As she neared the house she saw Gavin McCourtney rolling a wheel toward the wagon. He grinned at her and touched his fingers to his forelock in a mocking gesture of respect. She lifted her nose in the air and went past him. The soft ripple of knowing laughter that followed her made her want to turn and slap him.

CHAPTER
Eight

Dawn was lighting the eastern sky when Amy said good-bye to the family amid hugs, kisses and tears. Eleanor Woodbury, having thanked Liberty for her hospitality, waited tight-lipped and angry on the wagon seat. Gavin sat beside her and watched the family say their farewells with a knot of regret in his heart for never having known, and probably never knowing, what it was like to be so loved by family or friends.

"Bye, honey." Liberty had tears in her eyes. She hugged her sister. "I'm so glad you'll be with Rain," she whispered. Aloud she said, "Be careful—take care of yourself. We'll see you in a few weeks. You take care of her, Rain. Hear me, now." Liberty sniffed back her tears and kissed Rain's cheek. "And take care of yourself too."

"I'll do that, Libby."

"Take care of Mercy and Zack, Daniel." Amy wanted to hug him, but was afraid she would embarrass him. "And Mike, I'm counting on you to look after Daniel—"

Farr put his arms around Amy and hugged her affectionately. "Who's going to look after me?" he teased.

"Libby. I don't have to tell her; she doesn't let you get out of her sight. I'll miss you, Farr. Come on as soon as you can . . . and be careful."

"Listen to little sister," he said and hugged her again. "You'd better get on that horse or Rain will go off without you."

"Bye, everybody." Amy put on a wide-brimmed hat that had been Juicy's and mounted the horse Rain had chosen for her to ride.

To Farr she looked like a tall, slim boy until she turned and he could see the long rope of hair that hung down her back. He moved over and put his arm around Liberty, knowing that this parting was painful for her, yet knowing she wanted her sister to be with Rain.

"Amy!" Mercy ran to the horse and grabbed the stirrup. "I don't want you to go."

"Oh, honey, it's only for a little while."

Daniel came and gently pulled Mercy away from the horse's dancing feet. "Come back away. You've got to help Ma get things ready for us to go now that Amy won't be here to help her."

Mercy obeyed, then stood silently, holding tightly to Daniel's hand, her big cornflower blue eyes swimming in tears.

Rain gave Gavin the sign to move out. He shook hands with the long hunters, Farr and the boys, then mounted his dun horse.

"I'll leave word at Davidsonville, Farr. You do the same if I miss you on my way back." He raised his hand in a salute to Liberty and put his heels to the horse.

Amy moved in behind the wagon where a spare horse had been tied, turned in the saddle and waved. Tears blinding her, she saw only dimly the little group of people who waved back. She blinked her eyes rapidly, not wanting Rain to see her tears. She was happy and yet sad too, happy because she would be with Rain and sad because she was leaving behind all the love and security she had ever known.

Rain rode past her and moved up to speak to Gavin.

"The road is flat for a long stretch. We'll go at a good clip for a couple of hours, then ease off for an hour. The mules are strong, but at that rate they'll be worn down by the time we get to the big river. We'll trade them at Kaskaskia for a fresh pair."

"Aye. Lead on and set the pace." Rain rode ahead and the big Scotsman slapped the reins against the backs of the team and yelled, "H'yaw! H'yaw!" Gavin skillfully handled the reins until the mules settled into an easy gait, and the wagon rolled over the hard-packed road.

Gavin glanced at the woman who sat at the far side of the wagon seat with her skirts tucked about her legs as if they would be soiled by touching him. She wore a dark bonnet that shaded her face and a shawl about her shoulders. A grin jerked at his lips as her hand shot out to grab the seat between them when one of the wheels rolled over a stone. He waited until Rain was far enough ahead so that he was out of hearing distance before he spoke to her.

"Well now, lassie. Air ye goin' to pout all the way to the Arkansas?"

Eleanor turned to look at him with eyes as cold as a frozen pond. She tilted her chin at a haughty angle and spoke in a chilling tone.

"What I do or don't do cannot possibly be of any concern to you."

"Aye, but it is. Tis a pleasant journey I wish to be havin'."

"You are not being paid to enjoy yourself. You're being paid to drive this wagon. I do not wish to be bored by your inane conversation."

"And who's to be sayin' that ye'll be bored?" He turned to look at her set profile and studied her briefly. "Ye should be enjoyin' the wee things, lass. Ye be alive in a big, grand world. It'll speak to ye if ye listen. Ye can hear the wind whisperin', the bees hummin' and a frog ploppin' into the water. Tis a grand sight to see a bird soar. But ye'll have to be lookin' to see it."

"You may have missed your calling, Mr. McCourtney." The look she gave him was designed to put him firmly in the place of an inferior. "Perhaps you should be writing sonnets."

His soft, amused laughter infuriated her. She straightened her shoulders, held her chin at a proud angle and looked straight ahead.

"Ye'll be wearin' yerself out sittin' so ramrod stiff, or is it that corset ye're wearin' that's holdin' ye up so straight?"

Eleanor's mouth opened in surprise. She glared at him in icy contempt. "You are forgetting your place!"

"Aye. Tis a habit, I fear." Gavin chuckled deep in his chest. "Ye're a wonderin' how a mon like I be would be knowin' 'bout women and corsets. Even the women that I know wear corsets, lass. There's the highbrows such as ye are. There's the lowbrows, the doxies, the harlots, the chaste and the unchaste—all puttin' on the things to be coaxin' a mon to their bed, so he be havin' to take it off afore he can get down to the real business at hand."

"Shut up and drive!"

"Tis true, I tell ye, ye're torturin' yerself for naught. It matters naught to me or to Tallman if yer middle is small. Take off the thin' and breathe deep the fresh air. Tis spring, lass—"

"Damn you to hell and back! Shut up or I'll yell for Rain and he'll knock you on your ass!"

"Ahh..." Laughter rumbled up out of his deep chest. "Careful, lass. Ye be forgettin' yerself."

"What do you mean?"

"Why, nothin', ma'am. Nothin' a'tall." He continued to

laugh. "Tis a mighty fine day, I be thinkin'. The sky is blue, the birds are singin'—"

"I don't give a damn about the birds!" she snapped. Her eyes burned at him resentfully.

"Aye." He put his hand to his forelock and pulled, as he had done the day before when he was mocking her. She swiveled her shoulders around until her back was to him.

This only confirmed what she had known all along, Eleanor thought. Gavin McCourtney meant trouble. She had known it the moment Rain Tallman brought him and the wagon to her door the morning after Gilda died. He had been a crewman on the boat that brought her and Gilda to Louisville, and she had caught him watching her. The captain had told Gilda he was known up and down the river as a brawler. The few times she had been outside the small house she and Gilda had rented just off the square, she had seen him on the streets or in front of the tavern. If this common Scotsman continued to bother her, she decided, she would speak to Rain.

Amy Deverell was another matter. She had already spoken to Rain about *her*. He had a point, she reluctantly admitted, in bringing along a woman companion for her. It was important that her reputation be protected. But there was something about this particular woman that set her teeth on edge, and she pondered the reason. Could it be, she asked herself, that Amy was the type of woman she had always wanted to be—a woman in charge of her own destiny?

The man beside her began to sing. Eleanor's attention was captured, although she refused to turn and look at him. His voice was surprisingly good and the ballad he sang was a familiar one.

"Where, oh, where is my true love?
    My scalding tears, they burn.
No track or trace of her I've found,

Oh, when will she return?
Perhaps the wolves the heart have torn,
   that loved me aye so dear;
Should I die of grief, my soul will soar,
   straight to the arms of my
         El . . . ean . . . or."

Eleanor heard his soft, throaty laughter. She knew the song. He had revised the last lines to irritate her. She also knew he was trying to provoke her into exchanging barbs with him again. She would not give him the satisfaction, she decided. Nevertheless, it was maddening to have to keep still.

Gavin McCourtney, however, stayed in her thoughts. She could not help but wonder what kind of man he really was. He sang sentimental ballads yet was a notorious brawler, a shiftless ne'er-do-well known up and down the Ohio River only for his strength and his ability to drink and fight. He seemed to be a man with no roots, no ambition. All he had was brute strength and pride, she thought angrily. Brute strength, pride and a glib tongue.

The sun was warm at mid-morning and Eleanor removed her bonnet. They came to a small creek, pausing to let the animals drink. Gavin jumped down from the wagon, lifted the tin cup from the box on the side and carried a cup of water to Eleanor. She drank thirstily and then handed the cup back to him.

"Ye're welcome, lass," he said as if she had thanked him. "Aye, lass, ye're in for a time of it if'n ye don't unbend a bit and show ye're not what ye're makin' out to be," he added with a shake of his head.

"Go away," she hissed.

"Tis gettin' hárd fer ye to keep up the pretense, eh, me girl? To be sure, twill be harder as time goes by. I be tellin' ye fer a fact."

"What do you mean?"

"I'll not be the one to be tellin' ye, for ye'll soon be tellin' it to yerself."

His words stunned her. When she got over her astonishment and was able to speak, he was walking away. He headed toward the creek where Rain and Amy had knelt to drink.

Amy drank from her cupped hands as Rain did.

"Tired of the saddle?" he asked.

"Not yet. I'll ride till noon."

"It's the first day. Don't wear yourself out."

On the road again, Rain set a brisk pace for an hour, then eased off as the terrain became hilly. Gavin gave his attention to driving, keeping the pace yet trying to avoid the deep ruts or stones that would jolt the wagon. He took care not as much for the sake of the woman who rode beside him as for the wear on the wagon. Not a word passed between them; both were consumed with their own thoughts.

When they stopped at noon, Gavin and Rain unhitched the team, let them drink, wiped them down, and staked them out to graze.

Amy was stiff from being in the saddle for such a long stretch. She ignored her discomfort, led her horse and the spare to drink, then tied them so they could crop the fresh green grass growing near the stream. She walked a short distance alongside the creek, and when she was sure she was out of the sight of the men, relieved her full and aching bladder. She then splashed water on her face and hands to rid them of the trail dust.

Eleanor was still sitting on the wagon seat when Amy returned. She paused, intending to ask her if she needed privacy, but the dark-haired woman refused to acknowledge her. Amy moved on to the back of the wagon. The night before she and Liberty had cooked a joint of meat and several loaves of bread. They had packed the meat, bread and hard-cooked eggs in a metal-lined box along with freshly churned butter and a crock of berry jam. It would last the four travelers for several days. Amy spread a cloth on the tailgate and laid out sliced meat and bread.

Gavin returned from the creek carrying a bucket of fresh water. Eleanor lifted her chin and looked away from him when he passed, but stood when Rain approached and waited for him to help her down.

"If you . . . wish to be alone, Miss Woodbury, you can go down along the creek, behind that screen of cedars," Rain said and pointed toward the stream.

"Thank you." She held on to his arm for a long moment as if she were not steady on her feet. Then she smiled up into his face. "I'm just not used to such a rough ride," she said apologetically and grasped his arm with both her hands. "I'm glad Willy sent *you* to fetch me, Rain. I truly am glad." She looked up into his face, her lavender eyes showing admiration. When he didn't speak, she looked toward the place he had mentioned. "You'll wait and see that no one . . . ?" she asked fearfully.

"I'll wait."

Behind the wagon Gavin looked at Amy's suddenly red face. "Pay no mind to the lassie's wheedlin' yer man, lass. She be usin' her beauty to be gettin' her way with him. Tis all she has."

"It's plenty," Amy murmured.

"Aye. But there be naught to go with it, to me way a thinkin'."

Amy looked into twinkling blue eyes. "I think I'm going to like you, Mr. McCourtney."

"Well, now. That be fine news."

Amy continued working. She stacked the bread and meat together and handed Gavin a large portion.

"Go ahead and eat. We don't have time to wait until we're all here and the blessing said."

Amy looked past him and saw Rain, standing at the edge of the clearing, watching them. She wondered what he was thinking. Did he see her as tall, awkward and unwomanly compared to Eleanor? Feeling tired and a little teary, she poured a cup of water, picked up her own meal and settled herself by a tree. She put her cup down beside her, removed her hat and placed it on her bent knee. Her hunger had left her, but she forced herself to nibble at the food.

Eleanor came out of the woods and took Rain's arm. Her hair shone in the sunlight. The shawl had slipped from her shoulders and hung in a loop down her back. The neck of her dress was cut so that the white tops of her breasts were visible and pushed high by the tight corset that cinched her small waist. At the end of the wagon Rain waited for her to help herself to the food. She hesitated before taking a slice of bread and a small piece of meat and holding it daintily in her fingers.

"I'm not really hungry at all, Rain. But I suppose I should eat something."

"It's your last chance until after sundown," he said in a disinterested tone that brought her eyes to his face. A slow red crept into her cheeks that deepened when Rain picked up his own food and walked away, leaving her standing alone beside the wagon.

He went to where Amy sat and sank down, Indian fashion, beside her. He pushed his hat to the back of his head and took a bite of the meat and bread.

"Good food. I didn't know I was so hungry." His eyes locked with hers and drew all coherent thinking from her mind.

"Me, too."

"We made good time this morning."

"The road was smooth."

While Rain ate, his dark eyes moved around the area, but always returned to her face. Amy finished eating and took a drink from the cup. Their eyes met over the rim. When she lowered the cup, he took it from her hand, lifted it to his lips and drained it.

"I'll get some more water," he said and made a move to get up.

"I've had enough."

"Sure?"

"Sure." Amy's heart fluttered and she drew the tip of her tongue across her lips. Being with him and sharing the cup of water made her feel all mixed up and shaky inside.

"Farr told me that you can handle the team."

"I can handle them. I drove one of his supply wagons when we went to Vincennes."

"Either McCourtney or I will take over when we cross the Little Wabash up ahead."

Amy nodded. It felt strange to be with Rain away from the station. He seemed different, not so closed and standoffish. She wondered if he thought the same about her. She watched Eleanor walk back and forth alongside the wagon and tried not to think about how pretty she was. She looked down at her own clothes, the buckskin britches and the warm doeskin shirt. A breeze came from behind her and ruffled her hair. Absently she lifted a hand and looped a loose strand behind her ear. At least in her buckskin britches and loose shirt she was more comfortable than Eleanor.

Another thought came to mind that made her smile. She wondered how Eleanor had been able to hold her water since dawn. The breakfast meat had been exceptionally salty, and she had drunk several large cups of water. Amy herself had been able to relieve herself at the mid-morning stop and had still been anxious again by noon. Eleanor hadn't been off the wagon since dawn. She glanced at Rain and found him watching her.

"What are you thinking? What made you smile?" The smile he gave her was wicked, teasing, and jarred her to her senses.

"I . . . can't tell you."

"Why not?" He continued to look at her. Her radiant face and mischievous eyes made her look like the Amy of pigtails, freckles and a mouth full of questions.

"You'd think I was . . . shameless."

"Maybe. But tell me anyway."

His eyes smiled into hers with warm affection. They were so dark and shiny she could see her reflection in them. It was as if the two of them were cocooned in a small, intimate, happy world of their own. The luxury of being with him like this made Amy want to prolong it for as long as possible, store it up to think about later.

She shook her head. "I can't." Her voice was strained as she tried to keep laughter at bay.

"I could tickle it out of you like Juicy used to do." His smile widened and creases appeared in his cheeks next to his mouth. He looked young, boyish. She had never seen him smile like that.

"Do you remember that?" Laughter bubbled up and made both Eleanor and Gavin turn to look at them, but Rain and Amy had eyes only for each other.

"I remember a lot of things. You never held anything back. Always said what came to your mind."

"I can't this time. It was . . . an indelicate thought. Not one a lady should discuss."

"Not with anyone?"

"Well, not a man, unless—"

"Is it something Libby would tell Farr?"

"There's nothing that Libby wouldn't tell Farr. They're like one."

"I'll wait," he said, his smile gentle now. "But don't forget it so you can tell me . . . later."

Rain got to his feet, then held out his hand and Amy put hers in it. When she was standing beside him, he continued to hold on to her hand for a long moment, then he squeezed it gently before he released it. He had such a tender expression on his face that a delicious weakness flooded through her.

Amy was in a happy daze as she went about the chore of putting away the food box. She remembered each one of his words as if they were a treasure. Later, he had said, *Don't forget so you can tell me later*. It was almost as if he were saying that later they would be like Libby and Farr. Could she have misunderstood his meaning? She hoped with all her heart that she had not.

Gavin and Rain hitched up the team. Amy tied her horse to the back of the wagon, climbed up on the seat and took the reins in her gloved hands.

Eleanor, fuming because she was being ignored, stood waiting, refusing to climb up the wheel without assistance. Rain seemed not to notice. Before Gavin mounted his horse, he walked over to her, gripped her waist with his huge hands and lifted her as if she weighed no more than a doll. When she turned and bent to sit down she felt a sharp pain on her bottom.

"Ohh!" She let out a startled cry, whirled around and almost lost her balance. She grabbed on to the bow that held the canvas cover. When she had righted herself, the big Scot was behind the wagon and out of sight. Her anger flared. "Damn you for a whore's son!" she swore. "I'll see you horsewhipped!"

Amy turned to Eleanor. Suppressed rage was expressed in the flare of her nostrils and the tightness of her mouth.

"What's the matter?"

"He pinched me!"

"Oh? You must be mistaken."

"Damn it! I know what he did. He pinched me."

"I don't see how he could through all those skirts. How many petticoats do you have on? Four or five?"

"I might have known that you'd side with him. You just see what Willy has to say when we get there."

Rain motioned that he was ready to move out. Amy cracked the whip over the backs of the team. They strained at the harnesses and the wagon began to roll. Rain set the pace again and Gavin rode in the rear. Each man was armed with a rifle, shot bag and powder horn, and Amy's rifle was on the floorboards beneath her feet.

"Tell me about . . . Willy," Amy said once they were moving smoothly. Any conversation at all, she decided, made the time go faster.

Surprised by Amy's civil tone, Eleanor was silent for a moment before she began to speak.

"He's a refined, sensitive gentleman who has a great career ahead of him."

"Do you love him?"

"I will, once we're wed."

"How do you know that?"

"I just know it, that's all." For a fleeting moment Amy thought she heard a wistful note in her voice, but she dismissed the thought.

"I don't know why you think you'll love him *after* you're wed if you don't before."

"How do I know if I love him or not?" Eleanor snapped. "I don't even know him. Aunt Gilda said he was taken with me when I was a child."

"Haven't you seen him since?"

"No, but he writes charming letters."

"Well . . . he must know what he's doing."

"What do you mean?" Eleanor's head jerked around and her lavender eyes blazed with anger. "My blood is every bit as good as his. He needs a wife of breeding if he's going to get ahead in the military. There's more to being an officer than directing men on a battlefield, you know. I'll be in charge of the social part of his career. I'll bring some refinement to his home."

"I thought you said he *was* refined. What I meant was, you don't seem cut out for the rough life you'll have at an army post."

"Willy will take care of me." The tone of her voice conveyed her irritation. "I was taught that if I conduct myself at all times as a lady should, which doesn't mean riding astride in leather britches and letting my hair hang down my back like a savage," she added scathingly, "I would be taken care of by the stronger sex—men."

"Humph!" Amy ignored her sarcasm. "Maybe you will and maybe you'll be taken advantage of." Amy glanced at the woman beside her and wondered how old she was. She asked her. "How old are you?"

"That's what I mean. A woman of breeding would never ask another woman her age."

Amy laughed. "Why are you hiding it? You've got a few years on me, but what difference does it make? My sister, Libby, is almost eight years older than I am, and she's the prettiest woman in the territory."

"According to who?" Eleanor threw Amy a piercing look.

"According to her husband, that's who. He loves her to distraction."

Eleanor lapsed into silence, thinking how little she knew about the man she had promised to marry. It had been her aunt's idea to contact Will Bradford, but neither of them had the slightest idea that he would be sent to the frontier, or that he would expect them to go to some godawful place called Belle Point. They had been trying to figure out a way to return to Charleston and still have Will take care of them when Gilda came down with the fever. They spent almost all of their small hoard of coins on the doctors who promised they could make her well, and so there was nothing Eleanor could do when Rain Tallman came for her but to go with him.

As the afternoon wore on, Amy found herself feeling a little sorry for Eleanor Woodbury. She would hate to be traveling to a man she didn't know or love and be expected to share his bed.

It was sundown when they reached the Little Wabash. Rain came alongside.

"Pull up. McCourtney will drive across. I'll test the route first."

Amy pulled the team to a halt and wound the reins about the brake handle. She turned and climbed down over the wheel, glad to have her feet on solid ground. Gavin dismounted and tied his horse to the back of the wagon.

Amy watched as Rain's horse made its way carefully into the moving water. By the time he reached the middle of the stream the water was belly-high on the horse, then it began to recede. Before he reached the other side, Rain turned, moved downstream a few feet and came back.

Amy had put the bridle on her horse and was mounted. "I can lead Gavin's horse."

Rain nodded, then pointed his finger. "See that topped cedar? Head straight for that. The river bed seems solid, but it's slippery. Be careful. If you get into trouble, let Gavin's horse go. We can pick him up later. Come on, Gavin. The water will be higher on the mules, but I'll ride in front of them and they'll not be so likely to panic."

The crossing was slow but uneventful. Amy waited for Rain and the wagon, and when it rolled up the bank and on to the level trail he moved up beside her.

"It's good we got here when we did. It may be too high to cross by morning."

"How do you know that?" Amy asked.

"It rained up north. Didn't you notice the cloud bank or

the green leaves floating downstream? That cloud bank is moving around to the west. It's likely to rain before morning. We'll camp up there on that high rise."

The light was fading when they finally stopped. Gavin jumped down to unhitch the mules.

Amy glanced up to see that Eleanor had stood and was trying to back down over the wheel as she had done, but her voluminous skirts had preceded her and she had stepped on them. She hung there, searching blindly with her other foot for something to step on. She began to lose her grip on the wagon bow and let out a small cry. Gavin sprang to her and caught her as she fell backward.

"There ye be," he said and set her on her feet. "Ye ain't properly dressed out to be climbin', though ye went about it the right way."

She shrugged away. "I would have managed without your interference."

"And ye'd a been on yer stubborn arse, missy," he growled before returning to the mules.

CHAPTER
Nine

The evening air had a bite in it. While the men took care of the animals, Amy hastily built a small fire in a circle of stones and set a pot of water over it to heat. Eleanor hugged her shawl around her shoulders and walked impatiently back and forth between the edge of the woods and the wagon. Amy had never known a woman like her. She didn't offer to help with the meal or assist in any way. Her attitude showed that she fully expected the others to wait on her as if they were her servants. That irritated Amy, but not enough for her to make an issue of it. In a way she pitied the beautiful woman who was so unsuited to the frontier way of life.

Rain and Gavin picketed the animals close by, put the harnesses and saddles beneath the wagon, then began to build a shelter. Rain threw a loop over the top of a young sapling and pulled it down for Gavin to hold while he brought down the top of another some six feet away. They tied the two tops together, forming a bow, and quickly cut off the small limbs. By the time the water in the pot was boiling and Amy was dropping in small chunks of meat and potatoes, a crossbar had been set in two Ys, a canvas stretched over the frame and secured to stakes Gavin pounded in the ground. The men had put up the shelter quickly with only a few words passing between them.

The wind came up and scattered sparks from the cookfire.

"It seems we're in for a bit of a blow," Gavin said. "I best be lashin' down the wagon."

Rain looked toward the west. Blue-black clouds rolled toward them. "While you do that I'll lay in some dry wood for a breakfast fire."

Darkness had fallen when Rain returned with an armload of wood. He stored it under the canvas shelter. He brought the next load to the cookfire, knelt down beside Amy and poked short pieces of sticks beneath the boiling pot. Into the stew Amy dropped crushed dried sage leaves from the bag of seasoning Liberty had insisted she bring along.

"Smells good." Rain's hand came down on her shoulder and squeezed gently. "You may have to move it under the canvas, or it's liable to get watered down."

"It should be done enough to eat in another few minutes." She laid the seasonings bag aside and poked at the fire with a stick. "There's bread to go with it and, if the rain holds off, tea."

"I didn't ask you to come along to do all the work, Amy." Rain sat back on his heels and pushed his hat to the back of his head.

She looked into his eyes and smiled. "I know you didn't. But this is something I can do better than you."

"Oh, you think so? You may change your mind after you've eaten my roasted corn and fish baked in river mud."

"River mud? Ugh! Wait until I fix you some rolled in cornmeal and fried in pork fat."

"The first chance I get, I'll catch—" A loud clap of thunder drowned out his words and brought them both to their feet.

Eleanor ran to Rain and clasped his arm with both hands. "Oh, Rain, I'm so frightened."

"Of the storm?"

"Yes . . . and the Indians and . . . wild beasts . . ."

"The Indians here are peaceful. Occasionally you run into a renegade, just as you run into bad white men. But I believe we are reasonably safe here."

"But the storm—"

"You'll be all right in the wagon. Gavin has lashed it down. There's no danger of it tipping over."

"Tipping over? Oh!"

A dazzling flash lit the clearing, followed by darkness and a tremendous clap of thunder that made Eleanor press her hands over her ears. A few drops of rain hurtled down, plopping on her head. She let out a small shriek. When she lifted her shawl to cover her head the wind almost tore it from her hands.

"Get in the wagon." Rain gave Eleanor a gentle shove.

Gavin was waiting there to help her climb up onto a box so she could get inside.

Amy scooped up her cooking supplies, dumped them in the food box and carried it to the wagon while Rain set the iron pot and the teakettle under the canvas shelter. A blast of wind swept through the clearing before they could put out the cookfire and pushed a burning ember along the ground toward the wagon. Gavin quickly stomped it out with his heavy boots before the grass beneath the wagon could catch and burn.

There was nothing for Amy to do but climb up into the wagon with Eleanor and wait out the storm. In just a few minutes the rain came down in sheets, driven by gusty winds. Eleanor sat on the edge of her bunk with her hands over her ears. Amy felt her way in the darkness to the front of the wagon and tied down the flap. One of the men had lowered the flap at the back and secured it. It was pitch-dark inside the wagon. Over the sound of the rain pounding the canvas top, Amy heard little whimpering sounds of fright coming from Eleanor. She sat down on the bunk beside her.

"It's just a spring storm. It won't last long. Don't be afraid." To her surprise Eleanor turned on her with a torrent of angry words.

"I'm not afraid of this damn storm!" Lightning came again followed by thunder. "I hate going to Belle Point. I hate that damn riverman. I hate you! I hate this whole trip and . . . this is only the first day."

"Why did you tell Rain you were afraid of the storm?"

"Oh, you! You don't know anything about men at all," she snapped. "They love to feel protective toward a pretty, helpless woman. It makes them feel big and important."

"I admit that I don't know much about how to make a man feel *big* and *important*, but I don't lie, either," Amy said with heavy sarcasm.

She got up, moved to the end of the wagon and peered out. A flash of lightning illuminated the area. Rain and Gavin were beneath the canvas shelter, snug and dry. They had placed it with the back to the wind. She wondered how many makeshift shelters Rain had made over the last seven years.

"I'm hungry." Eleanor's complaining voice came out of the darkness. "Get me something to eat."

"No. You can wait and eat with the rest of us." The pity Amy had felt for the spoiled girl was gone.

"You've got bread and butter in that box. Are you refusing to give it to me?"

"Yes, I am. We noon tomorrow on what we have in the box. We'll eat when the storm passes."

"I'll tell Rain."

"Go ahead."

"I could have him if I set my mind to it, you know. I've yet to see the man I couldn't have if I wanted him."

"That must be a comfort to you."

"You don't believe me?"

"I believe you think you can have any man you want. But if it's true, then why didn't you pick out a rich man in Louisville and set your cap for him? Then you wouldn't have had to make this *awful* trip with all these *awful* people you hate so much."

"There wasn't a man in Louisville I'd wipe my feet on. None were as rich as Willy or had his background and breeding, either. For your information, *ma'am*, Willy Bradford is a very good catch."

Amy fumed. Conversation with the woman was impossible. She folded back the flap at the end of the wagon and looked out. The wind had died down and it was raining lightly. She fumbled in the supply box for bowls, spoons and cups for tea, slammed her hat down on her head and jumped down out of the wagon.

Rain had kindled a small fire just under the canvas. Amy squatted down beside him.

"I brought bowls and spoons," she said and set them down beside the pot of stew.

"Good girl. I was coming to get them as soon as my fire got going."

"Oh, shoot! I forgot the bread."

"What about Miss Woodbury? Is she coming out?"

"I don't know. If she doesn't I'll take some to her."

Rain put his hand on her wrist. "Don't wait on her, Amy. I'll ask her to come out and eat. She can come and eat with the rest of us or do without." He moved out from under the shelter and went to the end of the wagon.

"He's right, lass," Gavin said. "That miss needs to be doin' fer herself."

"I doubt she knows how."

"Then it's time she be learnin'. We be doin' her no favors by doin' for her, tis a fact."

"I hadn't thought about it like that."

Rain returned with Eleanor in his arms. He lowered her to the boughs Gavin had cut for beds.

"Thank you, Rain." She laughed a light trilling sound. "Oh . . . it's nice and cozy warm in here. And I'm so hungry."

Amy went back to the wagon for the bread, sloshing through the water, resentment making her linger longer than necessary. When she returned Eleanor sat with her legs drawn up under her, talking about how the storm reminded her of the one that destroyed her home, and how glad she was that it was over. She promised she would not be afraid the next time. Amy spread the bread cloth on the ground and broke off chunks of the bread, then took the bowl Gavin filled for her.

There was scarcely room for the four of them in the small space. Eleanor's skirts took up most of one side. Amy's elbow came in contact with Rain's when she lifted her spoon to her mouth. Eleanor chattered cheerfully, her eyes wide and childlike, her red mouth smiling. Amy suspected she was practicing her craft on Rain, intending to prove her boast that she could have any man she wanted if she set her mind to it. Because she was so uncommonly pretty, there was a niggling fear in Amy's mind that she could succeed. For the first time in her life she was jealous of another woman.

"I j-just have to admit, Rain, that it was the most awful day. But I know what to expect now. It will be better tomorrow. I'll get used to it. You'll see. The first of anything is the hardest. Don't you think so, Rain?"

"It takes a while to get used to the pace." Rain's answer was a long time coming. His face showed nothing. He sat cross-legged, looking out into the darkness when he raised his eyes from his bowl.

"Be patient with me, Rain."

"You're doing fine." Rain dropped a chunk of bread into his bowl and passed a piece to Gavin.

"This is the first time I've been off by myself—without Aunt Gilda." Eleanor's voice fluttered in her throat, and the words came out not much above a whisper. Her eyes wandered to Rain and clung beseechingly.

Amy closed her eyes against the scene.

"You'll be all right."

"Oh, I know that. I know you'll take care of me. It's just that . . . I'm so lonesome for Aunty Gilda, and this country is so big and . . . so wild."

"You'll get used to it."

"I don't know how you'll be able to find Willy way out there in Arkansas. I'd never heard of it when he wrote for me to come. I had to ask where it was." Eleanor's lavender eyes questioned and then she squeezed them tightly shut as if to hold back tears.

"I'll find him. Don't worry about it."

Amy looked up and found Gavin's eyes on her, blue and anxious. She tried to smile at him but could not.

"Here's my bowl, ma'am," Eleanor said. "I thank you kindly, but I just couldn't eat it all."

Amy took the bowl and set it on the ground. She didn't look up. Because if she did and Eleanor had a smug smile on her face she was afraid she would be goaded into saying something she would regret later.

"I think I'll go to bed, Rain," Eleanor said wearily.

"Don't you want tea?"

"I'll take some later. Aunty Gilda used to always bring me a cup of tea before I went to sleep."

Rain reached for the kettle and poured tea into one of the cups. "If you're going to have some, you'd better take it with you."

Anger flashed across Eleanor's beautiful features for only an instant before disappearing completely, and they took on a dejected, woeful expression. The change was noticed only by Gavin's sharp eyes.

"Oh, flitter. It'd be cold by the time I was ready for it. I'll . . . just not have any, I guess," she said petulantly. The embarrassing quiet that followed was broken by the sound of something crashing through the underbrush next to the shelter. Now fear washed across Eleanor's face and she asked in a rush, "What's that?"

"Probably a coon, curious about our fire."

"Can't you shoot him or something?"

"Why? This is his territory. We're the intruders."

Rain poured tea into a cup for Amy. He picked up the one Eleanor had refused and drank from it before he refilled it.

"I just guess . . . I'll go to bed." She looked directly at Amy. "Will you light a candle, ma'am?"

"No lights," Rain said firmly. "This fire is going out as soon as we finish eating."

"It's wet and muddy. I'll ruin my slippers."

Gavin moved out of the shelter. "It's stopped raining and, by gory, if the moon ain't out. I'll tote ye back to the wagon, Miss Woodbury. Twill save yer fine slippers from the mud."

"Tomorrow wear heavy shoes." Rain's tone was not kind.

"Heavy shoes? Whatever for?"

"So you can walk some of the time."

"Oh, I don't know if I can do that." Eleanor waited expectantly for Rain to reply, but he said nothing.

As soon as she got to her feet Gavin swept her up into his arms and headed for the wagon. When he reached it, he lowered her feet to the box they used for a step. His big hands clamped on her shoulders and kept her from turning to climb inside. Their faces were level and he brought his close to hers. He gave her a shake that whipped her head back and forth.

"What? What are you doing? You—you dolt!"

"Ye listen to me, ye little spawn a Satan. I can see ye

workin' yer wily ways on the lass' mon. Ye got yer own
mon waitin' fer ye, so ye leave this one be. Hear? The lass
loves him, tis plain to see. Ye'll not be a breakin' her heart
for naught."

"Get your hands off me, you ignorant oaf!" she hissed
angrily and hit at his hand. "Let go of me or I'll yell my
head off and Rain will send you packing—after he beats the
stuffings out of you."

"Yell, me beauty. He may cast me off, but I swear by all
that's holy I'll not be far behind ye. I'll be waitin' my
chance to catch ye, somewhere, sometime. I'll upend ye and
swat yer bare bottom with a hickory switch. Tis what ye
been needin' all the time."

"You dare to strike me and Willy Bradford will hunt you
down and kill you."

"If'n he be a mon a'tall he'll be thankin' me. For tis a
spankin' ye sorely need."

"You're stupid and ignorant. How do you know what I
need? And I'm not forgetting that you pinched me today!"

"Ye deserved it for yer stubborn ways. Now hear me, lass.
Leave the girl's mon be or ye'll be answerin' to me with
more'n a pinch on your bottom." He swung her up and over
the tailgate and dumped her in the wagon.

The wet canvas slapped her face and rain trickled down
her back. Her anger held back tears of frustration and discomfort. Slowly she got to her knees and then to her feet.
Frantic fingers worked at the buttons of her dress. She let it
and layers of petticoats fall to the floor. Then she worked on
the laces of her corset. Flinging it to the front of the wagon,
she reached under her pillow for the long loose nightgown
and slipped it over her head. She crawled beneath the covers
before she realized she still had on her shoes and stockings.
She removed them and lay down again, pulling the covers
over her head.

* * *

Amy, on her knees, placed the bowls and spoons in the empty stew pot and wrapped the remainder of the bread in the cloth. She hadn't lifted her eyes to Rain's since Gavin carried Eleanor away. Now she saw his hands pull the sticks from the campfire so it would die out.

"We can wash the pot in the morning." His voice came to her softly out of the darkness. "Sit by me and drink your tea. Gavin will not be back for a bit. He went to see about the horses after he dumped Miss Woodbury in the wagon." There was a hint of laughter in his voice.

"Dumped her? Why would he do that?"

Rain chuckled. "I can think of a number of reasons. It didn't hurt her or she'd have cried out."

"You hear everything."

"It's a habit I picked up when I didn't know if I would be alive come daylight. If I can't see, I listen."

"Uncle Juicy and I used to sit outside at night and he'd make me identify the different sounds. At the end, his hearing left him." She sank down on the boughs where Eleanor had sat and he put her cup in her hand.

"Are you tired?" His low-voiced query hung in the air.

"A little."

"It was an easy day compared to what's across the river."

"I'm looking forward to seeing the mountains."

"They'd be puny alongside the mountains farther west. But it's beautiful country. In some places you can see for miles. In other places the forest is so thick it's as dark as night, even when the sun is shining." He reached for her hand and she turned her palm up to meet it. "I want to show you the country along the Arkansas."

"I heard you telling Farr about it."

Her fingers found the spaces between his and gripped

hard, the tea in the cup on the ground beside her, forgotten. Abruptly he moved closer and put his arm around her, fitting her into the curve of his shoulder. Nothing seemed important to Amy except the feel of his big, hard body against hers, the regular thump of his heartbeat against her upper arm and this peaceful, relaxed feeling.

"Being with you gives me a feeling of contentment. It's a strange feeling, yet somehow familiar too," he said in a husky whisper. The arm holding her drew her closer. "Do you feel it, Amy?"

"Yes," she whispered and closed her eyes. "We've known each other for a long time."

"It's more than that. It's almost like I was lost and have found my way back home."

"I'm glad," she whispered. "I'm so . . . glad." Her attempt to speak was weakened by the depth of her emotion. She leaned her head against his shoulder and a wave of great joy washed over her. She felt so much happiness she was giddy, light-headed, unable to think clearly.

"I hear Gavin coming back. He moves like a buffalo." Rain laughed softly.

"I don't hear anything."

"He's there, by the cedar."

"I don't see him."

"Look at the outline of the tree. You can see his shoulder and arm." He moved his head until his cheek was against hers.

"I see him how."

He brought the hand holding hers up to his chest. Ever so gently he opened her fingers and pressed her palm against the base of his throat. It was such a sweet, simple gesture. It conveyed a deep longing to touch and be touched.

"I want to kiss you before he comes over," he whispered as he pushed the strands of long hair back from her face.

Amy was aware of the heavy beat of his heart and the

warm skin of his neck. When his fingers lifted her chin her lips parted and searched for his. He kissed her softly, sweetly, time and again. Her arm curled about his neck and the kisses became longer and more demanding. He gathered her even closer to him and their hearts thundered together. His lips were no longer gentle, they were hard, hungry. With a groan she could hear reverberating in his chest, he lifted his head and pressed his cheek tightly to hers.

"I liked doing that, sweetheart. I liked it too much!" He spoke with rough tenderness, his breathing fast. His fingers stroked her hair and rubbed her jaw. His lips traveled around her ear and then to her mouth as if he couldn't help himself. His lips played sweetly on hers for what seemed to Amy too short a time before he lifted his head and his arms fell away from her. "I'd better let you go . . . while I can."

They walked slowly to the wagon, Rain's hand at her waist. A few feet away from the end, he pulled her to a halt.

"I'm glad you're tall," he whispered in her ear. "I don't have to bend over so far to kiss you."

His mouth tenderly and almost reverently planted a kiss on her lips. The kiss was of a totally loving nature. A wave of tenderness for this big, quiet man flooded Amy's heart. He was lonely and longed for love as much as she did. Her fingertips moved in small caresses along his jawline to the dark hair around his ears, and her palms caressed the rough planes of his cheeks. He stood perfectly still while she placed a tender kiss on his lips before she moved away.

"I can stand a watch, Rain."

"No need for that. I sleep with one eye open."

"Good night."

"Night, Amy."

Amy moved into the wagon, careful not to wake Eleanor. She undressed swiftly and slipped into her nightdress. With shaking hands she unplaited her hair, dug her nails into her scalp for a few delicious moments, then lay down on her pallet. She pulled the blankets up over her and rested her head on her folded arm.

It was so new, this being with Rain. So wonderful. Even more than she had imagined it to be. He was not shy with her as he had been when he was young. She was the one who was tongue-tied most of the time.

"You shouldn't have let him kiss you, ma'am. That was a mistake." Eleanor's voice came softly out of the darkness.

Amy was shocked into silence by the knowledge that the woman had been watching her and Rain and had seen them kiss.

"Lesson number one," Eleanor continued. "Make a man wait. Make him want to hold you and kiss you more than anything before you give in. No man values a kiss given too easily. Lesson number two—"

"Shut up! I don't need your advice."

"You'd better take all the advice you can get with Rain Tallman. He's the kind that could sweet-talk a woman right out of her drawers—if he wanted her," Eleanor said with a light laugh.

"If you know so damn much about men, how come you've got to go clear to the Arkansas to get one?" Amy asked with cold sarcasm.

"I already told you that."

"Ah, yes. Money and breeding. It makes him sound like a high-priced stallion."

"It would be a long, long trip for a man like Rain without a woman to take care of his needs. Especially if he's used to having *it*. If you know what I mean. I'm taken, so that leaves you. He's working his way up to what he wants and you're so smitten with his good looks you'll give it to him."

Amy had never wanted to hit anyone as badly as she wanted to hit Eleanor Woodbury. She wanted to shout that she had known Rain and loved him for eight long years, and she wasn't going to let her spoil what happened between them by making it dirty. But what good would it do to tell Eleanor Woodbury anything? She was nothing but a shallow, spoiled woman.

She gritted her teeth and turned her back, hoping for sleep. But anger churned so violently inside her that sleep was a long time coming.

CHAPTER
Ten

Breakfast, before daylight, was fried bacon, bread and cups of strong, steaming coffee. Eleanor refused to get up when Amy called her. Rain stripped the canvas off their makeshift shelter, rolled it and tied it to the side of the wagon while Amy cleaned the campsite and Gavin hitched up the mules.

"I'll saddle your horse, or would you rather ride in the wagon this morning?" Rain paused beside Amy, his saddle on his shoulder and the bridle in his hand.

"No, I'll ride."

"I thought you might be saddle sore. You rode a good many miles yesterday."

"I'm a bit sore, but nothing that won't wear off in a little while."

"I don't want you to wear yourself out."

"I won't."

Amy's eyes followed him as he walked away. She had spent a restless night. The pallet she had lain on was hard, the quarters cramped. And in spite of her determination not to let Eleanor's remarks bother her, they had. During the long night hours as she turned restlessly, trying to find a comfortable position, she had come to the conclusion that the few kisses she and Rain had shared may have meant more to her than to him. Amy had thought about it until she was deep in despair and hours had passed before she fell asleep.

The wagon left deep ruts in the soft ground as the team slowly pulled it away from the campsite. Rain led the way and Amy took a position behind the wagon. It was a cold, damp morning. She turned up the collar of her coat and thought about Eleanor, warm and comfortable in her bed in the wagon.

Back on the road the ground was not so soft and the team picked up speed, but still the miles seemed to pass slowly under the wagon wheels. They passed a cabin, set on a rise above the road. A woman with a baby in her arms and a small child holding on to her skirt came out to wave at them as they passed. It was a slovenly looking place, Amy noted. The shed that housed the cow was leaning. A dead tree had been pulled up beside the house and it looked as though the settler cut just enough wood to satisfy their daily needs. The woman looked lonely, as if their passing was a highlight of her day.

At mid-morning they met a lone wagon going east. The wagon's canvas sagged on uneven hoops that seemed to shift with each jolt of the wheels on the rough ground. The man on the seat was big, square-shouldered, middle-aged and had a face full of whiskers. His wife sat beside him, her face all but hidden beneath a sagging bonnet. Two children stood behind the wagon seat, one holding on to the woman's shoulders; both had pinched, anxious faces. Halting his team, the man waited for Rain to ride up beside him. Rain motioned for Gavin to go on. He steered the team around the wagon and Amy followed. She looked over her shoulder to see the man extending a hand to Rain that looked as if it could knock a mule to its knees.

In a few minutes Rain rode up beside her.

"That man has more troubles than a dog has fleas. If I had stayed he would have told me all of them. Their cabin burned, Indians stole their stock, and the cow went dry. They're looking for a new place to settle."

"They've had bad luck, but the next place may not be any better."

"Everyone has a streak of bad luck once in a while. You either overcome it or give in and complain about it for the rest of your life."

When Rain left her to ride ahead, Amy thought about what he had said. Her father had been one to give in and complain. The thought that she might never see him again hurt her a little. He was her father even though he was the most selfish person she had ever known. She thought of Tally and wondered if he could break away from his mother's influence and seek a life of his own. She doubted it. She didn't think he had ever had an independent thought.

They came to a small, shallow pond and stopped to let the horses and mules drink. Amy got off the horse and led it and Gavin's horse to the water to drink alongside Rain's.

"You'd better see about Miss Woodbury, Amy. She may be sick."

"She was all right last night, and this morning she said not to bother her."

"She's not lying in that wagon all day or she will be sick. If she's all right, tell her to get up, put on some stout shoes and walk for a while."

Amy went to the back of the wagon and pulled up the flap. Eleanor was still in the bunk. She lay propped against the pillows, a blanket drawn up to her chin.

"What do you want?"

"Rain wants to know if you're all right."

"That's sweet of him. Tell him I'm fine."

"Then get up and dress. He said for you to wear some stout shoes today so you can walk a while."

Too late, Eleanor realized she had been led into the trap of admitting that she was not sick.

"I'll get up when I please and walk when I please." She flopped over on her side and buried her head in the pillow.

"No, you won't." Rain stood looking at her over Amy's shoulder. "You need to build up some strength for later. You'll not do it by lolling around and eating like a bird."

"I never eat much. I don't get hungry."

"A good brisk walk will make you hungry enough."

"I don't want to walk. I'm . . . not used to it."

"Today is a good day to start getting used to it. You'll walk for a short time this afternoon."

"You're mean and—"

"I can get meaner." Rain dropped the flap and mounted his horse. He motioned for Gavin to start the mules.

When they were mounted, Rain moved his horse to ride alongside Amy. His eyes roamed her slim figure. He liked the way she sat in the saddle—solidly, her feet dug deep in the stirrups, her back straight. She was lovely and proud, calm and capable. She was soft and yielding too. Holding her in his arms had been one of the most enjoyable moments of his life.

"Amy . . ." He didn't know why he said her name. He just wanted to. He could not tell her the other thoughts in his mind, not yet. She looked directly into his eyes. They were wide, clear, honest, deep amber eyes. "Ride up ahead for a while, Amy. Keep a sharp watch on the timber to the north. If we have any trouble it would come from there."

"Are you expecting some?"

"I'm always expecting some."

She put her heels to the mare and they sprang ahead. She

rode in a trot until she was well ahead of the wagon. Then she slowed the mare, keeping her eyes on the timberline to the north. She forced all thoughts of Rain from her mind and concentrated on keeping a sharp watch.

Half an hour later Rain moved up to ride point again and Amy fell back to ride behind. Eleanor was sitting on the seat beside Gavin. He grinned at Amy when she passed, but Eleanor sat as stiff as a board and looked straight ahead.

When they stopped for noon there was no water for the horses. Gavin unhitched the team and rubbed them down lest they get sores from the harnesses. After the horses were tied where they could eat the still wet grass, Rain started a small fire and set water on to heat for coffee.

Amy walked into the woods to find a place for privacy. She said nothing to Eleanor as she walked away, but was soon aware that she followed, silent and sullen. Behind a screen of sumac Amy stopped, looked around carefully, then placed her rifle within reaching distance. She finished what she had come to do within minutes, turned her back and waited while Eleanor was still fumbling with her skirts and pantalettes.

Eleanor appeared to be meekly subdued. She ate her meat and bread and then accepted a hard-cooked egg Amy gave to her. She sat alone, drinking her coffee and staring up the narrow woodland trail.

The sun came out. Amy took off her coat and tucked it beneath the wagon seat. The nooning had not been as happy as the day before. Tension flowed between Eleanor and the rest of them. Gavin hitched up the team, Rain put out the fire with a few shovels of dirt and Amy repacked the almost empty food box. Amy noticed how well Gavin and Rain worked together. The men didn't talk much; each seemed to know what to do. Everyone pitched in and worked except Eleanor.

Amy climbed on to the wagon seat and Gavin put the reins in her hands.

"We'll start out fairly slow, Amy," Rain said and mounted his horse. "Miss Woodbury will walk for a while. If you get tired, Miss Woodbury, hang on to that strap on the wagon."

Eleanor's eyes were pinpoints of anger. "I have to do as you say now, Mr. Tallman, but I may leave you when we reach a river town. How would you explain *that* to Will Bradford?"

"I'd tell him how lucky he was," Rain said simply and turned away. He lifted his hand and pointed west.

Rain kept his horse at a slow walk directly in front of the mules. Amy sat with the slack leather in her hands, thinking how foolish Eleanor had been to pit her will against Rain's. Amy was sure that once he made up his mind it was as unbending as it had been when he was a mere boy and had decided he would take Tecumseh's sisters home to Prophets-town.

Time seemed to pass slowly and silently. The only sounds Amy heard as the wagon rolled along were the creaking of its timbers, the jingle of the harnesses, and an occasional threatening caw from a bluejay in a tall cedar beside the trail. For the first time since dawn she was able to let her eyelids droop and relax.

Not much more than half an hour had passed when she was startled by Gavin's shout.

"Stop the wagon!"

Amy used all her strength to pull at the reins. Even before she had stopped the mules Rain was passing on his way to the back of the wagon. When she looked back, Eleanor was lying on the ground. Amy quickly secured the reins around the brake handle, jumped down and ran back to where Gavin was kneeling beside Eleanor.

"What's the matter with her?" She lifted one of Eleanor's limp hands, then answered her own question. "She's swooned. Get some water." Rain jumped to obey. Amy untied Eleanor's bonnet and pulled it off so she could fan her white face with the stiff brim.

"I be thinkin' I know what's ill with the lassie," Gavin said after they had wiped her face with a wet cloth and she had not revived. "She be laced so tight in a corset she can't be gettin' a deep breath 'n she be carryin' her weight in petticoats. What with them draggin' the ground 'n bein' wet was more than she could bear."

"What's a . . . corset?" Rain looked from Gavin to Amy with a puzzled frown. Amy dipped the cloth in the water, patted Eleanor's face and left the explanation to Gavin.

"It be a contraption made of whalebone 'n stout goods 'n laced tight about a woman's middle. Tis said some lassies wear 'em so tight as to crush their ribs. Aye, it's a torture the lass has been endurin'."

"Why? For God's sake!"

"Tis the fashion among the ladies of high standin'."

"Fashion be damned! Get it off her."

"The lass will have to be doin' it, mon, for tis next to her naked body."

"Amy can't do it by herself. Damn fool woman!" Rain swore again and flipped up Eleanor's skirt. "Get rid of some of those petticoats too. What are they tied to?"

"I'll do it."

Rain scowled when Amy quickly pulled Eleanor's skirt down over the petticoats. Having been raised with the Shawnee, he had never been able to understand the white woman's aversion to having their legs viewed.

Amy unbuttoned the front of Eleanor's dress from the neck down past her waist. She reached in and untied the top petticoat.

"That's one. Pull it off and I'll untie another." Gavin reached under Eleanor's back and lifted her. Rain reached beneath her skirt and jerked off the petticoat. They repeated

the process four times, leaving Eleanor wearing one petticoat, a light shift, pantalettes, and the corset. Amy kept
Eleanor's body covered as much as possible for propriety's
sake, and breathed a sigh of relief to discover she was wearing the corset over the light shift.

Rain looked at what Eleanor had laced herself into and
cursed. "Goddamn! A woman who'd wear that thing doesn't
have the sense of a goose. And to think some people think
Indian women are stupid."

He drew his knife and began to cut the laces, starting
where the garment came over the swell of her hips, up past a
waist he could span with his two hands, and on to where the
whalebone garment stopped just below her breasts. Amy
tired to tug the garment off and discovered it had shoulder
straps. There was nothing to do but fold back the top of the
dress and let Rain cut those too. The corset, damp with
sweat, was removed, and Amy hurriedly rebuttoned
Eleanor's dress.

Rain held the stiff garment spread in his two hands,
looked at it and shook his head.

"If that isn't the damnedest thing I've ever seen." He bent
the whalebones that were sewn into the material until they
snapped and then tossed the garment up into a cedar tree that
grew beside the trail. "Amy, see if she has more of those
things in her trunk."

"I don't think we should rummage in her things. If she
wants to torture herself, let her."

"I'll not be slowed down by a stubborn, vain woman
making a fool of herself. That may be the thing to do in
Louisville, but out here no one cares a whit about her
waist."

"She does."

"She can wear whatever she wants or what Will wants
when she gets to Belle Point. On the way there she'll wear

what I want her to wear, and it isn't that bone thing," Rain said curtly.

"Ye best be doin' it, lass. This one'll be wearin' the thin' for pure cussedness, so mad she'll be."

The smell of rose water wafted up from Eleanor's trunk when Amy opened it. Amid the lacy undergarments, fancy nightwear, dresses, and petticoats she found two more corsets, one plain, one edged in lace. She took them out to Rain. He looked at them in disgust, then his eyes went to Amy.

"Do you and Libby wear these things?"

She shook her head and fought the desire to giggle. "But I saw one in Vincennes and Libby said Governor Harrison's wife wears one."

"Miss Woodbury will not wear these again," he said and flung them, one at a time, up into the cedar tree, where they caught on a limb and dangled. The bizarre sight brought laughter bubbling out of Amy's throat.

"Someone will get the surprise of his life when he comes along here and a corset falls out of a tree and hits him."

Gavin chuckled and even Rain smiled—a little. Gavin pulled Eleanor's arms up over her head and pumped them back and forth while Amy patted her cheeks with a wet cloth.

Even in a faint she was beautiful, Amy thought. The skin that stretched over her high cheekbones was flawless and contrasted greatly with the thick, dark lashes that lay on her cheeks, and the high, arched brows above her eyes. The hair that swept up from her forehead was as black as midnight and glistened in the sunlight.

Eleanor stirred and tried to loosen her arms from Gavin's grasp. She frowned and made a small noise of irritation when he continued to raise her arms. She opened her eyes and looked straight up into his face.

"Ye'll be fine as silk, lassie. Take a deep breath 'n lie

still for a wee bit." Gavin spoke gently, as if he were talking to a child.

"What happened?"

"You swooned," Amy said. "Would you like a drink of water?"

"Yes, I would."

Gavin helped Eleanor sit up. "I'll be gettin' it."

Eleanor put her hands to her cheeks when she saw the pile of petticoats on the ground. "What . . . is that?"

"We took off your petticoats and corset," Amy said gently. "The petticoats were weighing you down, and the corset was so tight you couldn't breathe."

"Why . . . why . . . how dare you do that to me!"

"I dared, Miss Woodbury," Rain said. "Can you stand up? Your foolishness has delayed us long enough."

Gavin returned with the water. Eleanor drank, and then he helped her to her feet. She sucked in a long, full breath and painfully straightened and looked up at Rain. Outlined against the sky he stood tall, broad-shouldered and hatless. The wind ruffled his dark hair, giving him a faintly satanic look. There was a tightly strung alertness about him, something primitive and menacing. Eleanor shook with weakness and fear, but her pride forced her to defy him.

"You had no right to do that. I'll never forgive you. Never!"

"I don't want your forgiveness. If I'm going to get you to Belle Point, I want *obedience*, and I will have it. Do you understand, Miss Woodbury?"

"I don't seem to have much choice."

"No, you don't. Put her in the wagon, Gavin." Rain mounted the dun. "We have to make up for the time we lost, Amy. We'll push them hard for the next hour."

Amy gathered up Eleanor's petticoats and put them into the back of the wagon, then climbed on to the seat and waited for Gavin to help Eleanor. When she was seated and the wagon started, he went back to his horse.

Thoughts of Eleanor stayed in Gavin's mind. When he had lifted her up on to the seat there had been no con tortion of her beautiful features, no quivering lips, no tears, no out- pouring of angry words coming from her soft, red mouth. She had looked utterly lonely and defeated as she sat there with her hands folded in her lap. And Gavin, thinking about it, was touched by the realization that the arrogant beauty was frightened despite her habitual air of confidence.

"I kept you covered while we took off your corset and petticoats," Amy said. "They saw nothing that you need to feel ashamed about."

Eleanor turned her head slowly and looked at Amy with dull, uninterested eyes, but she did not speak. She turned away and wearily brushed a strand of hair from her face. They rode in silence across a broad expanse of open prairie and up and over a thickly wooded hill. They traveled until the sun, a red glow in the west, slid behind the horizon. And still they kept going. At dusk Rain turned off the main trail and into a small glade beside a rivulet of water that came down out of the hills.

Darkness came on rapidly. They set up camp as they had done the night before except for the makeshift shelter. Nei- ther Gavin nor Rain made a move to build one. The men tended the animals and Amy built a fire and put the kettle on to heat. A minimum of words passed between the three of them, and none at all came from Eleanor, who drew her shawl about her shoulders and walked down to the creek. Amy followed Eleanor, found the privacy she sought behind the bushes, then washed her face and hands in the cold water.

That night they ate the last of the eggs, the cooked meat and the bread Amy and Libby had prepared. As soon as the tea was hot, Rain put out the fire except for a few glowing embers.

"No point in calling attention to the fact that we're here," he said.

"Aye," Gavin said. "From here to the river the toughs roam as thick as hair on a dog's back."

"Have you been here before, Gavin?" Amy asked.

"Aye. A time or two, but not much beyond. I be workin' the Ohio from Pittsburgh to the big river." While he was talking Eleanor got up and went to the wagon. The big man's eyes followed her until she disappeared inside. "The lassie's pride be hurtin', I fear."

"Better her pride now than her neck later on," Rain said grimly. "It'll not be easy going cross-country to the Arkansas. I'm thinking we'll have to give up the wagon later on. I'd like to find some good riding mules for the women."

"Goddamn mule is the stubbornest critter there be." Gavin got out a long-stemmed pipe, packed it with tobacco, and lit it from a twig he set ablaze.

"They can be stubborn as a woman," Rain said, and flashed Amy one of his rare smiles. "But they've got horse sense too. A mule doesn't stray off or prance and kick when a snake crosses his path; he doesn't fall off a mountain trail. For the mountains, give me a good stout mule anytime."

"Ye may be right. But I'd soon walk as ride one of 'em."

"If I run into someone I know over on the river, or if you do, Gavin, and you know he's a good man, I'll hire him on to go with us. We'll need another watch."

"I can take a watch, Rain." Amy was cleaning up after the meal, rinsing the cups in the hot water from the kettle.

"I don't want you to have to do that, Amy. The trip will be hard enough even if you get a full night's sleep." Rain got to his feet and slung his rifle over his shoulder. "Stamp out the coals when she's through here, Gavin. I'll be back in a while. Where did you figure to bed down?"

"By the tree, yon." Gavin lifted his hand to a stand of trees a good six yards from the camp.

"I'll take the other side." Amy had straightened up and was looking from one man to the other. Rain put his hand on her shoulder. "Why don't you turn in, Amy?"

"What are you going to do?"

"I'm going to take a look around. Gavin will be here."

"Don't treat me like a prairie flower, Rain. I'm not going to turn up my toes at the first sign of trouble."

"I know you won't, Amy. When I expect trouble, you'll know it. Get a good night's sleep." He squeezed her shoulder and walked off into the darkness.

Amy watched him go. She knew Rain well enough to know that he did not lie. If he thought they were in any danger tonight he would have told her.

"He be a good mon, lass," Gavin said.

"He was hard on Eleanor today."

"Aye, but it had to be done. The lass twas wearin' herself down. The mon knows what he be about." Gavin got to his feet and stomped out the embers left by the fire. "Be ye ready to turn in?"

"Yes, it's been a trying day."

"That it has, lass. Night to ye."

"Good night, Gavin."

Amy was tired. Too tired even to think. She had scarcely slept the night before, and they had covered many miles that day. Inside the wagon she felt her way in the darkness until she came to the roll that was her bed. She threw out the pallet, eased herself down on it and took off her clothes. While she folded and stacked them in a neat pile, she wondered when she would get a chance to wash them. She slipped into her long nightdress, lay down and pulled the blanket up over her, stretched her tired muscles and sighed.

It was strange, she thought. The pallet wasn't as hard as the night before. Her next and last thought before the dark curtain of sleep dropped over her was that it was really rather comfortable.

Rain moved cautiously through the trees, as silent as a shadow. The forest was still except for the usual night sounds. An owl hooted from a nearby tree before flying off on lazy wings in search of its nightly meal. A pack rat cowered at the sound, traveled in a nervous circle, and then scurried away on some venture of its own.

Away from the camp, Rain broke into a slow trot, dodging through the trees and jumping over deadfalls. He ran parallel with the trail they had passed over that day. Occasionally he stopped, listened, sniffed the night air, and went on. Rain was following up on a minute but nagging thought, a fragile suspicion that his wilderness sense had told him to pursue, and five miles from where he had left Gavin and the women he saw a flicker of light in the forest. His hunch had been right.

He moved closer, waited and listened. And then he heard the sound of a horse stamping on the thick sod. The sound was almost inaudible save to one whose wilderness-honed hearing could distinguish the slightest noise. The sound told him that one horse was tethered north of the campfire.

Rain approached the camp from the west so as not to alert the horse. His was a silent, shadowy figure, his buckskins only a shade lighter than the surrounding darkness. He squatted low in the brush, practically concealed by a dead-fall, and concentrated all his attention on the figure beside the fire. One glance told him the man was a fool. A person with any sense at all would not be laying himself so open for attack. His fire was too bright and the green wood he was burning sent out smoke one could smell for miles. Anyone who wanted a horse or a gun had only to follow his nose to find one. The pilgrim sat silhouetted against the fire, a round straw hat on his head, a blanket about his shoulders and a cup in his hands. Rain noted the man's rifle was ten feet away, propped against a tree.

Soberly Rain considered what to do. The poor devil wouldn't live many nights if he didn't exercise more caution. He thought of warning him, telling him to stay close behind them until they reached Kaskaskia. But then again, it could be a trap. The man could draw a gun from under the blanket and shoot him. He didn't think that was likely, but he wasn't ready to risk it. He was not responsible for this fool, if that was really what he was. *Don't walk into trouble, wait until trouble comes to you,* Rain remembered Juicy saying to him when he first went to live at Quill's Station.

That afternoon Rain had ridden ahead, found a tree on a hilltop, climbed it and scanned the trail ahead and behind. There was nothing ahead, but behind them he saw that the wagon they had passed that morning had stopped in the middle of the trail. The farmer's wife was building a fire, the children scampering around, but there was no sign of the farmer. A horse was cropping grass nearby. The farmer had had only scrawny mules. It had to mean that they had met someone on a horse and he and the farmer had gone into the woods. The rider could have easily caught up with them today, but he did not. That was what had sent Rain on this night errand.

Rain backed away from the pilgrim's camp. Gliding silently through the trees, he hit the trail they had traveled that day and trotted back toward the wagon.

* * *

Amy awakened and knew it was the hour before dawn. The birds in the trees above the wagon were chirping. She crawled on her knees to the end of the wagon and looked out. Rain was squatting beside a fire and, strung out on a spit above it, the carcasses of two small animals were roasting. The aroma that came from the cooking meat made her stomach rumble. She dressed, picked up her hairbrush and quietly left the wagon.

"I brought up a bucket of water, Amy. It's there by the washbasin," Rain spoke with his back to her.

"Do you have eyes in the back of your head too?"

"I was listening for you. Your buckskins scraped on the tailgate."

Amy went into the bushes for her morning relief, then to the washbasin Rain had set out on a stump. She splashed her face and hands, dried them on the tail of her shirt, and then began to brush the snarls out of her hair so that she could braid it.

"Come on over here by me. I haven't seen you with your hair down since Christmas night." Amy's heart fluttered when she heard his softly voiced request. When she neared him, he reached out and filled his hand with the thick, long strands that spilled over her shoulders. His eyes, warm and smiling, held hers. "It's as soft as the down on a duck's belly." He lifted it to his cheek, then wound it about his hand. The curls clung to his fingers. "Anything as beautiful as this shouldn't be pinned up. I wish it could be free all the time," he said softly.

"I've got to plait it or it'll catch on fire when I cook." Her small laugh was free and happy.

"Let me do it."

Pleasure brought a faint run of color to her cheeks. "Do you know how?"

"Sure I do."

His hands on her shoulders turned her around. He gathered the shimmering mass, brought it behind her, and divided it into three strands. Slowly and carefully he began to braid. After each crossover he ran his hand down the full length of each strand. Amy stood as still as stone, closed her eyes and wondered how many other women had allowed him to braid their hair. A sudden flood of jealousy washed over her like a tide.

"You . . . seem to be pretty good at that. Have you had a lot of practice?"

"Sure. All Indian boys are taught to braid. I learned to braid hair from a horse's tail into a halter for my pony. Then it was leather whips, quirts, vines into ropes. I think I'm rather good at it. Stand still," he said when she tried to turn her head to look at him.

"I mean have you braided a . . . woman's hair?" she asked hesitantly.

"Do I dare to hope you're jealous?" he murmured close to her ear.

"Curious, is all." She was proud she could speak quite casually.

"I'm disappointed." He held the end of the braid in his hand and moved around in front of her, looping the thick rope over her shoulder. "What do you tie it with?"

"This is a thong Uncle Juicy cut for me. I use it in memory of him." She drew a narrow strip of leather from the pocket of her shirt.

Rain held the end of the braid while she tied it. When she finished, he let it fall back over her shoulder and framed her face with his cupped hands. He looked into her eyes as he bent his head and then closed them when he kissed her softly on the lips. His mouth was warm and loving on hers. As he moved his face against hers, she could feel the scrape of his eyelashes on her cheeks.

"Kissing you is getting to be a habit. I missed it last night." He murmured the words against her cheek and then kissed her again, his lips lingering as if reluctant to leave hers.

"It was your own fault. I was willing." Her breathless whisper breathed in his ear as her hand moved around him to stroke his back.

"You're a rare woman, Amy Deverell."

She looked into his dark eyes, trying to pierce the depths of his gaze to find what lay hidden there, waiting in an agony of suspense for him to say more, but he did not. He never said that she was pretty or that he loved her. He had only said she was rare and it was getting to be a habit to kiss her. For a timeless moment she looked up at him. Then she asked in a strangled whisper, "Rare like a white buffalo?"

"Like a white buffalo."

Her anger flared suddenly. "I suppose you think I'm proud to be compared to a buffalo!"

"Why not? They're noble, life-giving animals that have kept people alive for hundreds of years."

"And clumsy and dumb and . . . they stink!"

"Not to other buffalo. What has your back up?" he asked with genuine concern.

"You don't know, do you?" she spat out scornfully. When he didn't answer, she said, "You've always been able to make me so . . . so damn mad, so damn quick! You may be smart about some things, Rain Tallman, but you sure are dumb about women."

"I guess I am, for I sure as hell don't know what you're talking about."

"I'm not going to stand here and try to explain. It would take a week! Now get out of my way and I'll fix breakfast unless you plan to eat those scrawny rabbits that just fell into the fire." Her chin lifted stubbornly, her eyes determined, as if she dared him to say another word.

Rain stood with his hands to his sides looking at her rigid back as she bent to retrieve the burning meat. She was right, he thought. He knew less than nothing about women. He walked away wondering what he had said that had made her so angry.

CHAPTER
Eleven

They arrived at Kaskaskia in the early evening of the fifth day. The village had become the first capital of Illinois less than six months before when the state was admitted to the Union. Perched on the bank of the Mississippi, the town had first been settled by the French more than a hundred years before.

Amy viewed the town with interest. She was beginning to understand that a town grew up around a trading post as it had at Quill's Station. The broad Mississippi held the key to all the towns scattered along its banks, for on the waterway, boats arrived from New Orleans with goods manufactured in England and France that could be purchased with dollars or with furs. The river linked Kaskaskia with the world.

The main road through town led to the quay, and on it were several fine homes. There were also taverns, livery stables, a wheelwright, a large trading post, a blacksmith, and other businesses necessary to trade. It was all surrounded by a cluster of crude cabins.

On the southern edge of town Rain found a small, unoccupied cabin and told Amy to pull the wagon up close to it and stop. He came to her and, with his hands at her waist, swung her down.

"This is as rough a place as you'll find along the river, Amy. I want you and Miss Woodbury to stay out of sight. Understand?"

"You still don't believe I can take care of myself, do you, Rain?"

"Don't try to prove it to me here, sweetheart," he said and turned away to untie her horse from the back of the wagon. "There's a fireplace in the cabin. I don't know what shape it's in, but it'll be better than an open fire."

Sweetheart! Since the morning he had braided her hair, he had occasionally called her that when they were alone. Each endearment was a treasure she kept close to her heart. Amy had nourished her anger all that day, but when night had come and he walked her to the wagon and kissed her gently and sweetly, she whispered that she was sorry she had lashed out at him. He held her close and murmured that he had never liked anything that was so tame it didn't at one time or another try to bite him.

Eleanor had not forgiven either Amy or Rain for removing her petticoats and corset. She spoke to them only when necessary. Her attitude toward Gavin, however, seemed to have changed. They talked when he was on the wagon seat beside her, and she was quite civil to him at other times as well.

Because the fireplace in the cabin drew badly, Gavin climbed up on the roof and poked out the old bird nests that clogged it. The door hung on one leather strap and he fashioned a stout pole from a limb to prop against it on the inside. Eleanor refused to go into the dark, dirty cabin, and after walking about for a while, she climbed into the back of the wagon.

"I'm going in to see about getting passage across the river tomorrow," Rain said after he brought the harnesses into the musty cabin and piled them in one corner. "When I get back, it'll be your turn, Gavin. I guess I don't have to tell you that there are half a hundred men here that would cut your throat for the fun of it if they got the chance."

Gavin chuckled. "Aye. Ye don't have to be tellin' me 'bout river towns, laddie."

"Save me some supper, Amy. It'll probably be after dark before I get back."

Rain followed the path along the blacksmith's open-front building, his eyes searching ahead as they always did. He stepped on the walkway that ran in front of the mercantile, the tavern and the harness shop. The walk had been laid from the planks of old flatboats and trodden upon by the heavy boots of workmen, the callused feet of blacks, the moccasined feet of dark-skinned French *coureurs* and *voyageurs*, and wild, bragging boatmen from the barges that moved on the river.

Groups of men lounged in front of the three taverns. Some turned to look with more than casual interest at the tall, dark-haired man in buckskins who carried a rifle slung over his shoulder, wore a knife in his belt, and walked with long easy strides. He moved through the crowd, head up, never getting close enough to the buildings to get boxed in.

"Ain't that the gent they was talkin' 'bout up at Saint Louis?"

"If'n he got a notched ear it's him."

"Who is he?" the third man asked, whittling on a stick with a long, thin-bladed knife. "He don't look like nothin' but a woodsman to me."

"Name's Tallman. He's a fightin' son of a bitch. He can pick yore teeth with that knife a his'n at fifty feet."

"Fast too. Fast as a cow shittin' apple seeds."

"Army scout?" the man with the knife asked.

"Used to be. Heared he scouted some fer ole Zack Taylor. Guess he ain't spooky, but you ain't ort a push him none."

Rain paused at the end of the walk long enough to look across the street at a building with a new painted sign: PERRY FREIGHT COMPANY. Hammond Perry had moved into Kaskaskia. Rain wondered if he controlled the ferry as well. If he did, they would have a hard time finding someone to take them across. He didn't want to go on south with the wagon. The land was swampy close to the river, and to swing out would take more time than he was willing to spend. He'd have to figure out another way.

Hammond Perry stood beside the window of his freight office and watched Rain Tallman walk down the street. The kid he had sent to kill Tallman had failed. Hammond swore never again to send a kid to do a man's job, yet the opportunity had fallen into his lap when he had seen Tallman at Cahokia. He had no doubt that Tallman had gone on to Louisville and collected Will Bradford's bride. The man had the reputation of doing what he set out to do.

There were two men in the world that Hammond Perry despised above all others, and Rain Tallman was close to both of them.

Farrway Quill had tried to ruin Perry's military career the year before the War of 1812 by undermining his relationship to his superior officers. One time, seven years earlier, Hammond thought he could get rid of Quill and had had him arrested for treason. At the trial his witnesses turned yellow and fled, and Major Taylor had believed Quill's story. At that time the major had Hammond Perry and a fellow officer banished to Fort Dearborn for two years.

Will Bradford was the other man who had bested Perry at every turn. When it came time to select a man to take a company of men up the Arkansas River and establish a fort at Belle Point, Hammond was sure that he would be given the task. Will Bradford had managed to have him looked on with ill favor because of the way he had disciplined a platoon of men who had been insubordinate. Will Bradford had received the prize assignment, an assignment that would make his name go down in history instead of Hammond's.

Hammond rocked back on his heels, his dish-shaped face twisted with resentment as it always was when he thought of how fate had dealt with him. He was a small man with a receding chin that he tried to hide beneath a well-trimmed goatee. He dressed in clothes made in London and wore shoes made in Italy. He was rich and had plans to become richer. He was a man who loved revenge and he had plans for getting that too. With his hands locked behind his back, he rocked back and forth from the balls of his feet to his heels while his mind worked on his plans.

"This place isn't fit for hogs!" Amy viewed the dirt in the cabin with disgust.

Gavin laughed. "Ye be one of them what can't abide the dirt? Tis no castle to be sure, but the walls will shield ye, if'n ye have a yen for a wash."

"Wash? I'd love a bath, but how?"

"I'll fetch up a couple buckets of water, lass. Twill have to do."

Amy went to the wagon for clean clothes and a bar of soap. Eleanor was rummaging in her trunk and kept her back to her.

"Gavin has gone to get water for us to wash with. Won't it feel good to be clean again?" Amy asked in an attempt to ease the tension between them.

Eleanor ignored her as she had done the last few days, and after Amy gathered up what she needed she left the wagon.

When Gavin brought water up from the creek nearby, Amy warmed it with water from the teakettle. He poured it into a large washbasin and set it on the back of the wagon for Eleanor. She didn't answer when he called out to her, but later he noticed that she had taken the water inside the wagon.

The sun, completing its journey across the sky, was a red ball disappearing in the west. Rain had not returned. After her bath Amy had dressed again in her britches and a clean shirt. She washed her dirty shirt and undergarment in the bucket and hung them beside the fireplace to dry. The stew that had been bubbling for the last hour was sending up a delicious aroma, and Amy saw no reason why they shouldn't eat.

Gavin had been to the creek to wash and had shaved the whiskers from his face, using the soap Amy offered to soften them. His hair was wet, slicked back and tied. Amy liked the big man. There was a depth to him that she hadn't noticed at first, a gentleness. She still knew no more about him than she had been told the day she met him, that he was a riverman, a brawler. That he and Rain liked and respected each other was evident.

"Shall we eat, Gavin?" They had been sitting on the door-stone for the past half hour.

"Might as well, lass."

From the box on the side of the wagon, Amy took out bowls and spoons. Her first thought was not to call Eleanor. The stubborn, proud woman may have gone to bed. But then again, for the sake of Will Bradford, Rain's friend, she should make another attempt.

"Miss Woodbury, Gavin and I are going to eat. Won't you come out and join us?" Silence. Amy went back to the cabin. "I called Miss Woodbury, but she won't come out. I'll take some to her. I know Rain told me not to wait on her, but she must eat."

"Aye, the lassie be needin' a strong hand."

Amy dished out a generous helping of the stew and took it to the back of the wagon.

"Here's your supper, Miss Woodbury." Amy lifted the flap and looked inside. It took several seconds before her eyes could adjust to the gloom, but when they did, she saw that the wagon was empty. She turned to Gavin sitting on the doorstone. "She isn't here."

Gavin got slowly to his feet. "Mayhap she went to—"

"When did she go? We would have seen her leave." Amy returned to the cabin and dumped the stew back into the pot. "She's gone to town, Gavin. She sneaked out the front of the wagon."

"Nay. The lassie would not be so foolish."

"She did! What shall we do?"

"Ye be doin' nothin'. I'll be goin' to fetch her back."

"I'm going with you."

"No, lassie—"

"I'm going." Amy slipped her knife into the sheath strapped around her waist and picked up her rifle.

The idea of going into the village came to Eleanor when she heard Rain say he was leaving to arrange passage across the river. The last week had been the most miserable of her life. The thought of going on to Belle Point and marrying a man she did not love or even know was so repulsive that she dared not think about it lest she get sick. She should never have left Louisville. She knew that now, but at the time it had seemed romantic to go with the handsome stranger who was sent to take her hundreds of miles to a man who wanted to marry her, especially a man of wealth and position like Will Bradford.

Eleanor's heart fluttered with excitement as she washed and dressed in one of her most fetching dresses. Hidden in the bottom of her trunk were a few coins, enough, she hoped, to pay her passage to New Orleans. There she would sell some of her clothes and a few pieces of jewelry her aunt had left her for money to live on while she found a way to support herself. True, she was not the card player that Gilda had been, but she played fairly well. Her aunt had supported them for years by playing cards with high-class gentlemen who thought it a lark to play with the lady while her charming young niece looked on. Eleanor had told the story of her father's big plantation so many times that she half-believed it herself. She had known at an early age that her father was a scoundrel. He never did a day's work in his life, or so Gilda said. Her mother, however, was of good family, and Will Bradford was her first cousin. Gilda had set the wheels in motion that caused Will to ask for Eleanor's hand in marriage by telling him of her dire plight.

Eleanor waited until Gavin had gone to the creek and Amy was in the cabin. Then she took her money from the trunk, put on her prettiest bonnet and slipped out the front of the wagon. Within minutes she was walking down the road toward the main part of the town.

Kaskaskia's main road was choked with horses, freight wagons and men. When Eleanor turned on to the street her courage almost failed her. Yet she continued on, knowing this was her only chance to break away from the future that had been decided for her. By the time she reached the board-walk that fronted the mercantile, the eyes of every man on the street had passed over her and most of them stayed there. From either side of the street men watched her go by— freighters in heavy boots, boatmen, Indians, gamblers in beaver hats, French trappers with bright dark eyes and elaborately fringed buckskins. And everywhere there were dogs, medium-sized dogs, big dogs and runts, all searching for food.

Eleanor had never in her wildest imaginings thought there was such a place as this. The town was crowded to overflowing with men. She did not see a single woman as she continued on down the street. As she stared stonily ahead, a fearful tension gripped her. She had to get through the crowd to get to the quay where the boats were docked.

By sheer chance she missed being hit by the contents of a slop pail hurled out into the street from a second-story window. She sidestepped quickly and bumped into a man she was passing. She moved on, but not before she felt his hand nudge at her bottom.

A white-aproned man and a helper carried a drunk through the door of the tavern and tossed him into the street. A man riding a mule jumped the animal over him and continued on his way. No one paid the slightest attention to the unfortunate man in the street. All eyes were on the beautiful woman walking down the boardwalk.

"Howdy do, ma'am?" A man lifted his fur cap.

"Ya wantin' some company?" another asked.

"Lordy, if she don't smell purty."

"I ain't had me no clean woman in a long time."

"Hell, ya ain't *never* had ya no clean woman."

"I'd sure like ta have me a piece of that 'n."

Eleanor was not sure how it happened, but suddenly she was seized from behind, and before she could open her mouth she was inside a gloomy building with tables and a long plank bar. The two men holding her, each with an arm beneath her armpits, held her feet off the floor. Her wits returned and she screamed. There was a roar of laughter.

"Put me down—you filthy varmints! Let go of me!"

She tried to kick. There was more laughter and shouting

as men vied for a position close to her. She was surrounded by leering, unwashed, whiskered faces.

"What ya agoin' to do, Bull? What ya agoin' to do?" A lad with smooth, clean cheeks wiggled through the crowd.

"Don't ya know even *that*? God, Muley, I thought ya knew *that!*" someone said, and there was more laughter.

"Can I watch, Bull?"

The big man lifted Eleanor to stand on a table in the middle of the room. The man who put her there backed off and looked at her. The skin on his face sagged and the end of his nose had been lopped off. He wore a rag tied around his head, which was large and set on broad shoulders with scarcely any neck in between. He looked at her with small, bloodshot eyes that made her choke with fear.

"Look all ya vant, Muley," Bull spoke in a heavy German accent.

Act the lady, Eleanor told herself. If she acted the lady they would let her go. From the top of the table she looked down on the sea of faces, lifted her chin and spoke to the man called Bull.

"I want to leave now. I have friends waiting for me."

"She wants to go. She don't like us, Bull. Let me feel 'er before ya let 'er go."

"I ain't alettin' her go." Bull turned and glared at the man who spoke. "I found me a play-purty."

"Let me go! Get away from me!" Eleanor's fear made her voice shrill. She tried to get off the table, but Bull caught hold of her ankles and she almost fell on him.

"Line up, gents. Ya can feel her up to here." He raised Eleanor's dress to her knees.

Eleanor swung the bag of coins and jewelry she had looped over her arm. It hit Bull alongside the face and he grabbed it. The bag broke open. The contents spilled out on to the floor. Panic consumed her and screams of terror tore from her throat. They were scarcely heard over the roar of laughter that erupted when Bull lifted her skirts above her knees and told the first man to step up.

Men jammed the door trying to get into the crowded room. They came from up and down the street until fifty men stood outside the tavern door, craning their necks to see what was going on inside.

"Gavin! Gavin!" Eleanor screamed as the first man came to run his callused palms up and down her legs. "Gavin!"

Coming into town, Gavin and Amy first saw the crowd gathered in front of the building; then they heard the screams. Gavin began to run. Amy, having taken the time to poke her hair up under her hat, looked like a tall, slim boy running beside him. On the walk in front of the tavern, Gavin cleared a path with his fists and roars of rage. Amy followed close behind him, one hand on her knife, the other holding her rifle close to her side.

By the time they were inside the room, Eleanor was sobbing wildly and kicking at each man who came to feel her legs.

"Oh, Gavin!" she cried as they burst through the circle that surrounded the table. Her bonnet hung by the ties, her hair was loose, and a man standing on a chair was running his hands through it. Tears streamed down Eleanor's face.

With one sweep of his arm Gavin knocked the man from the chair. He fell to the floor with a crash, bounced up with his hand on his knife, and felt the prick of one in his back. When he hesitated, the tip of the knife pressed harder against him; he dropped his hand and moved away. All eyes were on Gavin and the man called Bull. They scarcely noticed the slim figure in buckskins who had nicked the man in the back with the knife.

"Back off or get a knife in yore gullet," Bull snarled.

"Ye can only get yer pleasure by bullin' a lassie, uh." Gavin made the statement in such an insulting way that Bull couldn't help but catch the meaning. They eyed each other, each recognizing the other for what he was. They both had been through a hundred barroom brawls and knew what to expect.

"Who are ya to be buttin' in?"

"Her mon, that's who."

"Yo're a liar. She's a street strumpet."

Gavin hit him. The blow would have knocked an ordinary man through the wall. Bull staggered into the crowd and was pushed back. A shot rang out and the bartender yelled.

"In the street! The whole herd of ya. I'll shoot the next man to land a blow."

"Get the lass out," Gavin said to Amy and waited until she helped Eleanor off the table. Pushing the two of them ahead of him, he went out into the street.

Amy took a firm grip on Eleanor's arm and pulled her out of the crowd that formed a circle around Gavin and Bull. Eleanor was still crying and wanted to leave. Amy shoved her, none too gently, up against a building.

"We're not leaving Gavin here alone to face what you got him into. You may have just got him killed," she snarled. "If he is, I'm going to beat you senseless. You stay here or, by God, the next man that wants you can have you."

"Oh!" Eleanor wailed and covered her face with her hands.

Amy stood on a box so she could see over the heads of the men. Gavin and Bull were squaring off.

"How ya want it?" Bull asked. "Fists, knives or whips?"

"Jest me fists, bully-boy, unless ye feel ye'll be needin' some help."

"Tear 'em up, Bull!" someone yelled.

"Whop his ass. He can't take keer a his own woman! Haw, haw, haw!"

The men on the sidelines were placing bets on Bull. He was a giant known up and down the river for his strength and fighting fury. The other man was big, but unknown.

Bull lunged, amazingly swift for such a big man, but Gavin was waiting for him and hit him with a jarring left punch to the teeth that flattened Bull's lips back. It didn't even slow the giant. Gavin dug in his feet and braced himself. They met head on and locked arms. They wrestled back and forth for a long while in a contest of sheer strength before they broke free.

Bull lunged again, his teeth showing in a grinning snarl. His right fist caught Gavin on the side of the head, knocking him to the ground. Gavin rolled over swiftly, came up and smashed a wicked left punch to Bull's belly that brought a loud grunt, then with his right hand he grabbed his crotch to throw him, but Bull's hand was in his hair, the fingers of his other hand searching for Gavin's eyes. He let go and hooked his leg around Bull's. They fell to the ground and rolled. Gavin came out on top and smashed blow after blow into Bull's face. The rag around his head came off and Gavin saw the reason for the sagging skin on his face. The man had once been partially scalped.

A knee came up into Gavin's ribs and a stabbing pain coursed through his vitals. He fell back, gasping for air. Bull sprang to his feet, swaying like a drunken bear. He lifted a heavy booted foot to crush the life from Gavin, but Gavin rolled over and staggered to his feet.

His mind was grappling with an idea of how to deal with the man. Brute strength wasn't the answer. His weak spot was his head. It also occurred to Gavin that even if he did beat the big man there were a dozen more men who would jump him before he could get the woman out of town. There were no rules of fair play in a place such as this.

Bull came in low and Gavin brought both fists down hard with a slanting blow to the top of his forehead. The thin skin over his skull split and blood streaked down Bull's face. Pain slowed him momentarily and gave Gavin time for another blow before powerful arms extended to catch him in a spine-crushing bear hug. The breath was being squeezed from his body. Gavin desperately butted the top of his head against Bull's skull until the man finally let go and fell back. His face was a bloody mask.

"I'll kill ya," Bull roared.

"Ye talk big," Gavin panted.

"I'll have the woman on yore grave!"

"Ye'll be in hell long afore me, ye hairless bastard."

Bull held his hand out to the side and the boy Muley slapped the handle of a knife into it. Bull made an unexpected swift move. Gavin would have been disemboweled if he had not leaped back, sucking his belly out of the path of Bull's knife. He was as good with a knife as the next man, but he had none. Now he was fighting for his life.

Amy jumped from the box, looked around for a place to hide Eleanor, grabbed her and pushed her between two buildings and behind a barrel.

"Don't you dare move from here! If you do I'll shave every hair off your head with my knife. Hear me?"

Eleanor nodded tearfully.

Amy ran back and wormed her way through the crowd to the inner circle, desperately afraid of what she would find. Gavin had managed to stay out of reach of the knife and had not sustained a serious cut. Not wanting to distract him, she held her breath while he dodged the blade. It caught his sleeve, the skin of his upper arm, and sliced a path across his chest before he was in the position she wanted. When Bull had danced his way around so that his back was to her and she faced Gavin, she drew her knife and held it up for him to see, then tossed it to him.

Gavin caught the knife with renewed hope. He had known the fight would be a bad one, and had leaped into it willingly, even eagerly, with his blood singing for vengeance. He had not expected a fight to the death, but if that was the way the bastard wanted it, so be it.

Amy watched. Gavin was more important to her than Eleanor. Unstanched blood flowed from the deep cut on his cheekbone and from the knife cuts on his arms and chest. Bull was in a rage to kill him. The fight had already lasted longer than any fight he had ever had and his reputation was at stake.

Yells of encouragement came from the crowd.

"Cut his guts out, Bull!"

"Whup him!"

Gavin lashed out and cut a ridge across the top of Bull's hand. Blood from his bleeding head was running down his forehead and into his eyes. He roared and swore, his anger and pain making him careless. Gavin rushed in and ducked beneath the swinging blade, his fist striking a powerful blow to Bull's crotch. The big man doubled over, dropped his knife and grabbed his genitals. The shouting ceased as if a curtain had fallen. Gavin kicked the knife out of Bull's reach and waited to see if the big man would get up.

There was a shrill scream of rage, and the boy Muley broke from the crowd with a knife raised to plunge into Gavin's back. Amy leaped and swung her rifle with all the force she possessed. *Don't do nothin' half-assed*, Juicy had once said, *hurt 'em afore they hurt you*. That was what she meant to do. The barrel caught the boy across the face and he staggered back, blood spurting from his nose. She whirled, her back against Gavin's, and stood in a crouch, feet spread for balance. The end of the rifle swung in an arc as the crowd closed in.

"Ayeee, lassie," Gavin breathed. "Ye done it now."

"Rush 'em," a man shouted. "He ain't got but one shot."

"You rush 'em. Damn fool kid's crazy enough to shoot."

"He's a gutsy one," someone said. "The man beat Bull fair and square. Let 'em go."

"Hell no, we ain't lettin' 'em go. I want me a turn at that big feller."

"You'll have to shoot the kid—"

"What'll we do, Gavin?" Amy asked in a low voice.

"I don't know. I'm agettin' me breath."

Rain, coming up from the quay, saw the commotion. He considered crossing the street to avoid the crowd, but as he stepped up on the boardwalk and looked over the heads of the men, he saw Amy and Gavin, back to back, in the center of the crowd. When he realized the danger to Amy, he at first was angry and vowed to beat her butt! Then a strange calm came over him as it usually did when he found himself in a tight spot.

The crowd was ugly. There was nothing to do but wade in. He shouldered his way through the crowd and walked into the circle.

"What's going on?" he demanded.

"What's it to ya?" someone countered belligerently.

"Twas a fight."

"Ho, *mon ami*, twas the devil of a fight." The Frenchman who spoke had a black beard and a mop of black curly hair. Perched on his head at a jaunty angle was a knit cap.

"Was it a fair fight?" Rain asked.

"No" a coarse voice shouted.

"Twas fair," the Frenchman growled. "I say, twas fair, by God! The lad busted the nose of a backstabber. Ho, it was a rare sight." He slapped his leg and cocked his head at Amy "He be a man soon, eh?"

"Then that's the end of it," Rain said.

"Not on your say-so." A man tried to swagger forward but was jerked back by a friend.

"Shut yore mouth, ya bloody fool! That's Rain Tallman yore mouthin' off to."

"Let's go," Rain said to Amy and Gavin. He nodded to the Frenchman and said, "Much obliged."

"Move, *mon ami*. I will watch your back."

Rain led the way through the crowd, Amy close behind

him and then Gavin. When they reached the boardwalk, the Frenchman was with them. Amy led the way to where she had pushed Eleanor behind a barrel when she went to give Gavin her knife. Eleanor was sitting on the ground, still crying.

Gavin went to her and yanked her to her feet. "Ye 'bout got us all kilt this time, me girl. Ye be needin' a thrashin' is what ye be needin'."

"Oh, Gavin." Eleanor tried to get close to him, but the Scot held her at arm's length with his hand wrapped about her upper arm. He propelled her down the street toward the cabin.

The Frenchman stared after Gavin and Eleanor.

"*Mon Dieu!* Tis easy to see why the big one fought like the devil. I would do the same for that one. It's been long since my eyes feasted on such beauty."

Rain held out his hand to the Frenchman. "Thanks."

"I would shake this place, friend," he said and grasped Rain's hand warmly. "That Bull is a bad man."

"We're leaving in the morning. Crossing over to the other side."

"That is good. Ah . . . take the young lad with you, or *she* be in danger here." He winked at Rain and burst into laughter, showing rows of white teeth through the black beard. His bright eyes on Amy flashed messages of admiration. He lifted his hand in a salute and sauntered back down the boardwalk.

Amy and Rain hurried to catch up with Gavin and Eleanor.

CHAPTER
Twelve

Amy moved silently beside Rain in the darkness, grateful for his presence. He was tense, alert, and he was very angry too. He had not said a word since they left the Frenchman. She was not sure if his anger was directed at her or at Eleanor. Every so often he stopped to listen and then moved on. A half moon was making its way up over the treetops, and the sky was growing lighter. An owl hooted; Rain paused, listened, and then . . . the same owl hooted again.

Eleanor's voice came out of the darkness ahead, followed by Gavin telling her sternly to be quiet. Gavin had a right to be angry with Eleanor, Amy reasoned. In fact, they all did. Her foolish action earlier had almost cost Gavin his life. He had saved her from certain rape and possible death. Amy did not know how he had managed to evade the killing slash of the knife until she could toss hers to him. And had he been seriously wounded or killed, all that stood between her and that pack of low-life scum, until Rain arrived, had been that one shot in her rifle.

As they neared camp, Rain became more cautious. Finally he stopped and gently pushed Amy against the trunk of a tall aspen that stood like a sentinel in the dim light. He indicated by a show of his palm that she was to stay there and then moved away silently. The minutes were long while Amy waited—long and lonely. Then he suddenly appeared out of the darkness and beckoned.

As they neared the cabin, they heard a steady, evenly spaced sound and a low agonized sob, followed by Eleanor's pleading voice. Amy knew instantly what the sound was, and so did Rain. It was the sound of a flat hand coming down hard on firm flesh at regular intervals.

"My God!" Rain exclaimed. "Has he lost his mind? She needs it, but—"

"Wait!" Amy put her hand on his arm to hold him back. "She almost got all of us killed tonight."

"I know. But I can't allow him to do that."

"Why not? She deserves every swat she's getting! Gavin is hurting—bad. He's got a hundred cuts and bruises because of her stupidity."

Rain looked down at Amy. She saw a flash of white teeth and knew he was smiling.

"Yeah. She deserves it. I should give you the same. I was so damn scared the hair raised up on the back of my neck when I saw you in the middle of the worst bunch of cutthroats along the river. Didn't I tell you to stay out of sight and not show yourself in those britches?"

"They were so busy looking at Eleanor they didn't even notice me."

"The Frenchman noticed, and he liked what he saw. I don't like any man looking at you the way that blasted Frenchman did."

Rain flung his arm around her and, with a growl of impatience, jerked her roughly to him. Silent, joyous laughter bubbled up in Amy's throat. She pressed herself tightly to him and slid her arm about his waist. Her head fell naturally to his shoulder and she leaned in sweet, glad comfort against him. His whiskers scraped gently against her forehead when he tilted his head to hers. Their lips met, clung in mutual hunger, parted, and met again in sweet, gentle kisses. He lifted his head and looked into her eyes with great tenderness.

"Disobey me again," he said, his lips moving down so close to hers that she could feel the movement when he spoke, "and you'll get what Eleanor's getting."

Gavin sat on the doorstone. He threw Eleanor face down over his lap, pulled up her skirt and petticoats, and his big hand came down hard on her buttocks.

"What? What are you doing?" She struggled, but his forearm across her back held her down.

"Yer a stubborn, headstrong lass, Nora, me girl. Ye been needin' this for a long while." His hand came down again.

"Ohh!" she wailed. "Oh . . . stop!"

"Ye been a shrew." *Swat!* "Ye been prideful and vain, is what ye been." *Swat!* "Ye be carin' more for the looks on the outside of ye 'n paid no mind a'tall at what ye was comin' to be on the inside." *Swat!* His words were punctuated with a slap on her behind.

"You . . . lout! Stop! Oh, you'll be sorry . . . for . . this . . ."

"Ye been holdin' yerself up above the rest of us like ye was a queen. Tis the end of it, me girl. Ye'll be doin' yer share of the work 'n keepin' yer lip buttoned." *Swat!* His hand came down hard on a white bottom that was shielded only by the thin cloth of her pantalettes.

"I . . . hate you! Oh!"

"I do not be carin'—" *Swat!*

"I'll tell Will! Damn you!"

"Ye'll not be swearin' a'tall. Hear?" *Swat!*

"I won't. Oh, Gavin, please—"

"Ye know what to be sayin'." *Swat!*

"I'm sorry! I'm sorry! Please, Gavin!"

"Ye'll be keepin' a civil tongue in yer head?"

"Yes. Oh, yes."

"Ye'll be doing what yer told?"

"Yes. Oh, yes."

"Aye. We'll see how ye be behavin' yerself, lass." His voice softened. "Ye be such a bonnie lass fer all yer wicked ways."

Gavin pulled her skirts down and turned her over. He fully expected her to jump up and run, but she curled on his lap and snuggled against him. Her arm moved up and about his neck and, crying softly, she buried her face in the curve of his shoulder. His arms held her close and he rocked her as if she were a small child.

"Don't cry, lassie, don't cry. Tis all over." He stroked her shimmering hair back from her face with gentle fingertips. "Ye learned a hard lesson this night. Yer pretty face coulda been the death of ye."

"I'm sorry. I didn't know it would be . . . like that. I wanted to go to . . . New Orleans. Now my money is gone and I'll have to go on to Will. All I could think of was you, Gavin, when that awful, ugly man grabbed me and made me stand on the table. I wanted you to come—"

"Now, now, lassie. Don't ye be cryin'. I heard ye callin' me name. The likes a them will na be touchin' ye ever again. Now, now, bonnie, sweet lassie, don't cry."

"He could have killed you! Oh, Gavin, your poor face." Eleanor lifted her face and looked up into his. Hers was tear-streaked and bloody from his shirt; his eye was swollen shut, and blood seeped from the cut on his cheekbone.

"Tis best ye get up, lass. Tis certain, yer fine dress is bein' ruined." Gavin hated saying the words. The sweet weight of the woman on his lap and her gentle fingers on his bruised face were sensations he would remember and cherish.

"I don't care about the dress." She slid off his lap. "I'll get some water and clean your face."

Amy and Rain came from the end of the wagon where Amy had tossed her hat.

"There's a fresh bucket of water in the cabin," Amy said. "Wash up and we'll eat."

Amy went inside and poked small pieces of wood in the glowing coals beneath the stew pot. She blew on them until they blazed. Soon there was enough light to see. Eleanor came in and picked up the bucket of water. She struggled to get it out the door. Her hair hung in strands, her face was swollen from crying and smeared with Gavin's blood. Her lavender dress was torn and bloodstained.

Amy prepared to serve the stew, trying not to feel sorry for Eleanor. She dredged up in her mind the thought of Gavin charging into the tavern to help Eleanor out of the trouble she had gotten herself into without a thought for himself, and she thought of his facing a man with a knife when he had none. Eleanor's behavior the last week had been that of a spoiled child, and Amy was glad Gavin had given her the spanking she deserved.

Rain appeared in the doorway. "Douse the fire," he said tersely.

Amy quickly did as she was told. She threw the water left in the washbowl on the flames. There was instant darkness. She felt her way along the wall until her hand closed around the barrel of her rifle. Quietly she slipped out the door. Rain's hand on her arm drew her away from the cabin.

"What is it?" she whispered.

Rain didn't speak until they were standing close together beneath the aspen tree.

"Listen."

Amy could hear absolutely nothing except the leaves stirring in the tree above them and the horses cropping the grass. She could smell nothing except the faint smell of wood smoke, a dampness rising from the steam, and a whiff of the stew that reminded her of how hungry she was.

"I don't hear anything."

"That's just it," Rain breathed in her ear. "The frogs down by the creek have stopped croaking."

"That's right, they have. Do you think we were followed from town?"

"No. That bunch would sound like a herd of buffalo coming through the underbrush."

Amy heard muffled voices coming from the side of the cabin. "Shouldn't we get Gavin and Eleanor?"

"Whoever is out there already knows we're here. I want him to think all of us are there by the cabin."

The sky was getting lighter by the minute as the half moon rose in the sky. Already the aspen was casting a shadow, and the outline of the cabin and the white canvas top of the wagon were clearly visible. Amy and Rain stood silently, Amy's shoulder against his arm. Her hand slid down his forearm and her fingers interlaced with his. After a while the frogs began to croak again, starting where they were standing, then gradually all along the creek.

"Whatever bothered the frogs is gone." Rain squeezed her hand and released it. He thought of telling her about the rider who had followed them for the last couple of days. After visiting his camp two nights in a row, Rain had come to the conclusion that the man was scared to be alone on the trail, staying close to them because it made him feel safer. He decided that there was no need for her to worry about it. So he said, "I'm hungry. Let's go eat."

They ate by the side of the cabin, quickly and quietly. When they had finished, Amy wiped out the bowls and washed the pot. Rain told them he had found a boatman who would take them across the river, and they had to be at the quay so they could shove off at dawn.

"Hammond Perry has moved his freight business here. The boatmen are all scared of him because he's rich and has connections in high places. He tells them who to do business with and who not to. He's spread the word that anyone who does business with me will regret it. I was lucky enough to find a man who refused to knuckle under and is moving on downriver. He'll take us across."

"Do you think Hammond Perry will give Farr and Libby trouble when they come through here?" Amy asked worriedly.

"They're not coming this way. They'll cross at Saint Louis. It's longer that way but the road is better suited for his heavy wagons. Don't worry. Jonas and Albert know about Perry. They'll nose around and find out what's best for Farr and Liberty."

"Aye," Gavin agreed. "They be a wily pair to my way a thinkin'. Yer folk be lucky to have them along."

"Do you feel like standing a watch?" Rain asked. "We'd better split the night between us."

"I can take a turn," Amy said quickly.

"No need for that, lassie. I be fit as soon as I take a wash at the creek."

"I've some salve to go on those cuts, Gavin," Amy said. "We don't want them to fester."

"Aye. The salve will be welcome." He stood and flexed his shoulders wearily. His bloody shirt hung in tatters from his massive shoulders, his hair had come loose in the back and framed a face that was even more swollen than before. He picked up his rifle and started off through the trees.

"Gavin, wait!" Eleanor jumped up and went to the wagon. She came out almost immediately, ran to him and pressed a bar of her scented soap in his hand. "Here's soap and . . . a towel." She draped it over his arm. "Do you have another shirt?"

"Aye. One other."

"Bring this one back. I'll mend it."

"Ye don't be owin' me, lass," he said gruffly.

"Please. I want to."

"Aye. So be it then."

Eleanor watched him leave. She turned reluctantly and, with head bent, slowly returned to where Amy and Rain stood.

"If you'll get the salve, I'll take care of Gavin's cuts," she said.

"All right. I'll get it."

When Amy left her alone with Rain, Eleanor found herself tongue-tied. Her mind went blank and she couldn't think of what she knew she had to say. Her eyes sought his face and found him staring at her, or so it seemed. The night was as dark as his eyes. His quiet watchfulness and his stoic expression frightened her.

"I've got to say that I'm sorry," she blurted.

"Don't say it if you don't mean it," he said curtly.

"But I do! I'm sorry I disobeyed you and went to town. I just never imagined anything so . . . terrible. The men were more like . . . animals!"

"You can't blame them. You paraded yourself. It's what a woman does here when she's loose."

"I didn't know."

"You do now."

Amy returned and held out a flat tin. "Here's the salve. There's a jug of vinegar over there under the food box. Be sure to wash the cuts out good with vinegar and water before you put the salve on."

"Thank you," Eleanor murmured. "I'll get something for a bandage so it won't get on his clean shirt."

Eleanor climbed into the wagon and Amy moved over close to Rain. "Let me take a watch."

"You can watch now. I'll go to the creek and wash. I've got clean clothes in my saddlebags."

"I'll wash your dirty ones the first chance I get."

Watching him go, Amy's heart swelled with pride and love. She and Rain were together, and she was able to do for him. They worked well together, and she thanked God for the training Juicy had given her.

More and more often Rain touched her as he passed, as he had done when he left her just now. The warmth from the pleasure of his hand on her arm was still there, and Amy covered it with hers, holding on as if it were something infinitely precious. Sometimes she could feel him watching her; she would turn, their eyes would meet and hold and smile. At other times he looked at her with mocking tenderness, and still at other times his dark, fathomless eyes flicked over her and away, reminding her of the shy youth of long ago.

Amy's heart soared when she thought of the soft words he had whispered in her ear, not over an hour ago. *I don't like any man looking at you the way that Frenchman did.*

Inside the cabin, with the door firmly closed so that no light would escape, Eleanor dressed Gavin's wounds by candlelight. The skin on his broad, muscular chest quivered more from the touch of her fingers than from the wounds or the cold. She gently washed the cuts on his arms, face and chest with the vinegar water, then smeared each with salve and bandaged them with strips torn from one of her clean petticoats. He sat on the box, his heart pumping wildly while the beautiful, fairylike creature hovered around him.

Gavin searched his memory for the last time a woman had

done for him what this one was doing. It had been many years, so many years that it seemed to be in another life that he had felt a woman's tender touch. There had been whores from time to time, but he had done the touching. They had been merely bodies he used to drive the devil from his loins.

While he had been at the creek, Eleanor had changed into a dark skirt and soft white shirt. Her hair was brushed and tied at the nape of her neck with a white ribbon. The shining dark tresses that hung to her hips brushed his bare shoulders and back when she turned this way or that while she administered to him. Her face was serious, her bottom lip caught firmly between her teeth. Gavin scarcely felt the pain when her fingers filled the cuts for watching the expressions flit across her perfectly formed features.

When Eleanor finished, she bent down in front of him until her face was level with his and stared at him intently.

"Gavin! Did you know that your nose is bent over to one side? Did that awful man do that to you?"

"No, lass." Gavin's wide mouth twitched, then broke into a slow, uneven smile that sent creases fanning out from his shining blue eyes and made indentations in his weathered cheeks. "That was done to me nose a long time ago."

Entranced, Eleanor watched this unexpected transformation of his battered features. Hesitantly, she lifted her hand and gripped the end of his nose with her thumb and forefinger. She wiggled it back and forth.

"It's there for good, isn't it?" she asked with a look of confusion in her eyes.

"I fear tis."

She straightened, still staring into his face, and tilted her head to one side as she studied him. "It suits you, though," she said as if she had decided something of great importance. "Gavin . . . how old are you?"

"Why, I be an old mon, lassie."

"How old?"

"I be thirty me birthday."

"That's not old. You're only seven years older than I am. Aunt Gilda always insisted that I say I was eighteen. I've been eighteen since I was twelve." Eleanor laughed. "Now, out here in the wilderness, it sounds so ridiculous. I'm twenty-three. Goodness! I've never said that out loud. Aunt Gilda would have swooned if she'd ever heard me."

"I don't be understandin' what difference twould make." Gavin got to his feet, trying not to wince as he reached for his shirt and slipped it over his head because he didn't know what else to do or say. "My thanks to ye, lass."

"Oh, Gavin!" Eleanor took his bruised and cut hand in both of hers, held his skinned knuckles against her soft cheek and looked up into his face. "My thanks to *ye*," she said softly, with so much emotion he thought she was going to cry.

"Now, now, lassie," he said gruffly. "Don't ye be frettin'." He put his other hand on the top of her head and patted gently. "Be off with ye. Ye've had a hard day, 'n the mon said we must be at the quay afore dawn." Gavin blew out the candle, pulled the pole away from the door and opened it.

It was decided that Rain would take the first watch so that Gavin could rest. As Eleanor went to her bed in the wagon, Gavin threw his blankets down on the soft grass beneath it.

"I will be needin' only a few winks, mon. Wake me when it's me turn."

"Are you turning in, Amy?" Rain was watching Amy reach into the wagon.

"No. I'm getting a blanket. I thought I'd stay with you for a while . . . if you want me to."

"Foolish woman," he teased and took her hand. "Come on."

They left the camp and took up their vigil beneath the aspen where they had stopped before. The forest was motionless, blurred into darkness, but the little area around the cabin was visible. Rain stood his rifle, butt down, against the tree trunk, sank down on to the soft mat of long grass and pulled Amy down beside him.

"It's getting cold. You're going to be glad you brought the blanket."

They sat for a while with shoulders touching. When he looped his arm around her to pull her close, she snuggled against his side. In silence they watched the shadows and listened to the sounds of the forest. Long ago Amy had developed an awed affection for the forest, marveling at its trickery, its beauty, and admiring its great towering trees. Tonight, because she was with Rain, she thought its awesome beauty magnificent. It wore a crown of a million sparkling stars. Heaven had never been nearer.

"What are you thinking?" he whispered.

"Lots of things. I was thinking about what Uncle Juicy said about trees. He said trees can live without man, but man would have a hell of a time living without trees."

"What else?"

"I'll not tell you now."

"That's two things you're going to tell me later."

"I haven't forgotten. Talk to me. What did you do and think all those years you were away?"

"I thought about all the people at Quill's Station. Do you remember coming to the barn the morning I left and asking me not to go?" His voice was a mere breath in her ear.

"I remember."

"You kissed me good-bye. You smelled sweet and your body was soft when you pressed against me. I thought about it for months."

She laughed softly. "I was so mad at you for going that for months after you left I'd call you a mule's ass every time your name was mentioned."

"Do you still think that's what I am?"

"Sometimes."

"If we didn't have to be so damned quiet I'd tickle you," he whispered with mock menace in his voice. His fingers found a spot beneath her breast and dug in. She wiggled, gasped, and grabbed his hand. Interlacing his fingers with hers, she brought it down to her lap.

"I can't stand that!" She turned her face into his shoulder to silence her giggle. "Something dreadful happens when I'm tickled."

"What? Tell me or I'll tickle you again."

"No. Please! That's another one of those things I'll have to tell you . . . later."

"Amy, Amy—" He rubbed his fingertips lightly over her cheek, then grasped her chin and tilted her face up to him. "Sometimes I can't believe this thing that's happened to me. I want to be with you all the time, and when I'm not with you, I'm thinking about you."

Amy felt light-headed with the exhilarating sense of release from a long nightmare. Her smile reflected her happiness. A sweeping tide of love for this man, this other part of herself, flowed over her.

"Does that mean you don't consider me the pest you once thought I was?"

"It means, Amy-girl, that I'm beginning to wonder how I could possibly live without you." The words came out huskily, his lips hovering a mere fraction over hers.

A shiver of excitement that was sheer heaven traveled down Amy's spine. She felt tremblingly alive when his urgent mouth covered hers. He pulled her closer and her flat palm on his chest moved up to the back of his neck. His lips moved away and then back to hers as if he couldn't stay away from them. He kissed her deeply and urgently, like a long-starved man. When he lifted his lips from her mouth, his breath came hotly against her cheek. She felt him take a deep, trembling breath before his firm mouth brushed hers again lightly.

It wasn't enough.

"Ahh . . . damn!" It was a groan that ended as his lips, hard and intense, found hers again, bruising their softness. His arms crushed her breast against his chest and he held her as if she were life itself. Gradually his hold loosened, and then his lips were at the corner of hers, tracing a path to her eyes, then back to close over her mouth. His tongue was insistent, demanding that she meet it with hers. She responded hesitantly at first, then with welcome, and finally passion. She clung to him mindlessly, her hand sliding into the neck of his shirt, feeling the warmth of his skin, the strength of his shoulders, and the soft hair on his chest.

Amy came out of her trance of pleasure. They were both breathing raggedly and unevenly. Her leg was across his lap and she could feel the throbbing hardness of him through his buckskins as he shifted her leg to bring it up hard against him.

"Oh, darling! I've loved you for so long . . ." She scarcely realized she had whispered the words.

"You do this to me every time I kiss you," he said simply, his voice a breath in her ear. His hand cupped her breast, his mouth opened over her lips, raking his teeth over their soft generous curves. The kiss fanned the flame of passion that burned in his loins and threatened to blaze out of control. She was his. This lovely, long length of strong yet soft woman was his. He liked everything about her body; her small rounded breasts, her smooth belly, her firm buttocks, her beautiful amber eyes. He felt that he knew her mind, her soul, her spirit as he had known no person other than himself. She had never known the touch of another man, and he vowed that as long as he lived she would be his alone. The thought sent a quiver of desire through him.

This feeling of tenderness was new to Rain. It was an emotion he had not felt before, and he wasn't sure how to express it. He could only stroke the hair back from her face

with unsteady fingers and kiss her lips time and again. A
fierce desire to protect her came over him, and without real-
izing it his arms tightened until she could scarcely breathe.
Here in his arms was more than he had ever dreamed of
having. He wanted to take her immediately, thrust himself
into her woman's body, satisfy the hunger that gnawed at
him and mark her as his own. But he knew that he couldn't
do that here. Reason dissolved the hunger that tormented
him. She was too precious to him, too virginal and sweet.
He wanted them both to taste the full pleasure of their mat-
ing. He pulled away from her, moved her leg from his lap
and concentrated on trying to ease the ragged gasps that
served as breathing.

"Rain?"

He knew she didn't understand why he had put her away
from him. He lifted her face with a finger beneath her chin.
Their eyes locked, hers moist with confusion, his tender.

"Are you mine, Amy?" he asked softly.

"I've always been... yours." Her fingertips gently
stroked his jaw, his cheek, the hair at his temple.

"I think I've always known that."

His words echoed to the very core of her being. She summoned all her determination to ask what she had to know.
Her voice came out thin and weak.

"Do you ... love me?"

He didn't answer for such a long while that her eyes wavered beneath the intensity of his. Her lower lip quivered
and, as she stared up at him, tears welled in her eyes. He
lifted a finger and wiped away a teardrop that trickled slowly
down her cheek.

"Ahh, don't cry. I'm not much for words, and I'm trying
to think of the right ones to say."

"All you have to say is yes or ... no."

"It isn't that easy. I don't know exactly what love is. I've
never used the word. I *like* things. I like the forest, the river,

the mountains. I like to see young deer sailing over a dead-fall, and I like taking a bath in a cool mountain stream. I like Farr and Libby—"

"Then . . . you *like* me?" The words came out, and on the heels of them a sob in spite of all she could do to hold it back.

"Please don't cry, sweetheart. It tears me up!" His hand cupped her cheek, his lips sipped the tears from her eyes. "I think I've always known that there was a link between us. Christmas night when I saw you standing in the doorway, I had such a strange, peaceful feeling. It was as if I had finally come home, not home to Farr's house, but really come home." He kissed her forehead. "You have seeped into my soul—that's what John Spotted Elk used to say to my mother. When I think that something could happen and you could be taken from me, I feel this terrible dread weighing me down so that I can hardly breathe. If that's what loving is, then I must love you very much."

Amy was quiet for the space of a dozen heartbeats. Then she was smiling through her tears, her eyes like amber stars shining up at him.

"You make me so mad! Why did it take you so damn long to say it?"

Then she was on her knees in front of him, her arms tight about his neck. She placed her lips on his, lightly at first, then with harder, deeper kisses. She kissed his eyes, his nose, his chin, then held his face to her breast.

"Whoa, now," he chortled happily when she turned and sat down on his lap. "I can't start kissing you again. I won't be able to stop with just a few kisses." He lifted her off his lap, sat her down beside him and tucked her shoulder beneath his. His fingers closed around the softness of her breast as if he had to touch her. "It's a damn good thing you're wearing the buckskins. I'm having a hard time keeping my hands off you."

She untied the belt at her waist, grasped his hand and slipped it under her shirt. His fingers quickly found the soft, warm flesh of her breast and closed around it possessively. A thrill tingled through her and she heard his quick intake of breath.

"Darling . . . am I too bold?" she whispered, her mouth open and warm against his neck.

"Ahh . . ." His palm rubbed her nipple, his fingers cupped and squeezed. His palm went to caress her other breast, then to the smooth satin plane of her belly; his wandering hand caressed as it explored. Her skin was the softest thing he had ever touched. "Too bold? Hell, no!"

"I like it when you touch me."

"I want to touch every inch of you, but . . . I can't now."

"Why not? I'm yours . . . and I want you to."

"It's too dangerous here. Someone could slip up on us."

"The frogs are still croaking."

"If they stopped I'd never know it." He pulled his hand from beneath her shirt, tucked the blanket around her and held her close to his side. "I can wait. When we mate I want it to be slow and last a long time. I want to look my fill at all that you hide beneath your shirt and britches. I'm going to look into your eyes when I'm fully joined with you and know that you're truly mine and that I'm yours." He said the words so solemnly that they were like marriage vows. "I may never get enough of your sweet body," he whispered raggedly.

"I hope not." She nipped his neck gently. "You said you didn't know pretty words," she teased. "Those were the most beautiful words I've ever heard."

"I wasn't trying to make them pretty. I just wanted you to know how I feel."

"I'm proud that you . . . want me that way."

"Once I have you, I fear I'll be as lusty as a bull moose in season."

"You don't scare me a bit." He hugged her close, laughed softly and she added, "You didn't laugh when you were at Quill's Station."

"No, I didn't," he admitted. "I guess I didn't have anything to laugh about."

They sat quietly, Rain's back against the trunk of the aspen, Amy's head on his shoulder. Time assumed a dreamlike quality. No unnatural noise intruded on their privacy, and the moments were filled with the simple pleasure of being together. The past hour had been utter bliss for them both, an almost surreal interlude. Rain had never loved, felt, enjoyed so deeply before. He had never been so intensely alive as he was when he held Amy in his arms, and he knew that she was giving herself to him openly and honestly.

Such an excess of happiness, he mused thoughtfully, came to only a few men. He thanked God that he was one of the lucky ones.

CHAPTER
Thirteen

The hour before dawn is the darkest, the stars their brightest. In the quiet of the morning, when the furred and feathered creatures are asleep in the forest, the slightest sound is obvious.

Rain's soft whisper brought Amy out of a sound sleep. Instantly alert, she sat up on her pallet and reached for her clothes. She dressed quickly and left the wagon. Rain loomed noiselessly out of the darkness. She strained her eyes to see his face.

A hand on her shoulder, he whispered, "We're about ready to move out. Gavin is hitching up. You drive. I'll be ahead, Gavin behind. Be as quiet as you can."

She drew back from him, looking up. His face was almost visible now. His arms drew her to him again, and he kissed her gently. They held each other for a few seconds, enjoying being close.

When Rain left her, Amy reached into the wagon for her powder flask and shot bag. She hung them over her shoulder and picked up her rifle. When she climbed up on the wagon wheel, she was surprised to see Eleanor sitting on the seat wrapped in a dark shawl, her white face a blur in the darkness. Neither woman spoke. Amy placed her rifle on the floor at her feet and took the reins when Gavin brought them to her.

Rain led them steadily along a narrow track. The only sound was that of the wagon rolling and the muffled sound of horses' hooves on the leaf-strewn floor of the forest. Black wilderness surrounded them as they moved through the nighttime of morning. Amy held her eyes wide open so she could see Rain's shadowy figure ahead. Soon she realized he was circling the town. After a tense time the eastern sky began to lighten and the houses in town took shape. Here and there faint lights shone from windows.

As they neared the river the air Amy pulled through her nostrils was damp and cool. She was too tense to realize fully she was about to cross the mighty river that separated east from west. For years she had heard Farr talk about the land west of the river. Now that she was about to go there, all she could think about was Rain ahead of them and the men out there who did not want them to cross.

They reached the river in the gray light of morning. A man came from one of the flatboats tied to the quay and spoke briefly to Rain. Gavin rode up to the side of the wagon.

"I'll drive it on, lass. Jump down and hold the horses."

Amy took the reins of Gavin's mount and untied hers from the end of the wagon. She moved the animals out of the way as the riverman and Rain tried to calm the frightened, balky mules and lead them on to the boat. The hollow sound their hooves made on the thick plank seemed to frighten them all the more. Only Gavin's strong hands on the reins kept them from bolting.

Amy was so intent on holding the dancing horses and watching the wagon being loaded that at first she didn't notice the rider racing his mount down the road toward the quay. Then she heard someone shouting her name.

"Miss Amy! Miss Amy!"

Amy was stunned when she recognized the rider. But not so stunned that her mind didn't register the curses that came from Rain's lips.

Tally Perkins slid his mount to a stop and jumped off.

"Rain," he shouted. "Ya gotta hurry!" Tally had lost his hat. His white-blond hair stood out on his head like a pile of straw.

"What the... Hell! What are you doing here?" Rain's angry voice boomed in the quiet of the morning.

"Men are comin' from the tavern. They're goin' to keep you from crossing," Tally gasped. "Hurry 'n cast off."

"How many?"

"Ten or more."

"Tie your horse if you're going to cross and help with these mules." Rain issued the crisp command and hurried to help Amy load the horses.

Tally and the boatman led the stumbling, frightened team on to the flat-bottomed boat. As soon as they were aboard, Gavin jumped down. He and Tally tied them to a stout post while the boatman cast off the ropes holding the boat to the dock. Gavin grabbed a pole to help push the heavily laden craft out into the river current.

"Lash down the wagon," the boatman shouted. "Poke a timber in the back of the wheels to keep 'er from rollin'."

Rain and Tally jumped to obey. They tied down the wagon and then grabbed poles to help push the boat away from the quay.

Everyone seemed to have forgotten about Eleanor who sat on the wagon seat, rigid with fear.

"Get down off there," Amy ordered sharply. Eleanor didn't move or answer, just looked at her as if she didn't see her. Amy climbed up on the wheel, grasped her arm and shook her. "Get off, damn you! If that wagon tips over you'll go with it."

"I'm . . . scared."

"Who isn't? Now get off. No one has time to mess with you, damn it." Eleanor stood and backed down over the wheel with Amy guiding her feet. When her feet felt the solid plank floor, she stood with her hands gripping the wagon wheel as if she were holding on to a life raft. Amy pried her hands loose and pushed her beneath the wagon. "Stay there. I've got to see about the horses."

Amy moved among the nervous horses, crooning, soothing, patting and stroking. The animals calmed.

Angry shouts came from a group of men running toward the quay. All four men on the boat put their backs to the poles and their combined strength moved it out from the bank. They were a dozen yards out on the river when the first shot was fired. Amy heard the impact as the bullet hit the water a yard to the side of the boat. Water fowl along the river rose with a great flapping of wings and fanned out in the sky overhead. The next shot hit the hull of the vessel, and the next one went into the head of the horse Amy was holding. The animal went down heavily, causing the boat to rock from side to side.

"Amy!" Rain shouted. "Get down! Get behind the horses."

Two more shots were fired that didn't come close to the cumbersome craft.

"I'll get ya, ya rat eatin' sons of bitches!" the boatman shouted. "Afore the summer's out ever' blasted one a ya'll get a pike in yore belly fer firin' on Red Cavanaugh!"

Another shot was fired. The bullet zipped into the water a dozen feet from the boat.

"Ye can't shoot no better'n ye can fight, bully-boy," Gavin shouted, and shook his fist at the man he had fought the night before and at the boy, Muley, who had tried to stab him in the back.

"Tell Perry ta send *men* next time he wants a job done right. Ya ain't nothin' but river trash standin' on the bank beggin' fer a handout from that cocky chinless bastard." The burly boatman was of undetermined age. He had a red beard, sparse red hair, and shouted his taunts in a deep booming voice. "Shit eatin' thieves! Whore's sons! Lazy, shore huggin' bastards! What ya agoin' to do now? Haw! Haw! Haw!"

The swifter current caught the boat and spun it halfway around. One of the frightened mules tried to buck. His fore-feet slashed at the floor of the craft.

"Get a sledge," Red shouted as he grabbed the steering oar. "Knock that mule in the head if he tries to break loose. He'll turn us over sure as hell!"

"Ye best do it, hoe-man," Gavin said to Tally. "Ye be knowin' more 'bout mules, 'n I be knowin' more 'bout boats."

Tally pulled his pole and went to the mules, making a wide loop around Rain. He hadn't counted on his anger. He had known that Amy would be madder than a stepped-on snake because he had tailed after her. The first thing that struck him when he arrived at the boat was that Rain was the one to fear. The way he had looked at him was scary! Tally almost wished he hadn't come.

The muscles of Gavin's big arms and those of Rain's stood out as they braced their feet and strained on the poles to bring the boat around so the current could grab it. Soon they were moving downriver and angling toward the western shore and the river was too deep for the poles. From there on they had to trust to the current and steering oar.

Gavin checked the ropes holding the wagon and the timbers behind the wheels. He bent to peer beneath the wagon where Eleanor was huddled.

"Be ye all right, lass?" Eleanor was so frightened that she had been sick. She looked at him with shamed eyes and little whimpering sounds came from her lips. She reached out a hand to him and he took it in his. "Ye've naught to fear now, lassie. We be across soon, 'n the devils won't be catchin' us."

"I'm sorry. . ." Her eyes flicked to the floor where the contents of her stomach had spewed from her mouth. "I was so scared."

"I been just that scared, lass. I been on the water more'n ten year, 'n if there be one thing I know tis rivers. I be lettin' no harm come to ye." Gavin looked around when the boat-man shouted, then turned back to Eleanor. "Stay here. Hold to the wheel so I be knowin' where ye be."

"The bush-bottomed sons a bitches is puttin' out to come after us." The boatman stood at the end of his craft and shook his fists at the objects of his anger.

"Do we have a chance of outrunning them?" Rain asked.

"None a'tall, mon. They be sittin' high in the water." Gavin spoke to the boatman. "Keep steady to the course. I know me a trick or two 'bout boat fightin'."

"We've got five rifles, counting Amy's, and one pistol. They've got twice that."

"Look what they be carryin', mon." Gavin's face creased with a lopsided grin, because of his cut, swollen lips. "Tis fer Perry's fancy horses I be thinkin'. Do ye still have the bow and them arrows about ye?"

"I see what you mean." Rain studied the boat, then cast the big man an admiring glance. "It was good of them to pick *that* boat." He pulled out his knife and shaved some thin slices of wood from the wagon box. "Get the iron kettle, Amy. We're going to build us a little fire. We'll use this and whatever else we can find that will burn."

"I've got a little kindling in the cook box. I always carry some."

"Good. Get it. Do you have any animal fat?"

"I've got that too. Libby put in a crock of lard."

Gavin reached under the wagon and pulled Eleanor out. She stood, swaying on unsteady legs and holding on to him.

"Buck up, lassie. We be needin' yer help. Get us some cloth. Some that'll burn fast. Hurry now." He picked her up and set her inside the back of the wagon.

Rain started the fire in the kettle with a small amount of gunpowder and the paper-thin shavings. Amy stood over it, shielding it from the wind and feeding it small pieces of kindling. She still did not know what was planned until Rain reached into a compartment beneath the wagon and drew out a bow and a quiver of arrows. He made small bundles out of the cloth Eleanor provided and tied them to the tips of six arrows. Amy dipped them carefully into the grease, coating them on all sides.

The other boat with a thick layer of straw on the deck and a pile on each end was rapidly reducing the distance between them. A score of men lay flat on their bellies with rifles ready, waiting to get within firing range.

"Stay where ye be," Gavin said when Eleanor attempted to get out of the wagon. "Lie down flat. The sideboards'll protect ye."

"Get in the wagon with Eleanor, Amy," Rain said without looking at her.

"No. I can shoot."

"Goddamn it! Don't argue. Do as I say!"

"You need my gun, Rain."

"I want you safe!"

"Miss Amy can shoot better'n anybody at Quill's Station, ceptin' Farr," Tally said.

"Don't be telling me what to do about Amy!" Rain snarled. The quelling look he gave Tally sent him scurrying back to the mules.

"I'll stay behind the horses. Don't—"

A shot fired from the other boat interrupted her words. The shot fell short, but Amy took advantage of the diversion and moved away quickly.

"Don't be wastin' a shot," Gavin advised from where he crouched beside the heavy post that held the wagon in place. "Can ye be shootin', Red?"

"As soon's I get them bastards in my sight."

"Aye. Hold yer fire, hoe-boy," Gavin called to Tally. "Wait till the mon lays down a flame, then shoot the ones tryin' to douse it."

From her position behind the horses, Amy watched Rain. He wet his finger and held it up to test the wind. He was watching the other boat approach, judging the distance between them. He looked over his shoulder to where she was standing. Their eyes met. She nodded and smiled, then looked back down the long barrel of her rifle that lay on the back of her horse.

No one spoke while they waited, letting the shots from the oncoming boat tell them when they were close enough for Rain to use the bow. When one of the shots came to within a few feet of the boat, he dipped the greased rag into the fire. It burst into flame. He fitted the arrow to the bow and stepped from behind the wagon. With his feet braced wide to steady himself, his powerful arm pulled back on the bow. When he released the flaming arrow, it arced in the sky over the water and then landed in the pile of straw on the stern of the boat. Gavin gave a triumphant shout and a volley of shots followed. Rain touched another torch to the fire in the kettle and sent it toward the boat with the same accuracy as before.

A volley of shots kept the rivermen from getting to the blazing straw. Rain's third arrow landed at the other end of the boat. The men were caught between two fires. Some tried to kick the burning straw off into the water. Amy's shot hit one in the leg and he tumbled into the muddy river. A small explosion of gunpowder sent sparks flying, causing more fires.

Suddenly Perry's henchmen ceased firing altogether and scrambled madly to get away from the flames that traveled the length of the boat. One man's clothing caught fire. He yelled and jumped into the river. Another was knocked overboard by a man trying to escape the flames.

Two more of Rain's blazing arrows found their mark. The burning straw sent up a cloud of black smoke that hung over the river before drifting toward shore. Small explosions were heard as the flames reached abandoned powder flasks. Yelling and cursing, the men, one by one, abandoned the boat and jumped into the river.

"Red! Wait! We give . . . up!"

"Give up what? Give up yore whorin' 'n drinkin'? Ya ain't got nothin' to whore with nohow, Bull," Red shouted with laughter. "I hope to hell ya drown. Ya ain't nothin' but rotten, stinkin' fish bait. If'n ya don't drown, or the snakes don't get ya, tell Perry that Red Cavanaugh ain't takin' kindly to bein' run off by the likes a him. I be back, by God! I be back with a full crew a cutthroats to stomp his ass!"

"I can't swim, Red!"

"Then drown, ya bastard."

"'Tis the law of the river—"

"Law, hell! Ya don't know law from a pile a horse shit!"

"I ain't forgettin' this."

"Ya will if'n ya drown or get snakebit. Haw! Haw! Haw!"

"Ya son of a bitch."

"Ya took the bastard's coin ta ruin me, Bull. Oh . . . looky there! Ain't that a water moccasin comin' at ya? Haw! Haw! Haw!" The boatman stomped his foot and roared with laughter at the way the men in the river tried to dodge a stick floating toward them.

Rain dipped a can of water from the river and put out the fire in the kettle. He glanced at Amy sitting on the floor cleaning her rifle. Juicy's teachings, he mused. When she finished cleaning, she reloaded and placed the rifle beneath the wagon seat once again. He watched her make her way around the mules to where Tally Perkins stood. Rain wondered if she had known Tally was going to follow them. He regretted now that he hadn't gone into Perkins' camp that first night and told him to keep his distance. But he hadn't known it was Tally Perkins. He never saw the man's face clearly. More than likely he'd been the one prowling around the cabin last night trying to have a private word with Amy.

"Tally, I want to know why in the world you followed me. Did Papa send you?" Amy was angry and she wanted him to know it. Her voice wasn't loud, but cold and impatient.

"No, Miss Amy. I . . . just wanted to come." The cowlike expression of devotion on his broad face made her cringe with embarrassment for him.

"Why didn't you speak to Rain before we left home instead of sneaking along behind?"

"He wouldn't of let me."

"Oh, for God's sake! You're so used to knuckling under to your mother you don't have any confidence at all. I'm surprised she let you come and more surprised that you got here without someone killing you for your horse and gun."

"I didn't tell her."

"You didn't tell her?" There was silence. "You've never done anything in your life without asking her," Amy said bitingly.

"I didn't tell her," Tally repeated firmly. Then, in tones of anguish, he said, "I knew I'd not ever see you again, Miss Amy. I had to come."

"Oh, Tally." Amy wasn't angry anymore. She just didn't know what to do. Her amber eyes studied Tally's face until he began to squirm.

"I ain't never goin' back!" he blurted. "I ain't *never* goin' back. Walter can farm for . . . him!"

Angry resentment flared in Tally's eyes. Amy knew he referred to her father. It occurred to Amy that the resentment had been there all the time, and he had not allowed himself to voice it. She felt a sudden wave of pity for all he had endured from her father and his mother. They had suffocated him, kept him on a tight leash and used him to work the farm. Amy doubted if Tally ever had a cent of his own in his life.

"I can't say that I blame you," Amy admitted finally. "I couldn't stand living with Elija, and he's my own father. I don't know how you've put up with him and your mother. I'll talk to Rain."

"Talk to me about what?" Rain was behind her, his hand at the nape of her neck. Amy looked over her shoulder and saw that his dark eyes were fastened on Tally's face. Anger and resentment burned in them.

"Tally doesn't want to go back to the farm."

"What's that got to do with us?" Rain asked.

"You and Gavin talked about taking on another man to stand watch—"

"It won't be him," Rain said firmly. He then spoke to Tally. "I choose the men I want to join me. You're not trailing with us or behind us. I would have stopped you the first night, but I didn't know who you were. I figured you were so damn stupid someone would kill you before you got to Kaskaskia."

"You knew he was following us?" Amy asked quietly, trying to control her anger.

"I knew someone was. I checked on him at night."

Tally finally found his voice. "I wasn't agoin' to show myself, Miss Amy. But I heared them fellers talkin', sayin' they was to get the woman. They said she was the purtiest woman they'd ever saw. I knew that had to be you, Miss Amy." His voice wavered, but a look of determination settled on his face. "I wasn't agoin' to let no hurt come to you."

Amy's face reddened. "They weren't talking about me. They were talking about Miss Woodbury."

Tally's eyes left Amy's face reluctantly and went to Eleanor. A frown drew his brows together over the bridge of his nose. He moved his head from side to side in denial.

"No. They was talkin' about you. You're lots purtier than she is."

"Oh, for goodness sake!"

"We appreciate your warning," Rain said. "But we'd have made out all right. When we land, you can take the north trail to Saint Genevieve and cross there or stay and find work in the lead mines. Either way, it's up to you."

Amy looked from Tally's worried face to Rain's stern features. "You can't send him off, Rain."

"I can and I will."

"But he knows nothing about working in the lead mines. He knows nothing but farming."

"I doubt if any of the men knew how to mine before they went to the mines."

"But he doesn't know how to . . . take care of himself."

Amy's words whipped Rain's anger into a rage. His eyes became as hard as steel, and the hand at the nape of her neck fell away.

"It seems goddamn strange to me that you're concerned about whether or not he can take care of himself." His voice was cold, his face remote.

"Why is it strange? I've known him as long as I've known you."

"And perhaps better, eh?"

Amy recoiled. For an instant she was stunned by his viciousness.

"Now you're being stupid." She tried to firm her quivering voice. Rain looked at her with unfathomable eyes and didn't speak. She tried reason. "I feel responsible for him. He wouldn't live to get to Saint Genevieve."

For a terrible space of time Rain was quiet. "Maybe you want to go with him and take care of him." His lips barely moved when he spoke. His voice was nasty and blistering.

"You . . . think that?" Amy almost strangled on the words. Rain looked at her with the blank stare she thought of as his Indian face. Hurt, anger and bewilderment surfaced in her amber eyes. Grim-faced and shaking with fury, she snarled, "Maybe I'll do just that, you . . . you dumb, bullheaded jackass!" She turned on her heel to walk away. Tally grabbed her arm.

"Miss Amy! Wait."

"Get your hands off me!" She slapped his hand from her arm. "And shut up! Just shut up!"

"What I said goes," Rain said after Amy left them. "You go your own way." He looked at Tally, and there was neither pity nor understanding in the glance. "From here on we travel fast and hard, and I carry no dead weight."

"I ain't got no quarrel with you." Tally's face was square and he had a square way of standing. There was a dumb animal patience in his eyes and in his voice.

"It's a damn good thing, because you'd not stand a chance. Take my advice and leave on your own. Amy is not for you."

"I know that I can't have her."

"That's right, you can't. Go back home." Rain left him and went to speak to the boatman.

Tally shook his head slowly, trying hard to understand something beyond his power. The only thing he had ever done on his own in all his twenty-two years was saddle up and ride away from the farm without first getting permission from his mother. It had taken all the courage he could muster. The thought that he might never see Amy again was what had goaded him to take the drastic action. He knew now that he could never have her. He had seen the way she looked at Rain, had seen Rain's hand on her neck beneath her hair. How could he ever hope to win her away from a man like Rain Tallman?

Amy was so steeped in her own misery that she didn't notice they were nearing the west bank of the river. She had seen the unyielding side of Rain before, so she wondered why she was so surprised by his cold treatment of Tally. His face was turned away from her now, but in her mind she could still see the wolfish snarl of his twisted mouth when he had said what he did about her going with Tally. She knew how unbending he was, and she burned with resentment for being placed in a situation not of her making.

The sun was up over the treetops when the front of the craft hit the heavy timbers of the dock with a jolt. Gavin and the boatman threw the thick ropes over the post and the boat stopped rocking. Amy untied her mount and moved it carefully around the dead horse. Rain was there, removing the saddle. He and Gavin, using the stout poles, rolled the dead animal off the boat and into the water, pushing it away from the dock and into the current.

The mules were untied and led up the short ramp to level ground. Amy followed leading her mount and Rain's.

"I'm obliged to you." Rain paid the boatman and shook his hand.

"I'm obliged back. Perry tried to have my boat burned fer holdin' out agin him. 'Stead, we burned his'n. I ain't never seen nobody but a Injun shoot a arrow like ya did."

"It was an Indian who taught me. Will you be able to get a crew here?"

The redheaded boatman looked over his shoulder. "Yeah. I'll pick up a couple."

Amy saw the leering looks Eleanor was getting from the disreputable wretches squatting in front of one of the three buildings that made up the landing settlement. This was a wild, rough land, and here were wilder and rougher men than she had ever known. Men lolled against the dock or sat in the dirt beneath the trees and, like the loafers in front of the building, watched and waited to see which direction the pilgrims would take. Amy's heart contracted painfully when she looked behind her and saw Tally standing beside his mount. He looked like a sheep among wolves.

She tied Rain's horse to the back of the wagon, mounted hers and rode back to Tally.

"What are you going to do, Tally?"

"I don't know, Miss Amy." He glanced at the men squatting in the dirt in front of the ramshackle building, then at the narrow trail that led north along the river.

"Come talk to Rain."

"No. I ain't abeggin'. I reckon I'll do what he says 'n try my hand at the mines."

"I can't go off and leave you here."

"There don't 'pear to be nothin' else you can do. I'm sorry if I gave you trouble. I never meant to. I sure never wanted Rain to be mad at you."

Rain rode up beside Amy. "Come on. I want to be rid of this place."

Amy looked at him for a long moment, then gigged her horse and rode to the front of the wagon.

"Give me my rifle, Gavin. It's under the seat." He handed the gun to her and she slid it into the holder on the saddle, reached into the back of the wagon for her powder flask and shot bag and hung them around her neck. She wheeled her horse and rode back toward Tally.

Rain moved his horse to block hers from reaching Tally. "I don't like the looks of this place. If we stay here much longer there'll be trouble. We're moving out. Now."

"Then go. I don't like the looks of it, either. I'm riding north to Saint Genevieve with Tally. I'll catch up."

A look of stunned disbelief came over Rain's face. "You'll do no such thing!"

"I'll do as I damn well please. You know as well as I do that Tally wouldn't get a mile from here before one of them," she jerked her head toward the loafers in front of the building, "killed him for his horse."

"Do you think you could stop it?"

"I know damn well I could. You don't have any confidence in me either. You still don't think I can take care of myself, do you?"

"Goddamn it! You don't have to take care of yourself. That's my job." His dark eyes, bright with anger, raked her face and his nostrils flared. Rain's fury was real. Amy had never seen him display such anger. Violence smoldered in his eyes. The tension in him was so strong that she was shaking from the impact of it. Still, she was determined not to back down.

"Mount up, Tally. Let's go. I'll catch up with you before night, Rain."

"Damn you to hell!" Rain directed his anger at Tally. His voice was cold. "You stupid son of a bitch. Every man in this place will be hot on your trail as soon as you leave here. Look at them! They're interested. They know she's a woman and because she's wearing britches they think she's as common as a brothel bitch. They're waiting to see what she's going to do. As soon as she leaves here, they'll be after her like a fish after bait. Do you want her raped by that bunch?"

"I . . . I ain't asked her to go," Tally stammered.

"Stop blaming Tally. I'm perfectly capable of deciding things for myself." Amy stared unblinkingly at him, seeing what her actions had wrought in him and not letting it deter her. "Come on, Tally." She wheeled her mount. Rain jumped his in front of her and grabbed the thin leather strap of the bridle.

"You knew I'd back down if you threatened to go off with

him, didn't you? You were right. I'll back down. He can come with us. But I'm warning you, he'll crack when things get tough. When that happens I'll dump him as if he were so much worthless baggage. Understand?"

"What about me? If I crack will you also dump me as so much worthless baggage? I didn't realize you chose your *friends* by how useful they were to you. Tally and I will do our share of the work, and we'll be no burden to you."

For a long moment their eyes locked—blazing amber burning into dark fire. His hand left the bridle and closed tightly about her wrist and lifted it up between them. She resisted the pull with all her strength.

"I've never laid a rough hand on a woman before, but by God, you're tempting me to beat you!" His voice quivered and his jaws snapped shut when he finished speaking.

"Don't try it. You might find me a bit harder to handle than Eleanor."

Amy looked Rain full in the face. It was a face she didn't know, a dark face turned livid with tight-lipped fury. Silence swirled around them as their eyes battled. Color drained from her cheeks, but she looked steadily at him and waited for him to make a move. His hand fell away from her wrist and he moved his mount back.

"Move out. We've attracted enough attention here." His voice was low, heavy, almost tired.

Amy was free of his grasp, but not the aura of anger that surrounded him like a heavy fog. She turned her mount and followed him, knowing that Tally followed her. She closed her eyes and gripped the saddle horn. Her breasts rose with a slow, indrawn breath. She felt sick.

The happiness of the night before seemed a dream to her now. She asked herself if she would ever understand this man who could be so sweet and gentle one day and so stubborn and vicious the next.

CHAPTER
Fourteen

It was almost noon. The sick feeling in the pit of Rain's stomach was still there. It had lain there since early morning. The fear he had felt when the horse Amy was holding was shot had unnerved him to the point that he had been unsure about his ability to shoot the fire arrows. He had had to put the thought from his mind that a mere few feet separated her from the bullet that went into the horse's head.

Now he wondered if that was the reason he had been so angry about Tally Perkins. Perkins wasn't much of a man. If he were he would have come right out and asked to join them. Instead he had sneaked along behind, probably hoping Amy would take pity on him, Rain thought irritably. He would do just as he had said if Perkins didn't measure up. This wasn't the trip to break in a new trail hand.

Another thought came to Rain that irritated him even more. He remembered his stepfather, John Spotted Elk, saying that a woman needed taming like a horse. Keep a strong hand on the bridle, pet them a little, and they would not mind the halter. But let them get the bit in their teeth and they would make a man miserable and themselves too. He had let Amy have her way this time against his better judgment. It was not a good way to start their life together.

They had not stopped since leaving the ramshackle settlement by the river where they had landed. Rain wanted to put as many miles as he could between his group and that place. The settlement was the hangout of raiders and thieves who had been run out of Saint Genevieve. He had been through it a few times on his way to the thriving mining town. The town had over three hundred houses, an academy, and eight or ten stores. The whole region was not in very good repute. Workmen from the lead mines were continually engaged in brawls and proprietors were frequently at odds. Nearly everyone carried a concealed dagger, sometimes two, while others wore a brace of pistols. Lawyers, boatmen, merchants, officers in civil and military authority, and river pirates all mixed at candlelighting time. One of the leading amusements of this wild, half-savage wilderness population was shooting at each other with rifles and pistols, or pinning an ear to the wall with a stiletto.

The trail Rain took south ran back from the river among trees with lofty limbs meeting overhead so that the sun came through in small, scattered patches. The floor of the forest was thickly bedded with old leaves and there was no undergrowth. They passed through quietly, but overhead the trees were noisy with brilliant, chattering parakeets. Rain led his party out of the forest and turned west, heading for the hilly country. He stopped at a spring that seeped out of a rocky bluff.

"We'll noon here," he said to Gavin.

The day had grown hotter by the hour, but here the air was surprisingly cool. The faint breeze smelled of pines and cedars, and Amy saw them scattered among the hickory, elm and a few types of shrub she had never seen before. To the west were the first of the low, rounded hills that gradually became higher, knobbier and rougher.

Amy handed the reins of her horse over to Tally when he reached for them. She occasionally watched him as she gathered wood for a small, quick fire. He was good with animals and seemed to be anxious to make himself useful. Even the balky mules obeyed him. He led the horses and mules to water and then tied them so they could graze on the tender grass.

Rain saw to his own horse and then, without a word, took up his rifle. In a few noiseless strides he disappeared. Feeling utterly miserable, Amy watched him leave. After relieving her aching bladder behind the bushes and washing at the spring, she returned to camp to start a small fire next to the bluff, using hickory because it made a thin smoke. The fact that Rain had ignored both her and Tally since leaving the settlement was making her sick inside. She tried desperately to pull her thoughts off her disappointment when Eleanor came to the fire with the big teakettle.

"Tell me what to do." The request was low and hesitant.

Amy took off her hat and rubbed the sleeve of her shirt across her forehead to cover her surprise. The open, honest look in Eleanor's eyes was also a surprise. Her hair was braided in Indian fashion, and the long ropes hung down over her chest. To Amy she was even more beautiful than when she wore it high and puffed. Her soft, white shirt was open at the neck and the sleeves were rolled up past her elbows. The toes of sturdy shoes showed beneath her dark skirt. It seemed to Amy that Eleanor had finally adapted to the trail. And she looked years younger.

"Amy? Gavin says I must help. And . . . I really want to."

"I'll be glad for your help. Two of us can get the meal ready much faster than one. Fill the kettle with water for tea while I cook the meat."

Eleanor hurried to the spring, walking around Gavin and Tally who squatted on their heels beside the wagon, looking closely at one of the rear wheels.

"Another day is about all the wheels can take without grease," Tally said.

Gavin had been watching the scene between Amy and Eleanor and was relieved to see Amy accept Eleanor's help. He saw Eleanor hurrying to the spring and tried to bring his attention back to what Tally was saying.

"I'll work on them tonight."

"Is that the truth, now? I don't be knowin' much about wagons and such."

"That's all I do know—wagons, mules and farming," Tally said wistfully.

"Ye'll be learnin' fast enuff. Rain's a good man, fer all his gruff ways. His job is to take the lassie to Belle Point. Tis rough land ahead. Ye was wrong not to be askin' to join afore we left Quill's."

"I know that now."

"It rankles him that his woman went against him. I can't be sayin' that I blame him. Twas shamed, he was."

"I never wanted to cause trouble for Miss Amy—"

"Tis done, lad. Ye do as the mon says if ye be wantin' to keep body 'n soul together."

Gavin's eyes strayed from Tally's worried face to Eleanor coming from the spring with the kettle. His eyes feasted on her face. The sun, coming through the foliage of the trees, fell directly on her head. Her hair had broken loose from the braids and was flying around her face. She pushed it from her white cheek with the back of her hand. Her eyes were on the ground, her lower lip caught firmly between her teeth.

As she neared, Gavin reluctantly turned his eyes away, not wanting her to see him watching. He cursed himself as a fool for allowing the warm feeling of joy to come over him when he looked at her. He hired on to take her to another man, he told himself sternly. On the heels of that thought came another. In the next few weeks he would have to store up enough sweet memories to last a lifetime.

Eleanor was awkward around the campfire, but she was willing help. Amy showed her how to stir up a batch of cornpone, wet it with spring water and spoon it into the hot grease after she lifted out the strips of meat. When the meal was ready the four of them ate it and drank the strong tea with hardly a word passing between them.

Nooning over, they prepared to move out. Rain had not returned. Amy wrapped a plate of food in a cloth and set it beneath the wagon seat. Gavin tied Rain's horse to the back of the wagon.

"Are we going without Rain?" Eleanor asked.

"Aye. Tis what he said to do."

Gavin didn't offer to help Eleanor climb up over the wheel and into the wagon. He watched her make several attempts, then turned away and grinned in satisfaction when she finally hoisted herself up and onto the seat as Amy had done.

"We should have left his horse," Eleanor said to Amy as they moved out.

"He'll catch up."

"You don't sound worried."

Amy didn't answer. She found her throat dry and lumpy.

"I don't blame you for being scared."

"I'm not *scared!*"

"He was boiling mad this morning." Eleanor threw Amy a quizzical glance."

"He'll get over it."

"Gavin says Rain is the best scout in the territory. I think that if Rain didn't want Tally along, you should have left him. After all, you didn't ask him to come. Or did you?"

"I'm not interested in what you think, and I don't want to talk about it."

"He's handsome! Heavens! He's handsome!" Eleanor sighed deeply. "Dressed in the right clothes he'd have every woman in Charleston after him." She turned the full force of her violet eyes on Amy. "Gavin says you're in love with him."

"In love with Tally? Humph!"

"Not Tally." Eleanor laughed softly. "Who would look at *him* when Rain and Gavin are around? I mean Rain. Are you in love with him?"

Amy looked Eleanor full in the face, her eyes suddenly hard amber agates, her voice equally hard and full of impatience when she spoke. "I've loved Rain Tallman since I was a child. If you've got any notion of working your charms on him, you'd better think twice about it. I'll fight you in every dirty way I can think of, and believe me, Eleanor, I can think of plenty of ways to make your life miserable between here and Belle Point."

"If you want him you'd better change your ways." The words were spoken firmly but kindly. "You don't know much about men, or you'd not have made an open issue about Tally coming with us in front of all those men at the settlement."

"I love Rain, but I don't kowtow to everything he says. He was wrong about Tally."

"You should have gone about it differently. There are ways of working things around so that a man thinks what *you* want was his idea to begin with."

"If you want us to get along, Eleanor, I suggest you tend to your own business."

"Don't be mad at me, Amy. I couldn't have Rain if I wanted him. Oh, I tried. I tried real hard on the way to Quill's Station. He looked right through me with those black eyes of his, as if he knew exactly what I was trying to do. I knew then that his heart belonged to someone else. It made me mad at first. I saw you and I thought, why her? What was it about you that was more desirable?" Eleanor laughed. "I'm glad now that he turned me down. You may not believe it, Amy, but I've not been turned down often. A man is more exciting if you *can't* twist him around your little finger."

"Exciting? Is that what you think love is?"

"Sure. Do you feel excited when you look at Tally? He looks at you as if he could melt and run all over the floor. Flitter! He'd lie down and let you walk on him or stick his hand in the fire to please you. Does that excite you? It's disgusting is what it is. Rain wouldn't tail after a woman who didn't want him, although I can't imagine a woman who wouldn't," she added with a giggle. "Rain calls the shots. He's a man, a real man, like Gavin."

"Speaking of Gavin. Don't be practicing your witchcraft on him, either." Amy spoke sharply.

"Do you want him too?" Eleanor's eyes narrowed curiously as she took in Amy's set features.

"Don't be foolish. I *like* Gavin. I don't want him heartbroken when you're handed over to Will Bradford."

"Gavin won't be heartbroken. He'll be glad to be rid of me. He thinks I'm utterly useless. He told me so."

"Not *utterly* useless," Amy said cynically. "Gavin has urges like any other man."

"He's not even hinted at such a thing," Eleanor said heatedly.

"He pinched you on the bottom, didn't he?"

"That was different. I'd been . . . hateful."

"Farr says reformed rogues make the best family men. Gavin's brawled up and down the river all his adult life. The only home he has ever known has been keelboats and taverns. When he settles down I hope he can find a woman who'll stand by him, give him a family, help him put down roots on some land. He needs to have a place to call his own and a woman who loves him above all else."

"You've got him all figured out, haven't you?"

"One thing about riding all day," Amy said thoughtfully, "it gives you time to think. You might try it, Eleanor."

"You don't think much of me, do you?" Eleanor asked, then went on without waiting for Amy's answer. "I guess I don't blame you. I've *been* thinking. Gavin is right. I'm useless. I can't think of one thing I can do better than you."

"With your looks you don't have to *do* anything," Amy mumbled.

"I used to think that," Eleanor said slowly. "All my life I've been used as a decoration. I didn't have to do anything but sit and be pretty and use nice manners. Aunt Gilda used to say the younger and more helpless I pretended to be, the more men would want to take care of me. It certainly didn't work with Rain . . . or Gavin."

An hour passed, then another. Amy squinted her eyes under the lowered hat brim and studied the terrain, trying to put thoughts of Rain in the back of her mind. The trail ran alongside a stand of trees so thick she could see into it for no more than ten feet. To the left was a meadow of rye grass. A flock of crows came and settled in the trees ahead, the sun shining on their blue-black wings, their noisy chatter breaking the silence.

Amy remembered Juicy telling her to watch the birds and they would tell her what was up ahead. He had said that the gathering of crows meant something nearby was dead or dying. She refused to let herself think the flock of cawing crows had anything to do with Rain, even though he had been gone for more than three hours.

When the shot sounded, the crows rose noisily from the treetops, clapped their wings and soared away like a drifting black cloud.

Amy sucked in a sharp breath and held it until her tortured lungs released it in short puffs. She thought her heart would choke her or stop thumping and never start again. The sound had come from the dense woods ahead and to the right.

Gavin stopped. Amy pulled the mules to a halt. They waited, but heard no other sound. Gavin gave the signal for them to wait and rode to the crest of the hill. At the top he took off his hat and waved for them to join him. Ten long minutes dragged by while the mules pulled the wagon up the hill. Finally they topped the rise and Amy could see what was ahead.

Relief washed over Amy like a warm tide when Rain came out of the woods to speak to Gavin. To her dismay, she suddenly felt like crying and was terribly afraid she was going to. She swallowed and blinked her eyes rapidly. He was safe! Discomfort, anger and all else paled in comparison to the relief she felt seeing him standing there. Her eyes clung to his tall figure as the mules continued their slow plodding gait toward him. She thanked the Lord her weepy mood had drained away by the time the wagon reached him and she stopped the team.

After speaking to Gavin, Rain walked toward the wagon. Tally had moved up from behind and sat his horse close to Amy on the wagon seat, so that he was between her and Rain when he walked past to get his horse. If Rain even looked at her she was unaware of it. He mounted his horse and rode into the woods.

"Rain brought down fresh meat," Gavin called. "We'll keep on. He be catchin' up."

Tight-lipped, her anger stirred anew at Rain's indifference, Amy slapped the reins against the backs of the mules with unnecessary force and the wagon moved.

Some time later Tally rode up to tell her to stop because Rain wanted to load the carcass of a deer onto the back of the wagon. Amy pulled up on the reins but looked straight ahead when Rain rode past the wagon, not giving him a chance to snub her again.

The day got no better as it wore on; if anything, it got worse. The trail was rocky and fine particles of grit flung up by the mule's hooves hit them in the face. Amy's hands in the leather gloves were sweaty and took on weight until her arms felt as if each were holding a hundred pounds. The trail ran along the curve of a low hill that was covered with bright spring blossoms. To the north was a wide marshland of reed and bogs that stretched to the low foothills.

By late afternoon Amy's bottom was beginning to feel as if it were glued to the wagon seat. Eleanor seemed to be dozing. When the sunlight dimmed, she glanced up.

"Is it going to storm?" Eleanor asked before Amy could speak. Then she gasped. "Oh, my goodness! What is it?"

A vast cloud of birds came winging from the south. Possibly a late flock migrating north, Amy thought. She stared at the sky, darkened by the bodies of countless birds. A growing sound of beating wings rose to a loud crescendo when the flock neared. She barely heard Eleanor's repeated whimpers of fright as the dark-haired woman covered her face with her hands and cringed back against the canvas that covered the wagon bed.

"Passenger pigeons!" Amy yelled.

The frightened mules suddenly picked up speed. Amy held them with all her strength but couldn't slow them. Tally raced up from behind the wagon and threw himself onto one of the mules.

"Haw! Haw!" he shouted.

Tally hung on to the harness, his feet braced against the crosstree. The mules slowed to a stop but continued to dance nervously. He slipped to the ground and stood between them, holding them in check. Amy sighed with relief and let the reins fall loose in her hands.

When she and Liberty had first come to the Wabash, they had heard tales about the incredible flocks of passenger pigeons. At that time it was hard for her to believe the vast numbers that were reported. Now she realized they were true. The pigeons were said to be a scourge, worse than a swarm of locusts to the settlers in the midwest. They had been known to strip entire farms, eating crops and everything else edible in a matter of hours. When they roosted for the night they would occupy the trees in an area of ten square miles. Many branches would be found broken the next morning from the weight of perched birds who crowded too closely. Farmers shot down as many as they could for food, and stuffed their pillows and mattresses with the feathers. But beyond that, the winged destroyers meant only ruin to the struggling settlers.

Some of the birds began to dart down at whatever was edible in the marsh. Rain tied his mount to the back of the wagon and got out his rifle. His shot rang out as soon as a bird came within range. It dropped to the ground with dying squawks. Gavin went to fetch it. He came back dangling the bird by the legs. It was at least twenty inches long with a blue-gray back and a red breast. It had a black bill, bloodred eyes and bright red legs.

As more birds descended Rain shot again and again. By the time the flock had passed over, a dozen shots had felled a dozen birds. They were put on the tailgate of the wagon along with the deer carcass, and Rain gave the order to start moving again.

The sun was setting when they came to a small river and a cleared area in which crops were planted between the stumps of felled trees. The settler's home was a dugout in the side of a dirt hill. Amy knew that many settlers in their first years did not immediately build a cabin because it took too much time. It was simpler and easier to merely dig out a hollow in a convenient place and put up a log front to create a snug home that stayed warm in the winter.

Rain rode ahead to meet the farmer who stood in front of his home with a flintlock aimed at him. The burly man's head jutted forward. He shielded his eyes against the setting sun with a callused palm. When Rain drew near, he lowered the gun and gave a shout of welcome.

"By Gawd, Tallman. I ne'er knowed it was you. Ain't seen ya fer a good long spell."

"Howdy, Badker." Rain dismounted and shook the man's hand.

"I got to be knowin' visitors is friendly."

"Don't blame you at all. I was glad to see that flock of pigeons passed your place. I was afraid I'd find you picked clean."

"Me'n the woman was holdin' our breath fer fear they'd light. Thank the good Lord they kept agoin'. None came down fer me to even shoot at."

"We got a few. There's a mite more meat than we can use. We'd be glad for you to take it off our hands."

"We'd be obliged, if'n yo're sure it's more 'n ya can use up." Badker's eyes went past Rain to the wagon. "Ain't never knowed ya to be travelin' with folk, Tallman. It's what fooled me. They goin' to settle hereabouts?"

"No. They're going on south. How are the missus and the boys?"

"Fine. Fine. Tell the folks to light," Badker invited heartily. "I'll have the woman stir up some vittles."

"No need for that. We'll camp down there alongside the river. Here are a half dozen birds." Rain took them off the wagon and placed them on the ground. "I'll dress out the deer and leave some of it in the morning."

"Why, thanky. I'll hone up my knife 'n give ya a hand. Vonnie!" he shouted. "Come on out. Ya've pined ta jaw with womenfolk. Here's two of 'em."

The farmer pulled back the doeskin flap covering the door of the dugout. A woman came out. She was not pretty, but she was pleasant looking. Her dress was neat and clean and made of dyed butternut homespun. It was faded from many

washings, as was her husband's shirt and the clothing of the
two children that hung on her skirts. Her straight black hair
was crowned with a crisp, snow-white cap that was slightly
askew, as if put there hastily while the visitors approached.
She greeted Rain with a warm smile and shook his hand, but
her eyes strayed to Eleanor and Amy on the wagon seat.

Amy saw loneliness in the woman's eyes. During one of
the long hunting trips she made with Juicy, she had seen that
same look in the eyes of women who had spent months in a
cabin without seeing anyone other than their husbands and
children.

"Hello. I'm Amy, and this is Eleanor."

"I'm Vonnie." The woman came forward, the children behind her and still holding on to her skirt.

Amy climbed down from the wagon and shook the
woman's hand. "Who is this?" she asked and peeked around
at the small boy who hid his face quickly.

"Denny and young Bud." Vonnie pulled the children out
from behind her and commanded, "Say hello to the lady."
The boys were so bashful they would only peek at Amy and
then hide their faces.

"Hello, boys." Amy had a special fondness for children
and it showed when she was around them.

"They don't see many folks," Vonnie said apologetically.

"Would you like to ride down to the river?" Amy asked.

Both boys looked at their mother. When she smiled and
nodded their faces broke into grins.

"Will it be a bother?" Vonnie asked.

"Of course not."

Gavin had tied his horse to the back of the wagon. He
lifted first one boy and then the other up on the seat beside
Eleanor. He climbed up beside them.

"Ye want me to be takin' them down, Miss Amy?" he
asked after he was already on the seat.

"If you want to. I'll walk down."

Vonnie and Amy waved to the boys. Amy knew that Vonnie was talking to her about what a treat it was for the boys to ride in the wagon, but Amy's attention was on Rain. She had looked up to see him watching her. His face was grim and bleak. He caught Amy's eyes with his and held them. He didn't look away until Badker, coming from the dugout, was beside him, talking and proudly showing him a large whetstone.

Tally had dismounted and hovered anxiously near Amy, holding the reins of his horse.

"Go on down, Tally," Amy said. "I'll walk."

"Is he your man?" Vonnie asked after Tally left them.

"No. He's my father's stepson." Amy turned her face toward Vonnie and looked at the other woman. "Rain Tallman is my man."

Vonnie's eyes went to Rain, then back to Amy to study her face. She nodded her head as if pleased and smiled with her eyes as well as her mouth.

"You're a mate for him. He's pure hickory, that's certain. We set store by Mr. Tallman."

"Does he stop here often?"

"Not often. But one time he come in the nick of time. My man was down flat on his back. It was dead of winter 'n he'd been ailing for quite a spell. We'd had no meat for weeks 'n I had dragged in all the deadfalls I could handle to use for firewood. Mr. Tallman come by 'n stayed more 'n a week helpin' out. You got a good man, miss."

"I think so," Amy said softly and swallowed hard. She smiled at Vonnie with her lips, but her eyes remained cheerless. "I'd better go on down and start supper." Then on impulse she added, "Why don't you come down and eat with us? We have plenty."

"I'd like that. Me 'n the boys picked berries this morning 'n I made a berry cobbler. I'll bring it 'n milk to put on it.

Send the boys back so they can help me 'n an I can get 'em cleaned up."

"I'll send them back," Amy promised, and started down the path toward where the wagon had stopped beside the river.

"Wait, Amy." Rain came toward her leading his horse. "I'll give you a ride." He mounted and held out his hand. She grasped it to swing up behind him. "No. Up here," he said, and took his foot out of the stirrup.

When Amy put her foot where Rain's had been he grasped her beneath her arms and lifted her up to sit across his thighs. His arms went around her and he pulled her, none too gently, back against him. He touched his heels to the side of the horse and the big dun moved slowly down the path.

Oh, God! Amy thought. She loved him so much. She tilted her head and rested it against his shoulder. After the tension of the day, it was heaven. Her mind fluttered to a stop when he pressed his cheek firmly to hers. Rain, her beloved, was holding her. She closed her eyes and gave herself up to the joy of leaning against his chest, his arms around her, her hands on his wrists, feeling the silky hair that covered them. Mindlessly, she lifted her hand to caress his other cheek. It was warm and rough and his whiskers scraped gently against her palm. Her fingers moved to his ear and fondled the nick in his earlobe. It occurred to her that the nick had been there for a long time, and she hadn't known about it until he came back to Quill's Station.

Rain moved his head and his lips slid across her cheek in search of hers with an impatient urgency. She turned her head and met them with equal insistence. His lips were gentle at first, then hardened, and her own parted under them, admitting him, submitting. She touched the tip of her tongue delicately against his mouth and felt him tremble. The strength and taste of him filled her senses. Locked in his embrace, glowing waves of pleasure spread like wildfire throughout her body. She was not even aware of the horse moving beneath them or the fact that they were in plain sight of the others at the wagon. Nothing existed for her except his warm, demanding lips and the powerful beat of his heart against her shoulder. Rain lifted his head. She could feel his eyes on her face. She quivered at the singing tension between them.

"Open your eyes and look at me." The command was made in a noncommittal voice.

Amy's heart beat wildly and a shudder rippled under her skin. She raised gold-tipped lashes and immediately became lost in the dark, narrowed pools of his eyes. For an endless moment their eyes held, their faces so close his breath was warm on her wet lips. She felt the throbbing beat of her pulses, high in her throat, fluttering to her very ears, as she watched his firm lips form words.

"You're *my* woman." He snarled the words bitingly. His eyes held a cold, austere light.

"Yes. Oh, yes."

"You'll be my wife from here on, and when we get to Belle Point you'll be my wife in name."

"It's what I've always wanted."

"You'll sleep in my blankets tonight and every night." He turned his chin slightly, his eyes never leaving hers, his face stern and angry. His arm tightened as if he expected her to pull away.

"Are you still angry about Tally?" She knew he was and didn't know why she asked. He ignored her question.

"We're a pair. We're mated for life." It was a simple, positive statement.

"I'm not sorry about . . . Tally."

Rain swore. "Goddamn it, I'm not talking about *him!*"

"I understand why he wanted to get away from Papa and

his mother." Amy's voice quivered, but she was determined to say what she had to say.

Rain swore under his breath. "He wants you for his woman."

"I feel sorry for him," she said softly. "I'll never be *his* woman."

"That's right. You won't. You'll never be any man's woman but mine."

"I've been yours for a long, long time."

"The Frenchman wanted you." He shook his head angrily and frowned deeply. "I'd not be surprised if that bastard showed up too."

"You're mistaken—"

"I mean what I said about my blankets. You'll make a place for us with my blankets and yours."

"All right."

He turned the horse into the shadowed woods and pulled him to a stop. Amy's hand went to his cheek. He looked at her for a long moment, then folded her in his arms, gently now, but securely. His heart was pounding, and that surprised her, because he seemed so confident. He jerked at the sash around her waist. When it came loose, his hand slid up under her shirt and his fingers gripped her firm, bare breast. He turned his head and covered her lips with his. His lips were not gentle, they were hard, forcing her mouth open. His tongue flicked hers as if he had to show his possession by invading her. His kisses and his hand on her nipple sent hot fires shimmering along her inner thighs and a wetness to her woman's cove.

He shifted his weight in the saddle and she felt the hard knot of his aroused masculinity against her hip. She drew back slightly.

"Don't let it scare you." His voice was a husky whisper. "I'm not going to throw you to the ground and have my way with you."

"I'm not scared." Then, in a hesitant whisper she said, "I'd not be mad if you did."

He pushed her face into the curve of his neck. "Oh, Amy, sweet woman. I get this way just looking at you." His lips were pressed to her cheek and his husky voice came to her through a cloud of unreality.

"I'm glad." It was unreal to her that she would be with him like this, talking about the hard object pressed to the side of her hip. Suddenly and unexpectedly, laughter burst from her lips. Her hands moved up to his cheeks, scraping across the growth of whiskers and into the thick, dark hair at his temples. Her fingers pulled.

"Ouch! What's that for?" His magnificent dark eyes were smiling.

"That's just a sample of what you'll get if I see you looking at Eleanor and . . . getting this way."

Unembarrassed and uninhibited, she eased her mouth up to his. Her lips parted softly as they touched his chiseled mouth. She felt the hand on her hip press her against his hard, elongated erection. His mouth opened against hers, yet he made no attempt to control the kiss although she sensed his growing hunger. It was hotly exciting and so maddeningly good to have her way with him that it goaded her to kiss him with a renewed, fiery hunger. Her tongue darted through his parted lips to taste and she rode the crest of the wildest, sweetest abandonment she had ever known. The need for air forced her to turn her face away and press her lips and nose against his cheek.

"Whoa!" His voice was a ragged breath in her ear. "I'm going to have to dunk myself in the river before I'll be decent enough to show myself to Eleanor and Mrs. Badker."

"Ah . . . poor Rain." Amy burrowed her hand down between them to feel the rock-hard object of his discomfort. When he grabbed her wrist and snatched her hand away, she laughed happily.

"Stop that, you little imp!" He spoke sternly, but there was a painfully savage grin on his face.

"I love you," she said earnestly, placing the tip of her nose against his. "I love you. I'm going to tell you that every day of my life."

He looked at her for a long moment, then tilted his face and kissed her mouth. It was a soft, lingering kiss. When he lifted his lips his face was so close to hers they were breathing the same air, so close she could not look into his eyes.

"You've got years of making up to do. I'm going to see that you do it."

CHAPTER
Fifteen

Hammond Perry, hands clasped behind him, rocked back and forth on the elevated heels of his shoes. He stood in the corner of his office, as far as possible from the nervous, fidgeting group of men gathered just inside the doorway. Hammond never stood close to anyone taller than he was if he could help it. He hated looking up at a man and giving orders. He hated more to have his plans thwarted by a bunch of ignorant louts. He silently chewed the cigar in his mouth and looked at the men with small, sharp eyes, letting the tension build. Finally, he took the cigar from his mouth and held it between his ringed fingers.

"I'm thinking," he said slowly, "that all you've got between your ears is shit."

Bull stepped away from the wall. "It ain't like ya think it was, Mr. Perry. We was agoin' to stop 'em from takin' Red's boat but somebody warned 'em."

"'Somebody warned 'em,'" Hammond mimicked. "Ten of you couldn't pull a sick whore off a piss pot, much less get a woman away from two men and a girl."

"It was like this—"

"Shut up!" Hammond roared. "You'll be lucky if I don't have every inch of skin flogged off your back!"

"Now see here—"

"You see here. You not only failed to get the woman, you took one of my boats out and lost it!" By the time Hammond reached the end of the sentence he was shouting. His voice was loud for a small man. He knew how to use it to intimidate, too. He did that now. "I thought you were the most man around here, Bull. Seems like I heard you bragging you could whip a bear with a willow switch. Hell! You let a Scot and a woman take Miss Woodbury away from you."

"How'd I know she was the one you wanted? 'Sides—" Bull's mind was so sluggish it took a while for what Hammond said to find root. "Woman?"

"The *boy* in buckskins was Amy Deverell from Quill's Station up on the Wabash."

"Woman?" Bull repeated dully. "Are ya sure?"

"Are you calling me a liar?" Hammond shouted.

"No, but I don't know no woman like—that."

"All the women *you* know are those sluts at the tavern."

"They ain't so bad!"

"I don't need your sass, either. The boat you sank carried eight ton. You'll work off the cost or I'll have you towed behind a keelboat to New Orleans and back until all that's left of you is a hunk of raw meat."

"We didn't sink it," Bull whined. "It was Tallman with them stinkin' fire arrows." The rest of the men bobbed their heads in agreement but were too intimidated by Hammond to speak up.

"All you had to do was kill him," Hammond said softly, smiling a most unpleasant smile.

"If'n ya knowed Tallman ya'd know it ain't easy," Bull grumbled. "If'n I'd knowed ya wanted a woman, I'd a got ya one. All kinds of 'em come through all the time."

"You stupid idiot!" Hammond's anger blossomed into rage. "I don't want *any* woman. I want *that* woman."

"Why? She don't look strong enuff ta stand up ta a good night a screwin', if'n ya ask me."

"I didn't ask you! Get the hell out of here! The lot of you make me want to puke. Go on! Get down to the docks and get to work. Now!"

Hammond waved them out the door and then stood at the window and watched them amble toward the quay. They stopped on the corner and gathered around Bull. He seemed to be trying to explain something to them.

"Bah!" Hammond snorted. He turned from the window and began pacing back and forth, his heels pounding on the floorboards. The wheels of his mind were turning, grinding out plans, discarding them, grinding out more. Five minutes passed, then ten before he came to a decision. He flung open a door to a room adjoining his office. The thin, gray-haired man bending over the ledger looked up. "Get that Frenchman, Efant, and bring him here."

After the man scurried away, Hammond sat down at his desk, leaned back in his chair, and propped his feet up on the corner of the desk. He tried to recall every scrap of information he had ever heard about Antoine Efant.

It was said the Frenchman, the second son of a wealthy New Orleans family, loved danger, adventure and beautiful women. It was also said he had been a spy for the British during the war, an assassin for a foreign government, and a scout for Zeb Pike. It was rumored that Efant was the leader of a raiding party that stole furs from the warehouses of both Lisa Manuel and the Chouteau family and sold them to the Hudson Bay Company.

Hammond lit another cigar and considered all these things that favored his hiring Efant to take Will Bradford's bride away from Rain Tallman. There was one more. The Frenchman had a weakness. He was honorable! Hammond chuckled. Efant considered a man's word his bond and had been known to kill a man for breaking it.

It was time, Hammond thought, that he take his place in the social life that was flourishing across the river in Saint Genevieve. He would do it with Miss Eleanor Woodbury on his arm. There were several methods he could use to make sure she was an obedient wife, pleasant in the company of others, docile in the privacy of their home. First he would take her himself, establish his possession of her. Ah, sweet revenge, he thought with a sigh. Then, if the woman proved to be troublesome, there were several ways he could tame her. One way would be to threaten to send her to a tavern like the Boar's Nest or to the streets in New Orleans. Ah, yes, she would stay with him all right, and she would be grateful for the chance to have a roof over her head and food for her belly.

Smiling around the cigar he held in his teeth, Hammond clasped his hands over his chest and began thinking of the different stories he could tell Efant to make him believe he had an *honorable* right to Miss Woodbury.

Antoine Efant was not a big man. He was of average height, but broad shoulders and legs like tree trunks made him appear larger than he was. His usual merry disposition was also deceiving. He had a quick temper and a quicker hand with a knife or gun. The mop of curly hair that hugged his head and the shiny black beard on his face made him appear young and carefree, but in truth he was a man nearing thirty years, the last ten having been spent doing exactly what he wanted.

He left Hammond's office with a sack of coins hanging on his belt. It was a considerable amount of money. But, Antoine mused as he stepped on the boardwalk, Hammond

Perry was the type of man who did not value a person if he came cheap. Antoine detested Perry, but the man had been dealt an injustice. Even a weasel like Perry was entitled to claim what had been given to him.

Antoine headed for the tavern where Perry's man had found him an hour before. The group around Bull stopped talking when Antoine walked by. The town was buzzing with the news that Bull and his cohorts had been sent out to stop Red Cavanaugh's boat from crossing the river and that Perry's boat had been set afire and sunk. Eight men had come ashore, one with a bullet wound in his leg. Two others hadn't been heard from, but no one seemed too concerned about them. Bull was hatching a plan to save his face, Antoine thought wryly. He would have to do something to regain his title of town bully, or else his friends would turn against him and he would be forced to leave town.

What Bull did or did not do was of no concern to Antoine. He never worked with more than two men. For this job he thought he would need only one—Hull Dexter. There was one thing about Hull he liked: the man followed orders without asking questions. One thing about him he did not like was the rumor that Hull had been in charge of a train of wagons about eight years earlier and had left the women and children to be massacred by river pirates. If Antoine ever found that to be true, he would shoot the bastard himself, not because of the women, but because of the children.

The beautiful, dark-haired woman the Scot had taken from Bull was the one Perry wanted brought to him. Antoine had not given her a thought since he saw the Scot drag her out from behind the barrel where she had been hiding and propel her down the road. But he had thought plenty about the tall girl in buckskins with the golden skin and daring spirit. Just thinking about her strong, slender body and flashing amber eyes excited him. He had known the moment she sprang to defend the Scot's back that she was the mate he had yearned for. At first he had thought she was the Scot's woman, and then he had seen the way the angry Scot had treated the black-haired beauty. There was affection in the rough way he handled her. Well, Antoine mused, that was the Scot's misfortune. He would not have her long.

Amy Deverell. Antoine said the name over and over in his mind. Hammond Perry had not been aware of the importance of the information he had given him when he told him the names of the group with Rain Tallman. Antoine had dreamed of having just such a woman as Amy Deverell beside him as he paddled down uncharted rivers, trekked across mountains, and explored the vast area beyond the river. There would be nights of passion with her strong, smooth body beneath him and a blanket of stars overhead.

"Ahh . . . *amour*."

Antoine dragged his thoughts from Amy and concentrated on the man he would have to best if he was to get either of the women. Rain Tallman was known for doing whatever task he took on. He would not give up easily. The man was already a legend west of the river. Zack Taylor had said he was the best shot, the best tracker, the best all-around scout west of the Allegheny Mountains. The only man known to be better was old Daniel Boone. Past eighty by now, he was still hunting and trapping up near Booneville. No doubt, Antoine thought sadly, he would have to kill Rain Tallman.

Rain knelt beside a branch of the White River and dressed the deer, throwing the offal far out in the water so the current would carry it away from the campsite. As he worked he was aware, as always, of what was going on around him. Tally Perkins had watered the mules, rubbed them down and staked them out to graze. With Gavin's help he had raised and blocked the back of the wagon, and now he was greasing the wheels.

The supper fire was sending up a thin spiral of smoke. Gavin had whittled a sharp point on a stick and run it through the bodies of six birds. With the spit supported at either end by forked sticks, the birds were roasting over the flames, sending up a delicious odor.

Rain pondered the question of why Bull and his bunch had been sent to get Eleanor. Somehow Perry had found out he was escorting Will Bradford's bride. It was the reason he had sent the kid, Mike Hartman, to kill him, and the reason he had sent Bull to keep them from crossing the river. Could a man's craving for revenge go that far? Rain wondered. If that were the case, Perry wouldn't give up until they reached Belle Point.

Uppermost in Rain's mind was the danger to Amy and Eleanor. One thing was sure: They would have to leave the comfort of the wagon and the wagon trails and cut across the mountains on horseback. Amy would make out, but how would Eleanor stand such a rigorous journey? There had been a great change in the woman since Gavin had taken her in hand. She was doing her share of the work, and she was civil to Amy and Gavin. Rain watched the women walking together, going upstream for privacy. Amy carried her rifle as if it were a part of her.

Rain leaned his elbow on his knee and watched Amy swinging along beside the shorter woman. He wondered how he could have been so stupid all those years as to stay away from her. She was a magnificent woman; strong and brave, honest and loving. She had been kind to Mrs. Badker, sensing the woman's loneliness. Would she be lonely in their high valley? He doubted it. He hoped that they would have many children of their own to keep them company, and they would be less than a day's journey from where Farr planned to set up his post on the river.

Amy had defied his authority today. Stubborn little baggage! The desire he felt for her was a deep pain gnawing at him even when he was most irritated with her. Tonight she would sleep in his blankets. He wanted the others to know that they were mated. No vows they could exchange in the presence of a minister or magistrate could be more sacred or binding than the vows they made today in the cool, dim forest.

Rain realized he must be grinning. He bent his head and continued his work. He was a fool, he told himself, to be so damn happy. The most dangerous part of their journey lay ahead.

"Have you and Rain made up?" Eleanor asked after she had dipped her washcloth in the clear water and lathered it with a small cake of soap.

"Yes." Amy shivered because the water she was washing in was so cold.

"You're lucky you've got someone who loves you," Eleanor said wistfully.

Amy looked up from where she squatted beside the stream and caught the forlorn look on Eleanor's face. She had been helpful and pleasant today and Amy was beginning to like her, something she had thought she would never do.

"There must be people who love you, Eleanor. You're so pretty."

"Ah, yes," Eleanor sighed. "There have been men who admired my face, but no one who loved or admired *me*, the person behind the face. Not even Aunt Gilda. She used my looks to draw men to play cards with her. There, I've said it. But that's all over now," she added gayly. "Oh, Amy, you don't know how glad I am to be rid of that corset and all those petticoats." She rose on her toes and did a few dance steps. "I feel light as a feather."

"Why did you wear them?"

"I don't know. I've worn five petticoats since I was ten years old and a corset since age twelve. I just never knew how grand and free I'd feel without them."

"You were sure mad when Rain took them off you."

"Yes, I was." Eleanor giggled. "Now I'm glad he did."

Amy stood up and slipped her shirt back over her head. "It was so funny to see Rain looking at your corset. He asked what it was. Gavin tried to explain that it was a garment ladies of high standing wore to make their waists small. Rain said, 'Fashion be damned! Get it off her.'" Amy did a good imitation of Rain's voice and laughter bubbled from both girls.

"I'm glad I swooned. I'd have died of embarrassment."

"It was a job getting the corset off you. Rain had to cut the laces."

"What did you do with it and the others? I was going to put one on just to defy him and I couldn't find them."

"Gavin said you would. Rain told me to get them out of your trunk. I didn't want to, but Gavin agreed with Rain, so I did. Rain threw them up in a cedar tree."

"He what?" Eleanor gasped.

"He threw them all up . . . in the . . . tree," Amy said between gasps of laughter. "It was so funny to see them dangling there. I said, 'Someone will get the surprise of his life when he comes along here and a corset falls out of a tree and hits him!'"

"I wish I could have seen it. Aunt Gilda would have had a fit. She paid a fortune for those corsets. What did Gavin say?"

"He said you were so stubborn that you'd put one on just for spite."

"Is that all?" Eleanor turned and bent over to adjust her stockings and Amy couldn't see her face.

"That's all. We'd better get back and see about the birds. The men will forget about them and let them burn."

They walked slowly back to camp. Amy wanted to ask Eleanor why she had taken the risk of going into Kaskaskia to find a boat to take her to New Orleans and why had she changed her mind about going on to Will Bradford, but their friendship was too new for Amy to ask personal questions. But it was strange, she thought, mighty strange. Of course, it wouldn't make any difference to Rain if Eleanor changed her mind about marrying Will. Rain's job was to take her to Belle Point, and he would do that regardless of how Eleanor felt about it.

The Badker family arrived with a pail of milk, a berry cobbler and a fiddle. The women kept up a lively chatter while they laid out the food. Amy was surprised and pleased at the way Eleanor treated Vonnie. Vonnie was hungry for news and Eleanor told her about the steamboats that were bringing passengers downriver from Pittsburgh and about the new glass jars they were using to preserve food.

"Why, I can't believe it," Vonnie exclaimed.

"It's true. A Frenchman discovered that you could put the food in the jars and seal them with metal caps lined with a glass. After you boil the jars, food and all, in water, the food keeps for months, maybe even a year."

"I'll have to tell Bud about that. Maybe we can get some the next time we go to Saint Genevieve."

Amy's eyes went often to Rain. He visited with Badker, but ever alert, his eyes and ears saw and heard everything that was going on around him. He had finished dressing the deer and after cutting off a haunch for them to cook and take with them, he had wrapped the remainder in the hide for the Badkers to take home. Gavin sat quietly smoking his pipe and Tally sat apart, his elbows on his knees, his big hands clasped while his thumbs twirled around each other.

After the meal, Bud Badker got out the fiddle and began to play. He played a lively tune and jigged. Vonnie and the boys clapped their hands in time with the music. To everyone's surprise, Tally got up and asked Vonnie to dance. She jumped up, put her hand in his and they began a wild gallop around the camp, staying within the circle of light made by the campfire.

"Sing, boys," Bud shouted.

The two small boys, their shyness forgotten, began to sing.

"Come join hand in hand, brave Americans all,
    And rouse your bold hearts at fair Liberty's call;
No tyrannous acts shall suppress your just claim,
    Or stain with dishonor America's name."

After the boys sang several verses of the song, their father asked, "How about 'Yankee Doodle,' boys?"

The small freckled faces broke into wide grins. The boys joined hands and swung them between them, a foot going up and down in time with the music. Their childish voices were surprisingly good.

"Should a haughty foe expect
    to give our boys a caning,
We guess they'll find the lads have larnt
    a little bit of training.
Yankee Doodle fa, sol, la,
    trumpet, drum and fiddle."

Amy watched Rain's face. He was smiling one of his rare smiles as he watched the boys. As if sensing Amy was watching him, his eyes turned to hers, snared them and held.

A message passed between them that they both understood. *They would have boys someday.* He would be like Farr was with Daniel and Zack, Amy thought, and he would be gentle with the girls. She felt a wild, heated longing stab her body and race through her veins with the speed of lightning.

When Vonnie sank down beside Amy, she had to tear her thoughts away from Rain.

"Whoeeee! I haven't danced with anyone but the boys for so long I'm out of breath."

"Your boys dance too?"

"Oh my, yes. Bud has taught them to clog and cut the pigeon wing. It's what we do when we get lonesome. He's teaching them to fiddle. Heavens! It's hard on the ears at times."

Tally stood in front of Eleanor. "Ma'am?"

Eleanor smiled brightly, stood and put her hand in his. "I don't know how."

"I'll show you. Put your hand on my shoulder. Now . . . first one foot and then the other."

In a matter of minutes Eleanor had the hang of it. Laughter sweeter than the fiddle music broke from her lips. Gavin moved back into the darkness so he could watch her openly without her seeing him. She was the most beautiful woman he had ever seen. Why, he asked himself, did this woman pull at his heartstrings? Why her? It was more than her pretty face; it was something deeper. At times he thought he saw a yearning in her violet eyes, a yearning to belong to someone. He knew the feeling well. He'd had it all his life. Yet she wasn't for him. There was as much distance between them as there was between a great laird and the peasants who tilled his fields.

Gavin turned and walked into the woods. One nagging question had stayed with him all day. Why had Eleanor tried to leave them? It was more than her anger at Rain for taking off her corsets and petticoats. She had said that her money was gone and now she would *have* to go on to Will. Did that mean the lass no longer wanted to marry Major Bradford? No matter, he thought. She would be taken to Belle Point and given the chance to tell the major if she didn't want to be his wife. A shudder of longing worked its way down the length of his body. Gavin walked deeper into the woods until he could no longer hear Eleanor's merry laughter.

Amy was relieved when Badker put down the fiddle. She would have danced with Tally if he had asked her and she wasn't sure how Rain would have felt about it. And at that point she didn't want to do anything to put a strain on their newly forged relationship. At times it had seemed as if the evening would never be over. Now the Badker family was getting ready to go back to their home in the side of the hill.

"I'll help pack the meat back up to the house, Bud," Rain said. "Take the birds, too. We'll not be able to use them."

"I'll cook some of the birds overnight in my wall oven, Amy," Vonnie said. "Stop by in the morning. You'll have meat to last for several days. Let me at least do that," she hastened to say when Amy started to protest that it would be too much trouble. "It's been such a treat to visit with you 'n Eleanor. If yo're ever this way again, our door is always open."

"My sister will be through here in a few weeks. Her name is Liberty Quill. Tell her we are fine and are looking forward to seeing her and Farr."

"I'll do that, I surely will."

Gavin returned while the good-byes were being said.

"I'll take the early morning watch," Rain told him. "I'm not expecting trouble, but you never can tell who'll come along."

"That be true," Badker said. "Lots a folks is movin' in, 'n lots a toughs drift down from that settlement below Saint Genevieve. I don't leave the woman 'n kids alone for long anymore."

"Rain, I was thinkin' the young feller could be takin' the first watch if it sets well with ye. I be stayin' with him a spell."

"It's all right with me if you want to take on the chore." Rain picked up one end of the pole supporting the deer carcass, Badker picked up the other, and they started up the path. Vonnie and the boys followed, one boy carrying the fiddle, the other the milk pail.

"Bye, Amy and Eleanor. We sure had a good time." Vonnie's voice came out of the darkness.

"She seems happy," Eleanor said.

"Why wouldn't she be? She's got her husband and her boys to do for." Amy climbed into the wagon and Eleanor followed.

"Oh my, I'm tired." Eleanor flexed her shoulders and stretched her arms. "Don't you want to sleep on the cot? We can take turns on the pallet."

"Well . . . no." Amy pulled her bedroll out from under the cot. "I'm going to sleep outside."

"Outside? Whatever for?"

"Because I want to!" Amy spoke sharper than she had intended. She was immediately sorry but didn't know how to fix it.

"I'm sorry I asked," Eleanor said quietly. She sat down on the cot and began to unbutton her dress. "It's your own business if you sleep with Rain. Believe me, Amy, I don't blame you. I'd do the same if someone loved me."

"We're going to be married—"

"What do a few words from a preacher amount to? Besides, we could all be killed before we meet up with one." Eleanor stood, pulled her dress down and stepped out of it.

Amy reached over and squeezed Eleanor's hand. "If you're not careful, Eleanor, I'm going to start liking you very much."

"I'd like that. I've never had a woman friend, or a man friend, either, for that matter," she added dryly.

"You have now. Rain and I are going to homestead in the Arkansas. We may not be far from the fort."

Eleanor lay back on the bunk. "When I was in Louisville, the idea of going to a fort in the wilderness seemed so romantic."

"And it doesn't now?"

"It's scary, Amy."

"It's reasonably safe there. If it wasn't, Major Bradford wouldn't have sent for you."

"I'm not worried about that. I guess there's not much use in worrying about anything at all. What will happen will happen." Eleanor giggled softly. "You know, I can't help but wonder what would have happened if Aunt Gilda had come along. She and Rain may have killed each other."

"I've a feeling Rain would have been able to handle her."

"You know, I think you're right."

CHAPTER
Sixteen

Amy spread her blankets with Rain's in a grassy spot beneath a fir tree a dozen yards from the campfire that was now only a few glowing embers. If she were sure this was where Rain wanted to stay, she would cut some pine boughs for their bed. She placed her rifle within easy reach and sat down to wait. It was a dark night, made darker still by the dense woods that surrounded their campsite. The night air was cold. Amy shivered and pulled one of the blankets up around her shoulders. The cold retreated and warmth came as she huddled beneath the tree and watched and waited for Rain to come to her.

She wondered where Gavin and Tally were. If she were keeping watch, she would move slowly, making a complete circle around the camp. Juicy had told her that was the thing to do when camping out in the open.

A figure suddenly came out of the darkness and crouched beside her. Instinctively, one hand threw back the blanket and the other reached for her knife.

"Whoa! It's me."

"Damn you, Rain! Don't sneak up on me."

"You shouldn't have let me. I've been watching you for several minutes."

"Why?"

"Because I wanted to, sweet girl." He slid his arm across her shoulders and his lips nuzzled her cheek. "Come on. I want to talk with Gavin, then I'll take you to a place where I'll have you all to myself for a few hours."

Amy's heart felt like a hummingbird gone mad inside her chest. She took his hand and he pulled her to her feet. He quickly rolled up their blankets and tucked them under his arm. Amy picked up her rifle. Rain led her through a thicket that grew close to the riverbank, across loose shale, and along the stream that spilled over and around slabs and shelves of rock.

Out of the corner of her eye Amy saw something move, something on the shore upstream. Amy tried to look directly at it, but saw nothing at first, then detected movement. This time she saw the shape of a man standing among the boulders.

Rain whistled the call of a night bird and another figure moved out of the darkness and stood beside the first one.

When they reached Tally and Gavin, Rain snorted. "You're trying hard to get yourself killed, Perkins. I saw you fifty feet away."

"I thought I was . . . hid."

"You moved. Boulders don't move," Rain said impatiently. "It's a good thing there's no one around. I want to talk to you and Amy, Gavin. There's something you should be aware of. I'd rather not alarm Miss Woodbury. I don't know how she'll stand up to what's turned out to be real danger for her."

"I be thinkin' the lassie be stronger than we first believed."

In short, terse sentences, Rain told them about Hammond Perry wanting the assignment to build the fort at Belle Point, and when he was passed over for Will Bradford, his hatred for the man almost exceeded his hatred for Farr Quill. He told them Perry was a vindictive man and would go to any means to satisfy his need for revenge.

"He knows Miss Woodbury is Will's intended bride. He's going to try and take her. He's already tried and failed. He won't give up until we get to Belle Point, if then."

"The mon would *kill* the lassie to spite a mon who bested him?"

"That or worse," Rain said bluntly.

"Holy God! Why did'na ye say so when we were at Kaskaskia? I would kill the mon with me bare hands!"

"At Kaskaskia I was reasonably sure that was his intention. The attempt to keep us from crossing the river proved it. Perry wants Miss Woodbury."

"What will he be doin'? The lassie would'na wed the mon."

"If not he would sell her to a brothel downriver. Either way it would be a victory over Will Bradford."

"He will'na be havin' her!" Gavin's strong words vibrated from his deep chest.

"There'll be another attempt made during the next few days. They know where we're going and they know that there's only one wagon trail. What I want to do is to travel fast for the next few days and maybe outrun them. When we get to Davidsonville we'll leave the wagon, get horses and mules, and go cross-country. The wagon and Miss Woodbury's trunks can be picked up later."

"Why not leave the wagon here with the Badkers, Rain?" Amy's hand wiggled into his and gripped hard.

"We need a horse for Miss Woodbury and a couple of good pack animals. We can get both in Davidsonville."

"She can have my horse." Tally's voice came out of the darkness where he had retreated after Rain had scolded him. "I can ride one of the mules and lead the other. They're good pack mules . . ." As Tally finished speaking his voice faded and Amy wanted to kick him for having so little confidence. Mules were something he knew about.

"They've not been broken for riding and we don't have time to break one in," Rain said sharply.

"I may not know much about how to get along in the wilds, Rain, but I know mules." It was the strongest statement Amy had ever heard Tally make. She was secretly elated. In the silence that followed Tally's outburst he added, "I've worked with mules since I can remember. I can ride one and lead one and you and your horses may have a hell of a time keeping up!"

"Hmm . . ." Rain was silent for a moment. "All right. We'll leave the wagon here. Gavin, do you know that shelf I showed you this evening? That's where Amy and I will spread our blankets tonight. Give a whistle sometime after midnight and I'll take the early morning watch."

Amy felt the blood rush to her face and was grateful for the darkness. Rain was making sure Gavin and Tally knew they were sleeping together.

"No need for that, mon," Gavin said without the slightest hesitation. "Me 'n the lad will be seein' yer not disturbed this night. Be off with ye."

Amy walked beside Rain over the rough stones, past boulders as high as her head and through a dense growth of sumac. Up a short incline near a bend of the river Rain stopped. The shelter was under a shelf of rock five or six feet above the river. It was not quite a cave; it was perhaps five feet from floor to ceiling at its entrance and went back three or four feet into the cliff. The floor was covered with cedar boughs.

"I was here today while it was still light," he said softly in answer to her unasked question.

Rain leaned their rifles against the stone wall and dropped their blankets on the boughs. He slipped his arms around her as if he couldn't wait and his lips fell hungrily to hers. They were demanding, yet tender.

"I've been waiting all evening for this time alone with you," he whispered.

"This is a perfect place. I'm glad you found it." Her eyes danced lovingly over his face and her hand inched up to curl about his neck.

The kiss they shared was long and deep and full of promised passion that flared whenever they touched. She took his kiss thirstily. His lips pulled away, his arms dropped from around her and he bent to spread their blankets on the soft cushion of cedar boughs.

"What is this?"

"My . . . nightdress."

Amy took it from his hand, sank down on the blankets, bent her head and unlaced her shirt. When she looked up, Rain was no longer there. In her haste her fingers fumbled with the laces on her moccasins and the belt to her britches. It seemed an eternity until she slipped the nightdress over her head and lay back on the blanket, moved to the far side and pulled a blanket up over her.

She sat up suddenly and sucked in her breath. Should she unbraid her hair? Yes, she decided. Rain would like that. She loosened her hair from the long braid and combed it with her fingers. She lay back down, her heart pounding like that of a scared rabbit, but she was not scared. How many long, lonely nights lay behind her? They were over now. She would be with her love forever.

Rain appeared suddenly and dropped down beside her. He was naked to the waist. He had washed in the river. She could smell the dampness of his skin.

"You're so quiet," she whispered.

"Years of practice." He quickly removed his moccasins and britches and lay down beside her. "The water was cold, but I didn't want to come to you smelling like a goat."

She felt a sweetness, a rightness when he turned to her and wrapped his arms around her. Amy wasn't prepared for the warmth or the strength of his hard, muscular body; his long legs against hers, his arms under and around her. Her trembling body was gathered tenderly to a warm, naked chest, matted with soft hair. The feel of his body against hers created a sweet, unbearable, erotic pleasure-pain in the pit of her stomach that spread through her femininity with throbbing arousal. His legs meshed with hers and she rubbed the bottom of her feet on the tops of his. Her hands stroked his back and shoulders, caressing him. Her face found refuge against his neck. She felt his hands on her buttocks, pulling her tightly against him.

"Your bottom is just a good handful," he whispered. Then laughed such a joyous laugh that she wanted to cry.

"I . . . love you." It was all she could think of to say.

"Ahh . . ." His arms locked her to him. "This is heaven. Pure heaven."

"I want to be with you forever."

"You will be." He smoothed her hair back from her face with his palm. She felt his excitement, felt his whole strong frame begin to quiver. "Amy, Amy, Amy—"

"I've waited a long time for you. Love me, Rain. Truly love me." Her heart beat with pure joy.

Amy met his searching lips and surrendered to the excitement of his touch, her mouth responding to the insistent persuasion of his. The kiss deepened. His hunger seemed insatiable and his caressing hands became almost savage.

"Your mouth is so sweet," he whispered, his lips moving to her eyes. She lifted her fingertips to his cheek and pulled his mouth back to hers. He responded instantly to the urgency of her desire. His tongue gently stroked her inner lips, the moist, velvet texture sending a throbbing message to her womb. He pulled on the cloth that kept his hands from her warm flesh. "Take this thing off, sweet."

He sat up, bringing her with him. Anxious hands lifted the nightdress and pulled it off over her head. He lay back and stretched out, pulling her on top of him. He positioned her thighs between his and pulled her up to lie on his chest. She covered him, the blanket covering her. His hands cupped her buttocks, pressing her against the hardness that had sprung alive when he first touched her. It lay now, long and throbbing, cradled between their bellies. She gloried in the feel of him, knowing that soon he would fill her aching emptiness. She lifted her head from his chest, her hands framed his face and she kissed him again and again.

"I can't believe I'm really here with you . . . like this." Even as she spoke her hands clutched him, her stomach muscles tightened, her breathing and heartbeat were all mixed up.

"I want to see you," he whispered. "God! I want to see your face when I love you." His callused fingers stroked her from her neck to her spine, learning the smoothness of her back and haunches; pressing her to the hardness that thrilled her to the marrow.

"You will, you will . . . soon."

He rolled her on her back and hovered over her. "I wanted this first time to last a long time. I don't think I can wait very long . . ." The words were groaned thickly into her ear. "I like the feel of your breasts against my chest, your belly against mine, your arms around me. Amy, Amy, why didn't I come back sooner?"

The deeply buried heat in her body flared when she felt the tug of his lips on her nipple. He kissed her breast, rolled the bud around with his tongue and grasped it gently with his teeth. Tremors shot through her in waves as his exploring fingers moved over her body, prowling ever closer to the ultimate goal. She welcomed them when they probed between her parted thighs and slid into the mysterious, moist secret place, touching what had not been touched before.

The thrust of her hips incited him to lift his mouth to hers in a kiss that stripped away everything but the need to assuage the ache building to unbearable heights within both of them.

"Now? Sweet . . . now?"

"Yes, yes." She opened her thighs and pulled him to her. Her arms wound tightly around his neck and she pressed herself against him. She was caught up in overpowering desire and the need for physical release. He lifted himself above her, sought entrance and paused.

"Will I hurt you?" His chest heaved as he attempted to control his breathing.

"Don't stop!" she pleaded. Her hands feverishly clung to him, holding him tightly while she kissed his mouth again and again.

Her emotional plea echoed in the far depths of his heart, bringing a mistiness to his eyes and a tightness to his throat. Her sweet response brought his innermost thoughts leaping to his lips.

"I love you. You fill my . . . heart, my thoughts, you make my life complete." With muttered, incoherent endearments he moved into her, reverently guiding her to accept the root of his being. With a moan and a hungry, eager thrust, he found himself enclosed, embedded in that sweet softness, that warm and hallowed place. Amy felt a slight pain that passed quickly, lost in the pleasure when she was stabbed again and again with that blade of fire. The magic circle of pleasure widened. She desperately wanted what they were reaching for, dreaded missing it, and quivered with expectation beneath the pressure of his body.

She thrust her body upward and found her hands clasped tightly to his buttocks. He was huge and deep inside her. Waves of frenzied pleasure ripped through her. The whole world was the man joined to her. His mouth was her mouth, his body and hers were one. This joining would forever be imprinted in her memory. She was a part of her beloved at last. He was at home in her body, moving gently, the tip of his arching hardness caressing her womb. She arched her hips hungrily and he wildly accepted what she offered. Her heart vibrated with all the love that was stored there for him.

Amy had not dreamed that being with Rain like this would carry her to such sensual heights. Their passion swelled, rocked them, enclosed them in a world where nothing existed but the two of them. She clung to him, aware only of the thrusting, pulsing rhythm that increased and brought with it spasms of pleasure that coursed like a gorgeous dance through her body. She felt his strong body halt, quiver, tighten. She felt the flood of his release and heard him moan her name over and over.

She wasn't really aware when it ended. The sweet, familiar smell of his breath and the light touch of his lips at the corner of her mouth awakened her. She tightened her arms and legs around him, holding him inside her, and hungrily turned her mouth to his. Her hands moved up into his hair and down the strong line of his back and shoulders, then up to clasp around his neck.

"It's even better than I dreamed it would be," he murmured when his lips finally left hers.

She laughed softly against his mouth, caught his lip between her teeth and nibbled gently.

"Rain. Darling Rain. Do you know how long I've loved you? How long I've waited for you to be just where you are? I'm so glad we've done this wonderful thing together. I'm filled with you—" Her breath caught in a sob and she couldn't say anything more. Emotion made her eyes fill with tears and her voice break.

"I'm glad we didn't wait. You're all woman, little Amy, even if you do wear britches," he teased. His lips rubbed hers in sensuous assault. He advanced his pelvis upward. To her delight she felt the full length of him, hard, pulsing, caressing.

"Rain...am I a slut for liking this?" She locked her hands in the small of his back and strained up against him.

"Oh, God, no! Where did you get that idea?"

"Most women don't like this. Libby does, though. She said that when she's with Farr he shuts out the world. I didn't understand what she meant then, but I do now."

"I want you to feel empty if I'm not there." His voice was a ragged whisper.

His heart thundered against hers, making wordless declarations of need and longing. This joining was wholly unlike before. Her hands moved lovingly over him, searching, caressing. She learned the mysteries about which she had only vaguely heard. In her newfound freedom to love and discover, her hand burrowed between them to the place where they were joined. She laughed with delight to discover thick, coarse hair cushioning her.

"We fit so well together!" she exclaimed, and rubbed her toes against his ankles.

"I told you I was glad you were tall."

"I used to hate being taller than the other girls. Now I'm glad."

He turned on his side, taking her with him, her soft belly tight against his hard one. They kissed for a long time, his tongue inside her mouth, moving gently while his fingers teased the nipple on her breast to hardness. He moved down and she pillowed his head on her breast. When he turned his mouth to her nipple, the pleasure was so acute that she tightened her arms about him and murmured unintelligibly in his ear. He laughed, a loving, knowing laugh. His lips tugged once again at her breast before he moved up so his lips could reach hers and he could implant himself more deeply in the cavern between her thighs.

"I wish I could see you," he murmured. "I wish I could see your breasts, your smooth belly. I want to see you naked with just your hair covering you."

"Rain, I want . . ." She arched against him when he flexed his hips.

"Tell me. Oh! Oh . . . be still, sweetheart!" he breathed in gasps when she moved urgently. "Yes, yes."

With a long breath he thrust fully into her. She responded. They both trembled violently and incredibly long waves of pleasure washed over them: raw, unheeding spasms that lasted until the final thrust of his pelvis. She felt the exquisite explosion, the sudden bursting inside her. She heard his cry and their fevered bodies took flight. They floated down from that high forgetfulness, clinging together in a closeness of body and mind, and lay shuddering in each other's arms.

Amy held him to her breast. He was dearer to her than her very heart. Holding him in her tight embrace, she marveled at how the entire world had changed for her. Then, as if in a dream, he was once again the tall, dark, sad-faced boy of long ago. Once again she heard the words he had said before he went away to discover what kind of man he was. His voice wasn't so deep then, or so confident. *You're just a kid, Amy. You're not ready for grown-up love.* She had loved him so desperately and wished time would pass swiftly so she would be a grown-up and he would come back to her. Finally he had come. Here in her arms was all she had ever yearned for.

Slowly his breathing steadied and he rolled onto his back. His arms pulled her to him, his hand sought her thigh to bring it up to rest on his. They were quiet for a long while, her head on his shoulder, his hand stroking her arm.

"Thank you for bringing me to this place, Rain. It's like having a home of our own."

"I wanted to have you all to myself. It might be the last time for a while."

"I wish we could find a place like this every night," she said wistfully.

"We're going to have to move fast, sleep when we can."

"I know. I'm being greedy. I love you so much."

"I love you too."

"Is it getting easier to say?"

"I've never been good with words."

"It's all right. I feel loved. Do you? Can you feel how much I love you, Rain?"

"Yes . . ." His arms tightened. He turned his lips to her forehead. "I don't feel lonely inside anymore."

"I don't either, but I didn't know exactly how to say it."

"Today on the boat I was wishing I hadn't brought you along."

"If you hadn't we'd have missed this." She stroked the silky hairs on his chest with her fingertips.

"It won't be easy getting Eleanor through Perry's men. He'll not send another bungler like Bull."

"I thought of that. I'll be a help to you, Rain. Uncle Juicy taught me a lot."

"I've been thinking of having you stay here with the Badkers to wait for Farr and Libby."

Amy was shocked speechless by his calm words. Then one word exploded from her lips. "No!" Her fingers in the hair that lay against his neck knotted. "No!" she said again.

His chest heaved with a sigh. "I knew you'd say that. It would just be for a few weeks. I'll come back for you."

Amy felt a knot of heat in her throat and incipient moisture under her lids. Then her pain surged into a mighty indignation.

"How could you even think of leaving me after we've been together like this? I've been telling you that I'm not helpless, that I can do some . . . things as good as you . . . can. You . . . don't even listen." Her voice was shaking so that the words came out with angry sobs.

"You must know that I love you. If anything should happen to you I couldn't live on. Don't you see?"

"If you leave me," she said, muffled against him, "I'll

follow. Do you want that? Here, I *will* die. With you, I'll have a chance. What would it be like for me? If something happened to you it would be weeks or months before I knew. You could be hurt and needing me and I wouldn't know. I couldn't bear that. How can you ask me to do this if you love me?"

"It's because I love you—"

"I'll not live on another day or night away from you. I waited and waited and waited," she sobbed, hiding her face in the curve of his neck.

"Ahh . . . Amy, love." He turned her face up to him and his lips found her teary eyes. "I want to keep you safe. I may have already planted the seed of our first son."

"It could be a . . . girl."

He chuckled softly. "Tall, stubborn, and with golden eyes like her ma."

"Don't you dare laugh at me!"

"Amy. Oh, Amy! You're one of a kind."

"What does that mean?"

"It means you don't have to stay here. It means that it makes me more scared than I've ever been in my life, but proud too that you want to take your chances with me."

"Didn't you think I'd want to be with you?"

"I hoped you'd want to, but—"

"Don't *but* me, Rain Tallman." She leaned over him and rested her forearms on his chest and looked down at him. She could only see the outline of his face, but she saw a gleam that could only be moisture in his eyes. "You make me so *damn* mad!"

"I'm going to have to take you in hand. Ladies don't swear."

"You told me that once before."

"And you said, 'I'm not a lady, I'm just a kid.'"

"You remember that?"

"Of course. I remember a lot of things."

"Like what?"

"One time you went behind the barn with Mercy, lifted your dress and you didn't have on any underdrawers. I saw this—" His hands moved down her back and gripped her behind.

"Why you . . . sneaky pissant!"

He laughed against her cheek, rolled her over and pressed her down on the blanket-covered boughs. His kisses became deeper and more urgent, his breath quickened, the part of his body pressed to her soft down hardened.

They loved each other long and sweetly as time marched unmeasured through the night.

CHAPTER
Seventeen

"The meat will last several days. There's bread to go with it." Vonnie handed the doeskin bag to Amy who tied it to the back of her saddle.

"Thanks, Vonnie. You take care now, and keep an eye on those boys."

"I will. You be careful too." Vonnie went to the horse after Gavin had lifted Eleanor to sit in the saddle and held up her hand. "We'll take care of your things, Eleanor."

"I want you to take them. I have a feeling I'll have no need for fancy dresses and lace petticoats."

"No need?" Vonnie echoed. "Of course you'll be back—"

"I want you to have them. I can get more if I want them. I have everything I need right here . . . in this bundle." Eleanor's eyes went to Gavin who was lashing her bedroll and personal items to the back of the saddle and then to where Amy stood beside Rain, her hand tucked into his.

Loneliness swept over Eleanor like a dark cloud. Amy had shared Rain's bed last night. What had it been like for her? What was it like for Vonnie who seemed so happy with her family? Eleanor tried to shake the questions from her mind. It was absurd to have such thoughts. Before she had been preoccupied with what material things a man would be able to provide for her, and not what it would be like to be loved by him. But that was before she had met Gavin. He wasn't like anyone she had ever known, with his great, strong body, his head of shaggy hair and his bold eyes.

Now, for the hundredth time, Eleanor recalled the gentle way Gavin had held her in his arms after he had spanked her. She had felt that he really cared for her. Just thinking about the words he had murmured, *Don't cry, lassie. The likes a them will na be touchin' ye ever again,* sent that extraordinary sensation through her body, as if for an instant she'd held the world in the palm of her hand. She couldn't remember a time when someone cared if she cried, except for the fact that it would make her eyes puffy and spoil her looks.

Eleanor had not thought of the joy of love; she had only seen the result—her mother's unreasonable devotion to a man who squandered her inheritance, frequented the gambling halls, and kept a woman for his pleasure.

"But Eleanor, I can send your trunk on with the Quills when they come by."

"No. Please, Vonnie, I want you to have it. Make shirts for the boys out of the petticoats. Heavens! You should be able to get two shirts from one."

"Well, I do thank you—"

"I doubt Farr will have an extra team to hitch to the wagon," Rain was saying. "Use it, Badker, as if it were your own."

"It'll be here when ya come this way again. Me 'n the missus thank ya." He placed a big hand on his wife's shoulder and smiled down at her affectionately. "She'll be naggin' to go to town now so she can ride in style," he teased.

"Stay close in for a few days," Rain advised. "I'll leave a

broad trail for a few hours so anyone coming here will know we have left the wagon and gone on. I don't want to bring trouble down on you."

"We'll take care. Ya be watchful, now."

Tally loaded one of the mules with the supplies Rain set out, threw a blanket over the back of the other and mounted. The mule danced about nervously but gradually settled down when Tally drew the pack mule close beside the one he was riding. Rain watched closely, then nodded to the others to mount up.

They waved good-bye to the Badkers and followed Rain down the river path. Amy rode behind Rain, followed by Eleanor, Tally and the pack mule. Gavin rode at the end of the caravan. Eleanor had never ridden astride, and now she marveled at how easy it was to sit in the saddle with both feet in a stirrup. Her dark, full skirt just barely covered the calves of her legs and she giggled at the thought of what her aunt would say if she could see her.

An hour before dawn Amy and Rain had come back to the wagon. Rain had told Eleanor about Hammond Perry and that he suspected Perry was going to try and take her from them. A few weeks ago Rain's words would have terrified her. Now she had calmly told them she would do what had to be done. For the first time Rain's dark eyes had shown a faint glint of admiration when they met hers.

Eleanor admitted to herself, as the horse climbed an embankment and headed into the dark forest, that she had never been happier in her life. Here in the woods, her hair in braids, in the plainest of dresses and not the faintest scent of rose oil on her body, she was happy. For the first time in her life she was not concerned with her appearance, and, somehow, she felt a proprietary feeling toward the others, a responsibility to them. It was important to her now that they think well of her. This admission surprised her even more than the others

The trail wound through clumps of poplar, maple, oak and other deciduous trees, with a few pines and cedars among them. Rain set a fast walking pace, and the horses picked their way around brush and deadfalls. Then Rain angled the horses upward. As they climbed higher and higher, pines, cedars and spruce alone faced them. The horses approached a rocky bluff, then began to skirt a path on a rocky cliff.

They rode for the better part of three hours, through beautiful scenery the likes of which Eleanor had not seen before. Suddenly they broke into an open plain and had a panoramic view of more hills and valleys in the distance, covered with the fresh green of spring. Rain drew his mount to a halt beside a trickling stream.

"We'll rest here for a few minutes."

Eleanor threw her leg over the horse's back as she had seen Amy do to dismount only to fall flat on her backside when her legs refused to hold her. The horse shied but was quickly caught by Rain. Gavin lifted Eleanor to her feet and stood holding her until blood flowed into her legs. Laughter bubbled from her lips as she looked up at his craggy, weathered face.

"It's good that I've got a tough backside, huh, Gavin?"

"Tis, lassie." His hands tightened on her upper arms and he smiled, his white teeth flashing in his weathered face. They stared at each other without speaking. He had watched her since leaving the Badkers. He had gloried in the sight of her shining hair, the contours of her curving back, the feminine roundness of her hips. Even without the deformity of the hideous corset her figure was shaped like an hourglass.

Eleanor stared into the eyes looking down at her. She was deeply disturbed by the power in his bright blue gaze. She and this man were so different, yet she felt that they deeply knew each other, that there was a kinship between them that could not exist between another woman and another man.

He was not handsome, certainly; he didn't need to be with

those compelling blue eyes. His appearance was rough, even crude, but inside he had a sweet and gentle nature. There was character in the hard sweep of his jaw, his firm chin, his nose that angled to one side. Eleanor was close enough to notice the fine lines at the corners of his eyes, the shaggy eyebrows that were too long, and she wondered if he would allow her to trim them.

Finally he broke the silence with a diminutive of her name. She barely noticed that he spoke it without the preceding title; it sounded so right coming from his lips.

"Nora?"

"Yes, Gavin?"

"Ye be all right now, lass?"

"Yes, Gavin."

"Walk a bit. We be goin' on afore ye know it." His hands slid from her arms. He walked away, leading her horse and his to drink.

Eleanor followed Amy into the bushes. "Maybe I'm crazy, but I'm enjoying this."

"Once, a long time ago, Rain left Quill's Station saying he had to find out what kind of man he was. I think you're just now finding out what kind of woman you are."

"I keep thinking that I should be scared, but I'm not."

"You will be when the time comes. Uncle Juicy used to say that only a fool wasn't scared some of the time. Um . . . don't squat there. That may be a poison weed."

"There's a lot I don't know. Amy . . . do you think there could be killing if Hammond Perry sends men to get me?"

"They'll not just walk in and ask you to go with them, that's certain. Rain won't let them slip up on us. He'll not let them take you."

"I can't imagine shooting a man."

"I can if he was shooting at me or Rain."

"I think I know what you mean."

"Don't worry about it now. We've got a long way to go."

"I wish we could go on and on and never get there," Eleanor murmured.

"What a thing to say," Amy chided. "Your Willy is waiting for you."

"I don't want to think about it," Eleanor said hurriedly. "We'd better get back. I want a drink of water before we start."

The sun, concealed behind the thick forest, was slowly sinking in the west. It had been hours since they had stopped for a rest and Amy was beginning to feel tired and hungry. She had passed out the sticks of jerky Vonnie had sent for an afternoon snack, and the salted beef had made her thirsty. They followed Rain along a ridge and into a valley, then up a steep incline. They went along the edge of the valley to where it curved to a line parallel with the slope of the mountain before turning up the mountain path.

Daylight was fading when they heard the sound of rushing water. The noise of the creek, the whisper of the breeze in the trees, the rustle of leaves underfoot, the chirping of the birds, and the scurrying of small animals were all comforting sounds to Amy.

Rain stopped directly under a huge tree drooping over the edge of a limestone wall.

"We'll stop here."

They stopped but sat their horses, looking at him. Although Rain seemed tireless, Amy and Eleanor were exhausted. Eleanor had been holding on to the saddle horn for the last few hours, but not a murmur of complaint had passed her lips.

Rain went to Amy and helped her down from the horse. "Are you all right?" he asked.

"I'm all right, but Eleanor . . ."

Eleanor looked at Gavin dully when he stood beside her horse. There was no feeling whatever in her cramped limbs. She was paralyzed, unable to move. He lifted her from the horse, carried her a short distance and set her down beneath the tree. Sharp flashes of pain attended every movement of her body, and she stifled the moans of agony by biting her lips.

"Ye did good, lassie."

"Oh . . . I don't think I'll ever move again," she whispered. "I don't want Rain and Amy to . . . know."

"It'll get worse afore it gets better."

"Oh, Gavin, will I ever be able to walk?"

"Ye need the kinks worked out a ye, lass. Sit here till I tend the animals. I'll be back fer ye."

The animals were stripped and rubbed down with handfuls of dried grass. Rain worked on his horse and Amy's. Gavin tended his horse and Eleanor's, and Tally the mules. Amy unpacked the food, but was hesitant about starting a fire until she had talked with Rain.

"Sit still, Eleanor," Amy said when Eleanor made a groaning attempt to get up and help her. "I can't do anymore until Rain tells me it's safe to build a fire."

"I don't know if I can move. Oh . . . I am useless!"

"That was a hard ride."

"Don't Rain and Gavin ever get tired? I think they could go on all night."

"Maybe they could, but the horses couldn't." Amy walked to meet Rain coming from where they had hobbled the animals. "Shall I build a fire for tea?"

"Yes. That's the reason I chose this place. Come, I'll show you." He led her around a large boulder and under a ledge. "Build it here. The smoke will hit the top of the ledge and scatter. The fire won't be seen until someone is close enough to hear the horses. But first—" He caught her hand and pulled her to him. His arms went around her and he lowered his mouth to her upturned lips. She shook from the force of his deep, starved, unrelenting kiss. "I've been thinking about that for hours."

"I've been thinking about . . . last night."

"Sweet, brazen, little hussy!" he chided with rough tenderness. Laughing softly, he framed her face with his two hands before planting a soft kiss on her mouth.

"I am what I am, Rain Tallman!"

"And I wouldn't change a hair on your head!" He hugged her fiercely for a long delicious moment. "We'd better get some tea made," he said when he released her. "I found some dry hickory that will make a quick fire. How's Eleanor?"

"She's never ridden astride. The last few hours were torture for her, but she didn't complain. I . . . I like her."

"She's not the same woman I brought out of Louisville. I even like her a little bit myself."

"As long as it's a little bit it's all right. I'd hate to have to put a nick in your other ear!"

"What a vicious child you are!" He grinned down at her happily.

"You didn't think I was a child last night."

"Noo . . ."

"And tonight?"

"You'll be a bit tired for loving tonight, sweet woman. Or will you?" he asked hopefully.

"I'm not a small, delicate woman, Mr. Tallman!"

"Thank God for that!"

Low moans and groans came from under the tree as Amy and Rain returned for the cooking gear. Gavin had cut some boughs and placed Eleanor facedown on them. He was on his knees beside her, vigorously rubbing and massaging the cramped muscles of her feet and ankles and working swiftly up to the aching thighs.

"Oh! Oh! Gavin, stop . . . stop! I can't bear it!"

"Ye must, lassie. We can't be lettin' the muscles tighten up on ye." His huge hands kneaded the muscles in her thighs and legs through the heavy skirt.

"But . . . my bottom is sore too and—"

"Hush now. I'll tend to it."

Rain knelt down beside Gavin. "Can't move, huh?"

"She be in a bad way, mon. Muscles tight as a bowstring."

"If I remember right, there's a hot spring up and in back of this bluff. The Indians use heat for sore joints and cramped muscles."

"I've heard of it. Can I be carryin' her up there?"

"I'll go up first and make sure the spring is still there. It'll help her to soak, and then you can work the kinks out of her muscles. She's got to ride tomorrow."

Amy walked with Rain toward the place where he would start up the bluff. It was narrow, steep and rocky.

"Can Gavin carry her up there?"

"Sure. He's as steady on his feet as a cat."

"He doesn't seem to mind taking care of Eleanor," Amy said.

"He's a good man," Rain said quietly.

"I think he's in love with her."

"I'm sure of it. That's why he'll treat her honorably. He knows that she's the intended of another man. He'll do nothing to cause her pain. I'd stake my life on it."

"Don't be staking your life on anything, Rain. It's too precious to me."

While Rain was gone, Amy carried meat and bread to Gavin and Eleanor. Gavin brought a cup of water from the creek and Eleanor drank thirstily, but ate little.

Rain returned. "There's a nice little pool of hot water up there. It smells like sulphur. It'll be rough going up that shale to reach it, but it'll help her to soak in it. I'll show you the way."

"Do you want me to go with you, Eleanor?" Amy asked.

"Not unless you want to. If you'd get my other skirt and shirt, I can get in the pool with these clothes. Oh, Amy, I'm one big aching lump! How do you stand it?"

"I'm used to walking and riding. Now you know why Rain wanted you to walk part of the time."

Gavin wrapped Eleanor in a blanket and lifted her in his arms. Eleanor felt as if she had been beaten with a flat board, and surrendered to her misery. She lapsed into a semiconscious state against Gavin's broad chest, feeling secure in his arms, confident he would take care of her. She was only halfway aware when he started up a long slope, the shale sliding beneath his boots, and that occasionally he turned sideways to keep the brush from slapping her. After a while she had the blurred impression that he was breathing heavily and wondered why. She found this speculation too great an effort and drifted into sleep.

Eleanor felt herself being lowered to the ground, heard the murmur of Gavin and Rain's voices.

"You could see a fire for miles up here," Rain said.

"Twill be a bright night when the moon is up."

"Can you make out?" Rain asked. "It'd be a hard climb for Amy. She's tuckered out but won't admit it."

"I be makin' out, mon. I'll soak the lassie 'n work the kinks from her joints. She be in shape to ride come mornin'."

"Gavin . . . she belongs to another man."

"I be knowin' it. Ye're not to be thinkin' I'd force meself on the lassie."

"I know that." Rain gripped his shoulder hard. "Sometimes fate deals us a losing hand, huh, Gavin?"

"Aye. Tis true."

"Here's your rifle and knife." Rain placed the weapons nearby. "Give the night signal if you need help."

Gavin removed his boots and shirt before he knelt down

beside Eleanor and stripped off her shoes, stockings and
heavy skirt. She moaned rebelliously, angry that he had
snatched her from her comfortable state of sleep. He unbuttoned her shirt with trembling fingers, feeling as if he had no
right to be touching her at all. Eleanor was aware that she
was being undressed, but it did not astonish her. Clothed or
unclothed, the pain was the same.

He lifted her in his arms with only her thin shift covering
her body and carried her to the pool. Waves of warm vapor
wafted up from the heated water. The smell of sulphur was
strong. Gavin sat on the edge and plunged his feet into the
water. It was warm, very warm. He waited a minute or so,
then slowly slid into the water with Eleanor in his arms. Her
eyes flew open and her hand clasped his forearm when first
her feet and then her bottom touched water.

"Is it too hot, lass?"

The sound of the words, the strong vibration of his deep
voice against her, reassured her. She could feel his breath on
the top of her head fanning the tendrils of her hair.

She shook her head. "No . . ."

"Ye needn't fear. I'll not let ye drop."

"I'm not afraid. I'm not afraid when you're with me,
Gavin. I love you," she murmured drowsily, unaware she
had said the words. His body's strength was massive, protective, all that was certain and secure in her life. She
wanted to stay in his arms forever. She dozed off again.

Gavin stood still for a long moment holding the precious
burden in his arms. Her cheek was pressed to his shoulder,
the palm of her hand lay flat against his naked chest, long
braids of shiny black hair floated on the water. A wild unreasonable emotion between agony and elation took possession
of him. It was like being caught in a whirlwind. For an
instant he thought about running away to some remote spot
in the mountains where he could have this soft, sweet
woman all to himself. Years of frustration and pain weighed

on his shoulders. Surely she knew how much he ached to love her!

Emotion and reason fought for dominance while he stood there. The lass was out of her head and thought he was another man. But had she not said his name? Gavin shook his shaggy head, unable to believe she meant the words for him.

He waded deeper into the pool until the water came up to his waist. Then he slipped his arm from beneath her knees and lowered her until her feet rested on the tops of his and she was immersed in the warm water to her shoulder blades. He held her upright against him with one arm wrapped about her waist and worked the muscles of her back and buttocks with his free hand. In her drowsy state Eleanor could feel the flow of water and the slow, almost caressing movements of Gavin's hands massaging her tired body, carrying away the last vestige of her pain. She contemplated this blessing briefly, then confident he could take care of her, she fell entirely asleep with her cheek against his chest, lost to all sensation.

When Eleanor awoke, she was lying on a bed of spruce boughs beside the pool and covered with a blanket. She was stiff and sore but hardly more than pleasantly so. Gavin sat at her feet, his head resting on the bent arm supported by his drawn-up knees. The moonlight shone on the white skin of his broad back and massive shoulders. She looked at him for a long time before she spoke.

"Gavin?"

He lifted his head quickly when she said his name, leaned toward her and peered into her face.

"Ye be awake? How do ye feel, lass?"

"Better. Much better. I can move without all that pain. I just barely remember being in the pool. Oh, it felt so good!"

"Aye. The heat takes the cramps away."

"Is it morning?"

"Twill be in a few hours."

"You haven't slept?"

"I dozed a time or two," he said, not wanting her to know that he had sat beside her for hours, his eyes on her face. He could not bear to waste a moment of the time alone with her.

"Come lie down."

"Nay. I thought to put ye in the pool again—"

"I don't need to go in the pool again, Gavin. Come lie down."

"Lassie—I canna. Me britches be dryin' yon on the warm stones."

Eleanor giggled. "Wrap my skirt around you. Oh . . . mercy me!" She suddenly realized she was naked beneath the blanket. "Where are my clothes?"

"Yer shift be dryin', too. Twas dark then. Ye needn't fear ye was naked to me eyes."

"I'm not worried about that. Come lie down on the top of the blanket. I know you're tired, you carried me up that steep hill."

"Yer weight twas nothin'—"

In the light of the moon she saw him looking at her but was unable to read his expression.

"Please, Gavin. Just for a little while."

Slowly he moved up on the bed of boughs, and she saw that he did have her dark skirt wrapped around his lower body. He eased himself down on top of the blanket that covered her, leaving a foot of space between them. He lay on his back, looking up at the stars, his profile sharply etched in the moonlight. A flood of tenderness for this big, rough man washed over her. She wanted to pull his shaggy head to her breast, hold him, comfort him, wipe away the lines of loneliness from his face. They were two of a kind, she and Gavin McCourtney; each traveling a lonely trail through life.

"Gavin? May I lay my head on your arm?" Her whispered

request was merely a breath, but it reached him. He rolled his head to look at her.

"Lass . . . it wouldna be proper."

"Who would know?" She inched closer to him.

"I would be knowin'."

"Let me be close to you for a little while." She lifted his arm up over her head and snuggled against his side, her shoulder beneath his armpit, her head in the hollow of his shoulder. "I get lonely and scared sometimes, but not when I'm with you."

"Rain be a good mon. He'll see ye through to Belle Point."

"I don't mean that." She tilted her face so she could look up at his. He was once again looking at the stars. "Talk to me. This may be our last chance to be alone together. I want to know what you think, what your dreams are." Her hand slid back and forth across his chest, her fingers curling in the silky hair that covered his nipples.

"A mon like I be dreams only of a tankard of ale 'n a full belly, lass."

"I don't believe that. I think you want a home, a wife and children. Amy said you'd be a good husband and father."

"Why would she say a thin' like that? I been on the river half me life." His arm had unconsciously drawn her closer to his side and his hand now rested on the side of her hip.

"Do you like living on the river?"

"Tis all I know, lassie."

"What about your folks?"

"Gone so long I canna recall their faces."

"Do you remember what I told you about a big plantation in Carolina? It was all lies," she admitted softly. "Aunt Gilda made up the story. She told it to everyone so they would think we were quality folk. But the truth is my father was a scoundrel. My aunt used to say he could talk a bird right out of a tree. The two of them bilked people out of money.

That's how we lived. My mother was ashamed, but she loved my father even when he brought other women to the house to sleep with him. She died, then he died, then Aunt Gilda. So . . . I'm nothing I pretended to be."

Her voice was so sad that Gavin turned his face and his lips brushed her forehead.

"Ahh . . . ye be what ye are—a fine lass. It has naught to do with what yer pa or ma was."

"Will Bradford thinks I'm somebody. He's distant kin on my mother's side. Aunt Gilda led him to believe the family still had a high social standing."

"It willna matter to the mon when he sees ye."

Her hand was moving back and forth across his chest, sending shock waves through his body and causing his flesh to quiver. He captured it with his own to still it.

"I hope he's gone when we get there."

"Nay . . . ye canna be hopin' that. Rain would have to be takin' ye on to him."

"At Kaskaskia, I thought to go to New Orleans and make my own way."

"Twas a foolish thought," he chided gently. "Ye be needin' a mon to care for ye."

"A woman doesn't have much say about her life. I know now that I have to go on to Belle Point. It's like I'm caught in a trap."

"Nay. The mon will be good to ye. Rain says he be a fine mon."

"But I don't love him."

"Tis said that few love when they wed, lass."

"The ones that do are lucky." Eleanor's hand slid from beneath his It inched up his neck to his cheek and gently turned his face toward hers. "Will you kiss me once as if you loved me and we were going to wed?"

"Nay, lassie . . . I canna do it. Ye be promised to a good mon—"

"Please, Gavin. We'll not be taking anything from Will Bradford. He doesn't love me. He feels obligated to take care of me because I'm distant family. The only way he can do it is by marrying me."

"Ah . . . sweet lassie. The mon'd be a fool not to love ye."

"Would you have loved me if I wasn't promised?"

"I wouldna dare. Ye be far above me. I've nothin' to offer a lass like ye be."

"You've got yourself. You're kind, you're brave, you have good thoughts. You see much more than I see. I've been thinking about what you said to me the day we left Quill's Station. You said to look at the world around me and to be glad I was in it. I'd never thought about it before."

They were silent for a long while. Finally she said, "I think I love you." He was quiet for so long she thought he had gone to sleep. She raised her head and looked at him. "Did you hear me, Gavin? I think I love you."

"Ye dinna know what ye be sayin'. Ye'll change yer mind when ye get to Belle Point 'n see the fine officer who wants to wed ye. There ye can stand back, draw a breath, not dependin' on me. There ye'll see me as I be."

"I'll see a man who is as honorable as any I've ever met. I'll see a brave man who risked his life because of my foolishness. I'll see a man who looked at me and saw the real me behind my face and I'll see the only man I could give myself to . . . wholly, if he wanted me."

"Nora! Ah, Nora lass, ye be temptin' me to betray the trust the mon put on me. Tis true I ache for ye, but—"

Eleanor raised up and leaned over him. Her hands caressed his cheeks, her breath warm on his lips.

"I'll not ask you to betray your friend's trust and kiss me. I'll kiss you. Let me. Please let me." She could feel his great body tremble as her lips slid over his chin to his.

Gavin could feel small firm breasts, warm clinging hands . . . the intimacy of that contact sent waves of shock reverberating through him. As if compelled by forces stronger than he, his arms tightened into a steely band around her, holding her with such force she could scarcely breathe. Her mouth, open and sweet, settled on his, sending a swift, mysterious liquid fire to his very center. His body throbbed and quickened with that almost painful burning. Her mouth was as sweet as honey, her touch as soft as cotton. Her lips moved gently, softly over his like the wings of a butterfly. Oh, God! How he wanted to lean over her, deepen the kiss, explore the sweetness of her mouth. But he could not! He closed his eyes tightly and stayed perfectly still. A groan escaped him when she made little smacking movements with her lips and then lifted them. Her face hovered over his, her eyelashes scraping his cheek.

"Your lips are . . . soft, not hard like I thought they would be. Your whiskers are soft too." She rubbed her palms against his cheeks. "Did you know I've not kissed a man before? Isn't that strange considering I was the lure for Aunt Gilda's card games? Lots of men tried, but I couldn't bear for them to touch me. Aunt Gilda was afraid I'd lose my virginity and miss the chance to get a rich husband who would take care of her." She looked into his eyes. "Did you like it?" He stared up at her as if in a daze. When he didn't answer, she drew back. "You didn't like it—"

As if in a panic, he clasped her to him. He held her so close she could feel the hard bones and muscles of his body through the blanket, thrusting against the softness of hers. His hoarse, ragged breathing accompanied the thunder of his heartbeat. The first gentle touch of her lips had shaken him like a leaf in a mighty gale, and it was difficult for him to utter a word.

"Nora . . . me darlin' girl," he whispered beseechingly. He was trembling. She looked down into his eyes and saw moisture there. It touched her unbearably. The age-old maternal urge to comfort him came over her. She wrapped her

arms about him and moved her leg up over his to warm him.
Her knee innocently nudged at his hard maleness, causing
him to shy away from her. Gently but firmly he moved her
leg away.

"Darling Gavin! Sweet, darling Gavin—I'm sorry."

"Tis na yer fault," he croaked.

"I didn't know you'd want me . . . that way." The realization filled her with an almost unbearable tenderness.

Gavin was beginning to smile now, a tentative, shaky
smile that tugged at her emotions as strongly as his embrace.
She kissed the corner of his smile, then lay down with her
head on his shoulder and stared up at the sky dotted with
millions of stars.

"I've wondered what it would be like to be with a man,
make babies with him," she murmured. "Aunt Gilda said it
was an unpleasant duty a woman had to endure, but I don't
think that's true if you love the man. Amy was with Rain
last night and this morning she looked at him like he was the
sun and the stars. I wish I was going to be with you like that,
Gavin."

"Shh . . . ye shouldna be sayin' such things."

"Don't shush me. I feel like I can tell you all my
thoughts."

"It's best ye be sayin' none such as that, lass," he said
gruffly.

"Call me Nora. Only you have called me Nora."

"The birds are stirrin'. It'll soon be morn."

"I wish we could stay here forever," she said wistfully.

"So do I, Nora girl."

CHAPTER
Eighteen

They started out at first light. Rain led them through a winding maze of ravines and across a series of sharp ridges. They crossed a deep, swift creek with high banks and followed a dim trail through the trees a few yards from its bank.

Eleanor had dreaded the time Gavin would lift her to sit in the saddle. When he had done so, she smiled in surprise. The pain had not been as severe as she had thought it would be.

Shortly after they had stopped for the noon meal, they came out onto a wagon track and Rain increased the pace. At one point they smelled the faint odor of wood smoke in the air, but it gradually diminished as they passed a homestead set high on a clearing.

Rain was riding ahead. In the middle of the afternoon he turned back, his worried manner indicating that something was wrong.

"Men up ahead on horseback. They're just sitting there, waiting."

"Indians?" Amy backed her horse so Gavin could come closer.

"No. They look to be a bunch of river rats. They're on horseback, but without saddles, which indicates they've stolen the horses."

"How many?" Gavin asked.

"Five that I saw. They didn't see me."

"Could be they'll move on," Gavin said hopefully.

"Not likely," Rain said dryly. "It's Bull and his cutthroats. They've come downriver by boat and cut across. They knew we'd go through Davidsonville and this is the only track." Rain removed his rifle from the holster and placed it across his lap.

Gavin brought up his rifle, as did Amy and Tally. Eleanor sat her horse quietly; her violet eyes, full of concern, sought Gavin's.

"Are these the men who have come to take me to Hammond Perry?" she asked calmly.

"They're Perry's men and I'm sure that's what they have in mind," Rain answered. "Let's move on so they'll see us. No point in delaying it."

Amy rode beside Rain. "Can we turn back?"

"They'd come on. We might as well face them and get it over with."

"What are we going to do?"

"Nothing until we see what they're going to do. I think by showing themselves they thought to draw me away, ambush me and swoop in to take Eleanor. Perry wants her alive. They don't dare shoot her."

Topping a small hill, they saw the riders coming toward them in a ragged line. Bull and the boy, Muley, were the only ones Amy recognized. The others could have been any of the loafers that hung around the river towns. Some carried pistols, some rifles. They came at a slow trot and then a walk. Rain stopped his horse. Gavin pulled up alongside him, and Amy fell back beside Eleanor.

Bull pulled a length ahead of the others and raised his hand in greeting. "Howdy."

"Stay where you are or take a bullet between the eyes," Rain said crisply.

Bull raised his hand to signal a halt.

"Ya ain't goin' ta be friendly? Hell! Twas us what was dunked in the river."

"What are you after?" Rain knew what they were after but was going to make him say it.

They were a dirty, unkempt, hungry-looking bunch, all of them. Rain had seen their kind: renegades operating out of the river towns. They turned their hands at smuggling, stealing horses and preying on travelers, roving like hungry wolves, picking off the weak and unwary. Now their eyes hungrily surveyed the women.

"We come to get Mr. Perry's woman," Bull said. A thin smile flitted briefly across his whiskered face.

"It'll take more than what you've got there to take her, Bull," Rain said evenly.

"Oh, we got more." Bull lifted his hand and waved. Two men rode out of the woods, one from each side of them, and joined the group behind Bull. "What ya say now, Tallman? Bull Ellert ain't no fool. Seven men ta three. Ah . . . maybe four, if'n ya call that one in britches a man." He laughed and the men behind him snickered. "If twarn't fer the woman we'd gun ya down here 'n now. We figure ya owe us fer the dunkin' in the river 'n burnin' Mr. Perry's boat."

"That was a fair fight, Bull."

"Are ya handin' over the woman?"

Rain took off his hat and wiped the sweat from his forehead with the sleeve of his shirt. He settled his hat back on his head before he spoke. "I have to admit the odds are pretty stiff. There are times a man thinks he's got everything going on a downhill grade and he comes to a creek he can't cross. I guess you've kind of outfoxed me this time."

Bull grinned over his shoulder at his men. "I figured ya'd see it my way, Tallman. I heared ya warn't no rattlehead."

"I never thought I was a rattlehead. I'm not going to die for a mere woman, even a pretty one. If Perry wants her, he can have her. Back off down the road and let me try to convince her that it's the only thing we can do."

"I ain't carin' if 'n she wants ta come. Send 'er on over."

"What are you worried about? You've got seven guns to our three. Give me ten minutes to talk to Miss Woodbury, then come get her."

"Ya figurin' to run?"

"Where the hell would we run to? The woman's threatening to cut her face up. Perry wouldn't want a scarred woman—"

Eleanor let out a long, piercing scream. "I'll kill myself!" She grabbed for Rain's knife and he grabbed her wrist.

"See how it is? I've got to make her understand you'll kill the rest of us if she doesn't knuckle under and go with you."

Bull watched Rain struggle with Eleanor. Finally Rain swung an arm around her waist and lifted her from the saddle. She fought and screamed.

"All right. Ten minutes." Bull said. "When we come back, ya turn the woman 'n the horses over to us 'n get yoreself good 'n clear a here."

"You'll want the guns too?"

"The guns too. Ten minutes to talk. I'd hate to take her to Mr. Perry with a cut face, but I will." He turned his horse and the group followed him back down the wagon track.

Eleanor continued to struggle in Rain's grasp for several minutes. When Bull and his men were a good hundred yards away, Rain let her down so that her feet could touch the ground. She looked up at him and grinned.

"How was it?"

"Good thinking. You almost convinced me." There was

no mistaking the admiration in his brief smile. "We've got to decide what we're going to do."

Eleanor moved over to Gavin and slipped her hand into his. He gripped it so hard she thought her bones would break.

"Be ye thinkin' the same as me?" Gavin asked.

"There's no thinking to be done. They'll kill us as soon as they have Eleanor. They'll not leave us to come after them another time."

"It's my thought."

"We don't have much choice. They outnumber us." Rain spoke gravely. "There's only one thing to do." He got off his horse and the others did the same.

"What's that?" Amy stood quietly, holding the reins of her horse.

"Kill them before they kill us. They're sure going to. As soon as Eleanor is clear, they'll open up on us."

"They've got us outnumbered, mon." Gavin's arm had gone about Eleanor, but no one seemed to notice, not even Gavin.

"Only by three if Amy and Tally shoot."

"I'll shoot," Amy said quickly. "I've got a pistol in my pack, and my knife." She patted the scabbard belted to her waist.

"And you?" Rain glanced doubtfully at Tally. "Can you shoot?"

"Yo're not agoin' to just shoot 'em down?"

"That's what they're going to do to us," Rain pointed out harshly. "You're damn right we'll shoot them down. You don't make deals with hungry wolves."

"I've . . . not shot a man. It ain't Christian."

"What they're going to do to us isn't Christian, either," Amy said stoutly. "I've not shot a man, but I can do it."

"I would if I knew how to shoot," Eleanor said.

"You can shoot my pistol." Amy began to untie the bedroll lashed to her saddle. "I'll load it. All you'll have to do is point and pull the trigger."

"It'll cut down the odds, Eleanor, if you can do it."

"Don't worry. Just show me what to do." Eleanor's lavender eyes sought Gavin's. She would do it for her love, she thought. Aloud she said, "I'd go with them if it would save you all."

"Right now you're what's keeping us alive." Rain turned his horse so the group watching didn't see him check the load in his gun. "Line the horses up in front of us casually, so they can't see what we're doing. Tally, bring the mules up as if you're leaving. Then turn them and come back as if you've changed your mind. That way they'll be between us."

Cold sweat broke out on Tally's face, but he did as he was told. "It don't seem Christian," he repeated, "not to give 'em a chance to back off."

"Hush your whining, Tally," Amy said sternly. "You wanted to come with us and I insisted you stay against Rain's better judgment. Now, damn it, act like a man and do what has to be done."

"But Miss Amy, I ain't never—"

"Shut up! Do what Rain tells you to do or you'll stay right here as buzzard feed."

The group stood behind the horses and prepared their weapons.

"If each one of us hits a man it will leave two alive and us with empty rifles. I can account for one with my knife," Rain said.

"I can take care of the other with mine." Amy looked Rain square in the eyes. "You've never let me show you what I can do. Trust me, Rain. Uncle Juicy saw to it that I can defend myself. He remembered how helpless Fawnella was when she was left alone and the Frenchman killed her."

"All right, sweetheart." His hand came out and gripped

her shoulder. "Chances are a couple of them will turn tail and run when the shooting starts. If that happens, let them go."

"Which one do I . . . shoot?" Tally was trembling like a leaf.

"When they come on, I'll parcel them out. You'll have to do more yelling, Eleanor. We'll be out in front like I'm trying to put you on the horse. Then we'll duck behind the horses and start shooting."

Rain had shot a few men. It was never easy. He understood Tally's feelings. Even the riffraff coming to kill them were men. Some might have families who would wonder what happened to them. He hated killing. He never killed an animal or bird or caught a fish unless he was going to eat it. He would kill these men because if he didn't they would kill them or, even worse, take Amy and Eleanor and use them in the most degrading manner. At the thought of Amy in the hands of such men a chilling calm took possession of him.

Gavin tried to block every thought from his mind except what had to be done. That he would die then and there was of no consequence if he could keep Eleanor safe. She was so beautiful that it almost hurt his eyes to look at her, and just now her magnificent lavender eyes had held a brilliant, soft glow of adoration when she looked at him. She was so great a miracle that it was unthinkable that someone so fragile and precious be handed over to the scum coming to get her. He would die protecting this treasure who had become the core of his life.

Minutes dragged by. Finally Bull and his scavengers started toward them. They fanned out to form a semicircle behind Bull. Everyone carried a gun of some kind, and every gun was ready. Rain was counting on the fact that he had convinced Bull they were willing to hand Eleanor over to them. That, he thought, along with knowing what was about to happen, would give them the advantage.

"Tally, take Bull," he said. "He'll be the closest, the biggest target and the easiest to hit. Remember, he's here to kill Amy and take Eleanor. I'll take the two on the left end. Gavin, take the one on the right before he flanks us. Amy, the one in the beaver hat is yours and the one next to Bull with the feather in his hat is Eleanor's. Eleanor, hold your arm straight out, take your time and squeeze off the shot. That leaves the kid. Unless he turns tail and runs, you'll have to knife him, Amy."

"I will if I have to," she answered calmly.

"I'll drag Eleanor out. When they get so close we can't miss, I'll give the signal. Hold the pistol behind you, Eleanor. Now . . . start yelling!"

Eleanor started screaming and fighting to break loose from the hand Rain had clamped to her arm.

"No! Noo!"

"Damn it! Come on!" Rain shouted, jerking her beneath the horse's neck.

"Stop! Noo . . . I won't go!"

When Bull was within ten yards, Rain let his hand slip from Eleanor's arm. Quick as a wink she darted behind the horse. At the same time Rain slipped behind the mules.

"Now!"

The roar of the weapons was deafening. The mules plunged, horses squealed, men shrieked and cursed and fell. Through the haze of black powder smoke, Rain watched his man jerk backward and fall from the saddle. He drew back his hand and sent his knife hurling at his second man, heard him scream, clutch his stomach and fall to the ground. The smoke was heavy, but Rain could see Bull, still in the saddle, lifting his gun. A second later Amy's knife went flying through the air like a well-aimed arrow and was buried to the hilt in Bull's chest. There was a look of surprise on his face, then his rifle slipped from his hands and he slowly slid from the saddle.

A man crawled on the ground, screeching, and was trampled by a terrified horse. Through the churning dust and smoke, Rain saw that one man was left, the kid. He saw him raise his rifle and fire, then drop it and spur his horse toward them, drawing his pistol from his belt. Rain grasped the barrel of his rifle and leaped into the path of the horse. He swung viciously and clubbed the kid from the saddle. Like a cornered wolf the boy sprang up, his teeth bared. Rain knocked him to the ground again, giving him a sharp whack on the head with his rifle butt. The boy lay in a crumpled heap, like a small, vicious animal.

One mule was down and the other began to buck and bray. Its hooves slashed viciously at the men on the ground.

"Help me," someone yelled. "Help me afore that gawddamn mule—" The man went slack as a hoof found its mark.

As far as Rain could tell the kid had fired the only shot. Rain quickly reloaded his rifle and walked out among the dead or wounded men. He checked each man and kicked weapons away from those still living. He retrieved his knife and Amy's, wiped the bloody blades on the dead men's clothing, then turned back to his own group. His eyes sought Amy standing tall and alert. She had already reloaded her rifle and was ready to use it. Tally stood apart from the others, head down, vomiting on the ground.

"It's over," Rain said. Amy nodded and lowered the weapon.

Gavin had been hit by the only shot fired by the renegades. He was down and Eleanor was bending over him, her face ashen. The mule had taken the bullet through the neck, but fired at such close range, it had passed through and hit Gavin in the side. Blood seeped from the wound, but he was still conscious. Rain knelt beside him and slashed his shirt with his knife so he could see the damage.

"Tis bad?" Gavin asked.

"I don't know," Rain said honestly. "The bullet is still in there."

"Do what ye have to, mon."

"There's no hurry yet. We'll get away from this place first."

"What about . . . them?" Amy jerked her head toward the dead and wounded.

"They're not our problem," Rain said coldly. He turned back to Gavin. "Can you ride?"

"Oh, no! Please don't move him!" Eleanor pleaded.

"Hush, lass," Gavin soothed gently. To Rain he said, "I can ride."

"He'll bleed to death!" Eleanor wailed.

"Tear your petticoat in strips and wrap it around him," Rain ordered. "Goddamn it, Tally, stop puking and get the horses. If you'd done your share, Gavin wouldn't have been hit."

Tears were streaming down Tally's face. "I ain't a killer. I couldn't a killed that boy like . . . you did."

"He had a gun in his hand. I knocked him out. When he comes to he'll be at your throat the first chance he gets."

Tally looked at Amy for help, but the eyes that looked back at him were cold. She turned away from him and went to Rain. He slipped her knife back in the scabbard that hung from her waist. His hands moved up to her shoulders and gripped hard.

"You're a woman to ride the river with, sweetheart. Old Juicy would have been proud, but not as proud as I am." He kissed her gently on the forehead.

"I had to stop Bull—"

"I know. It's over. Don't think about it. I'll see if any of them out there had a bottle of whiskey. Gavin's going to need it." He started away, then turned back. "Shoot that downed mule, Tally. You've still got a load in your gun."

They put several miles between them and the battlefield

where the bodies of the dead and wounded had fallen before they stopped. The ride was torture for Gavin. Amy led his horse and Eleanor rode alongside him. They camped near a little creek beneath a spreading oak tree. Amy and Eleanor gathered old leaves into a soft mat and spread blankets over them. Rain and Tally lifted Gavin from the horse and placed him on it. Not a grunt or a groan passed the big man's lips even though his face was ashen and drenched with sweat.

"I'll build a fire," Amy said when Tally and Rain led the horses away. "We'll need bandages, Eleanor. I've got a clean cloth shirt. What do you have?"

"I've got another petticoat." Eleanor's eyes were filled with tears. "He . . . pushed me behind him after I shot. He'll be all right, won't he?" Quaking fear raced through her; her knees felt like water.

"He's big and strong. I've seen weaker men recover from worse wounds." Amy slipped an arm about the small, dark-haired woman. "You were grand, Eleanor. Just grand! You came through like a real frontier woman. Uncle Juicy would have said you've got sand. Are you sure you weren't raised on the frontier and have been fooling me about Louisville?"

"I just had to do what I could."

"It was plenty. As soon as we get a chance, I'll teach you how to load the rifle and shoot. I'll teach you to throw a knife too. But right now we've got to see to Gavin. I'll start a fire. Take the coffeepot to the creek and scour it, fill it with clean, clear water. Rain will want to get that bullet out of Gavin's side and he'll need boiling water."

By the time the water was boiling, Rain had whetted his knife until the blade was keen. He held it and Amy's in the boiling water for several minutes, then went to kneel beside Gavin.

"Do you want another drink of that whiskey?"

"Lord no! That'd kill a mon!"

"I don't know if the bullet touched any vital parts or not. I don't think it has. The bullet was nearly spent when it hit you. I can feel it under the skin on your back. I'll have to make a cut and pull it on through."

"Do what ye need to." Gavin's voice was slurred from the whiskey.

"I'll help you, Rain," Eleanor said.

"No, lassie." Gavin's voice firmed up. "Go on down to the creek 'n wash yer pretty face," he said as if talking to a child. "It'll be no sight for ye to be seein'."

"Come on away, Eleanor. We've got to wash this petticoat so we can use it again tomorrow." Amy picked up the bloody cloth Rain had taken from around Gavin's middle and drew Eleanor toward the creek. "He doesn't want you to see him like that. He's afraid he'll holler when Rain takes the bullet out. Men! They're afraid to show a little weakness."

"But Rain needs help, and Tally won't be worth a flitter."

"Rain was right about Tally. He should have stayed on the farm."

"Oh, Amy! I love Gavin so much!"

"Eleanor! You haven't . . . ? Didn't . . . ?"

"No! But I would have. He wouldn't!"

"But . . . what about Will Bradford?"

"I don't care about Will. I love Gavin. I don't want to go to Will, but don't tell Rain. Please don't."

"I won't tell him."

Troubled by her promise and Eleanor's unhappy state, Amy left Eleanor by the creek and returned to camp.

Rain worked over Gavin with swift, sure strokes of the knife. Gavin bit down hard on the leather belt between his teeth and not a sound escaped his lips even when Rain drew the bullet out through the hole he cut in his back. A gasp was all that was heard when he poured vinegar on the wound. With his knife and Amy's he picked lint from the wound in Gavin's side, then doused it with a small amount of their precious supply of vinegar, blessing Amy for insisting that they bring it along.

"It's lucky that bullet was almost spent or it would have torn a chunk out of you," Rain said when he finished. "Amy, smear some salve on the cut I made in his back. I'll find a slippery elm. Tonight we'll boil the bark and make a poultice, but for now that's got to do." He wrapped a wide strip from Eleanor's other petticoat around Gavin's middle. "We'll stay here today and tomorrow. The next day we'll have to go on to Davidsonville. If he can't ride, I'll build a travois."

"He needs fresh meat to build his strength," Amy said, wiping the sweat from Gavin's forehead.

"I'll go—" Rain's words were cut off by Eleanor's scream that came from the creek.

Amy jumped to her feet.

Eleanor screamed again. The terrified woman was running toward them as if the devil were after her. "Indians! Indians!"

"It's all right," Rain said quickly and placed his hand on Amy's arm. "It's all right," he said again to Eleanor when she reached them. "He's a friend of mine. I knew he was there."

The Indian that came out of the woods riding a magnificent sorrel was tall, lithe in build, and wore doeskin britches and a shirt adorned with beads. He was lighter in color than most Indians with a pleasant, expressive face and lively intelligent eyes. He leaped from the horse when Rain went to meet him with an outstretched hand and beaming smile. The two clasped hands and pounded each other on the shoulders and wrestled each other like two cub bears.

"Greetings, Meshewa."

"Greetings, Tallman."

"Is my friend Meshewa getting so old he can't conceal

himself from a woman, and so ugly he frightens her out of her wits when she sees him?" Rain teased.

"Ah . . . such a pretty woman! My feet follow my eyes." His English was smooth and effortless. "She must forgive me for frightening her."

"Mary Blue Feather will skin you out and use your hide for whet leather if she catches you eyeing another woman."

The Indian was handsome. He was as handsome as Amy remembered Tecumseh to be when he visited Quill's Station years ago. At the mention of his wife, Meshewa's smile broadened and his dark eyes glinted.

"That is true, Tallman. She watches me like the hawk watches the rabbit." There was pride in his tone. "She makes me wear these in my hair to keep my thoughts on her." His black hair was parted in the middle and two short braids decorated with small blue feathers lay on his chest. He lifted one as he spoke.

"How is Mary Blue Feather?" Rain asked.

"Big with papoose." Meshewa made a motion with his hand to indicate a large stomach.

"Again?" Rain exclaimed. "No wonder they call you Meshewa, the stallion."

The Indian laughed, his dark eyes going from Rain to Amy standing beside him.

"Your woman, Tallman?"

"My woman. She's called Amy."

"Little Wife?" He looked at Rain and Rain nodded. "I've heard much about Little Wife from Quill's Station." Meshewa's dark eyes settled boldly on Amy's face. "My uncle, John Spotted Elk, spoke often of Juicy Deverell."

"He was his friend," Amy murmured.

"No papoose, Tallman?" Meshewa looked pointedly at Amy's flat stomach. "Want that Meshewa show you how to make papoose?"

Color flooded Amy's face, but she refused to turn from the Indian's knowing eyes.

"We'll make the papoose when the time is right," Rain said and threw his arm across Amy's shoulders. "Sweetheart, this *heathen* is the son of Minnie Dove, sister of my stepfather. We grew up together. His father, Black Fox, failed to teach him manners."

Amy held out her hand. "How do you do?"

The Indian took her hand in his and pumped it up and down. "How do you do?" he repeated. "She pretty woman, Tallman. She shoot good, too."

"You were . . . there?" Amy stammered.

"I watch to see what Tallman do. My uncle would be proud. You did fine too, Little Wife." He dismissed the shootings with a shrug of his shoulders.

"The woman you scared is Eleanor Woodbury. I'm taking her to Will Bradford at Belle Point."

"Ahh . . ." The Indian turned to look at Eleanor who was kneeling beside Gavin. "Will Bradford's woman?"

"Will sent for her."

"Do you know Will Bradford too?" Amy asked.

"Meshewa knows everyone this side of the Rocky Mountains," Rain said with a grin.

"Be glad, Tallman. I know Antoine Efant ask questions of you."

"Antoine Efant? The Frenchman who stole the furs out from under the noses of Chouteau and Lisa Manuel?" Rain's face was suddenly grim. "What's he been wanting to know about me? Where did you hear this?"

Meshewa shrugged again. "Saint Genevieve. What man usually want to know? Where you go? Why you go? When you go? He may want your woman." The Indian said the last with a teasing glance at Amy.

"He'll pay hell getting her!" Rain was suddenly angry. "Is Efant short, stocky, black curly hair, and wears a knit cap?"

"He not pretty like you, Tallman."

"Meshewa! Damn you!"

Meshewa laughed and clapped Rain on the shoulder. "Mary Blue Feather say Tallman make good lover. Huh, Little Wife?"

"Mary Blue Feather was right," Amy said boldly and smiled into the Indian's eyes.

Meshewa turned his attention to Eleanor. "If this one be Will Bradford's woman, why did big man carry her to hot pool and sleep with her under one blanket? Will Bradford kill him."

Eleanor jumped up. "He didn't!" she exclaimed.

"I see big man's prints, one bed." Meshewa shrugged again and turned back to Rain. "Big man hurt bad?"

"I'm not sure. I got the bullet out and the bleeding has stopped. Tonight I'll make a slippery elm poultice if I can find an elm tree. I don't want to stay here more than one more day."

The Indian stood over Gavin and nodded gravely. "Needs meat to make strong. Come, Tallman. Hunt with Meshewa. I show you slippery elm and elk."

"Fire a single shot if you need me, Amy." Rain picked up his rifle. "We'll not be far away."

"If he's a friend of yours, why didn't he come help us today?" she whispered when the Indian went to get his horse and the gun he had left lying in the grass.

"There was no reason to, sweetheart. It was best he didn't let Bull know he was there. If it had come to hand-to-hand fighting, he would have come charging in. It's what I would have done."

"Did you know he was there?"

"No. The first I knew he was near was when I stopped here. He knew this was a likely place to camp and was here ahead of us. He left his sign here on the tree and I stopped. We've left signs for each other since we were knee-high to a duck. Get the kettle on, we'll be back with fresh meat. Meanwhile, make Gavin some tea."

Eleanor sat on the blanket beside Gavin and held his hand. He had drifted off to sleep. She looked across at Amy with teary eyes.

"We weren't under a blanket," she said with a catch in her voice. "He sat up beside me all night. It was almost morning when I persuaded him to lie down and rest. We did nothing wrong, Amy. I swear it!"

"You don't have to explain to me—"

"But I want to tell you about it so you'll not think . . . badly of Gavin. I asked him to kiss me and he wouldn't. So I kissed him. That's all that happened."

"If you feel you and Gavin have done no wrong, that's all that matters, Eleanor. I'm going to build a spit and hang the kettle over the fire. Then I'm going to talk with Tally. Sit here and fan the flies off Gavin. Sleep is the best thing for him right now."

Tally had hobbled the mule and the horses in a small grassy clearing near the creek. He sat with his back to a tree, knees up, throwing the blade of his pocketknife into the dirt between his booted feet.

"That's sure a good way to dull a knife." Amy walked up to him and stood looking down at his bent head.

Tally wiped the blade on his pant leg, flipped it shut and put it in his pocket. He clasped his hands around his bent knees, refusing to look at her.

"When we get to Davidsonville, I want you to leave us, Tally. Maybe you can get work there until you can join up with some folks going back up north. If not, I'll give you some money to see you home."

"I don't need your money. I'm sorry I shamed you, Miss Amy."

"You didn't shame me. You shamed yourself."

"I'm not cut out for . . . killin' 'n traipsin' all over the country. I'm a farmer."

"Rain tried to tell you that. He tried to tell me too, but I wouldn't listen."

"I don't hold with killin' like he done. Ma said he was . . . hard. She said a wandering man wasn't no good to hisself or anybody."

"I don't hold with killing either, and neither does Rain, unless someone is trying to kill us!" Amy said heatedly. "I had to stop Bull today when you failed to do it. That gave the boy the chance to shoot Gavin."

"I couldn't just kill him," Tally said stubbornly.

"No. You'd have let them come on and kill us," Amy retorted sarcastically.

"We wasn't sure they was agoin' to."

"Oh, for crying out loud! You're just as bullheaded as my pa. You stayed with your mother because you needed her to tell you what to do. Go on back home, Tally. Your place is behind the plow."

"It wasn't so bad. It's a heap better than shilly-shallyin' all over the country without a spot of your own," he retorted.

"Rain and I will have a place of our own someday. We're settling in Arkansas."

"You been sleepin' with him, and you ain't wed!" Tally spat out accusingly.

"Yes, I have. I'm proud of it. I hope to bear his children; many, many children. I pity your wife if you ever get one. She'll be getting a gutless man."

Amy turned and walked rapidly away from him before she said something she would regret later. Tally would never be anything except what he was, and she had been wrong to think he could change.

CHAPTER
Nineteen

Amy lay with her head on her arm and gazed up at the brilliant night stars in the black vault above. The day had been spent quietly, resting and tending to Gavin. They had needed the day of rest because a human being could not go all the way through the valley of death and then return without suffering shock for a little while.

Gavin had slept most of the day. At mealtime Eleanor had insisted on feeding him chunks of tender meat and bread soaked in the broth. She spent the rest of the time sitting beside him, fanning him with the brim of her bonnet and bringing him cool water from the creek. She had been exceptionally quiet. In her eyes was the sad, haunted look of lost dreams and pitiful resignation. When darkness came she spread her blankets near his and lay down on her side facing him, as if she couldn't bear not to look at him.

Rain and Meshewa left the camp when darkness fell. Tally still sat beneath a tree, brooding. Rain ignored him and told Amy to go on to bed. He and his friend would circle the camp and be back soon.

Now Amy lay wondering when Rain and Meshewa slept.

They had sat up talking beside the campfire most of the night before, and today they had ridden away and not returned until late in the afternoon.

The camp was quiet except for the normal night sounds: the crickets, frogs, and the creek water flowing over stones on its journey to a larger stream somewhere to the south.

Amy, attuned to the night sounds, was suddenly aware that the cadence of the crickets was interrupted. She cautiously lifted her head to look behind her.

Rain came out of the shadows, crossed a patch of moonlight and walked back into the shadow again. He threw his hat on the ground beneath the tree, leaning his rifle against the trunk.

"How did you know I was coming?" he asked as he squatted down beside her.

"The crickets stopped singing as you passed."

Rain chuckled and pulled his shirt off over his head, then sat down on the blanket and pulled off his moccasins.

"Meshewa is gone. He likes to travel at night. He has the eyes of an owl."

"Where's he going?"

"Home. After the earthquake his uncle moved the tribe west to the Beaver Lake country. He carried a message to the tribes east of the big river and heard that I had passed through Kaskaskia."

"A war message?"

"No. A message saying it was time for the tribes to move west before they were boxed in by the whites. His uncle is troubled. Their home is north of Belle Point, but Meshewa said there's constant trouble between the Osage and the Cherokee and Will Bradford was doing all he could to keep peace." Rain lifted the blanket and lay down beside her; he wrapped his arm around her and drew her to his side. "Forget about all that now, sweetheart. Come here. I want to hold you."

"I didn't expect you to come to our blankets tonight," she whispered and turned her lips to the warm skin of his shoulder.

"Is that why you've got this thing on?" he asked, his hand hard against her buttocks pulling her tightly against him.

"I thought Meshewa would come back with you, and you wouldn't want to—"

"Wouldn't want to! Not until I'm old and gray and have one foot in the grave! Even with a cane I'm going to chase you around the house." He pulled her to a sitting position and pulled the gown over her head. "Do you want *to*, Little Wife? Do you?" he asked between chuckles, pushing her back down on the blanket and leaning over her.

"You know I do!" Her arms went around his neck, her palms smoothing the muscles in his shoulders. "But . . . I want to talk to you first—" His mouth closed over hers and his fingers found the nipple on her breast and squeezed it. "Rain! Stop or I'll not be able to . . . talk," she gasped when his lips left hers and followed his fingers to her breast.

"I told you that once I had a taste of you I'd be like a rutting moose. We can talk later. Right now I'm so hungry for you I'm about to burst." His hands caressing her warm naked body from the nape of her neck to her firm buttocks were both sweet and violent.

"Greedy man!" She laughed happily in his ear. "You've had me every night but last night."

"I want you every night!" he said hoarsely, pulling her tightly against him and moving his hips so that his arousal rubbed against her soft belly. "I almost hated Meshewa for keeping me from you."

His fingers made sharp invasions of her body, and she responded by touching his dark nipples, tentatively at first, and then more firmly as he hissed in pleasure. His mouth explored her neck and shoulders and deposited wet kisses in her ear. With her head held fast in the crook of his elbow he feasted on her mouth while his fingers searched the silken copper bush between her legs and then crept into the damp, dark crevice of delight.

"Rain, darling, I love you," she murmured and arched against him, aware only of the need to satisfy the hunger he was provoking.

She felt him moving down to enter her and spread her legs to welcome him. He was as hard and firm and wonderful as before. It felt so good to have him there. She pressed up against him and heard the answering groan that came from deep in his throat. He went in all the way and held himself there. When he withdrew she almost cried out, clutching his buttocks to keep him from leaving her. She wanted the surging rhythm, and her hips began to move.

His muted laugh against her mouth was one of sheer joy. He slowed the rhythm and she twisted and turned under him, trying to get him to increase the pace. Then suddenly he thrust with unbelievable force, pressing deeper and deeper against her womb. Amy was sure she would explode, that she would die of pleasure. But he didn't stop. They moved closer and harder and faster until time and forest and stars all exploded in a gigantic burst of color. She gave a sob of joy as he responded with a long shuddering sigh. When they were two again, they lay panting and holding on to each other.

They remained for a long while locked together. His body was a beloved weight against her, his head beside hers, a light breeze cooling the sweat on their bodies. After long moments he raised up to lean on his elbows. She smiled up at him and stroked his cheek with her fingertips.

"Have I told you today that I love you, Little Wife?" he asked shakily. "I love you so much it purely scares the hell out of me." His lips nibbled at hers for a long moment before he whispered, "My God! I could have gone through life without knowing . . . this if I'd not gone back to Quill's Station."

"I was waiting for you," she said simply. "I would have waited forever." She felt like crying for the lonely years spent after Juicy's death, hoping and praying Rain would return.

"Sweetheart! I didn't know!" He rolled to his back and held her close to his side. "You're not crying?" he asked anxiously when he felt moisture on her cheek.

"No. It's just nerves. I thought we were going to die yesterday and never build a home or see our children," she said in a small voice against his neck.

"I'm glad it's over. I don't think we'll have to worry about Hammond Perry now. If Gavin hadn't been shot, we'd have been to Belle Point in a week or ten days. We may have to leave him in Davidsonville."

"I told Tally to leave us when we get to Davidsonville. I was wrong about him, and I'm sorry. We should have sent him downriver with the boatman that brought us across."

"I've seen his type before. He needs to be in a place where he does the same thing day after day. He can't handle quick decisions. If you'd have been killed or even hit because he didn't have the guts to shoot I'd have killed him!" he said fervently. "As it is, he let the kid shoot Gavin, who's ten times the man he is."

"Gavin's going to be all right, isn't he?"

"I think so. If we bind him good and tight he should be able to ride tomorrow. We'll make it a short day. I have a friend in Davidsonville who'll look after him if he can't go on."

"Eleanor is worried about what Meshewa said about her and Gavin sleeping together."

"Meshewa read the signs as he saw them. Gavin has fallen in love with Eleanor, but I'm sure he'll not dishonor her. My job is to take her to Will Bradford, sweetheart. What happens after that is up to them."

"What if . . . she doesn't want to marry Will?"

"Then she'll have to tell him."

"She'll not want to leave Gavin in Davidsonville."

"She'll have to if he can't travel."

"Rain . . . why do you think the Frenchman was asking about you? Could he have anything to do with Hammond Perry wanting Eleanor?"

"I don't think so. I've heard about Efant. Now I think he was the Frenchman we met in Kaskaskia. He's a rogue. Some say he's a cold-blooded killer, some say he's an honorable man. But there's no need for us to worry about him until the time comes." He moved out from under the blanket and began to pull on his shirt and britches. Amy leaned up on one elbow to watch him.

"Where are you going?"

"I'm going to circle the camp. I'll be back soon."

Eleanor saw Rain leave Amy's blankets and move silently into the woods along the stream. She took a quivering breath and blinked back the tears. The hours had dragged by slowly as she lay on her lonely bed, listening for any sound that came from the man who lay a few feet away.

After Rain had left camp, Gavin threw back the blanket and leaned up on his elbow.

"Gavin?" Eleanor whispered and inched over to him. "Do you want a drink of water?"

"Aye. But I can be gettin' it."

"I've got some right here." She brought the cup and held it to his lips. He drank thirstily and lay back down. "Can't you sleep?" she asked anxiously, placing her palm on his forehead.

"I been sleepin' the day out, lass. I just be tired of lyin' here."

"Your forehead is still cool. Rain said to watch for signs of fever."

"Ye best be gettin' some sleep yerself. Ye been up 'n down——"

"You were awake?"

"Aye. Most of the time."

Eleanor folded out the edge of the blanket covering Gavin and lay down on her side on the top of it, pulling her blanket over them.

"Lassie, ye shouldn't——"

"Don't say anything, Gavin. I'm going to stay here. You may need me."

"Ye be making trouble for yerself."

"I don't care. Gavin . . . if you hadn't shoved me behind you I'd have been killed. The shot that hit you in the side would have hit me higher up."

"Ye don't know that, lass."

"Look at me." With a palm against his cheek she turned him toward her. Their faces were close. She moved her body closer and her breast nudged his forearm. "I love you. Yesterday I was sure we were going to die. But because you were with me, I wasn't really afraid."

"Ye stood up to it like the grand lass ye are."

"Do you love me? Do you love me just a bit?"

"Nora, lass, I got no right——"

"Why don't you have the right?" she whispered.

"'Cause I be what I be, and ye be promised to another mon. Even if ye werena——"

"When we get to Belle Point, I'm going to tell Will that I'm not going to marry him."

"Now why would ye be doin' a thin' like that?"

"Because I don't want to marry him. I want to marry you,

if you . . . want me. I think you do. We can build a life together, Gavin. I know we can."

"Ye don't be knowin' what ye be sayin'."

"I know perfectly well what I'm saying. I'm going to kiss
you. If you don't want to kiss me back, it's all right."

"Nay, Nora! The mon will be comin' back."

"Let him see; I don't care. Someday you'll kiss me.
Someday, you'll come to my blankets and hold me in your
arms all night long, just like he holds Amy," she whispered,
her lips floating above his. Her kiss was sweet, gentle, loving, clinging. She kissed him lingeringly, tasting his mouth,
learning the shape, but softly, gently. Reluctantly the kiss
ended.

"Ye be killin' me, my . . . sweet angel of a woman," he
muttered thickly and anxiously. The streak of flame spreading through his groin was making breathing difficult. "I be
achin' fer ye 'n holdin' meself from ye."

"You don't have to hold yourself from me."

"Tis almost more than I can bear." When he lifted his arm
she raised her head to fit it on his shoulder and snuggled
against his side. She could feel his great body shudder even
though there was a blanket between them.

"I'm not hurting you?"

"Nay. Tis not fittin' to mention the part of me that aches
for ye. Nora, lass, I don't know what to be doin'."

"To know that you love me is enough. We'll go to Will
and tell him that we love each other. He'll release me."

"Then what, lass? I've no way to be takin' care of ye in
the style ye be used to. The best I can do is to homestead. It
be a rough life for a lass such as ye."

"You're not to be worrying about it. Hear? You've got to
get well before we do anything. Oh, kiss me, sweet man.
Really kiss me!" She tilted her head and brushed her lips
against the pulse in his throat. He pulled her even closer to
his side and gave a hungry moan of anticipation.

"Take care, lass," he warned her with pain in his voice, "lest I be carried beyond endurance."

She felt his lips in her hair and his hand stealing up to gently encircle her round breast. He gently teased her ear with his tongue and teeth, then his lips crossed her cheek to her waiting mouth. His kiss was long and demanding, and she felt a flood of sensations sweep over her. He devoured her mouth hungrily, again and again, drinking in her sweetness until his senses reeled. Then all too soon it was over and he fell away from her. He lay beside her, his breath coming in agonized gasps.

"Ye be so sweet . . . so sweet."

"Kissing is wonderful," she said weakly while placing small kisses along the line of his jaw. "Gavin . . . what were you like as a little boy?"

"Ah, lass, twas long ago. I was like most boys. Happy."

"Tell me."

"Me mother liked music, me father was a scholarly mon. Many nights he would teach me to read by candlelight 'n me mother would sing to us. I believe they loved each other; it's what a child wants to believe." He hugged her close to him now, not caring if Rain returned and found them lying close together.

"I was a lad of nine years when we come from Scotland to start a new life in America. We were in the harbor, plannin' to leave the ship come mornin'. In the middle of the night there was a fire, 'n the ship went up in a flash. The flames spread 'n there was nothin' to do. Me father tossed me over the side, then went back for me mother. I never saw them again."

"Oh, my poor love! What did you do?"

"I was bonded to a kind lady. She died of fever when I was twelve 'n and I took to the river to earn me keep. That be it, lass. I be nothin' but a rough rivermon."

In answer, Eleanor slid her arms about his neck and covered his face with fierce kisses.

"'Nothin' but a rough rivermon'?" she protested heatedly, copying his Scottish accent. "You're the sweetest, most wonderful rivermon in all the world, Gavin McCourtney!"

"Lass, lassie—ye got to be stoppin' this."

"How can I when I'm so happy?"

"Ye can shut yer pretty eyes 'n sleep is what ye can do. Mornin' will find ye worn out."

"I'll shut my eyes, but I can't promise to sleep," she said, and snuggled against him.

Eleanor was asleep when Rain returned. He passed by, looked down, and saw her head cradled in the crook of Gavin's arm. He paused briefly and moved on, sure that he had seen Gavin's eyes gleaming up at him through the darkness.

Dawn had lightened the eastern sky when Rain came to the small breakfast fire. Eleanor was sitting on her blankets combing her hair and Gavin was coming from the creek. She stopped combing and watched Gavin anxiously.

"Morning," Rain said.

"Morning." Eleanor turned her head to Rain, then back to watch Gavin.

"He seems better." Rain added a few sticks of wood to the fire and set the kettle over the blaze.

"He . . . says he is."

"I dinna see the boy or his horse," Gavin said as soon as he reached them.

"He left last night," Rain said calmly. He tilted his head and looked up as Amy neared with their blanket rolls. "Tally left last night, Amy. I saw him ride out and head south."

"Why didn't you stop him?"

"It would have been foolish to leave camp and go after him," he replied briskly.

"You're right. I'm sorry, Rain."

"Why would he do a thing like that?" Eleanor asked.

"He wanted to go home," Amy said slowly.

"Twas a foolhardy thin' the lad be doin'."

"How far is it to Davidsonville?" Amy asked while she rolled the blankets and tied them.

"He can make it in one day of hard riding. We'll make it in two," Rain said. "You and Eleanor will have to ride double and lead the pack mule."

The four drank tea and ate cold bread and meat, then doused the campfire and prepared to leave. Rain and Amy brought up the horses and Rain helped Gavin into the saddle.

Throughout the morning they traveled alongside the fast-moving creek. When the underbrush thickened, Rain turned east, crossed the creek, and they came to the wagon track. Amy suspected it was the one they had been on when they were attacked by Bull and his men. The land was rolling and thickly forested. Several times they flushed deer from their beds, and when they passed alongside a marshy field, they roused a flock of teal.

Gavin's features were frozen into lines that could only be pain. He stayed erect in the saddle, but accepted Rain's help when they stopped for a noon rest. Eleanor hovered over him, bringing him water and food.

In the late afternoon Rain turned off the track and into the woods. They camped deep in the forest. As soon as the blankets were spread, Gavin lay down and was almost instantly asleep. Rain and Amy led the animals to water, then tied them close to camp. Amy discovered a berry bush and filled her hat with the dark, juicy berries. There was no fire that night and again they ate bread and cold meat. The berries were a welcome treat.

Gavin appeared to be much stronger when morning came.

Eleanor and Amy changed the bandage and were pleased to
see the wound was pink and healing. Again a slippery elm
poultice was applied and held in place by strips of Eleanor's
petticoat.

On the trail again, Rain traveled at an even pace, putting
the horses in a fast walk. It was a warm, sweet-smelling day.
Wild roses grew alongside the dirt track and bees hummed
over them. Amy watched as two male cardinals flew out of
the trees. They whirled and dived and circled each other.
They were joined by a female and the two bright patches of
scarlet chased the reddish brown until they were mere specks
in the blue sky. Nearer the ground a wren scolded as they
passed too close to her nest, and a squirrel, chased by a
blackbird, scurried up a tree.

The day was beautiful, peaceful. As Amy watched Rain
riding ahead happiness flooded her heart. He was her love,
and they were on their way to his high valley and dream
river where they would spend the rest of their lives together.
The only problem left to be solved was that of Eleanor and
Gavin. If Will Bradford was the man Rain said he was, he
would surely release Eleanor from her promise to marry him
so that she could be happy with Gavin.

In the middle of the morning Rain began to notice the
squawks of crows and the scavengers gathering in the trees
ahead. He waited several minutes before he lifted his hand to
signal a halt.

"Wait here," he said curtly, knowing instinctively that
something ahead was dead and that it must be something
larger than a small animal to attract such a large flock of
scavengers.

"What is it?" Amy called, but Rain had spurred his horse
into a lope and didn't answer.

The three of them waited anxiously for Rain's return, feeling vulnerable there on the track. Amy's eyes swept the trail
behind them and to the sides. There was silence except for

the noisy cawing of the crows. It seemed to her that Rain had been gone for a long while, but it couldn't have been more than a quarter of an hour before she saw him riding back toward them. He rode directly to Amy.

"It's Tally," he said quietly. "Someone must have sneaked up behind him and cut his throat. They took his horse and his gun."

Amy gave a strangled cry. "Oh . . . my God!" Her hand went to her throat as if she were afraid she would throw up.

"How horrible!" Eleanor exclaimed.

"There's no sign of a fight, not even a struggle. He never even had time to be scared," Rain said gently, as if to comfort Amy. "Wait for me over there." He pointed to a stand of thick aspens. "I'll bury him."

"It's all my fault! I shamed him or he wouldn't have left," Amy said over the sob in her throat. "I'll help . . . bury him."

"No," Rain said firmly. "It wasn't your fault and you'll not help bury him. Gavin," he looked the big man directly in the eyes, sending a silent message. "Take the women over there and wait for me."

"Aye, that I'll be doin'."

Head down, Amy turned her horse and followed Gavin. Behind her Eleanor placed a comforting hand on her shoulder. When they were among the trees, Gavin stopped and eased himself from the saddle. Eleanor slid down, but Amy sat her horse, her face turned away from them.

"I should have made him go back when we were in Saint Genevieve," she said raggedly. "It was too late after we crossed the river."

"Ye can't be blamin' yerself, lass. He was a mon grown."

"But he left home because of me."

"Ye can't be helpin' that."

"Poor Tally." The image of him sitting beneath the tree throwing his knife into the dirt at his feet came suddenly to

Amy's mind. "I told him to leave us when we got to David-sonville. He said he had in mind to do that."

"Why did he leave in the middle of the night?" Eleanor asked.

"I think he couldn't stand the sight of us, and he wanted to do something on his own. He must have camped right out in the open again. He hadn't learned a thing . . ." Amy's voice trailed away.

When Rain signaled from the road, they left the woods and joined him.

"I did the best I could, Amy." Rain's shirt was wet with sweat. "Here, I brought you this." He shoved Tally's pocket-knife in her hand. "It's something to give his ma."

Amy put it in her pocket without looking at it. "I'll proba-bly never see her again," she murmured, keeping her face turned away from him.

The crows had scattered by the time they reached the place where Tally had died. Amy kept her eyes straight ahead. She had known Tally for a long time. His dogged devotion to her had been a source of irritation, but now that he was dead she felt only pity.

Tears welled in her eyes and she cried softly.

CHAPTER
Twenty

Antoine Efant sat on the porch, his chair tilted back against the wall, cleaning his fingernails with a long, thin blade. The cabin belonged to Pete Hopcus, a man with whom he had worked before and who had gone to Davidsonville for news. Antoine waited anxiously for his return.

"Gawd, it's hot down here." The man who spoke was older than Antoine, had a permanent scowl on his whiskered face and the clothes he wore were not as neat and clean as those of the other man. Hull Dexter was a man who would turn his hand at most anything to get an easy dollar.

"Mon Dieu! Your complaining is beginning to irritate me. Are you not being paid for your discomfort?"

Hull ignored Antoine's question and mopped his face with the sleeve of his shirt.

"Don't the heat 'n skeeters bother you?"

"No. Go down to the creek and get a bucket of water."

"Pete ort a be back." Hull got slowly to his feet. "If'n he don't bring that jug a whiskey I'll break his scrawny neck."

"And if he *does* I'll break yours." Antoine continued to clean his fingernails with the knife.

"Jesus, Efant! Ya ain't human."

"There'll be no drinking until the job is done. I told you that at the start. You can hightail it out if it doesn't suit you."

"And get a knife in my back? I ain't heard of a body quittin' on Antoine Efant."

"Nobody ever has," Antoine said, then added softly, "and lived to tell it. Now, get the hell down to the creek."

Rain and his party reached Davidsonville in the late afternoon of the second day. The settlement appeared suddenly when they rounded a bend in the track. Amy didn't know what she had expected, but the town was little more than a few scattered log buildings clustered around a trading post. Davidsonville, covering no more than a dozen acres, was set in a clearing surrounded by thick forests. The trail meandered through the middle of the town, passing close to the store.

In front of the squat log building the earth had been chopped and chewed by horses' hooves and wagon wheels until it was powdery, and a fine dust cloud swirled around the hooves of their horses as they stopped.

Rain guided his horse to the hitching rail. As he tied the reins to the stout post, a man emerged and stood on the porch, his feet spread, his fists on his hips. He was a short man, built like a barrel, with long, dark, white-streaked hair and a protruding abdomen. His beard, tinged with gray, was braided in three long strands that dangled in front of his homespun shirt. He let out a whooping yell and pounded both hands against his chest as if he were beating a drum.

"*Mon Dieu!* Rain Tallman! I thought you'd been strung up and dried out by now. How you be?"

"Fine, Jean Pierre. You look as fat and sassy as ever."

"Ain't got no wish to be nothin' else. Come on in. Come right on it. Bring the womenfolk in outta the sun." He eyed Amy and Eleanor curiously.

A crowd began to gather to gawk at the strangers. More than ten families lived in the settlement and a representative from each seemed to appear from nowhere. Half a dozen Indians came from inside the trading post and stood watching, blankets about their shoulders, their faces impassive. At the sight of the Indians, Eleanor cowered against Amy.

"We need rooms for a night or two, Jean Pierre." Rain spoke while lifting first Eleanor and then Amy from the horse. Amy stepped up on the porch. Eleanor waited for Gavin and stayed close to his side.

"Funny you'd show up like this. Soldier feller from Belle Point brought in mail no more'n a week ago. A letter in it for you."

"That so?"

The trader couldn't understand the famed woodsman's lack of enthusiasm. To most folks a letter was a high point in their lives. Tallman acted as if he received a letter every day.

Rain took Amy by the elbow and urged her through the door and into the store. Gavin and Eleanor followed. Amy looked around with interest, comparing it unfavorably to Farr's store back at Quill's Station. It was not as well-organized and not nearly as clean.

It was cool and dark inside. The only light came from the open door and from one small glass window at the front. The place was crowded with barrels, stacks of furs, traps, and all manner of supplies homesteaders needed to survive. Harnesses and tools hung from the rafters. Rain had to dodge around those to get to the counter. A mingling of odors tickled their nostrils: leather, furs, spices and cooked cabbage. The store was also the post office, the first post office to be established in the Arkansas Territory.

Jean Pierre Hoffman went behind a counter and rummaged among a clutter of papers, hides and tobacco pouches. Finally, after numerous curses and threats of mutilations to those who had dared to meddle with government property, he came up with a thin white envelope and proudly handed it over to Rain. He watched expectantly with bright dark eyes, waiting for Rain to open the letter. But Rain slipped the envelope inside the neck of his shirt.

"How about the rooms?" he asked. "The ladies are tired, and they would be grateful for a chance to wash."

"I am honored to have the ladies as my guests." The trader bowed. His smile showed missing front teeth. "Tennessee!" he bellowed. "Bring water!"

The building had two wings. The left evidently housed the owner's quarters according to the sounds coming from that area. The voice of a woman scolding children could be plainly heard. Hoffman led them to the right wing. There was a long dark storeroom and at the end a guest room. The door he opened sagged back on its leather hinges. Amy and Eleanor went into the room.

"It's the best I got," he announced. "You gents can bed down in the storeroom."

"That will be fine," Rain said, crowding into the small room and moving along the wall to make room for Gavin.

The trader lingered in the doorway for a long moment, then went back to the store. Rain Tallman was a legend in the land west of the big river. That he had arrived at the settlement with two women would be the talk for months to come. Jean Pierre would be the one to tell about how he came riding in one day and as cool as you please said he wanted a room.

"Ahh..." Jean Pierre sighed. "He is a man, that one. Which one will he have, or will it be both?"

The room was small, the cracks in the log walls filled with mud plaster. One high window was covered by a thin deerskin. Under that a crude bench was nailed to the wall. The bed was built into one corner, a platform a foot off the floor, covered with a straw-filled pad. A candle in a glass holder sat on the mantel. If Amy hadn't been so tired and so depressed because of Tally she would have laughed at the irony of that touch of refinement in the rough setting.

A girl came to the door with a bucket of water and a tin basin. She had large dark eyes and long black braids. Her skin was light, but her Indian blood was evident. Rain took the bucket and basin.

"Thank you, Tennessee."

"Come sit down, Gavin." Eleanor gestured toward the bench against the wall. The big Scot eased himself down and Eleanor sat beside him. "This is only slightly better than camping," she said with a giggle.

"There's something about being enclosed in these dark walls that makes me edgy." Amy wrapped her arms around herself and shuddered. "How long will we be here, Rain?"

"It depends on what the letter says." Rain took it from his shirt and looked at the writing on the envelope. "It's from Will."

They all waited expectantly for Rain to open his letter. He stepped to the door and looked out, then slit the end of the envelope with his knife and pulled out the sheet of paper. He read the missive slowly, tilting the paper to the light so he could see. Then he read it again before he spoke.

"It's from Will," he said again and glanced at Eleanor. There was a frightened look on her face as if she expected a death notice. "The letter is addressed to me, Eleanor, but it concerns you. Do you want me to read it aloud?"

She nodded stiffly. Rain moved closer to the bench, stood with his shoulder against the wall, and began to read aloud:

Belle Point
22 May, 1819

Dear friend Rain,
    I reluctantly take pen in hand to inform you of the conditions here at the post. As deadly as any threat that might arise from the Indian conflict, ague and bilious fever have afflicted the men of the garrison, the settlers about the post, and the Indians. More than one hundred have already succumbed to this malady.
    Conditions here at the post have not progressed as I had hoped when I entrusted you with the mission of bringing Miss Woodbury to Belle Point. There are no women here at the post except for the wives of two enlisted men who work as laundresses, and no suitable housing. There is much unrest among the tribes and my duties keep me away from the post much of the time.
    The conditions here have made it necessary for me to make a grievous decision. Therefore, I must inform you that I am unable to have Miss Woodbury and her aunt with me at the present time. It may be years before this post will be secure enough for me to bring them here. Please assure Miss Woodbury that I am aware of my commitment to her and will honor it at a later date should she still be desirous of accepting my hand in marriage.
    In the meanwhile, Rain, if you will find quarters

for them in Kaskaskia or Saint Genevieve, I will
make the necessary arrangements with General
Smith at Belle Fontaine to set up a fund to meet
their living expenses. And you, my friend, will be
reimbursed for both time and money, and I will be
forever in your debt.

Your servant,
William Bradford, Major
Company A, Ninth Military Department
Belle Point, Arkansas Territory

Rain held out the letter to Eleanor. "Do you want to read
it?" She shook her head numbly, as if she hadn't yet absorbed the meaning of the message. Rain carefully slipped
the paper into the envelope and put it back inside his shirt.

"Does it mean I don't have to marry him?" Eleanor sat
with her hands tightly clasped in front of her.

"Will wouldn't have *forced* you to marry him. He's a kind
man who feels responsible for you." There was a faint note
of irritation in Rain's voice.

"I appreciate that," Eleanor said gravely. "I don't want
him to feel responsible for me. Aunt Gilda played on his
family honor to get his promise to marry me. I'll write to
him and tell him he doesn't need to worry about me."

"That's up to you. I'll take you to Saint Genevieve if
that's where you want to go. But first I want Will to know
about Perry."

"No!" she exclaimed. "I don't want to be obligated to
Will." Then, with the look of a new awakening on her face,
she blurted, "You may think I'm wicked and ungrateful, but
I feel free! Free!" The smile she turned on Gavin was radiant. "For the first time in my life I'm free to do what I want
to do. I don't have Papa, Aunt Gilda, Will Bradford, or

anyone saying I must do this, do that. You don't realize how wonderful it is."

"Well, I guess that's one way of looking at it. Write your letter to Will. I'll send one too and tell him he needn't provide for you, if that's what you want." Rain pulled himself away from the wall. "Gavin, I take it you and Eleanor are a team."

It was the first Rain had acknowledged that there was a special feeling between the Scot and Eleanor. Gavin's face turned brick red.

"Aye. I love the lassie," he said firmly, looking Rain straight in the eye. "But I not be knowin' 'bout hitchin' with her. I got thinkin' to do, mon."

"That will have to be settled. My offer still goes to take her where she wants to go."

"I'm not going anywhere without Gavin," Eleanor said quietly.

Rain shrugged and slipped his arm around Amy. "We've got some deciding to do too, sweetheart. We can leave word here with Jean Pierre for Farr and Libby and go on and start our cabin, or we can backtrack and meet them."

"I remember what you said the night you came to Quill's Station. I'm eager to see your high valley and the river where you sat daydreaming." Her eyes caressed him, full of love and happiness.

Smile lines crinkled the corners of Rain's eyes. He tilted his head and placed a kiss on the end of her nose.

"I was hoping you'd say that. I remember you sitting behind me, quiet as a mouse." He kissed her nose again. "Gavin, do you have a yen to homestead? There's plenty of room, and soon we'll be joined by Farr and Libby. Farr wants to build on the river where he can trade."

"Yes, he does," Eleanor said quickly. "And so I do."

"Hold on, lass. There be more to homesteadin' than wantin' to. I be studyin' on the matter."

"What's there to study on?"

"'What's there to study on?'" he echoed. "By holy hell, lass. I be tellin' ye I got no money to buy stock, tools, seed—Ye be needin money to be keepin' body and soul together till the land pays." There was something agonized in the blue eyes that looked down at her.

"Have you forgotten that you've got money coming? You haven't drawn a cent of your pay since leaving Louisville," Rain said. "Come on. Let's get out of here and let the women digest all that's happened. I'll bring in the packs so you can wash before supper."

The room was almost completely dark when Rain returned with their bundles. Amy had found tinder, flint and steel and had lit the candle, mentally thanking the landlord for the luxury, knowing that candles were costly on the frontier. They took turns washing in the basin, pouring the dirty water in the tin chamber pot that sat in the corner. A feeling of security about four walls and a closed door comforted them when they undressed.

"I never thought I'd be so happy." Eleanor was in high spirits. She had washed her face and was now brushing her hair. "Just think! I can do what I want to do, and more than anything in the world I want to spend my life with Gavin. I never knew there was a man in the world who was so strong yet so kind."

"Settling on new land is a hard life. There will be times when you'll be cold and hungry, maybe even sick. You saw how Vonnie lived."

"But she was happy. I've thought of how hard it would be. But everything we have will be due to our own efforts. The home will be our home, the children ours. Oh, Amy, I want lots of children. I wished for a brother or sister when I was young. It's so lonely being an only child."

Rain knocked on the door and said, "Vittles on the table

in Hoffman's quarters." The women blew out the candle and followed him through the dark storeroom.

In the landlord's quarters they sat on benches at the long narrow table and were served by Mrs. Hoffman and Tennessee. The trader's wife had an impressive build, a bronze face and dark, shoe-button eyes. She wore her dark hair parted in the middle and pinned in a tight knot at the back of her head. In honor of the guests, she had pinned a brooch at the neck of her long, doeskin dress. Her daughter was a willowy girl of no more than twelve years. Tennessee moved quietly and with dignity even though her linsey-woolsey dress was too small for her growing body. It was drawn tightly across her budding breasts and showed her bare legs and feet. Six more children, who looked to be scarcely more than a year apart, lined up against the wall waiting their turn at the table.

The meal was simple but good. In silence Mrs. Hoffman served venison steak, dandelion greens and sweet potatoes on wooden plates. Mr. Hoffman wolfed down his food, then leaned back in his chair and puffed on a clay pipe, sending clouds of tobacco smoke toward the ceiling.

"Did anyone come through here yesterday or this morning riding a horse and leading one?" Rain asked casually.

"Pilgrims come through all the time. Renegades, deserters and thieves too. We get 'em all. Don't usually pay no mind. Peter Hopcus was here today. He's a homesteader east of here on the Current River. He said a young feller came by his place last night riding a horse and leading one. Said he called out a howdy and offered a meal, but was glad when the youngun passed on. Hopcus said he was surly and mean looking."

"Any horses been stolen around here lately?"

"I ain't heared a any round here. Hopcus said some was took east a him by river raiders. You looking for somebody, Tallman? Pete might still be around, if'n you want to talk to him."

"No. We found a pilgrim up on the trail. Horse and gun gone. Didn't want to bed down if there was a cutthroat hanging around."

"I sure can't guarantee they ain't. But there ain't any that I know of. We don't put up with any tomfoolery. This is a post office of the government," he said proudly. "The militia keeps a sharp eye on this place. Did you get the name of the man killed? I'll put it in the Territory Record Book."

"I knew him. I'll give you the information later." Rain was sorry he had brought up the matter when he saw the pained look on Amy's face. "I want to send a letter to Will Bradford at Belle Point. Do you have any idea when a messenger will be going that way?"

"The mail will be comin' in from the east any day now. What goes on west will go up the Arkansas. But I hear it's floodin' now. Might have to wait a week or two."

Rain nodded. "Some friends of mine will be coming through in a few weeks. I'll leave a letter for them, too."

"You goin' south?" Hoffman's eyes went from Rain to Amy to Eleanor and back. The desire to know why Rain Tallman was traveling with two young women burned strong, but he didn't dare ask the woodsman.

"We've not decided on it." Rain shook his head when Tennessee offered more sweet potatoes. "If you ladies have finished eating, we can walk for a bit."

Amy and Eleanor stood. Disappointed, Jean Pierre got quickly to his feet and bowed. Amy looked around to thank Mrs. Hoffman and Tennessee, but they had disappeared behind the curtain that divided the room.

"Thank Mrs. Hoffman for the fine meal."

"*Oui, mademoiselle.*" Jean Pierre bowed again and wondered if the tall one in buckskins was Tallman's woman. She was a beauty in a completely different way from the black-haired woman who was small and had the face of an angel. The tall one was slim, but with generous breasts and rounded hips. Her movements were graceful, her smile quick and warm. Jean Pierre sighed for his lost youth.

Amy breathed in gulps of the warm night air as soon as they reached the porch. The heavy scent of the cooking and the closeness of the room had almost made her sick.

"I hate to be closed in like that. I love to be outside," she whispered, and clutched Rain's arm.

"You're a mountain sprite." He laughed and covered the hand on his arm with his. "Gavin, I left my rifle just inside the door. Wait here until I get it, and we'll walk for a short way and talk. This place is full of ears, and Jean Pierre likes nothing more than to gossip."

A few lights shone from the open doors of the cabins they passed as they walked down the moonlit road. Families gathered on the porches fell silent as the strangers passed. In the distance someone played a squeeze box and a woman sang. Children laughed and played and called silly things to each other. All were familiar, homey sounds that reminded Amy of her life at Quill's Station.

At the edge of the village Rain stopped.

"A couple of years ago a preacher lived only a few hours' ride from here. I'm thinking of riding out and seeing if he's still there, and if he's willing to come here to Davidsonville. We could be wed tomorrow or the next day. We'll be here a few days while I gather supplies to last until Farr gets here. What do you say, Amy mine?"

"Yes! Oh, yes!" Amy hugged Rain's arm. "We could be married before we go home to your land even though I feel we're already married."

"Gavin?" Eleanor shook Gavin's arm and looked up into his face expectantly when he didn't say anything. "What do you think?"

"I dunno, lass. It be happenin' too fast fer ye to be know-in' if it be what ye want. Ye be knowin' only today ye have freedom to be goin' yer own way. Ye should think afore ye be settin' plans what will last a lifetime." Gavin's Scottish brogue was never more pronounced as he strived to make Eleanor understand the seriousness of the decision.

Eleanor was quiet for a moment, then backed away from him and faced him with her hands on her hips.

"You don't want me. You think I'd be like a millstone around your neck. You don't think I'll hold up and be a suitable mate for you. Is that it?" she asked in a tight voice. "You didn't mean what you said . . . that night?"

"I dinna be sayin' what I dinna mean," he said sternly. "I be sayin' ye have a choice to make now. Ye dinna have to be takin' a rough rivermon with naught to offer ye."

"Damn you, Gavin McCourtney! You big, stupid ox! I could slap you! How dare you say I'm a cheap, common woman who played up to the only man available! That's what you mean, isn't it? If I had all the men in the world to choose from I'd choose you, you big . . . dumb . . . ugly jackass!"

Rain laughed. "It seems I've heard those words before. In a barn, wasn't it, sweetheart? You'd better marry her, Gavin, and get her away from Amy, or she'll be toting a rifle and wearing britches and swearing."

"And throwing a knife," Eleanor added, tossing her head haughtily. "Amy's going to teach me."

"Come on, sweetheart," Rain said to Amy. "Let's leave them to decide what they want to do, though I'm sure I know what it'll be. I'll ride out tomorrow and see if I can find the preacher."

"Can I go with you? We could all go with you and be married there."

"If we are wed here, sweetheart, Jean Pierre will record it in the Territory Record Book along with the land deeds, births, marriages and deaths. I want him to record the land in my name and yours, Mrs. Rain Tallman."

"Gavin can just go with you, Rain," Eleanor said and

looked defiantly at the big man. "He's not going to pussy-foot around and get out of marrying me because he thinks he's got nothing to offer. Are you, Gavin?"

"Nay, Nora, me girl. And if I be hearin' any more sass or swear words comin' from yer sweet mouth ye know what ye'll be gettin'."

"Yes, Gavin . . . darling."

The first stars of the night had just made an appearance when Pete Hopcus rode down the lane to his cabin. Antoine heard him coming. He slipped his knife in the scabbard and stood waiting. Waiting was what Antoine did best—waiting and listening and looking. The three traits had saved his life more times than he had fingers and toes.

Pete Hopcus was a thin man with a short beard and a long mustache. He wore baggy homespun britches held up with rope suspenders. People usually remembered him because of his big ears.

"Tallman rode in with a woman in buckskin britches and the purtiest black-haired woman I ever seen. Lordy! I thought I was tired a black-haired women, but this one's a beauty."

"Is that all?"

"All?" Pete echoed. "Ya ain't never seen a woman like—"

"Is that all that rode in?" Antoine gritted. "Tallman and two women?"

"Naw. A big feller was with them. He was walkin' easy, like he'd been hurt."

"The Scot," Antoine muttered. "They all survived the ambush that stupid pig set up. The kid wasn't sure. If they had harmed a hair on that woman's head I'd have roasted him over a slow fire."

"I'd like to have me a piece of that'n myself. Wheee... she's a beauty."

"I'm not talking about that black-haired bitch!" Antoine snarled. "I'm talking about Amy Deverell. Was she all right?"

"The one in britches? She seemed to be."

"Tallman did just what I'd have done, only I would've killed that damn kid!"

"And saved you the trouble, huh?"

Antoine shrugged. "The whelp was like the wolverine— mad to kill. So I killed *him*. I want no tales carried back to Kaskaskia."

Pete Hopcus gave the Frenchman a sideways glance and a shiver of apprehension slithered down his spine when he saw him eyeing him intently. Good God, Pete thought. Didn't the man trust him after all these years?

"Tallman said they'd need a room for the women for a couple of days," Pete said, not liking the uneasy feeling that had come over him.

"Anything else?"

"Tallman had a letter. Soldier left it more'n a week ago, Hoffman said, but I couldn't find out any more."

"It's more than I expected. Come on in. We'll go over what we're going to do."

Pete led his horse around to the back of the cabin, and once again Antoine went over in his mind his plan for carrying out his mission. That his golden princess was close to being his made the Frenchman's skin tingle. Nothing—or anyone—had ever excited him more. For a brief moment a boyish smile played at the corners of his hard mouth.

"Ma petite. Ma bijou," he murmured to the vision of Amy that floated in front of his eyes. "It will not be long before you are mine."

CHAPTER
Twenty-one

"I wish we could have gone with them, don't you, Amy?" Eleanor and Amy stood on the porch of the trading post watching Rain and Gavin ride away.

"Yes, but this will give us some time to wash our hair and our clothes. I'm glad I brought my blue dress. I've only worn it one time since Rain came home. I think he'd like me to wear it for the wedding."

"Aunt Gilda would be horrified to know I was getting married in that old skirt and a shirt that's lost two buttons." Eleanor giggled happily. "But it doesn't matter. I'm marrying the kindest, sweetest man in the world. I know that Gavin loves *me,* not a dressed-up doll," she said with a dreamy look in her lavender eyes.

"You would be pretty wrapped in a blanket."

"Oh, you! If we had some flowers I could make us each a crown."

"I saw bluebells and Queen Anne's lace just outside of town. I bet we can find jack-in-the-pulpits too. Would they do?"

"Oh, yes. I'll weave them into a wreath. It'll help pass the time until Gavin and Rain get back. I don't like being here without them. I think that storekeeper is an old . . . lecher!"

"Lecher? What's that?"

"Don't you know what a lecher is? Oh flitter, Amy! I swear to goodness. You know about a lot of things, but you don't know a blessed thing about men." Eleanor tilted her head sassily and looked up at the taller woman. "A lecher is a man whose mind is on what a woman's got in her drawers. In your case, your leather britches."

Amy burst out laughing. "I do declare, Eleanor. Sometimes you surprise me. How do you know that?"

"Because when your back is turned he's looking at your . . . bottom."

"Let him look. It seems he's been looking at Mrs. Hoffman's bottom too from the number of young ones he's got. Let's see if we can get a bucket from Mrs. Hoffman. We can wash our hair at the creek and pick the flowers while it's drying."

The population of Davidsonville had poured out of their homes at dawn. Now that the morning meal was over, they settled into the day's routine. The women worked in the gardens and watched with interest the activity in front of the store. The children played happily in the dirt in front of the cabins or rolled hoops down the dusty road.

Most of the men were gathered around a wagon which had been propped up so a wheel could be removed. A stick had been cut to use as a short axle and another had been tied to the wheel. Amy had seen this method of measuring land done many times. The men carried the wheel to the edge of town. With a man on each end, they started rolling the wheel. Each time the stick struck the ground it gouged a mark. It usually measured a hundred and twenty-six marks to the quarter mile. Many a homestead had been marked off using this method.

A man on a sorrel horse rode around from the back of the

store. He slouched in the saddle, nodded to a man who was tying his horse to the rail and went on down the road. Amy squinted her eyes and studied the rider. Something was familiar about him. Yet he was so ordinary he could be one of the hundreds of men who had stopped at Quill's Station at one time or the other. His head was bent but tilted in their direction. As the horse passed, his head turned. He was looking at them. A feeling of unease came over Amy. She watched him until he rode out of town, then she urged Eleanor back inside the store.

Hull Dexter reined his horse at the prearranged meeting place and waited for Antoine Efant and Pete Hopcus to appear. Mosquitoes swarmed around his face. He fanned at them angrily with his hat and cursed. Hull hated this hot, sultry country. He was beginning to hate and fear Antoine Efant as well. The man had changed since learning of Bull's aborted attempt to get the Woodbury woman. He had been so angry that he had killed the kid who told him about it. In the days that followed, while they waited for Tallman to show up, the anger had stayed with Efant. Hull was sure of one thing: He would be glad when the job was over and he could head north.

Antoine and Pete came silently out of the woods behind him. The twitching ears of his horse told Hull they were there and he turned to face them.

"What did you find out?" Antoine leaned lazily against a tree. Hull knew the pose was deceptive, that the Frenchman's nerves were strung tighter than a bowstring.

"Tallman and the big Scot have gone south to fetch a padre. Hoffman was tellin' people in the store that there'll be a weddin'."

"Gawd!" Pete said. "I'd give a year a my life to crawl on

that black-haired one. The woman in britches is Tallman's woman. She—"

Antoine's dark eyes hardened and sent an icy message to Pete. He stopped speaking and fumbled with the shot bag that hung from his belt.

"You may not have a year, Pete!" Antoine spoke teasingly, but Pete knew he was not teasing. "Where does this padre live?"

"He lives down on the fork of Eleven Point River. He does marryin' 'n buryin'."

"Is he known to Hoffman?"

"He's known to everybody north of the Arkansas."

"Do you know the country between here and Eleven Point?"

"Like the back of my hand."

"There's a bounty of five hundred dollars on Tallman. Bring back his right ear, the one with the nick in it, and it's yours."

"What about the Scot?"

"Fifty silver dollars."

"Do you want one of his ears or his nose?" Pete asked cheerfully.

"If he don't come for his woman, I'll know he's dead. Then you'll get your pay."

"Fair enough."

"You've got two rifles; you'll have two shots. Get Tallman with the first shot or you'll not get another chance at him.'

"I ain't no fool. I know what Tallman can do."

"You know where I'll be. Hull will take the Woodbury woman to the river. A boat will take them to Kaskaskia." Antoine looked up at Hull Dexter. "When it's done, I never want to see your face again. Stay clear of the Rocky Mountain country. That's where I'll be headed."

The Frenchman's eyes were as cold as death, and a shiver

traveled over Hull's skin in spite of the heat. Something was eating the Frenchman, something that had turned him ugly. He had never been surly and mean before. Hull had seen him kill with a smile on his face.

Without waiting for a reply from Hull, Antoine turned to Pete. "Drag the bodies off into the woods and shoot the horses. I don't want them coming back."

"I know what to do."

"Then go do it."

Pete left, but before he did he glanced up at Hull and Hull was sure there was a resentful look in his eyes. Hull got off his horse, tied the reins to a sapling, and followed Antoine through the woods.

Two horses were tied near the clear, fast-flowing creek. From that point there was a good view of the front of the store. Antoine squatted down on his heels and threw a stick out into the sunlight.

"We'll give it until the tree shadow reaches that stick. If they haven't come out you'll go and send one of those younguns rolling the hoop to get them. They'll come when they see the horse the kid brought in. That horse was the one the fellow was riding when he rode down to warn them at Kaskaskia."

Hull nodded, sat down and leaned back against a tree.

The shadow had almost reached the stick when Amy and Eleanor, carrying a bucket and an armful of clothes, came out of the store. The black-haired woman was laughing and swinging the bucket. Antoine had eyes only for the tall, slender girl in the buckskins. It was the first time he had seen her without a hat. Her skin was golden and a long, thick braid of sunstreaked hair hung to her slender hips. The way she moved fascinated Antoine. She didn't walk; she floated, without as much as a bob of her head. Her legs were long and were hugged by the buckskin britches as was her tight but rounded bottom.

Antoine drew in a sharp hissing breath when they turned and started toward the creek. What luck. Didn't it mean the woman was meant for him? God had arranged for her to come to him. He touched his fingertips to his forehead and then made the sign of the cross on his chest.

"Get back!" he whispered hoarsely to Hull.

Seconds later they were out of sight behind the thick drooping branches of willows that screened the creek bank.

"Lordy but it's peaceful here." Eleanor skipped ahead of Amy, turned and walked backwards for a few steps so she could look at her. "There's a freedom in the wilderness that I never knew in town."

"It's because you're not wearing that tight corset," Amy teased.

"Oh, that!" Eleanor giggled happily, then said thoughtfully, "You can be yourself here."

"You can be yourself anywhere. But it's harder in some places than in others."

"It sure was hard with Aunt Gilda. Oh, look behind you, Amy!"

Eleanor pointed through the trees at a young deer, almost invisible in the shadowy light, nibbling on tender leaves. Suddenly its head came up. It stood as still as a statue, then it leaped, disappearing from sight.

"Oh, pooh!" Eleanor exclaimed. "Something scared it. I hope it wasn't us."

Amy laughed. "It probably smelled us, it's been so long since we washed our clothes. Tennessee gave me a piece of lye soap. We can use it on our clothes, but I have a piece I brought from home for our hair."

"Tennessee's a pretty girl. I wish she had one of the dresses I left with Vonnie."

"If the old lecher watches me, Eleanor, his daughter watches you. I think you've got her treed."

"Treed? What does that mean?"

"It means she likes you. She's . . . fascinated, bewitched."

"Oh, I'm glad. I told her I thought she was pretty."

The sun filtered down through the tall trees as they walked alongside the creek looking for a suitable place to bathe and wash their clothes. Amy strode ahead, her rifle in her hand. They came to a place where a long, flat rock protruded out into the stream.

"This looks like a good place." Amy leaned her rifle against a tree trunk and threw her soiled clothes down on the rock.

Eleanor sat on the rock and took off her shoes and stockings. She stretched her legs out in front of her, wiggled her toes, then plunged her feet into the water.

"Oh, that feels good! Take off your shoes, Amy."

In the silence that followed her words, Amy thought she heard a noise. She turned and looked back toward the way they had come. Nothing seemed to be stirring. They were screened from the settlement by thick willows. When the sound of a horse's nickering reached her she relaxed, chiding herself for being jumpy, and sat down beside Eleanor. Yet the unease stayed with her.

The stone was hot. Amy could feel the heat through her buckskin britches. She dangled her feet in the cool water and the tension left her. They sat quietly for a while, enjoying the sun on their backs and the cool water flowing over their feet. Then Eleanor splashed the water playfully. Drops of cool water hit Amy's face. She gasped.

"You little imp! I'll get you—" Her words became lost in an incredible, horrifying instant that she was to remember for the rest of her life.

A heavy blanket was thrown over her head and arms like steel bands wrapped around her. Amy was caught completely unaware and lunged back against her assailant. They toppled from the rock. She fell with a heavy body on top of her. Breath left her. The cloying closeness of the blanket over her head filled her with terror. In the seconds before she was rapped sharply on the head with a blunt instrument and propelled into a swirling black void, she heard Eleanor's terrified scream and a man's voice above her spitting out a curse.

Then he said, "Goddamn it, Hull. Knock the bitch out like I told you. It'll save time and trouble."

Rain and Gavin rode single file down the game trail, through a maze of boulders that had fallen from a cliff, around a bulging rock, and into a scattering of trees. Ahead they could see a sweep of open country, a meadow reaching to lose itself in the foothills beyond.

Rain dropped back so he could ride beside Gavin.

"Is the going too rough? I don't want that hole in your side to break open. Eleanor would have my scalp."

"No danger a that, mon," Gavin grumbled. "I be wrapped so tight in them blasted strips I canna take a decent breath."

Rain laughed. "This is only the beginning. They say a bossy woman gets worse as the years go by."

The track crossed the meadow and went along the edge of the forest. It was a still, warm day. Fluffy white clouds hung lazily in the blue sky. Rain's blue-black eyes, ever alert, studied the area, looked all around and saw nothing unusual.

Sometime later, when they were a little more than a couple of hours from Davidsonville, his keen ears caught a foreign sound. They were in a pass between two wooded hills not far from the fork of the river and Preacher Witsel's place. The big dun's ears peaked and Rain signaled to Gavin to stop.

When Rain lifted his rifle from the scabbard, Gavin did the same. They sat quietly for the space of a dozen heartbeats before Rain turned his mount into the trees. Gavin followed closely behind, the cushion of dead leaves muffling the sound of the horses' hooves.

"Horses coming up the trail. Six or eight of them," Rain whispered. "We'll wait here and let them pass."

They dismounted, Rain to move back toward the trail and Gavin to stand at the heads of the horses. Now he could hear the sound of the hoofbeats and even the creaking of saddle leather. They weren't Indians, he reasoned. Indians didn't use saddles or shod horses. Gavin tied the horses to a tree branch and leaned his rifle against its trunk. He had to have both hands free to clamp over the mouths of their mounts lest they nicker a greeting to the animals coming up the trail.

Rain peered through the foliage, his eyes on the peak where the riders would come over the rise. All his senses were in tune—his sight, his hearing, his ability to smell danger—all were focused on what was coming toward them.

When the riders appeared, coming in single file, the stiffness went out of Rain's shoulders and a grin spread over his firm lips.

"My God! Will Bradford!" Rain dropped the butt of his rifle to the ground. From his lips came the song of the brown thrush, loud and clear and melodious. He gave a sharp whistle, then the thrush song again.

The man leading the detail of six men signaled a halt. The sergeant behind him moved up.

"What is it, sir?"

At that moment Rain stepped out of the woods and stood in the trail. "Will! Will Bradford!" he called. "I was hoping you'd remember that signal and not shoot me."

"Rain? By all that's holy! Rain Tallman." Will Bradford was a portly man in his mid-forties, clean shaven and heavily jowled. He was the most honorable man Rain had ever known except for his stepfather and Farr Quill. He was off the horse by the time Rain reached him and pumped his hand vigorously.

"You were the last person I expected to see coming up that trail. I got your letter and figured you had your hands full at Belle Point." Rain's face was wreathed in smiles. "Gavin," he called. "Come on out and meet Will Bradford."

Gavin moved out of the woods leading the two horses. He came on slowly, but his thoughts were racing ahead. What did the appearance of Will Bradford mean? Had he changed his mind about taking Eleanor to Belle Point? Gavin sensed the dream of having her as his wife fading away.

"Will, this is Gavin McCourtney," Rain said. "He came with me from Louisville. Gavin, you've heard much about Will Bradford these last few weeks."

"I ken that I have. Tis an honor, sir." Gavin extended his hand."

"A Scot," Will said and shook Gavin's hand. "Some of the best soldiers I ever had were Scots."

"I be glad to hear it, sir."

"Where are you headed, Rain? You can't already have settled Miss Woodbury and her aunt in Saint Genevieve?"

"No. Miss Woodbury is at Davidsonville, Will. Her aunt passed on before we left Louisville."

"I'm sorry to hear it. Poor child. She's more alone than ever. I've been called to a conference in Belle Fontaine. It would be too rigorous a journey for her to travel with us. I'm afraid I'm going to have to impose on you to escort her, as I suggested in the letter."

"A lot of things have happened, Will. Important things that you need to know. Have you taken your mid-morning rest?"

"No. We can stop here for a while."

Rain and Will Bradford sat on a deadfall apart from the

men who, after picketing their horses, lounged on the grass. Rain explained as concisely as possible all that had happened. He told him about Hammond Perry sending the boy, Mike Hartman, to kill him. He told about the attack at Kaskaskia and the one later when Bull admitted Perry wanted Miss Woodbury.

"The man's holding a grudge, Will. He's not going to forget you were given the assignment he wanted at Belle Point."

"My God, Rain. There are times when I wish he'd gotten it."

"Now, about Miss Woodbury. My intended, Mrs. Amy Deverell, is with her at Davidsonville. Under different circumstances I would leave the telling of this to Miss Woodbury. But the truth of the matter is she has fallen in love with Gavin McCourtney and he with her. They wish to be married."

"By Jove!" Will turned a smiling face to Rain. "That's good news. You think McCourtney is a good man?"

"The best. He's lived a rough life as a riverman, but he's honest and steady. He loves her and will protect her with his life. He fought for her against great odds at Kaskaskia and saved her from rape and possible death."

"That's good enough for me. I have to admit that having her settled is a load off my mind." Will wiped his forehead with the cloth he took from around his neck.

"Miss Woodbury was going to leave a letter for you at Davidsonville. She's a different woman now from the young lady Gavin and I met in Louisville. She was so spoiled, Will, I was tempted to take a hairbrush to her backside. Gavin did it, and you'd be surprised at the results."

"Straightened her out, did it?" Will chuckled. "I wonder if that would work on some of my enlisted men?"

"Gavin and I were on our way to the Witsel place. We

thought to have the preacher return with us to Davidsonville. You'll be able to give her in marriage, Will."

"Preacher Witsel?" Will frowned and shook his head. "We stopped at his place this morning. He was drowned in the flood last week."

"Drowned? That's too bad. Then there's no need to go on. We'll ride back to Davidsonville with you."

"If you're bound to be wed, Rain, I'll be glad to officiate at the ceremony. I have the authority in Arkansas Territory."

"I'd forgotten about that! The women will be plumb tickled." Rain's face creased with one of his rare broad smiles. "Gavin," he called. "I've got good news," he said when Gavin reached them. "I've explained the situation to Will and you can stop worrying. Will is pleased about you and Eleanor."

Will could almost see the big Scot's shoulders slump in relief. He stood and held out his hand.

"Rain says you're a good man. I'm pleased to welcome you to the family. If there is anything I can do to help you and Eleanor get a start, I'm more than willing to do it."

"I . . . er . . . well, I do be thankin' ye." Gavin was so dumbfounded he didn't know what to say. This man, an important major, was offering friendship to *him*. For an instant it boggled his mind. Then his face creased in smiles and he shook the major's hand heartily.

Pete Hopcus had arrived at the pass a good half hour before Rain and Gavin. He was not bragging when he told Antoine he knew the country. He used a little-known deer trail to come across and reach this place. He shimmied up a tree and settled himself comfortably on a broad branch to wait. He had a clear view of the track, and his two rifles were primed and ready. When the two men came in sight he raised one gun and sighted the chest of the man on the dun horse.

Pete waited, his finger on the trigger, for his prey to come closer. He dared not miss the first shot. Suddenly the pair of riders stopped and Tallman jerked his head toward the woods. Almost before Pete could lower the rifle they had disappeared into the dense growth.

Tallman knew he was there! The thought sent a ripple of fear down Pete's spine. But how could he have known? Pete wondered. He looked over his shoulder to be sure his horse had not gotten loose and wandered onto the trail, alerting the man. A minute later he heard the riders coming from the south. So that was it? Tallman had heard them and left the trail to let them pass.

Pete relaxed. As soon as the riders passed he would have his chance to knock the famed woodsman out of the saddle, slice off his ear and collect his reward. Maybe he would go to Memphis or New Orleans. He wanted to get as far away from Antoine Efant as he could. The way the Frenchman was acting he could kill him like he had killed the kid that came in leading the pilgrim's horse.

The soldiers rode over the hill in single file. At their head was an officer, either a captain or a major, Pete was not sure which. They passed not thirty feet from the tree where Pete was perched and went on down the narrow path. Pete was wondering if he dared shoot Tallman there. The patrol was bound to hear the shots. Damn! He would have to wait until Tallman returned this way with the preacher, which meant he would have to kill the preacher too.

While Pete was trying to decide how he was going to accomplish this deed, the column of soldiers stopped and Rain Tallman walked out of the woods. He called a greeting to the officer. The officer got off his horse and the two shook hands. Then, to further irritate Pete, the soldiers dismounted, picketed their horses, broke out canteens and lolled on the grass. Tallman and the officer sat down on a deadfall.

When the men mounted their horses again, Pete breathed a sigh of relief. His sigh turned into a painful gasp when Rain and the officer, riding side by side, rode out toward Davidsonville. It took Pete several minutes to realize what this turn of events meant to him. Tallman was going back to the trading post. Pete couldn't shoot him while he was riding with the soldiers. They would be on him in a flash, and his life wouldn't be worth a snap of his fingers. On the other hand, Efant would kill him if Pete went back to his homestead and told him Tallman still lived.

Pete began to shake. In the space of half an hour everything he had dreamed of having had been snatched from him. He had to get away, far away. He had to leave his homestead and the two years of work he had put into the place. None of that mattered now. What was a homestead compared to his life?

As soon as it was safe to leave the tree, Pete shimmied down. He found his horse where he had left him, mounted and headed south toward the Arkansas River. If he were lucky he could trade one of the rifles for a ride downriver to the Mississippi. There he would work his way to New Orleans and a ship that would take him to some foreign land.

Pete prayed to God that he never came face to face with Antoine Efant again.

CHAPTER
Twenty-two

The blood pounding in Eleanor's throbbing head made her gag. Slowly she became aware of the jolting gait of the horse and realized that she had been thrown across its back. Her hands were bound and the thongs cut into her soft flesh when she tried to move. She opened her eyes and tried to focus them on the ground as it passed. Suddenly her stomach rebelled and vomit spewed out and over her hands dangling beneath her face. A violent pain struck between her eyes and she slipped back into the blissful state of unconsciousness.

When Eleanor came to again she found herself lying on the ground on her side, her back against the trunk of a tree. The smell of vomit on her clothes and her hands almost made her sick again. She forced herself to lie very still, and lifted her lashes so she could peek at her captors.

"You left nothing behind?" The question was asked by a stocky, black-bearded man with a knit cap on his head.

"I told ya I didn't. Why're ya worried? Ain't nobody to follow. The post office man'll think Injuns carried 'em off."

Eleanor wondered how much time had passed. The light in the clearing was dim. Was it dusk or were they so deep in the forest that the light couldn't penetrate the thick branches? If it was dusk, Gavin and Rain would have returned to town. Surely they were looking for her and Amy by now. Tears slid from her eyes and into the grass beneath her cheek.

Why had God let this happen? Had she been so wicked that she deserved such punishment? That morning she had been so happy, looking forward to her wedding night. *Oh, Gavin, Gavin.* She never got the chance to show him how much she loved him.

At first Amy thought she had awakened from a nightmare, one that was both frightening and painful. Wincing with pain, she tried to move her arms and discovered her hands were bound behind her back. Her head throbbed and her mouth was dry. Her eyes opened onto a blurred world, then gradually began to focus. In the dim light that filtered through the trees she began to make out her surroundings. She lay on the ground, three horses cropped grass nearby, and two men squatted on their heels chewing on a long roll of jerky. Amy could see Eleanor lying on the grass not ten feet away.

"Goddamn it, Hull, you hit her too hard. I told you to knock her out, not kill her."

"She ain't hurt none. She puked is all. I'd as soon go on. I ain't likin' hangin' round here."

"The woman's been riding belly down on that horse for a good four hours. She's worth money in our pockets. I want her delivered to Perry alive. You're not to diddle in her. I mean it, Hull," he growled threateningly.

"She's too skinny. I like women with more meat on them."

"She was promised to Perry. Her papa signed the marriage papers. Perry gets in her first. Is that understood?"

"I said it was."

Amy closed her eyes. Deep within, she shuddered. Her captor was Antoine Efant, the Frenchman Rain's Indian friend had said was asking about him. Hammond Perry had sent him to get Eleanor. What did he mean about signing the marriage papers? she wondered. Perry must have lied to him. Eleanor had never heard of Hammond Perry until after they left Kaskaskia.

Amy had not seen the other man's face clearly. Antoine Efant had called him Hull. Could he be Hull Dexter, the scout who had deserted them when she and Liberty first came to the wilderness? Farr was sure that Hull Dexter was responsible for the massacre of the wagon train Daniel and his folks had been with. Daniel had been the only one to survive, and that was because his mother had tossed him in the berry bushes. If the man was Hull Dexter, he was capable of anything.

Amy was startled when she felt a wet cloth on her face. Her eyes flew open. The black-bearded man was kneeling beside her, wiping her brow.

"Do you want a drink of water, *ma cherie*?" he asked gently.

Amy looked at him with eyes wide open but dull. Her mouth was too dry to speak, so she nodded.

The Frenchman lifted her head and carefully squirted water into her mouth from a bag. She drank thirstily and he lowered her head to the ground. His fingers sought the lump on her head above her ear. She winced.

"I did not want to do that, *ma petite*. The skin is not broken. The pain will go away soon."

Amy thought that the blow to her head had damaged her brains. She had no idea what the Frenchman called her, but from the tone of his voice it was an endearment. From somewhere in the back of her mind she seemed to remember the man's accent. Slowly, while she stared up at him, it came to her that this was the Frenchman they had met at Kaskaskia, the one who spoke up for them after the fight between Gavin and Bull.

"Eleanor. . ." She was barely able to croak the word.

"Hull hit her a mite hard, but she's all right."

"Hull . . . Dexter?"

"You know him?"

Amy groaned and closed her eyes. She felt the Frenchman lift her and her eyes flew open again. He held her against his chest and smoothed the hair back from her face.

"Ma bijou," he crooned. "You are not to worry. Hull will not molest your friend. He will take her to her betrothed—"

Amy tried to push herself away from him. With her hands tied behind her she was helpless to move, but her brain was clearing rapidly.

"He's taking her to Hammond Perry?"

"It is the honorable thing to do. Do not struggle, my pet. I will not hurt you."

"You're a stupid pig if you think it's honorable to send her to a low-down miserable skunk like Hammond Perry!"

"The man is entitled to his property. Her papa signed the marriage papers long ago. Perry has waited for her to become a woman and is ready to take her as his wife." The Frenchman seemed eager for Amy to understand and not think badly of him. He caressed her cheek with his fingertips. "We will have much time together. After we talk, you will understand."

Amy tried to jerk her head away from him, her eyes blazing into his.

"I will not spend time with you and I will never understand!"

The Frenchman looked over her head and spoke to Hull.

"Squirt some water on the woman's face. Get her on the

horse and move out." The voice he used when speaking to Hull was harsh, not at all like the soft tones he used when speaking to Amy.

Eleanor cried out when the water was poured on her face.

"Ya been awake all along," Hull growled, yanking her to her feet. Her knees buckled under her and Hull caught her against him to keep her from falling.

"Give her a drink of water and fork her on that horse," Antoine commanded.

Eleanor began to struggle and screamed, "Amy! A . . . my!"

"Shut up!" Hull slapped her across the face so hard her head snapped around. "If'n ya make another sound this knife might slip 'n cut yer pretty face." Eleanor felt the sharp edge of a blade at her throat. "That's better. Ya can have a drink a water, then ya'll straddle that horse or ya'll ride belly down. It's up to you."

"Why are you doing this?"

"Money," Hull answered, and squirted water from the bag toward her mouth. She opened it and drank gratefully.

Amy had deliberately ceased struggling against the arms that held her. Her fear had now turned to outrage. When she felt the Frenchman's attention was fully on Eleanor and Hull Dexter, she steeled herself, brought up her knees and hit Antoine in the face. The force of the blow knocked him on his back. He took her with him and she fell on top of him. Using every ounce of her strength, Amy brought her knee up, aiming for the vulnerable organ between his legs. He rolled with her and her knee hit the ground.

"You . . . you bastard! Rain will kill you!"

"Ho . . . my *petite* wildcat!" Antoine swung her over him and lay on top of her. "Tallman will not come for you. You will forget him."

"I'll never forget him. Get off me, you son of a bitch!"

"Such words coming from such a pretty mouth. I'm afraid, *ma cherie,* you make it necessary for me to hit you again—but on the other side where it will not hurt you so much."

"Damn you!"

When Amy went limp, Antoine gently turned her on her side so that she was not lying on the hands tied behind her back.

"Ah, *cherie,* you will take much taming, but what a woman you are!" Antoine got to his feet and, walking past Eleanor without as much as a glance in her direction, jerked the reins of Tally's horse loose from the branch. "Put her on," he commanded.

Hull slid his knife into his belt and grasped Eleanor about the waist. He lifted her high and she swung her leg over the saddle. When she was seated he stuck her feet in the stirrups.

"Please . . . don't do this." Her tear-filled lavender eyes looked down at Antoine.

"He will not rape you, *mademoiselle.* He knows I will kill him. He has my permission to cut you or beat you if you do not behave, but he will not rape you or kill you."

"What . . . about Amy?"

"You are not to concern yourself with the golden one," Antoine said while binding Eleanor's hands to the saddle horn. Hull mounted his horse and Antoine handed him the reins. *"Mademoiselle,* stay in the saddle. If you fall you will break your arms."

"My . . . uncle, Will Bradford, will pay you if you take me to him. He will pay more than Hammond Perry." Eleanor had just thought of Will Bradford and wished she had mentioned him before.

"It is no use. The bargain was made long ago. You were promised to Hammond Perry. You will go to him."

"No! I was not promised to him. I don't even know him! Please! You don't understand—"

"Begone!" Antoine said sharply.

The horses moved out of the clearing. Eleanor looked over her shoulder and saw Amy lying on the ground. She was leaving the only true friend she had ever had.

"Bye, Amy," she called softly. "Tell Gavin . . . I love him."

Her chin sank to her chest and she began to cry softly.

Amy awakened from a dream where small red demons were prodding her with fiery sticks. Every muscle in her body ached and her head felt as if it would explode at any moment. Her arms were as heavy as lead when she attempted to lift them. Finally her hands reached her head. She cautiously touched the large bumps above each ear. Wincing with pain, her fingertips explored the one side of her head that was caked with dried blood. She decided the cut was small and the injury not serious. Her eyes eventually grew accustomed to the dim light that came from a small fire on the other side of the room, and she was able to make out her surroundings.

She was in a small cabin. She could see a table, a bench, and, in front of the small fireplace, a chair. The bed she was on was a straw-covered platform built into the corner of the room. When she was sure she was alone she attempted to swing her feet off the bed. It was then she discovered that her leg was attached to the wall with a short chain. Panic caused her to sit up quickly and pain shot through her head. She tugged on the chain with both hands, crying out with frustration when it held fast. Giving up for the time being, she moved down in the bed until she could sit with her back to the wall.

Amy thought back to the last things she could remember. Eleanor lying on the ground. Hull Dexter. Efant, the Frenchman, saying he was sending Eleanor to Hammond Perry.

"Oh, poor Eleanor," she whispered. Amy wished she could tell Eleanor not to worry, that Rain and Gavin would come for them. That morning Rain said he would be back before sundown. By now he knew they were gone and he was searching for them. Was it only that morning? Amy was sure that it was night now.

"Hurry, my love," she whispered. In her mind she saw his quiet, dark face, his blue-black eyes and his shy smile. How would he ever find her? Eventually Gavin would find Eleanor with Hammond Perry. Would it be too late for them to have a happy life together? Rain would come for her. She would not despair! She would have faith in him, and in his love for her. She held on to the hope fiercely. Meanwhile she composed herself and made ready to face her captor.

The door opened and the Frenchman came in. He carried the carcass of a small skinned rabbit. His eyes found her at once. He placed the rabbit on the table and moved quickly to the bed.

"You are awake . . . and hungry, no doubt."

"No doubt," Amy said dryly.

"I will fix you a meal, then we will talk."

"You'd better talk now, and fast. Rain Tallman will come and he will kill you."

"We have time, *ma cherie*. You will feel better when you have eaten." He ran a sharp stick through the carcass, hung it on a spit and moved it over the fire.

"Why have you chained me like an animal?"

Antoine turned and looked at her. "So you will not leave me."

"I'll put a knife in your back the first chance I get."

"Ho! That I know, *ma bijou.*"

"Stop calling me those stupid French names."

"My jewel? My love? But you are my love. I knew it the minute I saw you at Kaskaskia. Ah . . . what a woman, I said to myself. I have searched for such a woman to be my mate."

"I have a man. Rain Tallman is ten times the man you are."

He unrolled a cloth on the table and cut slices from a roll of dark cake. It was nut-filled and smelled of rum.

"Someday you will know that is not true," he said patiently. "Someday you will love me."

"Your brains are . . . clabbered! I'll never love you, you bastard!" Amy shouted so loud she felt as if her head would split apart.

"You are wrong, *ma petite chou.* Antoine is not a bastard. The name Efant is one of the most respected in all New Orleans. *Ma mère* and *mon père* were married in the church long before I was conceived."

"I thought sure you were the offspring of a jackass and a warthog," Amy said crossly.

Antoine laughed. "Some say it is so."

"You'll not be laughing when Rain gets here. He'll cut out your gizzard."

"Ah . . . do not count on that. Antoine Efant would not leave a trail. I am a clever woodsman."

"Rain will see my moccasins, my rifle—"

"He will see nothing," Antoine said, and nodded toward the corner where her rifle stood beside the bundle of clothing she had taken to the creek to wash.

"Where is this place?"

"You would not know it."

It would serve no purpose, Antoine thought, to tell her they had turned west at the point where Hull took the woman and went east toward the river.

He considered telling her that Tallman was dead so she would grieve and get it over with. He watched the firelight flicker over her face. She glared at him with the eyes of a cat. Better to let her realize gradually, he thought, that Tallman would not come. He must first make her feel comfortable with him; later she would love him. It would be better if she knew nothing of his arrangement with Pete Hopcus to kill Tallman and the Scot. Pete would arrive before morning. He had decided that Pete was too dangerous to him to live. He would quietly slip a knife in his back and let the river carry him away.

"I need to relieve myself," Amy said bluntly.

"Ah, forgive me. I should have known. There is a pot for that purpose." The Frenchman pulled a metal pot from beneath the bed and set it up on the straw mattress.

Amy looked at him as if he had lost his mind. "I'm not using that!"

"Why not? I went to great pains to find a receptacle for you to use."

"I want to go outside."

"*Cherie*, do not be difficult. If I take you outside I will go with you with a rope about your slender neck so you will not run away from me."

"I'm not using . . . *that* with you in here!"

"Such modesty! Soon we will know everything about each other and you will not mind."

"If that time comes I'll kill myself."

"Do not say such things," he scolded gently. "I will leave you to do your bodily chores. Ah . . . I do not know why

some women think it so shameful when it is done by all of
God's creatures."

"Get out!" Amy hissed. "You make me sick!"

Amy lay with her head on her arm. Tears ran from the
corners of her eyes and into the hair at her temples. She had
not allowed herself to cry, but now, feeling frightened,
lonely and hungry, she made no effort to hold back the tears.

She had refused to eat a bite of the meal Antoine prepared. When he brought it to her she had knocked it from his
hand. The more he coaxed, the more determined she was to
refuse. Finally he had pleaded for her to eat and told her
they had a long journey ahead of them. She lay down on the
bed and turned her back to him.

Now Amy was wondering if, by defying him, she had
done more harm to herself. Hunger pangs were gnawing at
her insides. She would eat tomorrow, she promised her
empty stomach. She needed her strength should the opportunity to escape present itself.

Antoine had spread a blanket on the floor in front of the
open door. He made no attempt to lie beside her on the
platform bed. She vowed silently to fight him until she died
if he did. The Frenchman had asked her if she wished to put
on her nightdress—it was in the bundle of clothes she had
taken to the creek to wash. Now she wished she had said
yes. He would have had to unlock the iron band that encir-
cled her ankle in order for her to remove the buckskin
britches. But at that time she feared he meant to sleep with
her, and the britches were a protection against his advances.

Amy thought of Eleanor. Would Gavin and Rain know
that Hammond Perry was behind their abduction? Would
they think that she and Eleanor were together and headed for
Kaskaskia? The questions floated around in Amy's mind

until they were a mass of confusion, making her head hurt again. Wearily she closed her eyes. Tomorrow, she thought. Rain would come tomorrow.

It was past noon. Amy had begrudgingly eaten the meal Antoine had brought her. The Frenchman was edgy. He had not tried to make conversation with her since early morning. He was gone from the cabin for long stretches of time. With the door open Amy could see the trees and a small patch of sky. She sat on the bed, and each time Antoine left the cabin she yanked on the chain. The chain attached to the iron band around her ankle had been run through a small hole in the wall and somehow attached outside.

That morning Antoine had left a knife on the table. As soon as he went out the door Amy had begun to slide to the edge of the bed. She stood on one foot trying to reach the table. Her fingers had just gripped the edge so she could pull the table toward her when Antoine walked in.

"Ho, *ma cherie*. I just remembered the knife. You would cut Antoine if you could?"

"I'd cut your rotten heart out!" Almost crying with disappointment, Amy had sunk back down on the bed.

The afternoon dragged slowly by. As evening approached Amy became more and more aware that things were not as they had been the previous evening. Antoine became surly and silent. Making no attempt to start a supper fire, he brought her cold meat and a piece of the rum-soaked bread. Amy ate slowly and watched him where he sat looking out the open doorway.

Antoine was in a murderous rage. Pete Hopcus should have arrived the previous night or early that morning. Antoine wanted Tallman's ear in his pocket before he headed west. If Tallman lived, at one time or another they would cross paths. The good part was that Tallman didn't know he had the woman. Antoine had taken great care to ensure that they not be trailed to this place.

He and Hull had gone up the stream for more than five miles with the women until they came on to a rocky ledge. There Antoine had taken the precaution of leading one horse at a time out of the water to be sure no strike marks were left on the stones. The only man who knew of this place was Pete Hopcus.

Antoine thought of the woman in the cabin. He ached to lose himself in her soft, warm flesh. He wanted her to love him, but being with her would be good whether she loved him or not. Why should he not know the pleasure of holding his golden goddess? he asked himself as he got to his feet.

When Antoine came and sat down on the bed, Amy drew back to the far corner. Catching her hand in his, he raised it to his lips. He pressed burning kisses into her palm, and his tongue left a moist trail up to her wrist.

"My heart is yours, little Amy. I cannot wait for you to love me. I will show you how it is."

"You won't show me anything, damn you!" Amy tugged on her hand. "Get away from me, you . . . you woman stealer!"

He shook his head. "Ahh . . . just one kiss from your sweet mouth—"

"I'd sooner kiss a rattlesnake! You make me want to puke!"

"Ma cherie! I can make you come alive. I want to spend my life with you. You will learn to love me and you will love what I do to you, even if you say you do not." He began to pull her toward him.

"You're a stinking hog. I'll kill you the first chance I get." Panic began to flood her mind. She made a fist with her free hand and struck a resounding blow to his face. He merely laughed.

"Ho . . . my love, you do not disappoint me. We will fight. We will love. We will grow old together—"

"I think not." The quiet words were dropped like a keg of powder in the room.

Antoine sprang to his feet and whirled like a cat.

Rain stood hatless in the doorway. His name was a silent scream in Amy's throat.

"The fox lives!" Antoine hissed. He crouched to spring, his knife in his hand.

With a flip of his wrist Rain sent his knife flying through the air with the speed of an arrow. The Frenchman halted when the knife went into his chest. His face seemed frozen, except for his eyes. They turned slowly to Amy and looked at her unblinkingly. Then on stiff, unsteady legs he took the two steps needed to reach his rifle. He grasped it in one hand and lifted it.

Rain fired. The noise was deafening. Gun smoke filled the room. Antoine's body was propelled against the wall and then hurled to the floor. A part of his face was no longer there, and what used to be the back of his head was a gaping hole.

Amy screamed for Rain as the Frenchman's blood spilled across the floor.

Rain leaped across the room. Amy found herself crushed against his hard chest while he covered her face with fierce kisses.

"Are you all right, love? Oh, God! I've been in hell waiting for him to leave that doorway. Sweetheart . . . love . . . are you all right?"

"Yes, yes!" She sobbed from relief, from weakness, from happiness. "I knew you'd come. Oh, Rain, darling, hold me tight."

"I came in time, didn't I? I got here before—" He held her from him so he could look into her tear-streaked face.

"Yes, yes. You came in time."

"Thank God!" He clasped her to him. "You are my life. You are laughter and song and sunshine. Amy, sweet Amy, you are the mate of my heart, my soul," he whispered hoarsely.

"I was waiting for you."

So many questions crowded in her mind that she did not know where to begin. How had he found her?

"Rain! Oh, darling ... A man named Hull Dexter took Eleanor away. He's taking her to Hammond Perry."

"Yes, darling. We found the place where two horses went east and one horse went west. I came for you. Gavin and Will Bradford have gone after Eleanor. Let's leave this place. I'll tell you all about it on the way back to Davidsonville."

"Will Bradford and Gavin?"

"Yes, love. Will Bradford and Gavin. We must leave here."

"My leg is chained to the wall," she said when he attempted to help her to her feet.

"That son of a bitch! I could kill him all over again. I'll get a light. He's got to have a key here someplace."

Amy was so weak she could scarcely walk, but she managed by hanging on to Rain's arm. Before they left the cabin Rain pulled a burning ember from the fire he had lit so he could find the key and tossed it on the straw bed. He picked up Amy's rifle and her bundle of clothes and led her away.

At the river he swooped her up in his arms and, holding his precious burden to his chest, waded across to where the big dun horse waited.

CHAPTER
Twenty-three

Rain and Amy rode into town at dawn. They had spent the hours after midnight beneath the shelter of a large aspen tree when a light rain had begun to fall. During the night Rain told Amy about meeting Will Bradford and returning to Davidsonville with him and his men. He told her, while she sat curled in his arms, about his utter despair when she and Eleanor couldn't be found anywhere in town.

"Gavin was like a man possessed. He and Will Bradford were sure you had been carried off by Indians when they couldn't find a scrap of anything to indicate in which direction you had been taken. An Indian would not have been so careful," Rain said. "I knew someone had made plans carefully. I could think of only one man who would be so clever: Antoine Efant, the Frenchman who had been asking about me in Saint Genevieve."

Amy turned her head and buried her lips in the smooth skin of his throat, remembering the dark, smoldering eyes of the Frenchman.

"He said he was too clever to leave a trail, but I knew you would come for me."

"I had help, sweetheart. In the late afternoon Tennessee, Jean Pierre's daughter, came running up from the creek. She was worn out and her feet were bleeding. She could hardly walk or talk. She had followed you and Eleanor to the creek, and had been watching when Efant threw a blanket over your head, then hit you to knock you out.

"She told me they had taken you and Eleanor up the creek on horseback and she followed along the bank. She knew I would have to find where they came out of the creek in order to trail you and bring you back. The child may have run ten miles or more. She showed me the place where the horses came out of the creek and headed north. I had been past the place in my search. Efant was clever; he left not the faintest sign that he had passed that way.

"After that it was easy. We found where one of you had vomited, and saw strands of black hair on bushes. Tennessee had told us Eleanor was riding belly down on the horse and you were riding in front of a black-bearded man with a knit cap. Gavin was beside himself with worry."

"How did you know I had gone with Efant and Eleanor with Hull Dexter?"

"When it was too dark to see we stopped until daylight. We found the place where one of you had struggled with one of the men. I figured it was you and Efant, because Eleanor wouldn't have been strong enough. Two horses went east from there and one west. We followed the two horses until I found more black hair on a tree limb. Gavin, Will and one of his men followed that trail and I turned back to follow the other. I came to the cabin about noon, saw Efant, and had to wait. Sweetheart, I sweated blood while I waited!"

"He was kind to me in a way. He actually believed I would love him. I think he was crazy."

"No, he was enamored. You fascinated him that night at Kaskaskia. I saw it in his eyes when he looked at you."

"I don't want to enamor anyone but you." She touched his face tenderly, seeing the tired lines written there.

It was mid-morning when Will Bradford and Gavin arrived at the settlement with Eleanor riding in front of Will. They were met by Amy, Rain and Tennessee. Anxious townspeople waited in front of the store for news. Gavin was suffering from the wound in his side and had reluctantly allowed his beloved to ride the last few miles with Will.

Eleanor was exhausted and was put to bed, but not before she heard the part Tennessee played in their rescue. She hugged the small girl and kissed her. When she released her, Tennessee backed shyly away and watched her with glowing eyes.

Later Will told Rain that when Hull Dexter realized three men were closing in on him self-preservation had prevailed. He dropped the reins of the horse he was leading and took off down a gulley. The sergeant chased him for several miles, then lost him in the woods.

"We know who he is," Will said. "Someday he'll be brought to justice. I only wish there was some way I could legally tie this to Hammond Perry."

"He'll outwit himself again, the same as he did when he tried to get Farr hung for treason. I'm thankful to have Amy and Eleanor safe."

"I don't think Eleanor knew or cared who I was when we first reached her," Will said with a chuckle. "She had eyes only for Gavin and he for her. After a while Gavin introduced us and her first words were, 'I love Gavin. You don't have to bother with me.' Bother, indeed! She's family, even if only distantly," he scoffed. "Now Rain, when and where are these two weddings to take place?"

* * *

The entire population of Davidsonville wanted to attend the wedding of the famed woodsman and Amy Deverell. They were equally interested in the beautiful woman from Louisville and the Scottish riverman. In order to accommodate everyone, it was decided to have the ceremony performed on the porch of the trading post where all could see. Tennessee would stand up with the couples. Her papa smiled proudly when both Eleanor and Amy insisted, and her mother began at once to make her a dress suitable for the occasion.

Wild turkeys, sides of venison and two whole hogs purchased by Will Bradford roasted on spits beside the trading post. The women baked sweet potatoes, suet puddings and berry pies. Children turned the grinder to make cornmeal for bread and the men gathered around the barrel of whiskey Rain bought from the storekeeper.

Will Bradford had delayed his journey to Belle Fontaine for several days in order to officiate at the weddings. His men had set up camp on the edge of town and were enjoying the festivities with the townspeople.

On the morning of the second day after Amy and Eleanor were brought back they were wed to their men. Will Bradford, a splendid figure in his major's uniform, spoke the words that made first Amy and Rain, and then Eleanor and Gavin, husband and wife. Both women wore crowns of wildflowers picked by the children and fashioned by Eleanor and Tennessee.

The feasting and dancing, which took place in the road in front of the store, lasted most of the day. Toward evening Eleanor left Gavin's side to seek out Will Bradford so she might speak with him alone. She found him in the camp his men had set up at the edge of town.

"Major Bradford? May I speak with you?"

"Of course, child." Will took her arm and they walked a short distance from the camp.

"I want to apologize. I don't exactly know how."

"Apologize? For what?"

"I know Aunt Gilda wrote to you telling you of our dire circumstances and that she prevailed upon your family honor to provide for us. The truth is, sir, my father and my aunt were gamblers. They used me to—"

"Say no more." Will stopped and turned her to face him. "I know exactly what your father was and what Gilda Woodbury was. I also know that your mother was a lady who made the wrong decision when it came to choosing a husband. I was not deceived in any way. I wanted to provide for the daughter of a lady I admired. That's all there was to it. I could think of no other way than to wed you. I was proud and happy today when I united you in marriage to Gavin McCourtney. The man is deeply in love with you. I feel you will be safe in his hands."

"And I love him. Oh . . . sir, thank you." Eleanor put her arms about his waist and kissed his cheek.

"Will," the major said and cleared his throat. "Or better yet, Uncle Will. I expect a houseful of nieces and nephews. Here comes your husband. He has a murderous look on his face. Unhand me, child, before he kills me."

Eleanor's laugh was like the song of a bird. She reached out her hand to take Gavin's when he came near.

"Gavin, Uncle Will wants us to give him a houseful of nieces and nephews."

The Scot's homely, worried face broke into a beautiful smile. "I'll try to oblige you, sir."

Gavin slipped his arm around his wife, hers went around him, and they walked away. Eleanor looked up at him with a lovely smile and sparkling eyes and thought about how terribly lonely she had been before him, but now she would never be lonely or frightened or feel unloved again.

Amy leaned on her elbow next to Rain and traced the features of his handsome face with her fingertips. Her husband was the most beautiful man in the world. She said her thought aloud. He smiled, and she saw it in the moonlight that played hide and seek in the branches above their heads. They had opted to spend their wedding night in the woods, leaving the room at the trading post for Eleanor and Gavin.

Amy's gaze moved from his strong jaw up to his high forehead, lingering lovingly on his thick black lashes through which she caught a glimmer of laughter.

"Are you looking at me so you'll recognize your husband if you see him again?"

"Oh, you! I like to look at you. Shall I tell you what I see? I see a man who is handsome, brave and strong, so strong he can allow his gentleness to show, as it did today with Tennessee when you told her she was so pretty you might change your mind and marry her. She adores you, and so do I."

Rain reached up and pulled her to him so that she lay with her head on his chest. After the wedding, while waiting until it was decent to steal away to their private paradise, they had spent joyous hours talking and sharing their childhoods, funny forgotten memories, treasured secrets, hidden pains.

"Your heart beats so fast," Amy said and moved her ear down until it covered the nipple on his chest.

"It will beat just like that for the next fifty years when I hold you, warm and naked, in my arms." He wrapped a long strand of her hair around his hand and brought it to his lips. "It almost stopped with fear when I came close to losing you forever." His voice trembled with emotion when he added, "and now with happiness that I have you here in my arms."

Amy felt his lips in her hair and his wandering fingers found her nipples. She lifted her mouth to his and his kiss was long and demanding. With delicious provocation she deliberately raised one knee and nudged the part of him that brought her so much pleasure. He responded to the touch with a muffled groan and rolled her to her back.

"You went through so much, sweetheart. I'm afraid I'm wearing you out." His arms crushed her and she could feel the thunderous pounding of his heart.

"No, you're not wearing me out," she whispered lovingly, "but . . . please keep on trying."

From then on nothing mattered except satisfying their desperate need for each other. They swirled in a vortex of pleasure created by caressing hands, lips, biting teeth and closely entwined limbs.

They made love late into the night, until sheer exhaustion sent Amy into a deep sleep and Rain into that void between sleep and awareness. She lay molded to his naked body, her cheek nestled in the warm hollow of his shoulder.

They were together, as they were meant to be.

AUTHOR'S NOTE

All the people in this story are characters from my imagination, with the exception of Major William Bradford.

On Christmas Day, 1817, Major Bradford and his command of sixty-four men put ashore on the sandstone rock landing below the bluffs of Belle Point in the Arkansas Territory. There he established Fort Smith to keep peace between the hostile tribes.

I took the liberty of creating an incident in Major Bradford's life. (I hope his ancestors will forgive me.) After reading of his deeds, I feel he might have acted as I portrayed him in the story had such an event taken place.

I wish to acknowledge the help given me by Janie Glover, Special Projects Manager, Fort Smith Chamber of Commerce, Fort Smith, Arkansas. The book she sent me, *The Fort Smith Story* by Edwin P. Hicks, was most helpful.

Also I wish to acknowledge and give my heartfelt thanks to Marge Theiss of Clear Lake, Iowa, and thank her for correcting all the "to nots" and "not tos."

Dorothy Garlock